Peter Palliser went to the ⸻
ating from university and ⸻
in New York. He has written several screenplays and has
worked as a story-editor on a weekly television series. He
now lives in London with his wife and two children. *The
Bid* is his first novel.

Peter Palliser

THE BID

PENGUIN BOOKS

To Wendy

PENGUIN BOOKS

Published by the Penguin Group
27 Wrights Lane, London w8 5tz, England
Viking Penguin Inc., 40 West 23rd Street, New York, New York 10010, USA
Penguin Books Australia Ltd, Ringwood, Victoria, Australia
Penguin Books Canada Ltd, 2801 John Street, Markham, Ontario, Canada l3r 1b4
Penguin Books (NZ) Ltd, 182–190 Wairau Road, Auckland 10, New Zealand

Penguin Books Ltd, Registered Offices: Harmondsworth, Middlesex, England

Published in Penguin Books 1989

Made and printed in Great Britain by Richard Clay Ltd, Bungay, Suffolk
Filmset in Sabon

PART I

<u>Struggle for Existence</u>

The spirit as well as the precise wording of the General Principles and the ensuing Rules must be observed.

From *The City Code on Takeovers and Mergers*

Chapter One

I

Howard Hicks shifted uncomfortably in his chair and crossed his legs. 'I wish you hadn't asked me over,' he said.

'Thanks a lot,' Roger Andrews pretended hurt feelings. 'Why the hell not?'

'You're forcing me to take sides. I thought you knew I didn't want to be involved.'

'You can't help being involved, Howard,' Roger said dismissively. 'You sit on the board of my company and on the board of Nick Bishop's company. You're Bishop's closest friend.'

'Well then,' Howard said, 'I can only hope I don't get the opportunity to make the offer.'

'Sitting on the fence,' Roger said. He pushed himself back from the table.

'Steering the middle course, Roger. Trying to stay out of trouble and do the right thing.'

'It'll always be half-assed,' Roger said. 'Never quite right, never quite wrong. Go for broke either way. That's how you get results.'

The two men were having dinner in a small company flat on the top floor of Corpcom's London headquarters. It was a rainy Sunday night in January. Outside the traffic was heavy with taxis and the headlights gleamed above the wet roads. At this time of night Knightsbridge was empty of pedestrians, but the lights silhouetting Harrods shone regardless. Directly across the street from Harrods, Corpcom's unprepossessing six-storey building was dark except for the misty light that filtered through the heavy curtains covering the flat's dining-room windows.

The kitchen faced the back and so could not be seen from the main road. There, Sam, Andrews' Chinese cook, had prepared the meal that was now being eaten. Roger had not given his guest much notice, but his cook had plenty of warning. Just like this so-called emergency meeting, the meal that accompanied it had been carefully planned.

Sam was now cleaning the kitchen, for his part in the evening was over. He had only to bring a bowl of lichis to the table when he heard Andrews call for him. Roger Andrews did not believe in ringing for service: he liked the power of his own voice.

During the meal, Howard, tense, had said little. Roger spoke as he ate, outlining the role he expected Howard to play in Corpcom's newest takeover attempt. Roger's call had been unexpected and Howard had not been sure that he should welcome it. Now he knew that he did not.

'Don't you think there is something Darwinian about a takeover, Howard?' Roger asked after a long silence. His was a deep and rasping voice, bearing the trace of an American accent. The question hung there, unanswered, poised between them.

Roger finished his last mouthful of rice, which he had been shovelling into his mouth from a small Chinese bowl with red dragons painted on it. He was born in the Chinese year of the dragon and he liked having his personality stamped on his china, the way other men have their initials embossed on their briefcases or shirts or towels. He used chopsticks, holding the bowl an inch from his chin, eating as the Chinese do.

He put the bowl back on the table and moved it away from him, like a small child who has lost interest in his food. 'Have you ever read Darwin?' he spoke again, shifting his weight as he repressed a burp.

Howard shook his head. He was still eating. Unlike Roger, he ate slowly, using a knife and a fork. His appetites were obvious from his physical appearance. His face was slightly

8

puffy and there was a benevolent air to his flabby features. He was not obese, but his square-shouldered, solid body indicated corpulence. He looked older than the mere forty he was. From Roger's perspective, as Howard's knife moved the little grains of rice and pieces of chicken from his plate to his fork to his mouth, he seemed a little like a fish in a tank, his eyes slightly bulging, his lips puckered out into what could almost have been a permanent 'o'.

'That's the trouble with an English education,' Roger said, turning away from Howard, unable to avoid a feeling of distaste at his guest's eating habits. 'You specialize too early. You stay ignorant about a lot of things.'

'We learn to think. Deep thoughts,' Howard responded quickly, and the smile on his face was ironic.

'And where does it get you? The mood of the times is shallow, Howard. Look around you.' Roger got up from the table, and walked over towards a humidor on the sideboard. He was not tall, no more than five foot eight, broad-shouldered, solid, with a head virtually bald. His features were dominated by an eagle's beak that sprang from between narrow eyes and jutted out over thin lips.

Howard did look around him. A 'company flat' was an apt description, for there was nothing individual about it. It just held furniture: the dark, heavy Victorian mahogany sideboard and mirror; the dining-room table, also dark, but less ornate; and the chairs, square-backed and square-legged. Someone had bought from a shopping list, much as one would buy food. There were no flowers, books, or magazines, no china dogs or brass candlesticks, no clutter, no mess. It was as if everything precious had been removed to the bank, and the rooms waited for someone to come in, open the windows and breathe life into the stale atmosphere.

Roger turned with a long cigar in his hand; Howard had finished his food, and was taking a drink of beer, hoping to make the spice of the hot chilli disappear. His breathing was hurried and he sighed audibly when he put his empty glass on the table.

Roger sat down again. He put his cigar in his mouth and left it there, unlit, sucking at it. After a few seconds, he shouted at the door behind him, 'Sam – we're ready.'

As Sam ministered to them, bringing in the lichis, clearing away the dirty dishes, Howard looked at Roger and thought about his proposal. He was being asked to help outwit his closest friend. Put more dramatically, it amounted to betrayal. Howard knew that Nick was bound to see it as such. On the other hand, he thought, it could be argued that Roger's request was reasonable. After all, Howard was an obvious go-between. That was the trouble; he was already stuck in the middle. Howard did not think he could refuse the task should the opportunity arise, and he was sure that it would.

Automatically, he reached out for a lichi and began to peel the brown, scaly shell. The soft white flesh appeared comforting and he popped the nut into his mouth and bit into it, the juice cooling his mouth more effectively then the beer had.

'Let's get back to the point,' said Roger, suddenly eager to bring the evening to a close. Watching Howard find comfort in food irritated him, and he had become bored with their conversation just as intensely, as he had been enjoying it a few minutes earlier.

'You mean, thinking?' Howard said.

'Takeovers,' Roger said.

'Takeovers and Darwin,' Howard corrected him.

'Right.' Roger laughed at his own impatience and relaxed again, his mood as volatile as the weather. 'Darwin. You should read him. Struggle for existence, natural selection, survival of the fittest. Change a word here and there and you might find a lot of it in an offer document. Finance directors talk a bit like that, don't you think? Look at Peter.'

'Peter McNeal?' Howard said. 'Peter doesn't talk like that. He's too smug. He just hands down opinions.'

Roger laughed. He enjoyed Howard's dislike of Peter, who was his finance director, and a man he relied on much more than he did on Howard. Howard was a pawn, someone to be moved around whenever necessary.

'Peter doesn't *talk* like that,' Roger chuckled, 'but he writes like it.' He paused, just for a few seconds. 'I love it. The language. The formality of our lives, fronting really basic actions. An estate agent tells you a house needs modernization. You know the house is a wreck. When politicians have "constructive talks", they haven't decided anything. And of course, when a businessman talks of rationalization, we all know he's about to lay people off.'

'You're right. Sugar-coating is a much nicer way of looking at things.' Howard smiled. He preferred the superficiality of banter, and the conversation was getting much too close to the bone.

'With pills, perhaps,' Roger said, pressing his case, unwilling to let Howard duck the issue. 'Politicians and businessmen know exactly what they're doing when they sugar-coat pills. Then they can use them effectively. Think of Watergate. Nixon kept saying he was innocent. Why should he resign? So Congress threatened to impeach him. So he resigned.' Roger took the cigar out of his mouth and popped in a lichi nut. 'Then he was pardoned,' he went on, chewing as he spoke. 'But he was never guilty. That was the beauty of his manoeuvre. Think of it: Nixon never technically guilty, always innocent.'

'He was forced out of office,' Howard said.

'But he wasn't punished.'

'You have to be found guilty for that,' Howard said with a smile.

Roger smiled back at him and opened out his arms wide. 'That's my point,' he said. 'You can get away with a great lie, but not a puny one.' He added, 'We all know what kinds of filthy tricks honourable people get up to, don't we?'

That was when Roger had got up to light his cigar. The air became thick with smoke and the audience was over; Howard knew it. He rose in his usual deliberate way, not rushing things, making sure there were no false moves. He was taller than his girth would have led one to expect. He stood almost six feet; but for the weakness in the lines of his face, he was an imposing figure, the cut of his dark suit hiding his more obvious curves. He wore a gold watch on a chain across his waistcoat. He took the watch out now and looked at the time. It was 10.30.

'I should be on my way,' he said.

'We'll talk soon, then,' said Roger, making no effort to detain him, not even with a polite offer of a last drink, which could then be turned down. He simply refused the hypocrisies of social life, unless it suited him to use them.

They did not shake hands. Roger waited for the lift doors, which opened directly into the hall of the flat, to close and immediately turned back towards the kitchen.

'Sam,' he yelled, 'let's go.'

They took the lift directly to the underground car park, standing in silence, an odd couple, Roger smoking his cigar, Sam standing next to him, carrying a canvas bag which held his wok, the only kitchen utensil he refused to leave in the flat. Sam, who had left his family behind when Andrews brought him over from Hong Kong, lived in the Andrews' house in Hampstead, and was brought down to Knightsbridge when he was needed.

A few minutes later, Roger was sitting in the back of the Rolls-Royce as it drove up Park Lane. He was pleased with himself. He had just completed the last task before setting the takeover in motion. Tomorrow the fight would start. He smoked his cigar, with his feet up on the foot rest.

2

On this cold January night outside a square, concrete building in Cannon Street, it was quiet. Cars drove by at long intervals, breaking the stillness for a few seconds, their engines echoing in the silence. There were no pedestrians; it was almost midnight, still Sunday.

In a corner office on the seventh floor, two men moved about in the dark. The light that came in through the metallic venetian blinds accentuated their silhouettes without giving anything away, as if it shone menace rather than light on to them. The men wore black clothes under their heavy jackets, and the only sound was the occasional squeak from the new trainers the thinner of the two men was wearing. Now and then, a powerful torch flashed, beaming its arc on the large desk, on the floor or on the wall. When the torch was turned off, the room seemed impenetrable.

From the street, the building was completely dark but for one light on the ground floor, which shone dimly through the glass doors of the main entrance. It came from the lobby, where an elderly man in a blue uniform sat at a table, occasionally licking a finger to turn the pages of an *Exchange & Mart*. When he reached the end of each section of his paper, he would slowly push his chair back from the table, get up with a sigh and start another round of the building.

As the bells of St Paul's struck twelve, the guard looked up from the 'Land and Property Overseas' section. He had been studying an advertisement for a time-share in Key West when the bells finally tugged him away from his dream of a Florida beach, full of carefree Americans surfing and swimming in a clear blue sea. He looked back at his paper, and decided that 'Mobile Homes' could wait until his return. He got up, picked up his keys, checked that the front-door alarm was set and methodically stepped through the fire-door into the ground-floor offices.

The two men upstairs had found what they were looking for: an unlocked drawer in the desk. It was at the bottom, and by the time anybody looked, the tiny instrument they were about to place there would have served its purpose.

The thinner man, who was holding the torch, watched as his partner pulled the drawer out. He did it with care, slowly, not to make any noise, but the drawer creaked anyway. Immediately, he stopped. The thin man walked to the door, put his ear to the crack, listened, heard nothing. He returned to the desk and, standing over his partner, flashed the light back on and shone it on the half-open drawer. The heavier man returned to his task.

The sound of a car broke the Sunday silence again. Without thinking, the man holding the torch turned towards the windows. The torch's beam turned with him and, for a moment, flashed across the blinds.

'For Christ's sake, turn that off,' the man kneeling on the ground barked a whispered reprimand. 'I'll use this from now on.' He drew a pencil torch from his pocket and turned it on to the drawer.

They were still at work when the security guard emerged on to the seventh floor from the lift. From the corner office the intruders heard the lift doors opening. The small light was turned off, the work interrupted. The thin man, who had still been standing, quickly crouched behind the desk. They waited in silence, without panic, but ready for action if it should become necessary.

The guard walked towards the corner office. He too had a torch, which he kept lit, rather than switch the lights on. The dark kept him more alert, he thought.

Following his ritual he stopped at each door in the corridor, gently shaking the handles, making sure they were locked. From behind the desk the two men waited.

Finally, the beam from his torch reached the corner-office door. He placed his hand on the door handle and tried the door. It did not open. He shook it. Nick Bishop's office stayed locked.

The two men behind the desk looked at each other. They had expected this visit, yet they were relieved when they heard the footsteps move away and saw the light disappear. They waited for another five minutes, until they heard the fire-door at the end of the corridor open and close. Then the heavier man turned his light on; simultaneously his partner stood up again, looking towards the door. They went back to work.

Just as the guard returned to his seat in the alcove of the building's lobby, lit his hourly cigarette and returned to his reading, the two men were climbing out of the building the same way they had climbed in: the bathroom window on the first floor had been left unlocked on a visit to the building two days earlier. Security, they knew, was not rigid enough to include a thorough check of all windows. The men clambered down on to the roof of their car, which had been parked under the window, and drove off home to bed.

They had left behind two separate listening devices in the headquarters of Armadale International plc, a diversified company specializing in engineering, chemicals, and computer technology.

3

When Howard left the Corpcom building, a few minutes before Roger, it was still pouring. He stood under the small concrete canopy and scanned the late evening traffic for a free cab. Finally the comforting amber light appeared and, ducking against the rain, he struggled into the cab and sat heavily in the seat. Closing his eyes, he put his head back in relief, oblivious to his rain-soaked clothes.

For the first time this evening, Howard felt safe. As he began to relax, regaining his breath after his sudden exertion, an image flashed in his mind. Nick Bishop, tall, handsome, with a lazy elegance, standing by the fireless hearth in the remotest corner of his club, his elbow resting on the mantelpiece, his glass of champagne standing next to it, one leg idly crossed over the other so that only his toe rested on the carpet. He looked as if he were posing for an eighteenth-century portrait, waiting for his footman to come in with the cane he was to dangle from his hand or the spaniel that was to sit quietly at his feet. It was a posture that had become familiar to Howard over the last two decades. And, in Howard's mind, as he turned the corner into the small drawing-room where Nick was waiting for him Nick would sense his arrival and, breaking the spell, come to life. His foot would fall flat on the carpet; he would stand facing his guest squarely. Then, suddenly, Nick would come to meet him, his hand outstretched, a wide, open smile brightening his stern, angular face.

They had known each other since they were thirteen, first at school, as relative strangers, than at university, where their friendship had grown. Since then they had been close, sharing every aspect, or almost every aspect of their lives. It was a friendship of opposites. Nick, even though he was capable of enjoying life, was austere, rigid, almost Victorian in the certainty of his attitudes, and with an earnestness that was charming and yet encouraged duplicity in others. Howard was more flexible, more sensual and less passionate.

Howard wondered if it would be enough to have been best friends since school, to have the same interests, read the same books, like the same women and eat at the same restaurants. Howard was afraid of the consequences of what he had agreed, albeit tacitly, to do. Friendship, like love, can be destroyed. People do not passively fall out of love, like a decayed tooth falling out of rotten gums. People destroy love, betray it; and few men will forgive betrayal. Certainly, Nick never would.

Chapter Two

I

'What time is it?' Julian Campbell called from the shower. He waited, then, hearing no answer, he leaned towards the door and shouted, 'Rebecca!'

'Seven fifty-nine,' Rebecca's voice called back. The paste of sleep was still in it.

'Seven fifty-nine,' Julian muttered to himself. He did not like the exactitude of the digital watch.

Eight o'clock. He had to get out of the shower. He lingered a little longer. He knew that Nick Bishop would just be arriving at the office. Always early. Always at work before anyone else. Julian had worked for Nick for just under two years and he had never arrived at the office before his boss. But then, it was Nick and not Julian who was head of Armadale International. Julian liked his work, but he could stay away from it with ease; he was only the assistant to the managing director. It was like being a principal private secretary to a prime minister, always in the centre of things, but never responsible for the decisions he oversaw. That was as committed a position as he wanted at the moment.

He turned the shower off and walked into the bedroom, drying himself as he went, water dripping on to the carpet. He found Rebecca still lying in bed, her eyes closed, refusing to get up. He sat down on the side of the bed next to her and looked at the digital clock: 8.13, it blinked. He kissed her.

'It's 8.15,' he said.

'Did you bring me some coffee?' Rebecca didn't open her eyes. She smiled.

'I'm not going to have time for coffee. I've got to pick Alan up on the way.' Julian stood up again, threw the towel on to the bed, and began to dress.

'Car-pooling?' Rebecca watched him now, her eyes following him, like a camera, around the room as he selected his clothes from a tall mahogany chest of drawers and the high white cupboards that lined the wall opposite the bed. Julian was handsome; he had a strong, open face with a high forehead, and a short well-proportioned body. There was a slight heaviness around the middle, but only slight. His light-brown hair was cut short. His movements were graceful and firm. It was good to watch him dress.

'I'd give you a lift too, if you'd get up,' he said, feeling her gaze, and flattered by it.

'With Alan. No thanks.'

'He's all right.' Julian rarely said anything bad about anyone.

Rebecca sneered. 'He gives me the creeps.'

'We're going to supper there tonight. Remember?'

'I remember.' She sighed. 'I'm not even married to you and I'm behaving like a dutiful wife. That's England for you.'

Rebecca Zager was American, from Boston, although she and Julian had met here in London.

Julian was dressed now. He moved over to the bed again. 'You don't have to come, you know.'

Rebecca stretched, pulling back her arms till they almost touched the wall, tightening the muscles of her legs, and kicking off the bedclothes. 'It's a free meal. I never could say no to a free meal.' She looked up at him, uncovered now, naked. Long, slender legs led up to wide hips and their length was emphasized by her stretching, her feet extending out in front of her. Her stomach was flat, and, because she was lying on her back, her breasts fell slightly to each side. Her eyes were still puffed from sleep but they were dark and beautiful, like her long brown hair which was strewn on the pillow in a dark, untidy mesh.

Julian looked at her for a moment, not moving, admiring

her. He leaned down and one of his hands touched her hip, brushed over the pubic hair. Then he kissed her and walked to the door. 'I'll see you.'

'I'll meet you there. Don't be late.'

At 8.30 Julian was outside a three-storey house in Islington, his engine running, rock playing on the car stereo, waiting for Alan to emerge. Julian's entire body was clamouring for coffee, his eyes itched, his legs were slightly stiff, his head was beginning to ache a little. His fingers drumming on the steering wheel, he watched the red door, newly-painted, of Alan's house.

Alan Turner: thirty, tall, blond, blue-eyed, married, no children. In his own way, Alan was an archetype, a man with a future: a new house, a new car, a good career and a wife in the property business.

'Money is no object here,' Julian thought as he watched the red door open and Alan come out in one of his many expensive, tailor-made suits. Today's was a dark-blue number, double-breasted, with a razor-thin pin-stripe. 'Money's the subject,' and he smiled at his own little joke. He was honest enough to recognize that Alan Turner did indeed look good.

Alan got into the car. He was bright, cheerful, ready for the day. 'Sorry. Had to get a quick one in to start the week,' and he chortled.

Julian made no response.

'How's Becky, then? Still gorgeous. God, where did you find her?'

Julian drove on in silence. He knew Alan didn't need a reply. This was more in the nature of a monologue.

'Still on for tonight, eh?' Alan went on.

'Yes. Of course.' Julian managed a smile, a quick turn of the head.

'That's why Fanny's got the Alfa. She's going to cook up a storm tonight, so she's going shopping this morning.'

'What does she tell her boss?' Julian asked. Fanny was an

estate agent in Islington, helping to raise the value of property and thus, indirectly, of her and Alan's investment.

'January's pretty slow,' Alan answered. 'She just tells them she's going to be late. Some of us have all the luck,' he added a little condescendingly. It was an ambiguous statement; he was still feeling the after-effects of sex, and love was in full bloom.

'I look forward to it,' said Julian. 'The meal, I mean.'

They drove on for a while in silence, Julian manoeuvring through the traffic. However hard he tried, he seemed unable to leave home earlier than 8.30, which meant that, on the days he picked Alan up, he fell on the worst of the rush hour. While he tried to find the gaps, Alan looked out of the window, peering at the other men and women going to work. Mostly the women.

'What's the Pope got to say these days?' asked Alan, without turning back towards Julian, his gaze fixed on an attractive blonde woman in a red BMW, right next to Julian's car. The 'Pope' was what some of them called Nick Bishop. Alan had coined the phrase; he had been very pleased with it.

'What about specifically? He has a few things to say about quite a lot.' Julian was always careful when he was asked such questions. Being so close to Nick meant that he was often privy to information that was best kept uncirculated. At the same time, because he was in that position, his friends and peers assumed that he owed them scraps of gossip. This tightrope act was perhaps the hardest part of the job.

'What about? The "rumours" of course.' Alan put the word in inverted commas.

'I don't understand why, every time there's mention of a takeover, everyone begins to panic,' Julian said with a little more vehemence than necessary. He was feeling the strain, and the exasperation was genuine.

'More than three million are out of work, and you're asking why everyone gets panicky. W-O-R-K. It may have four letters, Julian, but it's a living.'

Julian changed gear and accelerated past a chauffeur-driven

black Mercedes with a grey-haired man reading the *Financial Times* in the back. He liked to squeeze past the privileged. 'Most people wouldn't even be affected,' he said. 'We'd just go on as if nothing had happened, for Christ's sake.'

'People like you and me wouldn't. We may not be on the board; I mean, that's an automatic kick in the arse. But we have "opposite numbers". You *have* heard of them? People who have opposite numbers in takeover situations have a fifty-fifty chance of becoming redundant. And that is a word I don't like. I can't afford it.'

'You worry too much.'

'I worry when you avoid my questions – especially when I was just trying to pass the time of day.' Alan waved his arm at the block of cars that surrounded them. 'God, look at this.'

The fumes from the exhaust surrounded the cars; cyclists in their fluorescent-yellow straps weaved annoyingly in and out of the few feet allowed by the cars, while motorbikes roared by on the outside. Both men were becoming irritable.

Last Friday Armadale's share price on the London Stock Exchange had been 213. This was 41p up from a month before, in early December. Rumours of a takeover had started with the new year. They had died a bit later, but the price had remained high.

'I can just see it now,' Julian suddenly said, his hand waving in the air to add drama, 'Business gridlock. Company after company in a takeover bid. Headline reads, "Circle of Gluttony in the City. Business world at a standstill".'

'Very funny,' Alan retorted, unimpressed. 'You're still avoiding the issue.'

'There's nothing to tell,' Julian said with a heavy sigh. 'Nick knows about as much about it as you do. The last rumour I heard was weeks ago: "Australian company hungry for Armadale Engineering." It was just a rumour and the share price is almost back to normal.'

But Alan was not to be put off yet. 'The share price is not back to normal. It is in fact abnormally high.'

'Not if we're doing well.'

'But we're not particularly,' Alan said. 'And that newspaper headline came out exactly thirteen days ago.'

'Probably something somebody said over a lager in Brisbane.' Julian dismissed it impatiently.

As the traffic moved again, he calmed down. He managed a half smile. 'I haven't even had a cup of coffee yet, and you're talking to me about a takeover.'

Julian realized, though, that what was rasping inside him wasn't just the need for caffeine. The unsettling rumour of a takeover had upset him too. It was not that he might lose his job. Julian had never minded that – a lost job was freedom regained – but up to now a takeover had been something theoretical, something he didn't really like, and also something distant.

'What you haven't had, old cock,' Alan burst into his thoughts, 'is a Monday morning workout. Now I can tell. Exercise clears the brain, old friend. I recommend it, and Rebecca can clear the brain better than most, I should think.'

Julian winced at Alan's remark, but the image of Rebecca lying in bed as he had left her flashed in front of him for a second. He wished he had had a little more time this morning.

The darting shape of a cyclist, bent over his handlebars, passing him on the left, brought him back to his immediate problems. With a pump of acceleration he found a gap and made the light, crossing the road as it turned red. They were almost there.

At five minutes to nine, Julian drove into the underground car park beneath the Armadale building. The security guard waved at them from the booth where he was reading his newspaper.

Not far behind them, a blue Ford Escort came down the ramp towards the car park. There were two men in it: one a man in his late forties with a thick, greying moustache and sad, basset-like eyes that had deep pouches under them, the driver younger, trimmer, with spiky fair hair and very pale skin. He wore an earring in his right ear and was chewing gum. He stopped the car next to the booth and opened his window. The older man leaned across him and handed the guard an envelope: in it were five twenty-pound notes.

'Do us a favour, mate,' said the sad-eyed man. 'Let us park the car down here for the day.'

The security guard looked from the man to the money and back to the man. A hundred pounds was a hefty bonus for allowing a car to park for a day. As much again as he took home in a week.

'No questions asked,' the man added.

There was a moment of silence. The guard weighed up the reality of cash against the abstractions of morality and conscience.

'Go all the way to the end and turn left,' he said, pointing towards the darkness. 'There are some empty spaces.' He checked a piece of paper in front of him. '211 to 225,' he said.

'Thanks, mate,' said the older man. He patted the driver on the arm and the car drove down into the garage.

The security guard had been careful and placed them well away from the main part of the garage. They were in a dark spot, hidden from view by a concrete pillar. Only someone parking next to them would notice that there was anyone there. The older man took out a small radio receiver, earphones and a tape-recorder from a British Airways bag. He made the connections and put the earphones on. He listened for a few seconds. The driver, his mouth moving rhythmically as he chewed, looked towards him. When the older man put his thumb up, the driver leaned back against the head rest of his seat and closed his eyes.

Julian and Alan came up from the car park and into Cannon Street; Armadale stood before them. On this cold day, with the early-morning sun already covered by a mass of grey cloud, Julian found it more unappealing than usual. He looked up towards the top floor. Nick Bishop would be there, he knew, at his desk in the seventh-floor corner office. Nick had no appointments until ten o'clock that morning but he always came in at eight to have a couple of hours of solid work before the day filled up with meetings and telephone calls. His jacket would be off, hanging on the back of his chair, the ashtray on the desk clean; Nick had stopped smoking many years ago. Julian smoked but he knew he would give up in time. It was rebelliousness now that kept him going.

Alan followed Julian's gaze. Alan worked on the seventh floor too, but he knew that Julian was thinking about Nick. 'The fact is,' Alan said, 'you don't like takeovers. It upsets your old-fashioned sense of fair play.'

Julian looked at his watch. It was nine o'clock exactly. He checked the traffic and suddenly ran across the street, taking Alan by surprise and leaving him on the other side. He hurried into the building and then waited inside the lobby.

Alan entered, slightly indignant; it was somehow an insult to his masculinity to have been outdistanced.

'I couldn't stand to wait any more,' Julian apologized. 'Come on. I must have some coffee.'

2

Nick heard the telephone ring in the outer office. He went on with the sentence he was writing, aware of the number of times the phone rang. His secretary, Sarah, was probably not in yet. He glanced at the clock on his desk: 9.03.

On the fifth ring he picked up the receiver. 'Nick Bishop,' he spoke firmly, the two words clipped. At the other end, he heard a little 'Oh' of surprise, a woman's voice.

'Mr Andrews for Mr Bishop,' she said.

'This is he. Andrews, did you say?'

'Yes, sir. Mr Roger Andrews.' And then hurriedly, she added, 'Would you hold on, please sir.' The telephone was dead suddenly, and Nick was left holding on.

Roger Andrews was the chairman and chief executive of Corpcom. At the mention of the name, Nick had known that what was coming was going to be bad news. They had never met, but Andrews' reputation was there for everyone to read about. 'Raider' was a favourite description. 'Predator' was an image the press also liked. Nick even remembered a magazine article about Andrews, entitled 'Portrait of a Predator' and, as Nick waited, the face on the cover now appeared before him as he had assessed it then: an intelligent face, but ruthless and uncaring. Nick was a moral animal, and he had no admiration for Roger Andrews', whatever his successes.

A forceful voice came on the line: 'Bishop. Roger Andrews here, of Corpcom.'

'I know.' Nick waited.

'There's no need to beat around the bush, then. This is a courtesy call.' A scorpion's courtesy, with its sting in the tail. 'Corpcom is making an offer for Armadale International. This doesn't have to be unfriendly, Nick.'

Andrews' use of his Christian name infuriated Nick. 'It's already unfriendly,' he answered.

'This doesn't have to be a fight. That's all I'm saying.' Andrews was firm. He remained unimpressed and went on, 'There's nothing personal about it. Corpcom's a large company, it's growing fast, and the combined businesses would . . .'

'Please.' Nick spoke loudly into the telephone, 'send me the document. Don't speak it to me.'

Nick paused. He waited, expecting Andrews to say something, but there was silence at the other end. Nick waited another moment and then slammed down the telephone. He stood up, his body rigid with rage, and turned towards the windows, but before he had reached them he changed direction and headed out of his office. Leaving the door open, he strode out past Sarah Dawes, a petite women in her mid-forties, who was just sitting down to her desk, her handbag open in front of her. Every day, as soon as she arrived at her desk, Sarah corrected her face, making sure that she put right whatever ravages the morning tube ride had wrought on her earlier careful preparations. Her powder compact and a tissue protruded from the bag; her hand was poised to get them out. She looked up, startled, as Nick went right by her without his usual greeting.

'Good morning, Mr Bishop,' she said to his back.

'Julian in yet?' Nick barked, without turning, walking towards Julian's smaller office, across the way from his own.

'I don't know . . .' Sarah looked worried. Nick's behaviour was decidedly unusual.

Nick opened the door to the office, but the still-darkened room gave him his answer immediately. Without bothering to close the door he turned and strode back towards his own office.

'He's late. Tell him to come in as soon as he gets here.' Then he added, like a child prompted by his parents, 'Please.' The thrust of civility calmed him and he managed to close the door behind him without slamming it. He stopped, leaned against it, and tried to think of what he should do next, of what that telephone call actually meant.

Nick had never been on the receiving end of a 'hostile takeover', and this was definitely hostile; and unwanted: it would bring chaos, upheaval, paralysis. During the next several weeks, assuming he did not capitulate, and he had no intention of doing so, the entire fabric of Armadale and its subsidiary companies would be thrown into disarray. His people would read their newspapers with anxiety from now on, fear compounded each day as they wondered if their future had been settled, whether their jobs were safe or not. Even if his company were forced to grow more effective as it tried to counter Andrews' offer, Nick did not believe this to be the right way to improve efficiency. It would be like antibodies fighting a virus, and Armadale would not settle down again until the virus had been routed. Perhaps then it might find itself trimmer, less diseased, but the hospitalization could not be anything but painful.

Nick's rage was released all over again. He picked up the telephone and punched in a series of numbers he knew well and waited peevishly for the connection to be made.

'Gerrard's Cross, 6854,' came the familiar, mournful voice

of Norma Hicks. Nick considered hanging up, because if Norma answered it meant that Howard had already left. He spoke all the same, just in case he was wrong.

'Norma. It's Nick Bishop.'

'Hallo.' Norma liked Nick as little as he liked her. Although Howard and Nick were old friends, their friendship had not extended to their wives, who had always been less enthralled by this friendship of opposites.

This morning Nick just did not have the patience to cater to the usual formalities he and Norma dealt in. He was abrupt.

'Is Howard in?'

'He's on his way in to London.'

'By car?' As he asked the question, Nick was already turning the pages of his address book, searching for the number of Howard's car telephone.

'Yes. He likes to take –'

'Thanks. I'll try him there.'

Norma heard the click, and put her own phone down. Nick Bishop's rudeness did not surprise her. In her mind, he was always rude and unpleasant. He was stuck up, too. She returned to filling the dishwasher with the breakfast dishes.

Behind the closed windows of his car, Howard was being driven through the slow-moving commuter traffic. Idly he watched the drivers of the cars next to him as they came and went. His face was drawn into unnatural lines, its creases more used to laughter and mockery than to seriousness or melancholy. He was worrying about Nick, wondering whether the call from Andrews had come yet, trying to imagine his friend's reaction: he could see the rage, the outrage even, for Nick would regard the offer as insulting, verging on the unethical.

Howard admired Nick's ability to draw clear moral boundaries on every issue. He himself was incapable of such decisiveness; it was something that he did not really understand. Nevertheless he admired it; a moral code was a 'good thing'.

And he was behaving as he was supposed to behave in these circumstances. For once, he had a moral reason for being non-committal and this was an irresistible combination. Yet Howard was uncomfortable. He had known that Corpcom was to make a bid for Armadale, and although he had not sat in on the Corpcom takeover meetings he had shared the secret and kept silence against Armadale. He was well aware that his decision not to get involved was based not on any conflict of interest between the two companies, or between an old friend and a boss. It was based on his conviction that Andrews would defeat Nick.

But last night Howard's position had been compromised. He had been dragged in to the fight as a negotiator, empowered to make an offer. Nick would see this as a commitment on Howard's part and, in a way, he knew that Nick would be right. He wished he had never been invited to dinner by Roger; he wished he had had the foresight to refuse the invitation. But how could he have known what he would be asked to do? And how could he have avoided the request once it was made?

When the telephone beeped in the car, he turned away from the traffic and, before his driver could reach for it, said, 'I'll get it.' Howard liked gadgets like car telephones and every time it rang, he felt a little thrill of anticipation. He reached towards the receiver and then he stopped himself. He waited. He sat there in mid-motion for a moment, his eyes darting from the telephone to the traffic outside. Could this be Nick? Howard's driver looked in the rear-view mirror, saw Howard poised but immobile. The two men caught each other's eye, and just as the driver's hand moved from the steering wheel, Howard picked up the receiver and spoke into it.

'Howard?' Nick's voice was urgent.

'Nick. How are you?' Howard was jovial, his voice carrying the tone it always did with his friend, but his stomach had tightened. 'I was just thinking about you . . .' He stopped, waiting for the interruption, expecting it like a predictable line in a play. And it came.

'I've just had a call from Roger Andrews. They're making a bid for me.'

'Andrews . . .?' Howard's voice caught. He cleared his throat, putting his hand on the mouthpiece first so as not to be betrayed.

'Yes. Andrews, for Christ's sake. Do you know anything about it?'

'What do you mean?' Howard was suddenly frightened, a deep, unconscious fear, like a child's.

Nick heard it. He was silent, realizing that Howard had known this was going to happen. 'How long have you known?' he asked.

'I haven't sat in on any discussions. You know I wouldn't do that.'

'But you knew.' Nick persevered.

'Yes . . . I knew.' Howard's breathing became short. 'But I couldn't tell you. You know I couldn't.'

'We're friends.'

'It wouldn't have been ethical.' Howard could hardly believe he was using this argument with Nick. Just for a second, he enjoyed that particular irony. And it prompted what he said next. 'You know that, Nick, you of all people.'

Nick was not convinced but he was silenced. He had never imagined that Howard had known. He was silent for so long that Howard went on, confident that 'right' was on his side now.

'You don't have to fight this, Nick. It doesn't have to be a hostile bid. Accept it and make the best of it.'

'You're asking me to recommend this to the shareholders? You must be joking!'

'I'm thinking of you, that's all.' Howard was beginning to tell the truth by default. Why should Nick not get out and save what he could? There was a deal to be made. Howard could arrange it. It was the way out. These thoughts suddenly poured into his brain, and he became almost enthusiastic, eloquent. 'You are supposed to have their best interest in mind. And this is a pretty generous offer.'

'Andrews is a terrorist. He's not interested in what we do at Armadale. All he wants is a quick return. He'll sell off engineering, he'll amalgamate our chemical arm into his own and rationalize the whole of the computers division. Half our people in head office will get laid off. And he's going to be using the money saved to finance the whole deal. I'm going to be paying for it. My shareholders know what I've done with this company,' Nick went on, still ranting at the injustice of the position he found himself in.

'What your shareholders care most about is how much they can get, Nick. Half of them are probably Corpcom shareholders as well,' Howard said. 'Nobody cares about a company any more.'

'I care. I've spent twelve years working for Armadale. It's mine. I'm not going to sell it to Andrews just because he needs to eat something new. Let him go somewhere else.'

This was the reaction Howard had anticipated. He had known that he would not be able to persuade his friend to give up, hand over the company and go elsewhere. That is what Howard would do, take the money and run. It's what made sense; business sense, even.

'Who are you doing this for? Your shareholders don't care who you are or what you've done, only how much money you can make for them and how quickly. Andrews can make a ton of money for them. He can do it much more quickly than you could. They know that . . . You know that.'

'What would you have me do?' Nick barely opened his mouth as he spoke. He held the phone as if he were going to hit someone.

At that moment, there was a knock on the door and, as Nick turned towards it, he saw Julian enter, a look of worry on his face. Julian was not used to having Sarah report that a foul-tempered Nick had complained of his tardiness and wanted to see him immediately. When he saw the expression on Nick's face, he was more worried. He made as if to move back out again, but Nick stopped him.

'Stay.' He spoke without covering the mouthpiece and went back to his conversation. Julian stayed like an obedient dog.

Howard sat back in the car, wondering if this were the moment. Could he make the deal, negotiate, like a successful troubleshooter? Was this the hour of his glory? He spoke nonchalantly, trying not to betray himself.

'You could recommend the bid, save everyone – including yourself, by the way – a lot of money. And then you resign gracefully, ready for another day.'

'Gracefully. That's the way to do it.' Nick was scornful.

'Like an old pro fighter,' Howard said. And as carelessly as he could, knowing this to be the hardest moment, he went on, 'Go when the going's good. There'll be a settlement, of course. A golden handshake.' He snapped out a laugh. He had risked making the offer, Roger's offer. Should he be more specific, and mention that the offer went beyond the normal contractual agreement Nick had with Armadale? He had been empowered to. At the same time, he asked himself anxiously whether Roger would honour it. He had reneged on his word before.

'It's beginning to sound like a bribe.' Nick spoke very deliberately.

'For heaven's sake, Nick. It's perfectly normal. What's it got to do with bribery?' And in the same breath, he added, 'We could arrange for it to be offshore, you know. Andrews has a lot of interests abroad.' Howard wondered if he was going too far too soon.

Nick laughed. He was beginning to find this conversation quite extraordinary. Surely Howard was not being serious?

'I can't accept that.'

'You can, Nick, you can,' Howard pressed, almost pleading with his friend.

There was a pause now. 'How little you know me,' he said, quietly, expressing no other emotion but sadness, and the remark brought an end to the conversation.

'Nick . . .' Howard's voice at the other end of the telephone was fainter now, 'I wish you'd think about it.' He could think of nothing else to say.

'I will.' But both of them knew that Nick's mind was made up and that, as on all matters of principle, he would not change it. 'I'll be in touch,' he added and hung up.

'We're being taken over, Julian,' he said. It was a confirmation of what Julian had already guessed.

Howard put the receiver back on the console between him and the driver. He sat back morosely, letting his arms hang limply on the armrests. He had hoped for some good sense; not passion, just common sense. Howard loathed passion. In the end, it brought nothing but pain and unhappiness. Compromise was the thing he loved; it kept life the appropriate shade of grey, like an autumn sky. He stared at the cars again and made another decision.

'Gordon,' he said to his driver, 'call the office and have Janet cancel my appointments. She can say I'm in bed with the flu, or whatever.'

'Yes, sir,' the driver said, and as he moved to pick up the car telephone, Howard added, 'Then take me to Holland Park.'

Chapter Three

I

Nick and Julian looked at each other in silence. Neither spoke because neither knew quite what to say. Nick looked at the clock on his desk: 9.14, it said. Automatically, Julian looked at his watch, and they spoke at the same time.

'Nine fourteen,' Nick said.

'A quarter past nine.' Julian remained approximate even now. 'It'll be on the topic screen in a quarter of an hour,' he added.

The 'topic screen' was the monitor that every company listed on the Stock Exchange, every bank, every investment house, every broker, had in their offices to stay in touch with the market, the modern equivalent of the ticker-tape. At 9.30, the broad details of Corpcom's offer for Armadale would be typed into the computer and broadcast over the City, over Wall Street, Chicago, and Paris, in Tokyo, and Singapore, wherever Armadale's stock was traded. In twenty minutes, the affair would be in the public domain. Nick, who, despite his shareholders, had always considered Armadale a family business, felt this exposure keenly.

'Bastards,' he said.

Julian, although he would never have dared admit it, was relieved. The tensions raised by the rumours of the last month were dispelled. The offer had come and the worst was known. And the challenge, the risks of a takeover, the turmoil it inevitably would bring, were exciting. It was a novelty for Julian, not knowing exactly what the future would bring. Unlike Alan, he preferred a certain amount of uncertainty and the thought that he might lose his job added piquancy to the situation. He had to admit to a thrill of anticipation, and he felt it to be treacherous – somehow an illicit pleasure.

'Richard is in New York and Tom is in Oslo. Otherwise everyone should be in the country.' Julian was making a quick run-through of the members of the board, knowing that they would have to be summoned as soon as possible. Richard Frye was Armadale's finance director and Tom Stillwood the chief executive in charge of Armadale's engineering arm.

Again Nick looked at the clock on his desk. He made a quick calculation. 'Book Richard on Concorde and wake him up at six. You'd better try to get Tom first. Use the phone here.' Nick didn't want any telephone calls made where they could be overheard. There was no need for rumours to start before they had to. When they did, they would spread quickly enough.

Julian tried to reach Stillwood in his hotel room, but it was one hour later in Oslo and he had already gone for the day. He left a message to ring as soon as possible.

'I'll ask his office what his agenda is,' he said to Nick, and went back to the telephone.

'I'll do that. You get Concorde organized,' Nick grabbed the phone.

Julian decided that Sarah could make the plane reservation. It would not give anything away. He stepped out of the room and made the request. As Sarah moved to her telephone, Julian went on, a smile of unconcern forced on to his face, 'Would you see if Mr Clemens is in the building yet, and ask him to come up as soon as possible?'

'What shall I tell him . . .?' She looked puzzled. Summoning one of Armadale's managing directors without any explanation was not something she was in the habit of doing. By now, most of them were engrossed in meetings. Their day was well under way and difficult to interrupt.

'Just that Mr Bishop needs to speak to him as soon as

possible,' and with that uninformative reply, Julian gave Sarah a reassuring smile and went back into the office.

Nick was still on the telephone, standing impatiently by his desk, occasionally tapping a folder that lay on it with a pencil. He was looking out of the window at the rain, forecast for the afternoon, that had already darkened the day and was soaking the streets.

'Harold in yet?' Nick questioned Julian.

'Sarah's calling him up,' he answered after he had closed the door. 'It's all right,' he added in response to Nick's questioning look, 'I didn't say why.'

'They'll all know in half an hour anyway,' Nick spoke to himself more than to Julian. He was wondering what the point of secrecy was at this stage. As soon as the Stock Exchange opened, the word would be out, but he seemed to need those extra minutes of privacy.

A voice on the telephone interrupted his thoughts. 'Yes,' he spoke into the telephone. 'Tom Stillwood. Armadale Engineering. He was supposed to meet with Mr Dinesen this morning.' Nick spoke slowly, shouting a little, the way he automatically spoke to foreigners. 'Yes, I'll hold on.' He could barely conceal his irritation. 'Let's get the others in,' he said to Julian. 'You can use the phone over there.' Nick pointed to the second telephone on the low coffee table at the other end of his office.

The room was divided into two sections. Nick's desk was in front of the windows, facing the room. Before it were two wood-framed armchairs. On the wall, within reach of the desk and to the right of it, there was a bookshelf with reports in spiral binders, several annual reports, an atlas, a dictionary, a *Who's Who* and several recent books about business and businessmen. It was a spartan work area, Nick revealing himself here by what he did not have. The austerity of the environment was repeated at the other end of the room, which was equally functional, if slightly more comfortable. A sofa and two armchairs upholstered in neutral serviceable tweed provided a more relaxed seating area where Nick might receive guests, but there was something hard and rationed about it, reflecting disinterest. Indeed Nick had never thought about his room: its function, as far as he was concerned, was purely utilitarian.

Julian went over to the coffee table and sat down on the sofa. Rather than pick up the telephone, he took a pad of paper from the low table and began making notes, listing the numbers of the board of directors who would have to be gathered in. With Frye and Stillwood away, most were non-executive members. Andrews had chosen his moment with care, Julian realized. There was no truly practical advantage in making an offer when key people were away, since they could always return in a few hours – but the psychological advantage existed; the tactical ploy of attacking when the generals were absent created a little more confusion, more helter-skelter activity. It was bad for morale, and morale was the root of two important elements in a takeover – self-image and public image. A great deal of money was going to be spent in the next few weeks, or months perhaps, in trying to persuade the public and the shareholders that Armadale was a healthy, prosperous enterprise, fit to survive.

Julian looked up at his boss, wondering if Nick were capable of outsmarting such an experienced takeover man as Roger Andrews. 'Let me wait for the connection,' he said, seeing that Nick was still holding on to the telephone.

'It's all right,' Nick answered. 'You start. I'll take Tony Morris and George Freeman. You can have the others.'

'What about Howard Hicks? He's on both boards, isn't he? That's a little tricky,' Julian said. 'Shall I let him know?'

'Don't bother,' Nick answered sharply. 'He can't come anyway. He'll know that.'

Julian was about to question him further, but he had turned away and was speaking into the telephone. 'Tom. I've been trying to get you for ages.' Without listening to Stillwood's apologies for being unavailable at a time when he was, as he should have been, on other business, Nick launched into a mixture of rapid explanations and passionate imprecations against Corpcom and Andrews.

Julian picked up his own telephone and began trying to reach the other board members. He did not want to hear what Nick was saying; listening to Nick's outburst was like barging in on someone who was naked.

Howard was relieved he did not have to attend the Armadale board meetings, would not have to face Nick's animosity. And today, with any luck, he would be able to stay out of touch with everyone, at least until after lunch. As he stepped out of his car in front of a tall cream-coloured house in Holland Park, he turned to his driver who was holding an open umbrella out for him.

'If my wife calls, I'm in a board meeting,' he said, knowing Gordon would know what to do. Gordon nodded dutifully and watched him go carefully down the wet steps to the basement flat.

The door was opened by a young woman of about twenty-five, with short reddish hair and a pale freckled face that lit up when she smiled. And this she did when she saw Howard standing at the door, a comic cuddly figure under his big black umbrella, uncomfortable and forlorn.

'Howie,' she cried out, 'I didn't expect you today.' She embraced him with unembarrassed affection, her thin robe opening as she did so, revealing small breasts that made almost no impression on her figure, a prominent rib cage and thin, spindly legs.

Howard urged her inside ahead of him, out of the rain and away from Gordon's supervisory gaze. It was a small flat, with one bedroom at the back, which led out into a square patio garden. It was very warm, which explained Sheilah's dress on a raw winter's day. Howard began to sweat immediately and scrambled to get his coat off.

Sheilah helped him attentively, taking the coat from him, and hanging it up on a hook in the hall. Then, with both hands flat on his back, she pushed him into the sitting-room. This was simply and inexpensively furnished, mostly with modern pine furniture. The beige carpet was new and gave off a slightly metallic smell. There was a bookshelf crammed with well-read paperbacks against one wall, and on the coffee table an almost encyclopaedic array of magazines spilling over on to the floor.

She steered him to an armchair, untied his tie and sat on his lap. She kissed him on the neck, forcing a smile out of him, and he began to relax.

2

Alan Turner was among the first to find out about Corpcom's bid.

Every day, soon after 9.30, he would wander into the small room that housed the topic screen, to check the latest market news. He played the stock market a little, and the morning visit to the screen was one of several throughout the day to follow the progress of his 'horses'.

When he looked at the screen this morning, he saw the message spread across it, broken by the monitor's lines:

Corpcom PLC offering 250p per share in Armadale International plc.

Having seen it, he turned away out of habit. Then he stopped and looked again. He read the words a third time, swore and closed the door of the small den-like room, as if being alone would make the panic that was surging through him any easier to bear or any more likely to disappear.

He took a packet of cigarettes out of his pocket. He remembered the conversation he had had with Julian that morning. He extracted a cigarette, lit it and took the first long drag. He leaned his head back against the door and blew the smoke out slowly. Corpcom. There was no way out. Armadale couldn't compete with that, and Nick was as likely a match for Roger Andrews as David had been against Goliath, except that Nick had not been given mastery by the Lord. As Alan tried to consider the likely events of the next week, the thoughts came into his brain with such speed and randomness that he could no longer stay still.

'Alan. Are you all right?' said someone he walked into.

Alan looked up blankly. 'What?' he said. 'I'm fine. Fine. I'll see you later,' he added and hurried on, his behaviour no more understandable than before. The man looked after him for a second, as if he were trying to puzzle it out. He moved on, walking past the topic screen, not aware that a glance at it would have answered his question.

As soon as Alan reached his office, he closed the door and went to the telephone and rang home. He hung on for several rings more than necessary: Fanny might be in the bath or something. But she wasn't. She had gone out shopping for this evening – to 'cook up a storm'. He banged the phone down and swore. He paused, and punched three numbers.

'Mr Campbell's telephone.'

'Sarah. It's Alan Turner.' Alan knew everyone and used Christian names with most of them. 'Julian in?' He could not conceal his impatience.

'He's in with Mr Bishop at the moment. Can I get him to ring you back?'

'Please . . .' and he hung up, forgetting his usual farewell. He envied Julian's position now. He never had before, but he yearned to know what was going on in Nick's office. To relieve the frustration he went out into the corridor and headed for the first occupied office he could find. The rumour was beginning to spread; the virus had caught hold.

By 9.45, Julian and Nick had reached all the board members. A meeting had been set for early evening, by which time Richard would have got back from New York. It made sense to wait for Frye, the finance director, and it gave the other board members the time to adjust their schedules.

'What next?' Nick said. 'John Grahame,' he answered himself. John Grahame was Armadale's investment banker.

Following his own train of thought, Julian said, 'We should probably draft an internal memo – let people know what's going on.'

Nick hesitated.

'Everybody'll know by lunchtime, anyway. It should come from the top,' Julian argued.

'No,' Nick answered. 'Not before the board meeting.'

'That's not until this evening, sir. It's going to be pretty panicky around here by then.'

Nick was not afraid of making the decision to fight the takeover, but he felt that he should not. The board had been summoned. A state of emergency was about to be declared. He did not want to make any statements until his directors had gathered and talked. Morale was important, but it had already been shaken. Strategy was what really mattered now.

'We're fighting a war, Julian.'

The intercom on his desk buzzed and Sarah's voice announced Harold Clemens, the managing director of Armadale's chemical business. He did not wait for Nick's response but walked straight in, a short, broad-shouldered man bulging out of an ill-fitting grey suit, whose baldness accentuated the roundness of his head. His voice carried a slight Scottish lilt and, while he did not look like a bull terrier, he somehow reminded people of one.

'Harold, come in.' Nick spoke. 'Close the door, would you?'

As Clemens turned, the intercom's buzzer sounded again and Sarah's voice spoke through it, 'Mr Grahame is on the phone, Mr Bishop.'

At the mention of John's name, Clemens flashed a look at Nick, and then at Julian. He was beginning to think he knew what this was all about. To be called so peremptorily at 9.48 – he checked his watch – with the rumours of takeovers that had been circulating, the conclusion seemed obvious.

Nick took the telephone immediately, 'John. You've seen the news? I was just about to ring you.'

'Corpcom's offering 250p a share,' Julian explained to Clemens. 'Takeover, I'm afraid.'

'So that's what they were all in a cabal about.' Clemens said in reply. 'I saw some of the marketing people in a huddle, as if they were making an evil brew or something. By eleven o'clock it'll be all over the building.'

He stopped talking and turned towards Nick, who was still on the phone with Grahame. He turned back to Julian. '250p. How much is he valuing us at, then?'

'I haven't worked it out yet.' He took a calculator from his jacket pocket and punched in the numbers.

Clemens said nothing as he waited. He was never long-winded; words usually spilled out of him in bursts, and when he had finished their flow stopped abruptly. He could be silent for a long time, listening to others talk, or waiting for an answer with patience, and the stillness of his red-cheeked face was often assumed – wrongly – to be placidity.

'Just over half a billion,' Julian answered. 'Between 530 and 540 million,' he added. Quickly, he redid the calculation. It came to the same figure and he nodded to Clemens. 'It's not bad,' he added.

'But it could be much better,' Clemens said.

'Not much better.' Nick had hung up the telephone and had heard the last exchange. 'It's close enough to be bloody tempting. John is on his way,' he added.

Julian started for the door. 'I'll get Sarah to set up lunch for us in here.'

'Have her cancel my appointments,' Nick said after him. 'You'd better tell her,' he added.

Julian nodded and left. The feeling returned, the thrill, the novelty. Already every action seemed crucial, even the ordering of a meal.

'Sarah,' Julian said, with a false air of nonchalance, 'Mr Bishop asked if you would cancel his appointments for today.' He smiled pleasantly.

Julian and Sarah played games with each other in the office, keeping up an atmosphere of friendly baiting. It was a form of flirtation. Even now, Julian could not resist it. Sarah looked back at him, and Julian knew he had not fooled her. Sarah's blue-grey eyes, which brightened her otherwise plain-featured face, scanned Julian's.

'I'll do it right away,' she said. 'Alan Turner called for you a few minutes ago,' she added, probing. 'He seemed in a bit of a flap.'

He was about to discuss the food when Sarah said, still in the same apparently businesslike, unconcerned tone of voice, 'What should I say to people? The cancelled appointments,' she added with a smile.

'A bit of a crisis.'

'Thanks a lot, Julian. You're a true friend,' Sarah finally admitted her curiosity, bringing the cat-and-mouse game to an end.

Julian leaned forward towards her and, after a quick look around, said, 'Corpcom's trying to take us over.'

Sarah stared back at him. 'A takeover,' she muttered. She was silenced by the enormity of it.

Julian brought her back to matters in hand by discussing the details of the working lunch she was to order, but once he had gone back into Nick's office, she sat motionless, her hand poised on the telephone, her mind on the news Julian had just given her. She felt as if she had been mugged. It was not right, not fair. She got up and went to the staff washroom to compose herself.

When she returned, the door to Nick's office was open, and Nick was leaning over her desk, looking over her diary.

'I'm sorry, sir,' Sarah apologized for her absence. 'Do you need something?'

'It's all right,' he said. 'I was just . . .' He did not finish his sentence, but waved his hand vaguely over the diary.

'I'm sorry,' she said again. 'About the takeover, I mean. If there's anything I can do . . .' she let the sentence hang, unfinished.

'Thank you, Sarah,' Nick said, a little stiffly. 'I'm afraid we're going to be working rather long hours for the next couple of weeks.' He shifted back to action suddenly and said, 'Since you know, why don't you come in and help Julian coordinate.'

The cabal that Clemens had noticed had now removed to Alan Turner's office. It consisted of four people, including Alan. Four men standing and sitting around Alan's desk as if it were a coffin and they the pall-bearers.

'They're bound to make some sort of announcement.' Alan spoke.

'We already know what it'll say.' This was Jim Ferrar, the only one of the four whose face was not appropriately mournful and whose lean, bearded figure was half-seated on the desk, one leg dangling off it, the other touching the floor. He was almost an incongruity in the group. His tone was undramatic, ironic, almost bored.

Jim was a computer analyst, responsible for the entire computer network of the Armadale group of companies. He had designed it and his days were spent ministering to it, perfecting its capabilities. Even though it was more than likely he would have to go if Corpcom's bid succeeded, it was even more likely that another company would snap him up. He had refused many offers from headhunters, offers that would have increased his salary along with his responsibilities. But he enjoyed his work, he liked Nick Bishop and Armadale, and he was faithful to them. Leaving a company because someone he did not know had offered him slightly more money was not the way he did things.

He ha little time for the atmosphere of post-mortem that was dominating the conversation. That Corpcom might succeed was indeed a possibility. Although he realized it was a good possibility, it was at the moment no more than that. Not all the data was in.

For the others, their expertise was more indirectly valued; their future prospects were less certain. Redundancy is never attractive. For Edward Falcon, pushing fifty, a family man – a wife and two teenagers to feed, clothe and house – the prospect was frightening.

Edward had heard the news from Alan. After failing to

reach Julian, Alan had rushed into Edward's office. He announced the news with breathless, almost triumphant impatience. He could have been announcing the death of a film star, or a terrorist bombing somewhere in Central London.

He had spoken in subdued tones, with solemn, well-articulated words: 'We're being taken over . . .' followed by an appropriately dramatic pause. Edward had looked up at Alan and felt a sudden uncontrollable vertigo, as if he had been falling in a dream. His heart had slowed down, missed a beat, and then another, he had gasped for breath, inhaling deeply. As Alan had continued talking, not noticing the effect his words were having, Edward opened the top drawer of his desk, took out a box of pills and popped two in to his mouth.

Half an hour later, Edward was sitting in Alan's one visitor's chair, directly facing Alan, who was at his desk. Nothing said between them had brought solace, only increased anxiety. Edward was one of three managers in Armadale Chemicals. Corpcom was a large producer of chemicals, and it was clear that if the takeover was to succeed, some managers would have to go in the rationalization process which justified takeovers. At the moment, hardly listening to the other's conversation any more, Edward was already unemployed and unemployable in his mind. He saw himself telling his wife, saw her hold back the tears of disappointment and turn away. He imagined what he would say next. But then the image cracked and he was back in Alan's room. Jim was talking.

'This isn't getting us anywhere. I've got work to do.' Jim got off the table. He wore a tie, with trainers beneath brown trousers and a sports jacket, a man who was never quite shabby but was incapable of being smart either.

Edward got up too. He suddenly wanted to get out of this claustrophobic room, back into his own territory, his own small office.

The two men walked out together, Edward a hunched and already beaten figure in contrast to Jim's erect, compact energy.

'We might as well start looking for other jobs,' Alan called after them.

'I couldn't do that,' said Philip Porter, with an edge of disapproval.

Philip, the fourth man in the room, was overweight, balding, with the cheerful countenance of a man conditioned to look at the best side of everything. Often he did not recognize unpleasantness until it had passed him by. A colleague of Alan's in the marketing department, older, less ambitious, Philip had worked for Armadale for twenty years, longer than Nick, longer than almost every executive in the company. He had watched Armadale grow, like his own back garden. He bore it the same kind of affection. The thought of deserting now shocked him.

'I don't owe them anything,' was Alan's answer. As far as he was concerned, he was earning his living. Ethics had nothing to do with it.

'I wish life were that simple,' Philip said with melancholy as he too began to leave. Then his optimism returned, as regular as the waves in the ocean, 'Nothing's happened yet. We shouldn't be so gloomy.'

Alan looked after him. He didn't understand Philip's optimism or his melancholy. For Alan, life was simple. His primary duty was to himself. Once that was satisfied, then he could afford luxuries like fidelity. Shaking his head at the world's credulity, he picked up his telephone and tried to reach Fanny. There was still no answer.

'Where the hell is she?' He had no intention of getting back to work today.

Chapter Four

On the Monday morning, Roger Andrews had woken early. His wife Margaret still snored gently beside him. He had decided he would be happier if he got up. He had shaved, showered and dressed quickly and gone downstairs to the kitchen to make his own breakfast, not waiting for the house-keeper to bring it up on a tray as was customary. Making breakfast was as close to cooking as Andrews came, but he enjoyed it all the same on the rare occasions when he took the time. It was a peaceful, relaxing activity that required him to concentrate on something different. Some men played patience, some gardened, he made breakfast when he could. He darted around the large, almost professional kitchen, hesi-tating occasionally over the whereabouts of utensils. He found some boiled potatoes in the fridge and fried them up to go with scrambled eggs and sausages.

At seven o'clock, his car picked him up and drove him rapidly through the sparse traffic down the Hampstead hills towards Knightsbridge and Corpcom's headquarters. The sun was shining weakly. Later it would rain, but Roger did not notice the weather. The morning papers lay on his lap unread. He was reviewing what would happen over the course of the next sixteen to twenty hours.

He did not really know Nick personally; he had met him a couple of times at business conferences, but they had never exchanged more than a few words. He could sense Nick's antipathy, something that had been confirmed by Howard's over-hasty denial the night before.

But Roger had not lived his life based on the feelings of others. As far as he was concerned, feelings were a luxury most people couldn't afford. What Howard had told him last night, though, was that Nick would be a hard man to shake off once challenged. Roger thought about the call he would make to his new opponent at nine o'clock. That would be the launch. He shifted in the back seat. He suddenly felt like an actor about to go on stage, the mixed emotions of anxiety and anticipation pumping adrenalin into his blood.

He was the first into the building, let in by the night watchman who was about to go off duty. He took the lift up to the fifth floor and strode into his office overlooking the street.

Double-glazing kept the traffic noise out of the room. It was a large office, dominated by a partners' kneehole desk, with drawers on both sides. The leather centre-piece was well-worn and almost completely bare, but for a dark mahogany humidor, a gold pencil tray next to a pad of paper, and two telephones. Facing the desk was a pair of modern armchairs covered in black leather. At the other end of the room was a large antique table, also bare. It was as stark an office as Nick Bishop's, yet more comfortable and welcoming, and much more expensive. The walls were white, encouraging the light to brighten the room and on them were displayed three large blow-up photographs; black and white prints of the cities of Toronto, London and Philadelphia. It was Roger's way of imprinting his personality on the office, modern reminders of his past, of where he and Corpcom had sprung from.

He had led a peripatetic life from the very beginning. An only child, he was born in Toronto of an American father and an English mother. His father, an engineer from Philadelphia, had met his mother while in Europe on a job. Returning with her to America he had then been tempted by the adventures of Canadian exploration. He spent much of the thirties on field trips in the North-West Territories, leaving his family in Toronto. Eventually, a divorce had separated the family, and Roger and his mother had left for England. During the

Second World War, Roger was sent back to his father, who had returned to his native Philadelphia. Kindergarten in Toronto, primary school in London, secondary school and university in America had shaped Roger's nomadic life. He had learned to depend on himself and to feel at home everywhere.

He had started in the fast-food business, and through acquisition had fed his urge for change, going from food chains to food distribution, to food production, until his company spanned the United States. As impetuously and determinedly as he had become a businessman, he sold out when his mother, who was still living in England, became ill. Taking everything he had, he began again, working out of England and Europe this time. His new empire, built once more on food distribution, but encompassing chemicals, computer technology, and building materials, reached across Europe and back towards the United States, via the Far East. This was Corpcom.

There was an extra device on Roger's desk this morning. A tape-recorder was connected to the speaker of one of the telephones. Going straight to that phone Roger pressed the speaker button and punched in a code number. He listened as the connection was made. There was no ring at the other end, for the code he had used, though it reached through to Armadale headquarters, did so silently, activating the microphone that had been placed in the lone telephone in the Armadale boardroom just before the two intruders had dealt with Nick's office. From the comfort of his own office, Roger would thus be able to monitor Armadale's emergency board meetings. Now there was nothing but silence. Armadale was still sleeping. Nevertheless, he did not kill the connection, but instead started the tape-recorder. Armadale's boardroom was wired for sound.

'He stood for a couple of moments, listening to the silence crackling through the speaker. Then he turned the volume on the speaker down and walked around the desk to his chair. He sat down, opened the humidor on his desk and took out the first cigar of the day. He did not light it immediately but stuck it in his mouth and chewed on it.

Roger had still not lit his cigar when Peter McNeal arrived at 8.30. Peter's demeanour was jaunty. He almost bounced into the room, a sardonic smile on his face. He was athletic-looking, and seemed almost Prussian with his fair hair and blue eyes. He had a tan which at this time of year could only have come from a skiing holiday or a sun lamp, and Peter was a man who rarely took holidays. He was very much a product of his age. He had entered business after spending six years educating himself for the job: a first-class degree in economics at an English university and an MBA at an American one. Peter believed in the infallibility of numbers and the inodorousness of money. Above all he believed in his own success. Roger liked him for this. And also because he could be trusted not to confuse business decisions with moral choices.

This morning, Peter had dressed for the occasion. He wore a flamboyantly tailored brown suit, a green tie with a blue shirt and, as a final touch, a turquoise pocket handkerchief puffed out of his breast pocket. Roger surveyed the young man who was his finance director, and much more than that: a combination of pupil, adviser, consultant, and chief minister, as well as occasional servant. In their own way, the two men were friends.

'You're a dead giveaway. Every time we make a bid, you come in looking like a South American parrot.'

Peter laughed. 'I dress for the occasion, that's all. In corporate wars one can afford to be well-dressed.'

'When's Rupert coming in?' Roger returned to business. Rupert Smythe was Corpcom's banker and adviser. During any takeover, men like Roger Andrews were supposedly bound to heed their banker's advice. More often than not with Roger it was the other way around. Of course, Andrews was an experienced takeover artist, but his was also a very large account. It certainly did not pay to argue too much with that kind of client.

'Soon after nine,' Peter answered. 'We'd better not let him into this room,' he added with a smile. He was looking at the tape-recorder on the desk. The caution was unnecessary: Roger operated stringently on 'need-to-know'.

Roger and Peter were very confident indeed, but their exuberance today was more a lust for battle than premature triumph. They both enjoyed the process of a takeover, especially when it was to be contested. Had they been questioned on this by shareholders, they could have honestly replied that they never favoured a contest over a friendly acquisition. They went after companies because they wanted to own them, not because they wanted a fight. But, like cats playing with mice, they both enjoyed the battle, always ensuring that the odds were on their side.

'How did it go with Howard last night?' Peter asked.

'As expected,' came Roger's answer. He shuddered, 'The guy gives me the creeps. I don't know why I keep him on the board.'

'Because everybody's a friend of his.'

'Jesus. I can't think why,' said Roger.

'What did he say?' Peter persevered.

'He said Bishop wouldn't go for it.' Roger said it begrudgingly. They had spoken about this before, and Roger had persisted in trying for an early victory by trying to persuade Nick not to fight the bid. 'We'll see,' he added with a stubborn tone of finality.

Following the lead he had been given, Peter turned to something else. 'I spoke to Simon Harner yesterday afternoon. He wants an interview with you.' He added in answer to Roger's questioning look, 'I told him I could probably arrange it.'

'Let him call us,' Roger said. 'I'll talk to him on the phone and set up a meeting for later this week. Give him an exclusive. Put him on our side.'

'He'll love it,' Peter said.

'That's pretty good timing,' Roger went on. He liked good omens. He was not superstitious, but he did not think one should ignore the signs that fate put in one's path.

'I prodded him along a bit,' McNeal said with a smile that could not avoid being smug. He had rung Simon, who was a university friend, knowing that if he chatted long enough the journalist would not be able to resist asking for an interview. He would know he was being manipulated but he would think the knowledge meant he was in control. That is what Peter counted on.

'We won't talk to the press today then. Just Harner. The others can wait till tomorrow.' It was all fitting into place. Roger wanted to give a press conference, but had been against doing it on the day the offer was announced; better to keep something back, not fire all his shots in one go. A press conference was not expected, or even necessary, but it would be useful. Roger liked the drama of it.

The delay of the press conference was also a tactical move. Nick and his board would have taken some decisions by the end of the first day. To have to make alterations, even psychological ones, because of new information would keep them off balance a little longer. Roger wanted to prolong Armadale's period of indecision as much as possible.

2

Throughout the rest of the day, people who had not expected to do so walked into the Armadale building on Cannon Street. Bankers, solicitors, stockbrokers, accountants, public-relations people had cancelled appointments and answered the summons that, like a call to arms, rang out from the Armadale corporate headquarters.

John Grahame, Armadale's banker, had arrived soon after ten with two colleagues. Fifty-five, tall, unruffled, he was the image of a merchant banker, with a patrician nose and uncommitted brown eyes, dressed in a conservative dark-grey suit, a blue striped shirt and a navy pindot tie. He brought with him to Armadale a calming influence and unimpassioned advice.

As soon as Sarah saw him coming towards her, flanked by

his two younger colleagues, she was standing up and moving towards the door of the office.

'Mr Bishop's expecting you, sir,' was all she said as she opened the door for him.

When he came into the office, he found Nick and Julian sitting at the coffee table, looking over the twenty-five pages of Corpcom's offer document, several copies of which had arrived soon after 9.30.

Nick stood up John came in. They shook hands silently. It seemed for a moment as if the doctor had come to look at a patient and diagnose an illness the family already suspected. John turned from Nick and nodded to Julian. He saw the document that Nick still held in his hand, his index finger marking his place.

'The offer document,' the banker stated, bluntly.

'Yes. Julian will get you some copies,' Nick answered. He looked over to Julian who had already stood up and moved towards an open cardboard box on the floor.

'They certainly aren't wasting time,' John Grahame said. 'None of this twenty-eight days nonsense. They must have very good security.'

He was referring to the rules that govern takeovers, laid out and explained by the Panel on Takeovers and Mergers, in a document entitled, 'The City Code on Takeovers and Mergers and the Rules Governing Substantial Acquisitions of Shares'. According to this code, Corpcom had twenty-eight days from the announcement of its bid for Armadale to publicize the details of the offer. That Roger Andrews had been able to post the offer document on the day of the announcement itself meant it had been in preparation for nearly two weeks. Grahame was right; there had been no leaks of Corpcom's intentions.

He looked up from the document after a quick glance. 'We should get an announcement up on the topic screen.'

'We're rejecting the offer,' Nick said quickly.

'We need the board to do it formally,' John responded. 'We should just advise shareholders to take no action pending formal advice from the board.' He looked over to his female assistant who nodded back to him. 'That will alert the institutions that we'll be fighting it.'

'All right,' Nick said, allowing himself to be led for the moment.

As in the scores of takeover bids and mergers that he had supervised, John was beginning to go through the steps of defence. With the offer document in his hand, he looked around the office for somewhere to sit.

'Since we've got this in hand,' he said to Nick, 'perhaps we should read it first and then talk.'

There was tension between the two men. Although Nick relied on the banker, John also represented an uncertain threat. He knew Armadale from the outside as much as from the inside. He assessed it financially and on its potential. The past had no sway for him, as it did for Armadale's employees. Grahame's fidelity – for there was fidelity – was to Armadale's performance and to its shareholders. It turned his advice into a source of anxiety and fear. There was no emotional appeal against it; if one's own financial adviser were to recommend selling, there was little one could do to prevent a takeover. To Nick, this amounted to something less than full commitment, however correct it was. He liked to be able to trust people unreservedly.

'We'll put you in the boardroom,' Nick said. 'We can work out of there. It's the best place.'

'While we do that, you should get your people and the accountants to check it over,' John said. 'We're going to have to do it anyway.'

'Julian,' Nick said, handing the task over to his assistant. He led the banker and his two assistants out of the office and down the corridor to the boardroom.

'We've got fourteen days to get our defence document out,' John said to Nick. 'That doesn't leave us much time.'

'I know.' Nick sounded irritated.

*

Harold Clemens had been right. The entire building knew of the bid by eleven o'clock. For a while, Armadale seemed to be alive with a murmur of protest. It settled down again, but the nervous edge that had started at the top in Nick's office, spread through the company and remained. The atmosphere was tense and quarrels flared like fireflies.

The men gathered in Nick's office, forming ranks, setting up their lines of defence, dividing the work that had to be done. Led by John and his two assistants, they made ready for the board meeting that evening and for the next several days: outlining a hierarchy, organizing committees, lines of communications, drafting statements of renunciation, press releases, letters to stockholders, an examination of Corpcom's actual offer and, finally, prodded by the bankers, the first steps towards an examination of Armadale itself.

3

Although Corpcom's own pulse had been running faster than usual, by lunchtime activity in the building was back to normal. The chaos belonged to the other side.

Throughout the day, at three-hour intervals, the young man with the spiky fair hair and the earring from the Ford Escort parked in Armadale's garage had returned to Corpcom with a package of tapes. As instructed, he went to the fourth floor and asked for Peter McNeal, who came out in person each time. They were recordings of all that was said in Nick's office, transmitted by the radio microphone placed in the bottom drawer of his desk to the receiver in the parked car beneath the building.

Listening with Roger in his office, Peter gloated over the evident panic – he felt as if he had let a fox loose in the neighbour's hen coop. Roger was more interested in how matters developed, than in how people were affected by them. Armadale was in a state of shock, as it should be. This was part of the expected run of events. After about forty-eight hours it would slowly subside. His side would try to prolong it, if possible.

By lunchtime too, the telephone calls from the press had been fielded. Apart from Simon Harner, who had rung and to whom Roger had spoken briefly and promised an interview on the following Thursday, journalists had been stonewalled, referred to the official press release of that morning, and asked to wait until the following day's press conference.

By lunchtime, Rupert Smythe had left Corpcom, satisfied that he could no longer do anything useful there. In the last several weeks, he had spent many hours with Roger and Peter, going over the preparations for the offer, the valuation of Armadale, the financing of the takeover itself. But now, his advice would not be needed until there was a reaction.

Still, Smythe had spent most of the morning reviewing the materials Roger would be using at the press conference, which was scheduled for ten the following morning. The principal elements were figures: past and future sales, past and future profits, earnings per share for Corpcom and for Armadale. They provided the rationale for Corpcom's offer for Armadale and the reasons shareholders should sell to Corpcom. All these would appear in the slide programme that would accompany Roger Andrews' talk. The television cameras were to be allowed in and Smythe wanted to be even more careful. Any misleading information could backfire on them if the Takeover Panel censured Corpcom's behaviour. The bank's name was behind any financial assertion and it was therefore Smythe's task to ensure these figures were acccurate and that Corpcom could do what it promised.

Smythe was younger than Grahame, his opposite number on the Armadale team, less assured, and more rigid. He found it hard to keep pace with Roger's more flamboyant manner and his sudden moves. To Roger he was a tool, scarcely a serious adviser. Andrews had performed so many takeover bids that he rarely felt the need of advisers any more. He used them as a foil for his ideas; with Smythe, he found it almost irresistible, when spending any length of time in the banker's company, not to provoke him in some way.

'I'm going to put that fool Bishop through the wringer,' he

said, during their third meeting of the day. 'You should have heard him on the telephone.'

'You don't want to be too direct, Roger,' Peter fed his boss the line like a good straight man.

'Why the hell not?' Roger exclaimed. 'I'm not afraid of putting my cards on the table.'

Smythe felt compelled to intervene. The last thing he wanted was Roger making unnecessary allegations about Armadale. 'Roger, I think you should just stick to the facts tomorrow,' he said cautiously.

'Bishop's the wrong man for the job. That's a fact,' Roger continued.

'That's open to question, I think,' Smythe was becoming irritated. 'After all, over the last four years, the company has been increasing its profits and its dividends almost every quarter. I don't think you can. . . .'

'Five per cent is the best they've done. The earnings per share went down three years ago.'

'But they've been up for the last two years,' Smythe said.

'Less than 5 per cent,' Roger countered. 'We're paying out almost 40 per cent more every year. That's what I call good management.'

'I thought we'd agreed that you'd be stressing rationalization. That combining the businesses would provide a strong platform for expansion. You don't want to do anything that will allow them to shop you to the Takeover Panel. Stick to the facts and don't get too personal.' Smythe was adamant.

'So the Panel will smack my hand and I'll say, "I'm sorry. I didn't mean it." The Panel's a joke.' Roger looked over at Peter and then back to Smythe. Looking at Smythe's serious, stricken face, he began to smile.

'Roger, I wish you wouldn't do that. It really isn't a joke.' Smythe was annoyed at being nettled in this way, especially since he knew that Roger was quite capable of carrying all of it out, regardless of advice or common sense. 'Anyway,' he added indignantly, 'the Takeover Panel is far from being a joke and you know it.'

'You're right, Rupert,' Roger said. 'The first rebuttal should come this afternoon.' He went on, back to business as rapidly as he had started in on Smythe. 'Keep 'em off balance,' was almost a motto, and he practised it in everything he did. 'I doubt they'll get the letter to the shareholders out before tomorrow.'

'Everything else all right?' Peter asked Smythe, building him up again.

'Looks like it,' he replied. He was looking forward to getting back to the office. He got up to leave.

Peter rose as well, 'I'll see you out.'

As Smythe stepped into the lift, the man with the spiky hair and earring came out of it with yet another package. Full of anticipation, Peter took the package back with him to Roger Andrews' office.

'Tapes,' he said as he walked in, waving it in the air.

They heard Roger's call to Nick, and they listened with glee as Nick vented his fury after he hung up. Both men were rapt, as if listening to a favourite radio programme. When Nick called them 'bastards', Peter smiled with satisfaction and Roger let out a laugh that shook his belly.

'Poor Howard . . .' Peter said. 'He sounded so miserable.'

'He's a weasel.' Roger said. After a moment he added, 'Shit. You were right. Howard was right. He didn't even begin to go for it. Jerk.'

'Everybody told you so.' Peter said. 'Doesn't matter. No harm's been done.'

'Every man is supposed to have his price,' Roger said. But there was a lightness in his voice, very little disappointment. He seemed unconcerned that his plan had not worked. But then, his master plan was working. Nick's refusal to play along was a small diversion in the overall scheme. This takeover had taken months to organize. It was going on schedule, even up to the scene Roger and Peter had just overheard.

'I wish you'd told Howard we'd bugged Bishop's office,' Peter said, his voice sounding bored.

'We couldn't do that. Even Howard has a vague sense of ethics. You've got to watch him. He'll do the right thing if you give him an excuse.'

'Oh, I know,' said Peter. 'But we're going to have to listen to that conversation all over again. You know how proud Howard is of his photographic memory.'

Chapter Five

I

Late that same Monday morning, Howard was still in bed. Sheilah was dressed, preparing lunch in the kitchen. They had made love, a long, slow half hour of delayed passion, drawn out with sensual skill by Howard. He wanted to kill his anxiety and nervousness about the takeover and had lost himself in Sheilah's skinny flesh, moving only slightly, his hands exploring lazily, as if he were forcing himself to relax by slowing himself down. He had slept afterwards, and now, while Sheilah was cooking, he sat up in bed, naked in the warm flat, reading.

Sheilah was a good cook. She was self-taught, a 'natural', her talent developed during the hours spent alone in her basement flat. She fed Howard meals he knew he should not eat yet was unable to resist. He put on weight regularly this way, but it was unlikely that Norma would notice or, if she did, that she would suspect the cause. The Hicks marriage was one of habit rather than love. Yet had Norma known of Howard's constant infidelity, she would inevitably have been angry and hurt; discovery would have made her isolation concrete.

Howard had just started a new chapter when the telephone rang. Sheilah would answer it in the kitchen. Howard rarely got telephone calls here. He usually did not bother with them, but today he stopped reading and waited to hear whether it was for him.

'It's a man called Peter McNeal,' she called to him.

Howard winced. He had known it would be one of them.

'I'll take it in the sitting-room,' he called back. He waited an instant further, heard Sheilah say, 'He won't be a moment,' and got out of bed, swinging his legs out of the covers and sitting up. He paused again, sighed; he wished he did not have to answer it. Finally he stood up and walked, still naked, to the telephone in the sitting-room. His body was slightly pear-shaped, with oddly thin legs beneath the bulk of his torso.

'Hello,' he said in a tired, resigned tone of voice as he settled into a comfortable chair. He made no attempt to conceal how unwelcome the call was.

'Sorry to bother you, Howard,' Peter McNeal said. 'We wondered if you'd spoken to your friend.'

Peter was going through the motions of pretending that he and Roger did not already know the outcome of Howard's conversation with Nick. It was a measure of his attention to detail.

Howard was on the defensive. Having undertaken to take the call from Nick and, if possible, make the offer of a deal, he should have reported on any conversation he might have had. 'I've been very busy, I'm afraid, since I spoke to him. I'm sorry about that. But perhaps we should talk about this in person,' he said carefully, delighted that he might be able to delay.

'Perhaps we should . . .' Peter thought it highly unlikely that anyone would be listening in on this conversation, but he was cautious. If his side was capable of bugging, so were other people. He knew that Corpcom was clean, but there was no knowing who was listening in on Howard's mistress's telephone. 'Why don't you come in for lunch?'

Howard automatically glanced towards the kitchen.

'Can't make lunch, I'm afraid,' he said. 'How about 2.30?'

'Fine. Come in then.'

'Good.' Then Howard added, slightly surprised at Peter's lack of curiosity, 'We were right, by the way.'

'Ah, yes. I assumed so.' Peter said and hung up.

'Do you have to go, Howie?' Sheilah was in the doorway,

looking at him. A call for Howard usually meant that he would be forced to leave.

'Not until after lunch,' he said. 'I'll get dressed.'

'Good.' Sheilah went back into the kitchen delighted.

Howard walked back into the bedroom. He went to the bed, picked up the open book and read a few words. It was pointless; he could not concentrate. Sadly he closed it, dropping it back on the bed.

Howard looked about him as he entered the Corpcom building. He could not escape the thought that perhaps there were spies about, watching, trying to find out who was coming and going. Although he felt that no one could reproach him for his behaviour up till now, his going to Corpcom and not to Armadale today indicated a choice of sides. He did not want this choice made public. Especially he did not want to feed Nick's already burning sense of betrayal.

The conversation with Roger and Peter took place in the boardroom.

Peter was the first to come in. He shook hands with Howard. 'Sorry to bring you in here,' he said, 'but this is our war room. We thought we might as well "de-brief" you in it.' He smiled.

'Boardrooms always make me think of food,' Howard said, as he sat down at the long rectangular table surrounded by chairs. 'They look like dining-rooms,' he added.

Peter looked down at Howard from behind, saw his broad back, noticed a mole on the back of his shortened neck, the skin creased where the shirt collar was a little tightened, and smiled at the remark. He imagined that most things reminded Howard of food.

'I see what you mean about "war room",' Howard said as he looked at the wall in front of him.

It was covered with sheets of drafting paper, charted with numbers and graphs, some indicating share prices, others sales and profit figures for both Armadale and Corpcom. Howard did not really see why they could not have met in

Roger's office. It seemed a little odd but he did not think about it for long. It did not occur to him that the reason might be a telephone bug, an 'infinity device', linked to a speaker on Roger's desk.

Roger came in almost at a run. 'Howard,' he said as a greeting, 'Peter tells me he didn't go for it.'

'I'm afraid not, Roger,' Howard said, but there was little disappointment in him. He began reporting the conversation, even describing where he had been when it took place.

Peter betrayed his lack of interest in Howard's report by allowing his gaze to wander, watching the early winter darkness fall over Harrods. Roger performed better, showing more interest. It did not matter. Howard did not notice Peter's boredom, for he could not imagine that they both already knew what he was telling them with such zealous accuracy. As Peter had said, Howard's memory never failed; it was a source of pride to him.

He enjoyed this particular report as well. He loved his friend Nick for his very difference from himself, for his uprightness, for his honour. To hold him up as an example of incorruptibility before men like Roger Andrews and Peter McNeal gave him a sense of satisfaction. He made a point of mentioning that Nick had described Roger as a 'terrorist'.

Andrews sneered at the remark, but he made no further comment.

When he finished his account, Howard said, 'I did warn you, Roger.'

'It was to be expected,' Roger snapped back. 'But I wanted to try it.'

'I just hope Nick isn't going to blame me for the whole thing.' Howard was feeling sorry for himself and wanted to remind Roger of the favour he had performed for him.

'You didn't have to do it,' Roger Andrews said. He felt no sense of gratitude, and was not willing to coddle Howard. He despised him for his lack of backbone; he used Howard's elasticity but did not respect it. Now that he had heard

Howard out, he gave him short shrift. He was even practical in that. If Roger needed to cover up the bugging, still he had no need to be nicer to Howard than he usually was.

Howard could have refused to get involved, and sat squarely on the fence. Now he realized that his behaviour had earned him nothing but the resentment of a friend and the contempt of a foe. He left Corpcom with eagerness, in a rush almost.

When he arrived home at 5.30, Howard burst in on Norma having a bath. She heard the front door open, knowing that it was unusual for Howard to come home so early, and she had a moment of panic, fear gripping her at the thought that it might be an intruder; in the bath, she felt even more alone and vulnerable than usual.

'Who is it?' she called out in a shrill, frightened voice.

From the other end of the house, Howard was calling her name: 'Norma?' He went from room to room. Eventually they recognized each other's voices. Howard went into the bathroom and Norma's fear turned to guilt at being caught in a bath in the afternoon.

'I wondered where you were?' Howard said, looking down at his wife's naked body, her heavy breasts bobbing up in the water like buoys, the nipples warning lights for ships passing in the night, her large stomach wrinkled above, her pubic hair, a thick greying bush, her legs overweight, but still a reminder of shapeliness past.

'I want to go to the cinema tonight,' Howard said, out of context.

'There's something I want to see on the telly,' she replied.

'We can tape it.'

'It's raining, Howard.'

'So what?' Howard did not want to be at home this evening.

'You want to go out to the cinema on a rainy, cold January night,' Norma looked up at Howard in amazement. He was normally so lazy; it was impossible to get him out of the house once he had returned. 'We haven't been to the cinema for over a year. You don't like the cinema.'

'Rubbish. I don't like bad films, but I love the cinema,' he said. 'Please, Norma. Let's go out.' He searched his brain for a good explanation. He did not even know what films were playing. 'I feel like it. I just feel like it. I can't explain.'

So it was settled. They went to the early evening show and then out to supper afterwards.

It was an expensive meal in the restaurant of an inn built out of a Tudor house. The dining room was small, its white walls contrasting with the dark heavy beams. Soft light came from a mock, gas-powered log fire in the fireplace and candles burned at each table. Howard ordered lavishly, as if he could get rid of his anxiety with calories: coquilles Saint Jacques, a gratin Dauphinois with his lamb, and even cheese after a chocolate torte. When he ordered a burgundy as well as champagne, Norma asked him, 'What are we celebrating?'

'Nothing,' he answered. 'I just wanted to spend some time out of the house with you.'

It was not a lie. Howard wanted to be out of the house so that he need not hear any more about the takeover, but he also wanted to be safe. Norma was his companion of many years, and habit was at times as warming as love.

Chapter Six

I

Richard Frye's day had disappeared in a supersonic rush. Armadale's finance director had left New York at nine a.m. Five hours later, at seven p.m., he walked into the boardroom.

The board meeting started a few minutes later. It included all its members, executive and non-executive, except for two. Robert Sands, the only American on the board, had not come over from New York. He was on a telephone hook-up for most of the meeting. And of course, Howard was not there.

While they waited for Richard to arrive, the members of the board sat in their assigned places, reading. Nick had met them all as they came in. He had shaken hands with them and showed them into the boardroom, where they each exchanged a couple of words with John before they moved on to do their homework.

Nick had then retreated to his own office, where he continued to go over the re-organization of Armadale with Julian. John remained in the boardroom, standing, deliberately looking out of the windows towards the Thames and the Embankment; he did not want to catch the roving eye of any of the members of the board and be forced into conversation yet.

The boardroom was a large, rectangular room, as anonymous and unattractive as the building; the windows were steel-framed, covered with white blinds, and opened with difficulty. John had pulled his blind up so that he could better stare at the twinkling lights that skirted the river. The room was compressed between a mottled brown carpet and a low white ceiling made up of square insulation tiles. Under the central lighting track ran a long table with curved ends. Against the bare inside wall, a low cabinet stretched along the length of the room. On it a solitary telephone sat. After a day spent in and out of the room, which even now he could see reflected in the window pane, John thought that a successful takeover might lead to Armadale abandoning the building, which could only be an improvement.

He turned to face the others when Richard entered, Nick and Julian following behind him. Richard's face was notable because it was so hairy. Heavy eyebrows formed a horizontal line across his face with hardly a break over the nose, matching his thick brown hair, which grew low over his brow, and the little tufts that even grew out of his ears. He was broad-shouldered and just under six feet tall. His public-school accent had a nasal twang. Even though he had been travelling, he wore a grey suit and a waistcoat over a blue shirt, topped with a white collar.

He walked in, threw a glance at John, and went over to his seat, picking up the offer document before sitting, looking around at the other men at the table with a half smile of greeting.

'Sorry to have kept you waiting. I came as quickly as I could.' Richard did not take anything too seriously.

'How was the flight?' asked Sir Edward Reald politely.

At sixty-six, Sir Edward was the oldest member of the board. A former head of research at International Chemicals, he was Armadale's consultant and ambassador, mainly for their chemical interests. But he was colourful and eccentric enough to be an asset in more general discussion; he often came at problems from an unusual perspective, throwing out solutions nobody else would have thought of. His face was sharp and angular, every bone outlined against the taut skin, and there was a gravelly tone to his voice which seemed to inspire respect.

'Squashed,' Richard responded. 'But very fast,' he added.

Nick called the meeting to order.

'I've asked John to be with us for obvious reasons,' he said. 'This is an emergency meeting to respond to Corpcom's bid for us and we need John's advice on how to handle the problem. I'd like Julian Campbell – whom you all know – to sit in as well. He works closely with me anyway, and if you approve, I'd like to suggest him as main coordinator during the time of the offer.' Nick paused and looked around the table. He expected no objections but he had to make sure.

'We'll get to that in due course,' he went on. 'You've all read the offer. I'm sorry, Richard,' Nick turned to Richard, who was reading it as Nick spoke.

'Go ahead,' Richard said, without looking up.

'So we know what we're dealing with.' Nick paused for an instant. He took a breath, 'I don't need to tell you that I am completely opposed to recommending the offer. Of course, we all have a responsibility to our shareholders. I don't deny that, but I do deny that we would be treating them badly if we try to hold on. As I see it, the price is reasonably fair. But then, why should we sell? In a year's time we can get a better price. The only way Andrews can do this is by selling each division off separately. Where will Armadale be then? The fact is, he's not interested in Armadale, but in the growth of Corpcom. His company grows by acquisition. He has shown that many times. What he's also shown is that his growth is at other people's expense. Andrews' taking over Armadale may be good for Corpcom's shareholders, but I promise you it won't be good for ours.'

'Of course Andrews is an asset-stripper,' said George Freeman. He was a round-faced man with glasses who, because he spoke methodically and with an upper-class accent, often sounded pompous. 'But I haven't noticed shareholders too bothered about that these days. What do Hawthorne's say?' he asked.

'I spoke to them this morning,' Nick said in reply. Hawthorne's were stockbrokers, and were Armadale's link to the Stock Exchange and with the institutions who were the principal shareholders in Armadale as well as in most of the country's public companies. 'The fund managers can go either way. As you say, I doubt they care very much which way. What we have to do is persuade them they can make more money with us.'

'Can we?' Sir Edward asked, never afraid of the facts.

'I think we can,' Nick answered. At the moment, he was not prepared to think otherwise. It was a determined sentiment, and while the others were willing to go along with it, their conviction was not as strong.

'I certainly think it is questionable whether Roger controlling this company will help it grow in the way it has in the last few years under Nick's management.' John had finally spoken.

It was a slow, even delivery, and it comforted everyone. Their independent adviser had backed them. They all breathed more easily.

'Before we go on and give you an outline of the kind of organization we are going to have to set up in the next few days,' John continued, 'it's my responsibility to warn you . . .' He paused in mid-sentence, '. . . a policeman reading you your rights, as it were,' he allowed himself a smile, trying to downplay the solemnity of the caution. 'Secrecy and security are now vitally important. Anything we say, casually sometimes, to a friend, out loud somewhere, can potentially affect share prices. We all know this. It's important to try to stick to the principle of "need to know". It's not just a question of dealing, I should add. It's important for what we are trying to do. Andrews knows that. We just have to look at ourselves to know how successful his security has been. The truth is, we didn't see it coming.'

'We all understand that, John,' said Jasper Thomas, Armadale's solicitor, a pale, thin man with high cheekbones and fine fair hair. Even his eyelashes were blond, and the effect gave a slightly eerie quality to his face.

'As I said, it's my duty to make the warning,' John was unmoved by the solicitor's petulant tone. 'I've said my piece. We can move on.' There were no objections. 'Julian, why don't you take over?' he said.

Julian was sitting away from the table, an acknowledge-ment that he was not a member of the board. He was there as a back-up. He got up now and moved towards a large flip-chart that was set up on an easel behind Nick.

Before he could say anything, Nick said, 'Julian's going to be heading up what we're calling the Defence Committee. Everything we do is going to be cleared through it.'

'And I'll be reporting directly to you, of course,' Julian said to the room, anxious to keep his task in the proper hierarchical perspective. He flipped up the first blank sheet and revealed a diagram of the new, militaristic organization. It looked like a family tree, with rectangular boxes represent-ing groups rather than people and black horizontal and vertical lines indicating links and relationships.

At the top of the pyramid was the 'Armadale Board' and directly below it Julian's own 'Defence Committee'. Lines went out left and right from that committee towards Fair-childs, representing John and his assistants, and towards Hawthorne's, the stockbrokers. These institutions were the two main advisers, symbolically flanking the tree. Then there were other boxes, for each important task that had to be carried out: the defence document, the Corpcom research group, the contacts section, the PR team, the advertising campaign. Julian went from one to the other, explaining the task of each boxed section. Finally, he came to the last rec-tangle, right at the bottom of the chart, the South Pole to Armadale Board's North. The letters there said 'MMC'.

'MMC,' started Julian, 'refers to the Monopolies and Mer-gers Commission.'

'I think we need to be fairly realistic,' John cut in. He paused, just long enough for the others to turn their attention away from Julian and the flip-chart towards him. 'Our share price leapt up today by 30p. It'll probably keep going. Corpcom's has stayed pretty steady. I don't want to make any rash statements at the very beginning, but I think we should work very hard to get this bid referred to the Monopolies Commission. It would give us breathing space and drag the battle on for months. I don't think Andrews would wait that long. He'll move on.'

'Are you saying that we're going to lose if we don't get the bid referred?' Sir Edward asked, trying to pierce John's equivocations.

'No, I'm not. Most bids are not referred,' John replied. 'We can't assume this one will be. But it's a good way of stopping them if we can manage it.'

'It's tricky,' Freeman said. 'It's a lobbying effort, not a straight request.'

'Absolutely,' John said. 'We must not be seen to be trying to get a reference.' He looked over towards Nick. 'If any of us is interviewed about it, the standard reply is that it's not in our hands. It's a matter for the authorities.'

'We should get on it right away,' Nick was back in charge of the meeting.

'Let's get this straight, though,' John continued. 'We are trying to enable the Secretary of State to reach the right decision. That is our aim, and we should not forget it.'

'Why the hypocrisy?' asked Sir Edward. 'We can lie to others without lying to ourselves, surely?'

'We'll be more convincing if we believe our own lies,' answered John.

His response created a lull. It was as if the strangeness of the behaviour he suggested had at last made concrete the reality of what was going on, that in five or six weeks, they might no longer be sitting here every month, that Armadale might no longer be their company but somebody else's, that the name of Armadale might no longer exist.

By 9.30 the board meeting was winding down. The rest of the battle-plan had been discussed. It was not complicated: build the image of a solid and profitable company, persuade the shareholders that this was the case. There was little else to be done at the moment, although a great deal of work would have to go into that simple operation. John suggested waiting for Andrews' press conference before firing any shots against

Corpcom. Everybody, with the exception of Nick, was relieved. He wanted to move immediately, but the others needed a breather, time to collect their thoughts. Julian would go to the press conference and try to glean as much information as he could.

When Nick sensed the weariness of the board, he raised one last topic: Howard Hicks.

'Most of you know, I imagine, that Howard is on Corpcom's board. That's why he's not here tonight.' He paused.

'What is it, Nick?' Sir Edward said.

'Howard's a very old friend,' Nick said. 'But . . . I wonder if there isn't a conflict . . .'

'You can be the best judge of that,' Sir Edward spoke again. He was firm.

'There's no conflict if he doesn't sit in on the board meetings during the takeover period,' said George, another non-executive board-member.

The non-executive members were aware of Howard's predicament. They all sat on other boards and could encounter a similar conflict. The general rule, written into the City Code, was that the board-member with a conflict did not sit in on the relevant discussions. Freeman was the only member of the board who had experience with takeover fights. He was on several other boards, and over the last two years had been involved in three separate takeover bids. He saw no reason for a resignation.

Everyone realized that Nick had raised the issue of resignation, even though he had not said anything specific. It made them feel uncomfortable.

'I don't want to feel as if we had any enemy agent inside,' Nick tried again and wished he were devious enough to have put it differently, to have said that he didn't want Howard to feel as if he were in a difficult position.

'If he sits out, there's no reason to feel it,' Harold Clemens said. He also saw the solution as simple. Howard could just stay away. He knew Howard only a little, and did not warm to him much, but he saw no reason why he should be forced to go.

'He must have known about this,' Nick said.

'Did he?' Sir Edward was direct.

Nick paused. Then he said, 'Yes.'

Julian looked up at this. He knew now why Nick was asking for Howard to be booted off the board.

'Of course he would know. They've been planning it for ages.' This was Jasper Thomas. He continued, 'As soon as he knew he would be bound not to tell us.'

'That's why I see a conflict,' Nick was ignoring the board's reluctance to do anything against Howard.

'Had he told you, he would have given Corpcom away,' Jasper continued.

'He could have resigned.'

'From which board?' asked Jasper.

'I don't care,' Nick was vehement now. 'One of them.'

But Jasper was unrelenting. 'If he had resigned from Armadale, he would have either had to give the truth as a reason or to lie. The truth would have betrayed the other side. I don't think one should ever demand of someone that he lie for us.'

'We've all just agreed to do it,' Nick said in exasperation.

Someone else spoke. 'Jasper has a point, Nick.' It was Richard, who, considering he was the finance director, had said little thus far. He had confirmed financial details when necessary, but had kept his attention on the materials in front of him, letting the others speak. Julian wondered at his unaccustomed silence.

'Also,' continued Jasper, 'had Howard resigned from Corpcom's board and Corpcom's bid were successful, then Howard is off not one, but two boards. That would be a little unfair, I think.'

Jasper stopped, pleased with his contribution. He had enjoyed outlining this particular Catch-22.

Nick was furious, but he knew that he had lost.

'If there's nothing else, I think that's it for tonight, then,' he said.

'Good. Let's drop it,' Sir Edward spoke clearly, and faced Nick as he did so. He understood Nick's resentment of

Howard, but he was not willing to give in to it. There was something childish in Nick that at times annoyed Reald.

They were all aware of the tension, but the meeting came to a close. The men went out of the boardroom in pairs. Grahame held back and left with Nick.

'You should get the place de-bugged,' he said in a low voice as they emerged into the corridor.

Nick looked at him in surprise. He had not thought about it. He had been too concerned about Howard to consider another treachery.

'Just a precaution,' Grahame added.

2

Roger and Peter listened in on the whole of Armadale's board meeting. The two men were sitting in the armchairs across from Roger's desk. The empty chair stared back at them from behind the desk. For the last four hours, Roger had paid close attention, getting up once to grab another cigar from his desk, then returning to his chair. Peter was more restless. He had walked about the room several times, stretching his legs. As Nick had raised the discussion about Howard, Peter had sat down again. At the end of the board meeting, when the last voice had spoken and the footsteps had died away, he watched Roger get up, go to the desk and hang up the telephone, thus disconnecting the hook-up.

Roger turned and said, 'I thought they'd never go home.'

'No surprises,' Peter replied.

'We need to stay on top of the Monopolies thing,' Roger said. 'We want to make bloody sure they don't get a referral.'

'We've gone over this a hundred times.'

'Going over it and doing it are two different things,' Andrews snapped. 'I know they shouldn't get a referral, but I want to stay on top of it. You can't trust a bureaucrat.'

'I'll stay on top of it,' Peter said to him.

'You know, Peter,' Roger said, 'you could have just said "yes" before. Why d'you have to argue with me?'

'It's the Socratic method. I just want to make sure you mean it.'

Peter got up from the chair. He was ready to go.

'I'm glad I stayed for the ending,' he said as he walked towards the door. 'Such human drama,' he added scornfully. He was surprised that Nick could conjure up so much emotion about Howard, and he found the anger of the one and the guilt of the other quite comic.

'Don't underestimate emotions just because you don't have any,' Roger said.

Peter shrugged. He regarded his detachment as an asset and he knew Roger did as well. 'See you tomorrow.'

It was eleven o'clock when Peter left Corpcom. Although he lived in a flat in Knightsbridge only ten minutes walk away, he took the lift down to the garage where he kept his car and drove to Notting Hill Gate. He drove a dark-grey Porsche, which went with his Prussian good looks. He believed it impressed women, amongst other things, and he was right as far as the women he chose to go out with were concerned. He was handsome, well-off, and he had a nice car; there were plenty of women who found the combination irresistible.

He rang the bell of a small two-storey house from which came the loud sounds of rock music. He had made sure she would be home earlier this evening. He had begun to feel an intense sexual desire just before the beginning of the Armadale board meeting and had nursed it throughout the evening, letting his mind wander occasionally during the more predictable moments. Now he sought release.

An attractive woman with langorous eyes and a long elastic body opened the door.

'Come in,' she said. When she had closed the door, she did not say anything else, she put her arms around his neck and, leaning her body against his, kissed him.

Peter led her up the stairs. There was no fumbling for buttons; once inside the bedroom, they kissed against the door, closing it that way; removing each other's clothes as they went. In less than three minutes, they were both naked and on the bed.

Peter McNeal made love with half Howard's skill but with twice his energy. He usually went home after. Whatever else he did, he always preferred sleeping in his own bed, and he drove away again about an hour later.

When Peter had left, Roger turned back to his desk. He picked up the telephone and dialled the coded number again, triggering the receiver in Armadale's boardroom. He listened, waiting for a sound, but he heard none and hung up. He sat down and picked up the other telephone.

His day was almost over. As he waited for the connection, he bit off the end of the cigar he had taken earlier, spat the tobacco out into the waste paper basket, his aim true, and stuck it into his mouth.

'Hallo,' the voice at the other end of the telephone was irritable.

'It's Roger Andrews here.'

'Oh, hallo.' The voice was more conciliatory now.

'Are they debugging yet?'

'First thing tomorrow.'

'Who's doing it?'

'I suggested the people.'

'Same ones?' Roger checked.

'Yes.'

'Maybe something could be left behind . . .'

The best time to set a bug is when you de-bug. Roger knew that, but so did others. To bug again this time would be riskier.

'This time. But it'll have to be the last.'

'No problem,' said Roger. 'Thank you.'

The two men hung up at the same time.

Roger sat at his desk for a minute, savouring his sense of power and control. Everything was going smoothly, according to plan. He knew the unexpected would come, and he looked forward to that as well. It was the spice this whole business needed to keep it interesting.

Finally, he lit his cigar, the last of the day. He sucked the air in, enveloping his head with smoke. He could go home now.

Chapter Seven

I

Julian did not arrive for supper at Alan Turner's house till just after 10.30. He had spoken to Alan at the office before the board meeting to tell him he would be late.

'Perhaps we should do it another night . . .' Julian had said.

'No,' Alan had replied breathlessly, 'come over when you're finished.'

'It might be pretty late,' Julian persisted. He knew Rebecca would jump at the chance of a postponement.

'Doesn't matter,' Alan had insisted. 'I want to know all about it.'

Julian was the horse's mouth and Alan wanted to hear what he had to say. Which was exactly what Julian dreaded.

Julian had tried to ring Rebecca earlier, but she had been out. He was still on the phone with Alan when he heard Nick paging him: Richard had arrived from New York.

'Alan,' he said quickly, 'could you ring Rebecca and tell her what's going on? I just don't have time. Tell her I'm sorry.'

'She doesn't know?' asked Alan, as if he could not believe someone he knew could not be aware of what was happening. 'Of course, I'll tell her.' He was delighted at the opportunity to tell someone else the news.

Julian winced at the idea of Alan giving Rebecca the message. He could just imagine the reception she would give him when they were next alone. He rang Alan again just before he left.

'I'm on my way,' he said. 'Is Rebecca there?'

'Absolutely,' Alan said and Julian heard the drink in his voice. 'I couldn't reach her either. She got here before I did. She's been here all evening.'

'Christ,' said Julian to himself as he hung up.

He drove fast and, at that time of night, it did not take him long. Alan opened the door. His tie was loose, his top button undone and one side of his shirt hung out of his trousers. He held a glass in his hand.

'At last! Becky was beginning to get worried.' He spoke too loudly.

Julian took off his coat, which Alan grabbed from him and then dropped. As he bent down to pick it up, Julian apologized.

Alan led Julian down a spiral staircase to the basement, which had been converted into a large, tiled, modern kitchen, with a dining room extension.

'Tell me,' Alan said. 'Come on. I want *all* the dirt.'

'There isn't much, really,' Julian said. He wished Alan would not question him. He felt exhausted. He was saved, at least temporarily, by Fanny, who heard Alan pressing him.

From the dining room, where she and Rebecca were waiting for them, she called, 'Leave the poor bugger alone, for Christ's sake. Let him have something to drink first.'

She and Rebecca sat at a large round table. In front of them were the remains of an elaborate meal. The plates were greasy from the salad dressing, which had mixed with thick gravy from the roast birds; there were three sets of glasses in front of them, each one filmed with a residue; the candles in the slender silver candlesticks had burned unevenly and wax had fallen from one on to the tablecloth; even the bowl of red hot-house roses Fanny had placed as a centrepiece had been pushed aside.

'Sorry I'm so late,' he said to Fanny.

'You poor thing. You must be starving,' she answered.

For someone who cooked so much and so well, Fanny was incongruously thin. She had long straight reddish-blonde hair, which fell to the middle of her back and which was cut in a fringe at the front; her face was delicately boned with freckled pale skin and a slightly upturned nose. Her eyes were what saved her from being rather plain: they were a bright blue and seemed to have a watery film of gentleness. As usual, she was dressed for the occasion, a short black dress, very simple and well cut, which plunged deeply at the neck. From her ears dangled long pearl drop earrings.

'What did I miss?' asked Julian. 'Looks delicious.'

'It was,' said Rebecca. 'I wish you could cook like this.'

Rebecca's mouth was turned down; she was having trouble keeping the facade up. And her left eyelid was slightly droopy, which meant that she had also been drinking. He looked at her. She was dressed almost perversely plainly, wearing black jeans and a black cashmere V-neck; she wore no make-up and no jewellery, except for pearl studs in her ears. Her long, wavy, dark-brown hair was almost black and her eyebrows were thick over her dark eyes. In his mind flashed the thought that she was beautiful, even more attractive for the very irregularities in her features: she did not need make-up. He went over to her to kiss her and she kissed him back, lingering as their lips met.

'You O K?' she asked.

'I'll survive, but a drink would help.' He sat down heavily after giving Fanny a kiss.

'What do you want?' Alan asked him. He was still standing, leaning on the chair next to Julian's.

'Anything.' He reached for the bottle of red wine on the table and turned it to look at the label. Alan always produced very good wines.

Before he could read it, Alan grabbed the bottle and began pouring some wine into a large glass.

'Chateau Lynch Bages, '75,' he said and gave a mild involuntary burp. 'Excuse me,' and he burped again, more loudly this time. He put the glass of wine in front of Julian and questioned him again, 'What is happening? You've got your drink, so now tell me.'

'He is valuing us at just over half a billion.' Julian's voice was tired. He took a drink of the wine and almost instantly felt exhausted; the alcohol seemed to absorb the remains of energy stored up in his veins.

'I know that, for Christ's sake; £536 million to be precise. And a few hundred thousand pounds. I knew that this morning,' Alan was annoyed. He was relentless, monomaniacal in his obsession with the personal repercussions of the bid. In his mind, Armadale had already been taken over; Nick had been fired and he had been fired along with him, abandoned in the foul world of the unemployed, forced to tread the pavements like a salesman, in search of work, humiliated, rejected, poor.

'Alan, will you shut up?' Fanny said. 'I'm getting sick of hearing about it.'

She found him embarrassing and almost cowardly in his reaction. He was disappointing her in front of other people, and she wished he would stop, but she did not know how to make that happen. For two hours now he had been holding the floor, talking at her and Rebecca about the ruthlessness of Roger, the inefficiency of Armadale, about Nick, who thought he could still live in a world of gentlemen, the make-believe world in which people are trusted to keep their word, in which men do the right thing, resign when they are doubted, do not steal when the opportunity is presented, do not lie to save their own skins. 'The man's a dinosaur!' he said at the height of his oration, his voice rising with indignation.

'Perhaps when Julian comes, he'll calm down,' Fanny had thought.

But as Fanny put a plate of re-heated pheasant, which even she could not prevent from drying up, in front of Julian, Alan started again.

'Tell me now, Julian. What is the deal? Exactly.'

'You haven't seen it?' Julian asked. 'It should have been published.'

'Where the hell am I going to get a copy?' Alan asked indignantly. 'You people were hoarding the bloody thing all day.'

Julian swallowed while Alan waited for an answer. The pheasant was delicious, as was the wine, and Julian realized now how hungry he was.

'In equity, he's offering 47 for 100,' Julian said.

'47 for 100,' said Alan. 'I can't figure it out, what's that make it?'

'A little better than equal. The cash is a premium. But I don't know for how long.'

'We closed at 240,' Alan said.

'That's right,' said Julian, speaking with his mouth full of roast potato. 'Up 27.'

'You guys,' Rebecca broke into their conversation, 'if I'd wanted to spend my evenings with accountants, I could have stayed in the States, moved to New Jersey, or something. What the hell are you talking about?'

'OK,' Julian broke in. He held his hands up to them for silence. 'This is it. Listen carefully. For every 100 shares of Armadale, Roger Andrews, who is the Chairman of Corpcom, is offering 47 shares of Corpcom. Since Armadale was trading on the Stock Exchange at 213p yesterday, and Corpcom at 458p, that makes it a pretty fair exchange. In fact, Corpcom is paying a little more than it has to. Because Corpcom has made it obvious that it intends to hold more than 15 per cent of the shares in Armadale, Corpcom has also – before it is legally forced to – made a cash offer of 250p for each Armadale share. That's what the numbers meant.'

'Terrific,' Rebecca said. 'I'm enlightened. Aren't you?' she turned to Fanny.

'I don't understand a bloody word,' Fanny laughed.

'I'm not surprised,' Alan said. 'Listen, girls, why don't you go into the kitchen and make some more coffee or something?'

'I think we will,' said Rebecca, deciding that escape was better than incomprehensible explanations from Julian or being patronized by Alan.

'How much is he borrowing?' Alan went on without a glance at the departing women.

'I don't know. I suppose we'll find out tomorrow, at the press conference.' Julian reached for the bottle of wine and poured himself another glass. 'Is there any more?' he looked back towards the kitchen, 'It's delicious, Fanny,' he called.

She brought him another full plate and he attacked it with as much vigour as the first. Alan questioned him while he ate.

In the kitchen Fanny and Rebecca noisily loaded the dishwasher.

There seemed to be no particular order to Alan's questions. He asked about the strategy that had been worked out, what the chances were of a referral to the Monopolies and Mergers Commission, about Nick's attitude, the board meeting, whether Armadale would sell off some of its assets to build up some cash. His curiosity was exacerbated by Julian's monosyllabic answers, monosyllabic because there was no more to say than 'no', or 'yes', 'they didn't talk about it', or 'I don't think so'.

He finished eating and looked at his empty plate. 'I was starving.'

'I heard Hicks wasn't at the board meeting,' said Alan. He could think of nothing else. There would be no other topic of conversation this evening. If it had been anyone else, Julian might not have minded. Alan's relentless insistence irritated him.

'Hicks is also on Corpcom's board,' Julian did not elaborate.

'You see!' Alan was triumphant. 'There is a problem.'

Julian was annoyed. 'For heaven's sake, calm down. Howard Hicks is unlikely to be a problem to anyone. Have you ever spent any time with him? He couldn't move quickly enough to be a problem, he's practically inert.' Julian had raised his voice. He and Alan were now in confrontation, Julian enticed into an argument against his will. It seemed inevitable with Alan, who made pronouncements on everything. As time passed, it became more and more difficult to ignore them.

'People take sides all the time, Julian.'

'Some prefer to stay out of it. Why would you want to get involved, anyway?'

'Money,' Alan said. 'That's why most people do things.'

Julian sighed in exasperation. He said, 'Hicks did not show up to the board meeting because of a conflict of interest. He will not be showing up at other board meetings for the same reason. There is no problem.'

There was a certain finality to Julian's words. Alan therefore turned towards Rebecca who was coming in with some coffee, to deliver the final word, 'Your Julian is gullible. You should try to corrupt him a little.'

'He's corrupt enough for me,' she said with a little smile. Fanny laughed and Alan was robbed of his triumph.

'Listen,' Rebecca went on. 'I know this is important. But I've had it. I don't want to hear about it any more.'

Alan got up from his chair, went to the cupboard across the room and fished out the bottle of brandy. He poured himself a large dose.

'I'm tongue-tied,' he said.

But the evening was over. There was no more conversation and soon Julian and Rebecca went home.

After they had left, Alan started talking again. He sat in the kitchen on a tall stool, leaning against the counter while Fanny put the remaining dishes into the dishwasher. He was still drinking, knowing that he would have a hangover the next morning, but too drunk to care.

'Why does this sort of thing always have to happen to me?' he asked plaintively.

Fanny who was bending down when he said it, waited until she straightened up. 'You're hysterical. And you're drunk. Go to bed.'

'You don't understand the first thing about it. You'll be hysterical when I'm out of a job and we can't afford to pay the mortgage.'

'You haven't lost your job. Why don't you wait until you do lose it?' She was trying to placate him. 'Anyway, I work. I make more money than you do.' She laughed. She had meant to lighten the mood, but it had the opposite effect.

'Bastards . . .' he cried. 'It's always the little people who get screwed.'

Fanny put the plate that was in her hand on the counter and went and put her arms around him.

'You try to build a career and they take it away from you.' He spoke to himself, really.

She hugged him, and whispered in his ear, 'Go to bed, darling.'

He did, walking heavily up the stairs. Fanny finished tidying up the kitchen and then followed him. She found him asleep on his back, snoring from the drink. His clothes were in a pile on the floor next to the bed. She was relieved; she wanted to go to bed alone tonight.

'Next time you're going to get stuck at the office, let me know, O K?' Rebecca said in the car.

She had contained herself until now. She felt sorry for Fanny; she liked her and she thought her wasted on a man like Alan. Now she vented her irritation.

'I didn't have time,' Julian said. 'I'm sorry.'

'You had time to call Alan,' Rebecca persisted. 'Call me first. I could call him rather than having him calling me.'

'I tried. You were out.'

'Leave a message,' she insisted. 'You English still don't know how to use the phone.'

Julian realized that she was right. If he had spoken to her, they could probably have got out of the evening.

'You're right.'

'You bet I'm right,' she went on, delighted that for once, Julian had admitted it. 'We could have stayed home.'

'Alan wouldn't have allowed it.' Julian fell into the debate. 'You would've agreed to go, just as I did.'

'Typical. You said I was right and then you regretted it. Call *me* first, next time.'

Julian said nothing. He had learned by now not to argue a bad case; only lawyers needed to do that.

They drove the rest of the way in silence.

As they undressed, Julian wondered if he would have any

trouble getting into the press conference the next day. He fell into bed, exhausted. No anxiety would keep him awake tonight. His eyes were closed when he asked Rebecca if she wanted to come with him. She was a journalist. It might interest her.

'Sure,' she said. 'I'll be your date.' She turned to him but he was already asleep, breathing gently.

Few members of the defence made love that night. Sex was for the aggressors.

2

Edward Falcon got home from work later than he had ever done before. He had not been able to bring himself to leave until the board meeting broke up, although he knew it was pointless. He had not told his wife Edna anything when he had rung her. On the way back to Stockwell in the underground, he worried about her reaction.

He had called her name as soon as he opened the door of the two-storey house. There was no central heating and the narrow hallway was cool. Edward stood with his coat on, looking at Edna, who faced him with a dishtowel and a plate in her hand.

He had expected her to be immediately concerned, perhaps to cry; instead he found that the real anxiety was his.

'Maybe you can retire early,' she said, looking at the brighter side. 'They'll give you a settlement, won't they?'

'What kind of settlement?' he asked gloomily. This was not the reaction he wanted. He was not finished. His working life, his own life, was still in its prime; he was not ready to be pensioned off.

'I knew this was going to happen,' he said later as they sat together in the dining-room after his supper, incongruously formal, since the rest of the family had already eaten. Edward did not like to eat in the kitchen: they were finally able to afford a house with a dining-room and he believed it should be used. Their two teenagers were next door, in the drawing-room, watching television. That is where he and Edna normally would have been too, but this evening they sat at the table, a small glass of beer in front of each of them, another unusual occurrence in the middle of the week. 'Everyone's being taken over these days. It's the new breed of City people, only interested in money.' He paused, but Edna said nothing. This was not her field; she did not know what to say. 'Look at Alan Turner, you know, in marketing. He doesn't care about the company. He just cares about himself. That's how it is these days. How much can I make? And how quickly? Nobody gives a damn about the product, about what we manufacture, what we sell, about why we make a profit.' His voice rose in anger and he coughed as he tried to get his breath. 'They forget, all these City whizz-kids, that there would be no money if we didn't make something people wanted to buy.'

'Maybe the takeover won't work, then,' said Edna. 'If you're successful.'

'It's not like that,' Edward said, his voice full of bitterness. 'They make more money by taking companies over, playing around on the stock market.'

He stopped his tirade, looked deeply into his beer, as dejected as if he had already lost his job. Edna reached her hand across the table and put it gently on top of his.

'It doesn't matter, Eddie. We'll be all right,' she said.

3

As they were driving home, Howard had said to Norma, 'I think I'll take the day off tomorrow.' He leaned his head back against the rest, closing his eyes; they stung a little.

Norma was driving their new Rover – Howard bought a new car every two years – and it was slightly unfamiliar. She lacked confidence; she did not like driving, but she always did if they went out; she remained sober, whereas Howard always drank enough to be unsafe at the wheel.

'What's the matter with you?' she asked, without looking at him, her eyes fixed on the cat's eyes that flashed ahead of her. They had not discussed the takeover. It was a subject that Howard wanted to avoid, while Norma did not realize how much it mattered.

'You've been acting strangely all day,' she went on. 'Is there something wrong?' She remembered Nick's curt phone call. Even Nick had been unusually abrupt with her.

'It's this takeover,' Howard answered. 'Nick's very upset about it. He's taking it very badly, I think.'

'I'm not surprised.' For once, she sympathized with Nick. 'He's spent, what? Ten years? At least ten years building up that company. And now someone's going to take it away from him.' She paused, negotiated a turn, and added, 'Roger Andrews, of all people.'

Howard remained silent. His eyes were still closed; he might have been asleep.

'I remember you were pretty upset after Andrews took you over,' Norma went on.

'He broke his word,' said Howard, opening his eyes and looking over at her. 'He'd offered me a job on the board of Corpcom. Then he said I'd serve the company better by sticking to the Breweries. Bloody liar.'

'You were upset at losing the company,' Norma said. 'That's what I meant.'

They drove on in silence until they had turned into their drive and could hear the crunch of the gravel under their tyres.

'Nick's blaming me, you see,' Howard said, his voice rising in indignation. 'He thinks I should have told him this bid was coming.'

'I suppose you could have done,' Norma said. She switched off the engine, and suddenly the night was quiet, the silence of the countryside embracing them. Howard sat up at Norma's remark.

'I couldn't,' Howard raised his voice. 'I'm not allowed to. I'm on the board of both companies. Don't you see?' He was appealing to Norma; he wanted her to back his decision.

'I suppose so,' she said, adding, 'Nick is supposed to be your best friend.'

'Well, that's the trouble,' Howard said. He resented having been put in this position. It was as if his personal dilemma was at the centre of the takeover.

'I certainly don't think you can be blamed,' she said. 'But I would have told my best friend, I think.' She shook her head, put her hand on the door handle. 'Nick is so difficult anyway. He's always on such a high horse. Come on,' she continued, opening the door. 'Come *on*,' she said again, as Howard did not move.

Slowly Howard got out of the car. I'll give him a ring in the morning, he thought.

4

Roger Andrews had enjoyed his day. Mondays weren't always this good. It was well after midnight before he stood in front of the full-length mirror in his dressing-room wrapping a warm dressing-gown around himself. Next door, Margaret had just turned out the light, having waited up for him. He had found her reading a thriller in bed and, when he sat down beside her, her gentle blue eyes looked over her spectacles.

'What's the share price?' she asked him.

'Ours or theirs?'

'Both, of course,' she said.

'We're down five to 453. That's pretty good,' he said as she nodded her head. Roger smiled with satisfaction as he went on, 'They're up to 240p already. That's almost thirty.'

'A good day at the office, then,' she said and glanced back at her book.

He patted her thigh and kissed her on the cheek. He took off his jacket and went towards the dressing-room door, hearing her close her book as he turned the light on.

'Goodnight,' he called, and closed the door to the bedroom.

Ready for bed now he contemplated his own image. He did not see the flesh sagging over his waist, nor the dark circles under his eyes. He was looking at the general on the war path.

He had thought about the next few weeks for a long time now; he was happy to be in the middle of action again. Planning was satisfying but did not compare with the execution of the plan, for if the bid succeeded then the plan and the execution of it were proved correct. Each time he found it equally exciting and satisfying. If he had not, he would soon have stopped. Andrews' life had not only been driven by the desire for success and fortune, much of what he had accomplished had been done as part of a war against the mundane. He quickly moved on if anything became uninteresting. This volatility had helped him earn his reputation as a ruthless operator. He abandoned companies as quickly as he took them over. Andrews' considerable skill – perhaps it was an art – was his ability to combine financial gain with his need for change. It made him unpredictable, and therefore dangerous.

Chapter Eight

I

Sophie Bishop waited for Nick. The children were asleep and she was watching television. She looked at her watch. It was well after eleven o'clock already and he had telephoned only a few minutes ago to say he was leaving the office. Even now, it would take him close to forty-five minutes to get home. Longer, probably, because of the fog.

They lived just outside of London, in Kent. Their village, Downe, was a hamlet refuge from urban life: a few clusters of stone houses spread in a circle around a small village; a pub, a post office, two small shops and a school. That was it. At night, as soon as one left the built-up areas, a blanket of deep fog fell on the countryside; the city itself seemed to repel it. The turning to Downe, to the right off the main road, took one immediately into a world of high hedges bordering narrow winding lanes, in which two cars passed only with difficulty. The approach to Nick Bishop's house forked off one of these narrow winding lanes, an unpaved track which, after a hundred yards opened out into a large grassy area bordered with flower beds, which were bare now, and which fronted a two-storey, wide, solid stone house covered with ivy.

Inside a wood fire burned in the living-room. Sophie sat in front of it, alternately turning her gaze from its hypnotic flickering light to the glare of the television, on which she was not really concentrating. It was a well-proportioned large square room. French windows led out to the garden at the back. Thick dark burgundy curtains drawn across the windows kept the cold and the darkness out. Sophie was curled up on a deep, low velvet sofa, directly in front of the fire, letting the warmth envelop her, her eyes barely open, like a cat on its favourite cushion. Just one lamp was lit on a tall side table. A cold draught came through the door, left half-open in case one of the boys cried out for her.

Sophie yawned and yearned for her bed. Selfishly, she wished Nick had not called and she could have gone to sleep early; instead she would be tired in the morning and probably short-tempered with the children. She knew Nick would want her to wait up for him. He would need to talk; she had heard it in his voice and from what he had not said.

Sophie came to with a start when she heard the front door open. She looked at her watch; it was not yet midnight. Nick had driven fast. She had sat up and was leaning forward to put more wood on the fire when he walked in.

'You were asleep,' he said. There was a hint of disappointment, as if sleep were a betrayal.

'I was dozing,' Sophie said, and yawned, covering her mouth with her hand. 'You got here quickly. How fast did you go?'

'I didn't notice,' He was curt, irritated by the question.

Sophie sensed his need and she put her arms around him. 'I'm sorry,' she said. She embraced him, and then asked, 'Are you hungry?'

He had not thought of hunger, but now realized that he was and nodded.

'I'll get you something.' She left for the kitchen.

Nick turned on the main lights, brightening the room. He hated dimly-lit rooms. There was a trolley against the wall, next to the side table, where whisky and brandy glowed in crystal decanters, reflecting the light falling on the little silver tags around their necks. He took the whisky and poured himself a drink.

It was perhaps unfair, but he had wanted more from Sophie, not just sympathy, but understanding. He wanted Sophie to feel all the anger, the anxiety, the desire for vengeance that raged within him now. It was as if some urgent sexual desire was being left unsatisfied. If they had made love immediately, in a violent coupling, he might have felt some release. Now he wondered if he might have felt more easy if he had spent the night awake at his desk in his office.

Sophie was an outsider to Armadale. Being married to the managing director did not change that.

'Tell me what happened?' she said, dutifully if not enthusiastically, when Nick came in to the kitchen. She had lit the grill and was cooking a steak for him.

'You know what happened. We're being taken over.' He began to circle around the kitchen and Sophie patiently waited for him to settle. She was hurt by Nick's aggression, but tried to ignore it.

'At least, that's what Andrews is trying to do,' Nick said. He had seen Sophie's look. He was annoyed at himself.

'What are his chances?' she asked, helping him along, while throwing some lettuce leaves into a bowl.

There was a pause. Nick had been about to say that Roger did not have a hope, but honesty got the better of him. 'Pretty good,' he said instead, 'unless we can get the bid referred,' he added. 'I need to have it referred to the Monopolies and Mergers Commission. Otherwise I'll lose.' He faced her as he spoke.

It was a shock to Sophie. She looked up from the cup in which she was mixing the salad dressing and, for a moment, they stood there in silence, eyes looking into eyes, lips closed, bodies tense, immobile.

'Nick,' she said, a new fear in her voice, 'are you sure?'

'There's money in it,' he said with bitterness. 'People don't care about Armadale. They care about how much money they can make if they sell their shares. It's called the free market,' he added bitterly.

'Aren't you making money for them?'

'Not as quickly. Not as easily.' He took a large gulp of his drink and added 'Howard was right.'

'Howard?'

'Yes, Howard . . . The bastard.' Nick left the kitchen to get another drink. Sophie looked after him. 'Howard knew about this all along,' Nick shouted to her from the other room.

'Howard . . .' So that was what was eating him. 'Pour me one, would you, please?' she called back to him.

Suddenly she was impatient, eager to discover what Howard had done. It would be a vindication of her feelings, of that she was certain. She had never liked Howard, and had never understood why Nick was so bound to him. Howard, she thought, was all that Nick was not: unattractive, weak, dishonest, untrustworthy.

'It's ready,' she called. She took the plate to the pine table against the window at the end of the kitchen. She leaned over the table and pulled down the blind. She did not like looking out at the night.

Nick returned with her drink. He swallowed his own down and put the glass on the wooden counter next to the sink, opened the fridge and grabbed a beer to accompany his meal.

'I'll get you a napkin,' she said, her voice vague and distant. She was thinking that, whatever Howard had done, she was glad.

She wanted to put her hand up to his face and comfort him, but he walked by her to the table. Another moment lost, she thought. There were so many of them.

Nick ate rapidly, not speaking.

'What about Howard?' she said. She had waited long enough.

Nick made no answer, at first. He continued to eat hungrily. Then, without looking up from his plate, 'Howard's taken sides, that's all,' he said. 'He knew about the Corpcom bid,' Nick went on, 'and he decided to say nothing about it.'

Sophie was disappointed. 'But isn't that what he's supposed to do?' she said. 'Stay out of it, I mean.'

'He's a friend, damn it!' Nick looked at her. 'He should have told me. But no. He sat on the fence instead. The way he always does.'

'Howard's on the board of Corpcom, darling.' Sophie was now defending Howard. Nick was making a mistake; she wanted to save him from it. She did not want him to hate his friend for the wrong reason. Howard would betray Nick, she felt sure, if the occasion should present itself, but she was not sure that this was it.

'I would have resigned,' he said emphatically. 'I would have told him.'

Sophie grabbed his arms and looked up at him. She was not a small woman, but Nick was still four or five inches taller. She fixed her bright eyes on his and said. 'You wouldn't have done, Nick. I know you wouldn't. Put yourself in his position.'

'He made me an offer. A deal. A bribe, Sophie,' he added.

She felt sorry for him again. He seemed so forlorn. She put her arms around his waist and embraced him. He let her, allowing his pain to wash over him like a shower.

Suddenly he moved away, breaking the embrace, irked by his own indulgence, by Howard, by Sophie's sympathy. The urge for something more robust, more physical than mere sympathy came over him again.

'You'd better go to bed,' he said. 'You must be tired.'

'What about you?'

'I'll be up soon,' but he said it without conviction.

Sophie sensed his change of mood. It was her turn to be hurt by it. Nick was so adept at isolating himself, at feeling that others could not satisfy his needs, that he willed his seclusion. She was the one forced to make up, to bring them closer one to the other; sometimes she could not bridge the flow of things that were left unsaid and that separated them.

She began to tidy the kitchen, but he stopped her.

'I'll do that,' he said. 'It'll give me something else to think about.'

She did not argue, and was half-way out of the kitchen when he called her back, 'If we lose, I'll be out of a job. You know that.'

She nodded, but still said nothing. She did not care. At the moment, she wished Nick were different, less exacting, less intense, less rigid.

'You don't care?' He said it aggressively.

'Of course I care,' she answered. 'But it's not so important. We won't be poor. And you'll get another job.'

'I might not,' he said.

She shrugged: he was arguing with her out of principle. 'Yes, you will,' she said. She hesitated at the door and then said, 'Good night.'

She went upstairs to John's room and went in to check on him. The seven-year-old was lying on his side, both arms in front of him, dangling down the side of the bed. Sophie kissed him on the head and left the room, closing the door to a crack. She did the same with Alistair, whose room was down the hall, past her own; she found him snoring gently, just as she had left him last. She closed his door. He was nine, old enough not to need it open any more.

Finally she went into her own bedroom. She stood in the doorway, looking back towards the staircase. She and Nick had drifted apart during the conversation, yet she was not sure exactly where. They had been close when he had walked in and now they were distant. She realized she had not satisfied him, as if her love-making had been dull.

Nick settled into a comfortable armchair in the living-room, opposite the sofa Sophie had occupied earlier. The cushions were still flattened where she had been. The fire was dying; only embers, burning red, were left in the grate next to the ashes. He sat, hands dangling from the arm rests, trying to think of what to do, but too tired to complete a thought. His mind was repeatedly intruded upon by flashes of his past, images of Howard as he had been when they had been friends; there was no doubt in Nick's mind that their friendship would not survive. He could not conceive of how it could, just as Howard, however anxious and fearful, could not imagine it ever ending.

He saw Howard at school, walking down a corridor, treading heavily towards the open door of a classroom, both hands in his pockets, his jacket sagging between his elbows; a comic, self-conscious, but unashamed figure. Then came Howard at Oxford, in his own flat by then. He had moved out of college after the first year to be on his own, away from the clutches of authority. With his three flatmates he had lived out his freedom well, in a different routine from the other students. Nick could see Howard draining a glass of whisky and reaching for the bottle to pour himself more; lying asleep in the lavatory, his elbow on the toilet bowl, having just vomited because he had drunk as much as he could after his final exams.

Later, after university, Howard had rented a flat in London to spend a sabbatical year before he went to work in his father's breweries.

'On sabbatical from what?' Nick remembered asking him then.

'From everything,' Howard had answered. 'Mainly from work. It's probably my last chance until I'm too old to enjoy it.'

Howard had been in his dressing-gown, lounging in the armchair of his sitting-room. Magazines were strewn on the floor beside clothes and records, which were left out of their sleeves to gather dust and scratches. Next to him, sitting on the arm, almost on his lap, was Howard's girlfriend, wearing nothing but one of Howard's striped shirts. She was the reverse of Sheilah for, in those days, Howard liked big-breasted, large-hipped women.

'Sit down, Nick,' he had said, 'you look uncomfortable,' staring at Nick's crotch. Howard was unable to resist a rough laugh, bringing his girlfriend into the joke with a stroke of his hand on her thigh.

He married a girl like that, Nick thought. Norma was even fuller now, twelve years and three children later. Was that why Howard went for Sheilah's thinness, to escape the weight of wife and married obligations?

At Nick's wedding, Howard had been best man and had given a speech that was a little too salacious. At the last minute, he checked himself and in the end had made the toast emotional and moving.

'I am the "best man" here,' he had said and, turning towards Nick at the centre of the long table, next to Sophie, who was beautiful because she was so happy, 'but that's only a title. Nick deserves it more than anyone.' He had paused, and with a natural theatricality, raised his glass as if in Roman salute, had gone on, 'To the best man, then.' He had encompassed the assembly and drunk deeply from his glass, his head tilted back at the neck.

That was a long way from the telephone call they had had this morning.

Nick had accepted Howard's affection and returned it. Now, self-importantly, he consciously thought of Howard as his Judas.

Nick found that he had been staring at one spot in the pattern of the sofa. He looked up from it with indistinct patterns of blue dancing in his eyes and saw Sophie standing in the doorway in her nightgown. Her dark hair fell along her cheeks, its ends tickling her shoulders. He could see the definition of her body, but he felt no desire. It was no longer automatic – it depended on his state of mind more than it used to.

'I was thinking of Howard,' he said. He would gladly go to bed now. 'Do you remember the toast he made at the wedding?'

She waited for him at the door. He stopped next to her and put his hand on her shoulder.

'I don't understand,' he said. 'He could have told me.'

'Just because someone loves you doesn't mean they deserve to be loved back,' she said. Immediately, she wished she had not spoken. It had sounded so harsh.

Nick turned and went on upstairs without a word.

Chapter Nine

I

Nick slept better than Sophie. He was exhausted and no amount of anger or bitterness could keep him awake.

For Sophie, whose turmoil was more immediate and personal, it was harder. She felt distanced from Nick. These days, it seemed, especially true in times of stress. It should have been the other way around. That they should have gone to bed so separate, without speaking to each other, with no semblance of shouldering the burden together distressed her and kept her awake. Eventually, she too fell asleep, and she did not hear him get up at six o'clock.

It was the children who woke her. They were better than a clock; they still woke at the same time every morning, although Alistair perhaps was beginning to lose that regularity.

As they always did, they had walked sleepily downstairs where they usually found their parents: Sophie at the cooker, Nick at the table, eating his breakfast. Nick left the house at 6.45 every morning. Sophie cooked for him and thus he had a little more time to see Alistair and John in the morning; otherwise they were only together on the weekends, since the boys were asleep when he got home in the evenings. To a certain extent, they were used to his absence.

This morning, they went downstairs and found Nick alone in the kitchen. Although he was an affectionate father, he was not enough accustomed to children to feel absolutely comfortable when he was with them.

'Hallo,' he said. 'Did you sleep well?'

'Where's Mummy?' asked John.

'Upstairs. Asleep.'

'Why is she asleep?' said Alistair.

'She was up late,' answered Nick. 'I let her sleep.'

Without saying another word, both boys turned and headed upstairs.

'Hey!' Nick called after them. 'John. Alistair. Come here.'

They appeared in the doorway. They said nothing, just looked at him, the question in their presence and their faces.

'Leave Mummy alone,' Nick said. 'You didn't even say "good morning" to me.'

'Good morning,' they said in unison and turned again to go upstairs.

'I said leave Mummy alone.'

'Who's going to make our breakfast?' asked Alistair. They were both back in the doorway again.

'I can do that,' Nick said.

'Aren't you going to work?' That was John. There was a trace of hope in his voice.

'Of course I'm going to work.' He looked at his watch. 'In fact I've got to go very soon.' He thought about what he had just said. 'All right. Off you go,' and he waved them upstairs.

They raced each other into their parents' bedroom and pounced on the bed, waking her that way.

Sophie woke with a start, looked at the clock on the bedside table, then over to Nick's side of the bed.

'Where's Daddy?' she asked.

'Downstairs,' Alistair answered.

'I'm hungry,' said John. 'What's for breakfast?'

Sophie got out of bed quickly. She wanted to catch Nick before he left. To see him off, if she could do nothing else.

'You're still here,' she said when she entered the kitchen. He looked up and, although he did not smile, she saw the tension of last night had been dispelled – at least for the moment.

'Did you have breakfast?' she asked.

'I didn't want to wake you.'

'You snored,' she said, and smiled, 'I had trouble getting to sleep.'

'I'm sorry.'

'Daddy always snores,' said Alistair, bored with his parents' exchange.

'No, I don't,' Nick said.

'Only when he sleeps on his back,' said Sophie. She felt relieved. This was family life; interrupted conversations, snatched moments, but a kind of unity anyway. Last night had frightened her, because it put this order into jeopardy; it seemed so easy to disrupt and destroy.

'I've got to go,' Nick stood up. 'I've got to drive myself this morning.'

He left the kitchen and went upstairs. Sophie started her delayed routine and began to make breakfast for the children.

Five minutes later, Nick was gone. There had been no more intimacy; the day and its child-filled bustle had started. Her kiss lingered as he said goodbye.

'Good luck,' she said.

He said nothing. His face had set already: he was thinking of what he had to do, and he wanted to leave. He kissed her again and left.

2

Alan Turner had a hangover. The moment he moved, his head throbbed with pain. His face was drained of blood and his mouth felt dry. He groaned when he tried to sit up and groaned when he forced himself out of bed. But this was not the first time and, with Fanny's help, he tried to alleviate the symptoms. He spent a long time in a bath, which helped only a little, while making him sleepy again. He drank the strong, sugary tea Fanny had made for him instead of the usual coffee. Eventually, he managed to leave for work on time. Fanny even drove him to Highbury Corner, for it had started snowing.

Alan took that personally too. He liked the snow but in the proper place: Switzerland, or the French Alps at least – not in town.

It was an overground train, not an underground, that took him into the City in twenty minutes. Holding his head with his hand, Alan looked out of the window gloomily. The snow was thin and insubstantial. It disappeared as soon as it hit the ground, melting so rapidly that it seemed never to have travelled the last few feet.

At Moorgate, Alan decided against changing trains as he usually did and chose to walk, even though it was still snowing. He needed it, he knew, to put the final touch on his recovery from last night.

He was right and by the time he reached the Armadale building, his headache had gone. The only trace of discomfort was the slight sting in his eyes and weakness in his legs. He was even early. He went straight up to his office, closed the door and picked up the phone. He had decided, somewhere on Old Jewry, that he had to do something concrete to protect himself. Nobody else would.

He made a telephone call to a friend of his, a headhunter with the exotic name of Annie Chinoise. They set a time for lunch on Thursday. Satisfied with his resolve, Alan began working on the sales figures for Armadale's engineering arm for the last year. This was something that would have to have been gathered for the annual general meeting anyway; he was just doing the job early this year.

At 9.30 he left his office to check the repercussions of Corpcom's offer on the Stock Exchange. He found Edward and Philip already in front of the topic screen. They too had come in early.

'What are we trading at?' asked Alan as soon as he saw them.

'241,' answered Philip without turning his head away from the monitor.

'It's gone up already,' Alan said. From the haze of the night before, he remembered Julian quoting him 240.

They stood in front of the screen, which hung from the ceiling. With their heads tilted upwards, their bodies still, they stared in silence as if at a man about to jump from a high ledge. They waited for the rescuers to perform a miracle, to stop the man from jumping.

Nothing life-saving appeared on the screen. It throbbed its green and white characters down at them. Finally, they turned away.

'It makes me sick,' said Philip. 'What's the matter with these people? Why can't they leave us alone? Corpcom doesn't need Armadale.'

'It needs something. It's called growth by acquisition,' Alan said, turning his resentment at the bid towards Philip, who least deserved it. Philip's lack of imagination, his inability to conceive of trouble until it stared him in the face irritated Alan; it was unbearably naïve.

'What they should be doing is creating new business, not buying it,' Edward said with bitterness. He was working hard to remain calm, to still the panic that threatened to erupt inside him every time the reality of the takeover was forced back on to him.

'Too expensive, that,' Alan said. He was almost jocular, as if he were enjoying this. 'That would mean creating jobs,' he went on. 'Building plants, finding a market, using imagination. But that's expensive. Why spend all that money, when you can just buy the bloody thing ready made?'

Jim Ferrar, striding briskly down the corridor, paused at the sound of Alan's voice and asked, 'What's the share price?' When Alan answered him with ponderous finality, Jim nodded, 'Not bad,' and strode off again towards his office.

'He doesn't seem to care much, does he?' Edward said. He resented the fact that Jim was not depressed and gloomy like the rest of them; he had no right not to be suffering.

'Why should he? He can always get another job,' said Alan.

'So can you,' Philip said to Alan. 'Jim does care, anyway.' He protected his friend. 'He's just getting on with the job.'

'Bully for him,' Alan came back at Philip. 'Who told you I can get another job? It's not so easy, you know.'

'You're young. You'll be OK. It won't be so easy for us.' Philip nodded towards Edward.

'Thanks a lot,' Edward said, piqued that the truth haunting him should come out of someone else's mouth. To make sure he would hear nothing else unwelcome, he left them there.

Philip looked after him and said, 'Poor Ed. I hope he'll be OK.'

'At this rate, he's going to be in hospital soon.' Alan thumped his chest. 'Heart, you know. He's always popping pills. By-pass material if ever I saw it.'

Uncomfortable, Philip looked at his watch. 'We'd better get a move on,' he said. 'There's a strategy meeting in five minutes.'

He hurried on his way. Alan went more slowly; he was not going to be rushed. A few paces on, he began to hurry as well, his resolve broken by necessity.

3

It was still dark when Nick arrived at Armadale. He found that many of his employees had arrived earlier than usual too, spurred on by lack of sleep and an anxious need to respond to the attack. They were his troops now, in the trenches. Only an amateur could talk about a team. This was no sport, no game being played on playing fields. There was too much at stake for that.

By eight o'clock, he was at Fairchild's, a maze of corridors and fire-doors, being led by a uniformed security guard up and down short flights of stairs, around several corners and into a small, quiet, wood-panelled room, where John was waiting for him. They were joined by his two assistants and a few minutes later by Richard. It was here that they would meet almost every morning during the next several weeks to discuss the day's strategy and prepare the series of meetings with brokers, accountants and institutional shareholders.

That morning John led a review and elaboration of the organization they had discussed the previous evening during the board meeting. Each activity was slotted, each committee given a principal activity.

'As we agreed yesterday,' John said, 'the most immediate task is to value the company and prepare our profit forecast. The accountants and valuers can assess the properties, but you have to come up with the figures to counter Andrews' own evaluation. We have to have a story to tell the shareholders.'

'What about the shareholders?' said Nick. 'We have to start talking to them.'

'There's really not much point at the moment,' John said. 'Let's get the defence document out. Once we've published the figures, then we can talk to the shareholders. Don't forget you can't give them price-sensitive information. Unless it's been published, they can't know about it. That's insider dealing.'

'That doesn't seem to have stopped some people,' Richard said with a smile.

'But it must stop you,' countered John Grahame.

'Of course it will,' said Nick impatiently. He had no time for pleasantries. 'I still want to talk to the shareholders while we get the forecasts ready. You said it, John,' he went on, 'we haven't exactly communicated with them in the last few years. We can at least bring them up to date without breaking the law.'

They agreed to arrange a series of meetings with stockbrokers and institutions to start building the lines of communications that Nick admitted he had ignored. Corpcom's bid had showed them all how poorly the City had been kept informed about them. Roger, on the other hand, was a well-known figure there. Whatever people might think of him personally, no one doubted his business skills.

For Nick, there was another problem; while ensuring the preparation of a coherent defence against Corpcom's offer, he had to maintain the normal functioning of Armadale.

With Julian at Roger's press conference, Nick chaired the first meeting of the defence committee that same morning at Armadale. This was the core group of his army, in charge of coordinating the drafting of the defence document. Two weeks was all they had to respond to Corpcom's offer document, which had been posted so early. With this job came the day-to-day tasks of monitoring the newspapers, gathering hard information for Armadale's brokers to feed to the shareholders, and, not least, probing into Corpcom itself to discover its secrets and weaknesses along with what truths, half-truths or lies there were.

At 9.15 the group sat in the boardroom. There was a representative from each division. Alan and Edward were there, seconded from their departments. Harold Clemens sat at the other end, flanked by the junior members.

'We have over 15,000 employees in Armadale,' Nick started after the usual preliminaries and politenesses. 'And about twenty-five managing directors, scattered over the whole country. We need to make sure that we all keep together. That means communicating properly. I don't want them discovering things in the press that they should have been told internally. Believe me, Andrews will be trying to divide us. To a certain extent, he has already started, by separating us in his offer document. What he calls the core and the fat.' He turned towards Alan, and went on, 'Alan, I think you should be concentrating on that side initially. We need a stronger network.'

'We don't want to ruffle any feathers,' Alan said, 'Some of those MDs can be pretty touchy about their independence.'

'Let's make sure they still have feathers to ruffle, shall we?' Nick was curt. He did not want to hear the problems. He knew them already. He wanted to hear the solutions.

'Perhaps you should go and see them,' Harold said. 'A quick visit might help that side of things.'

'I don't have the time,' Nick replied quickly. Then he considered his initial reaction. 'Let's keep it open, shall we? If Alan really feels it'll make a difference, we can dream up something.

'I want to cover a lot of ground, and I don't have much time,' Nick went on. 'If we can keep the discussion of specifics to a minimum this morning . . . then I can let you get on with it.' Nick looked at Harold at the other end of the table. For years Harold had been exhorting him to leave the small details alone. Nick liked to plunge into the very centre of a problem, dealing with every corner of it, until he knew it well; it was not that he disliked delegating authority, he just could not keep out of things.

Harold looked back at him and smiled, nodding his head gently.

'I want to address the issue of the referral to the Monopolies and Mergers Commission,' Nick started up again. 'I cannot emphasize enough how important this avenue is to us. A referral is our safety net and we want to set it up.' Nick was not telling them what he had told Sophie; that he feared a referral was his only hope.

'We're going to have to work very closely with the bank on this,' Nick went on, aware that the mention of John's team of experts brought a wave of resentment in them all. The bankers were outsiders, inspectors come to snoop. They were suspect allies, for their only personal involvement was their pride, and at any given point, their job itself might force them to switch sides. Their primary responsibility was not to Armadale's board of directors or its employees, but to Armadale's shareholders. They had seen it all before and so at times were unable to avoid a tone of condescension, of superiority which could extend to a disregard of the people who worked within Armadale itself. They could afford, for example, to insist on truth and honesty while the other side broke every rule in the book.

Edward, who represented Armadale Chemicals at the meeting, said 'How can we persuade people it's our product that matters? That's the important thing. The product.'

'I'm afraid,' Nick responded, with as much bitterness as was in Edward, 'that it's more than our products we're going to have to adapt to the wishes of the marketplace. It's ourselves, Armadale. Our job is going to be to persuade people, and especially our shareholders, that we are important. An important company which will make them more money as it is than if it changes hands.'

Alan said very little. He was becoming even more worried. The product be damned. The company be damned. It was the spread of the investment and the return on it that mattered. Alan was glad he was planning ahead.

4

Rebecca was up first this morning. She stood at the window, naked, her hand parting the curtain just enough for her to see out without being seen. She loved the snow, for it reminded her of winters in Cambridge, Massachusetts. That's where she had been born; her parents now lived in Concord, a few miles away. She had lived in England for several years, but nostalgia was beginning to pull at her. The snow increased the yearning for home – drifts of white snow on the streets, sledging in the park, each activity something that could be trusted to return every year, like Christmas. Here, all you could rely on was the rain, and the taxi cabs.

Julian woke to find her gazing out. She was as still as a statue, lost in her memories, her profile etched against the dark curtain, one leg bent at the knee, and he turned away for a second and then looked back at her. It was as if he could not bear to look at her for too long; he wanted to grab her, smother her, so great was the intensity of his passion. Her dark hair waved generously down beyond her shoulders. Her body was so elegantly curved. Her breasts were not large, but they were full, dropping gently, her hips were rounded and wide, her pubic hair dark, thick and untrimmed. He was aroused just looking at her.

'It's snowing,' she said, smiling with pleasure. 'I hope it'll stick.' She turned towards him then, and saw him looking at her with such transparent desire.

'What time is that press conference?' she asked.

'Ten o'clock,' he said. His voice was thick; he cleared his throat.

'D'you need to go to the office first?' She came back towards the bed.

'I don't think so.'

Suddenly she was right next to him, and her hand was on the inside of his thigh and running up his body. She buried her face in him; his skin had the smell of sleep and that particular morning silkiness. He brought her face up to his and kissed her; her lips fluttered on his, and then she straddled him and her breasts swept gently along his body, her hair stroking him as well, her lips barely touching him. He held her shoulders as her tongue played with him. Then he grabbed her; he turned her over, his hands ran to her hips and down her thighs. He buried himself deep in her, inhaling her smell. Their breathing came in gasps; they looked at each other, stopped, holding the moment. They smiled They kissed, and they made love slowly, as slowly as they could manage.

Chapter Ten

I

Just before ten o'clock, Rebecca and Julian went into the panelled room of the Stationers' Hall, where Roger Andrews was to hold his press conference. In the hall, about thirty people milled about as at a cocktail party, chatting in groups, and drinking coffee from white china cups. Julian suddenly felt unfamiliar and self-conscious. He wondered if he stood out from among the crowd. But no one looked at him, except men who were really looking at Rebecca. Even in her subdued colours, a grey wool suit and a black silk blouse, she was noticeable.

He began to feel more relaxed. He realized with amusement that he could not tell the businessmen from the journalists. The women, three of them, were journalists he guessed and Rebecca confirmed this; she knew two of them. Rebecca herself worked as a freelancer, placing her articles – mainly about the arts – with American newspapers as well as English.

Julian noticed Peter talking to two men, both with notepads. He did not think Peter knew him, but he decided to move on. He led Rebecca down the stairs, into a long rectangular hall, dark with panelling which rose above head height. At one end a stained glass window showed the first printing press. In the hall was a camera crew; four men, in trainers, jeans and heavy jackets. They seemed oblivious to everything and everybody; there was nothing of interest here, a new set-up, that was all.

In a little ante-room, there was a telephone call-box. A

woman in a black turtleneck and black-and-white long plaid skirt was talking animatedly on the telephone. She was sporting a heavy fur coat on her shoulders and looked as if she were out shopping, rather than on the job in the City. Julian watched her as she hung up, ran her hand through her thick blonde hair and then came back to the camera crew.

'They're allowing cameras in. You can set up now,' she told them.

Without a word, the men picked up their equipment, metallic cases, tripods, cameras, and moved in unison. This was their third move, but they showed no irritation. It was all part of the job anyway. Setting up was no different from shooting.

'Who's she?' Julian whispered to Rebecca.

'Angela Truman. She's with one of the I T V stations.'

They followed her into the room where the press conference would be held. It was a long room in which folding metal chairs had been placed in rows for the occasion. They faced a table set to one side of the room and at an angle; behind the table were two chairs. There was a microphone in front of one of them. Across the way, facing the room, was a bulletin board. Charts on this showed in numbers and graphs the success of Corpcom's many and diverse enterprises. On one diagram Armadale was described in its three principal components; lines drawn from these to Corpcom's indicated how the merger was intended. Julian made a note of this, but there was nothing secret about the information. He was here to take in atmosphere, to gauge the reaction to Roger, and how the bid was perceived by the press.

Rebecca walked automatically towards the front of the room, but Julian held her arm.

'At the back,' he said.

They sat and watched as the seats filled up. Julian was looking the audience over, hoping there was no one there he knew. Several of Corpcom's employees were scattered around the audience, wearing name-tags on their lapels, there to answer questions, to act as back-up if they were needed. A young journalist sat in the front row; he had a camera, and wore a long overcoat, which he kept on throughout the conference. There was another, with his tie slightly undone, a cigarette dangling from thick lips, despite the 'No smoking' sign; he coughed occasionally and then took a quick puff of his cigarette, as if that would soothe the problem. Angela Truman sat close to the front too, draping her coat on the back of her chair.

They waited for Roger Andrews.

He came in once everyone was seated. He walked the length of the room, confident and ready. Behind him came Peter McNeal, who was a little less relaxed, more aware of being in the limelight, and less accustomed to it.

Roger remained standing. He looked at the audience, like a teacher before his class. He knew they did not like him. He broke too many rules: he was aggressive, showy, direct and Canadian. Had he been all those things and English, preferably titled, they would have forgiven him these sins. He would have been 'flamboyant', 'controversial', perhaps 'suave'; he could even have allowed himself some sexual high-jinks if he had had the inclination. But he remained a foreigner, despite his English mother.

'Thank you all for coming,' he began. 'My name is Roger Andrews.' He paused for a second and then went on, 'I was taught at school that when you write an essay, it's always good to start with a quotation from someone famous. So I'm going to start with a quote. 'A man pretty much always refuses another man's first offer, no matter what it is.' Now today any sensible businessman will tell you that, but in fact it was Mark Twain who said it first.'

Nobody laughed, but there was that murmur, that shifting in an audience that implies appreciation. Andrews noticed it, and went on. He knew that he could only charm his audience, not win them over to his side. After all, he was a predator.

'I know,' he continued, 'that Armadale International will turn down my offer and advise its shareholders to do the same. It's not official yet, but it will be soon. I'm going to tell you why they're crazy and why the shareholders are going to agree with me.

'Corpcom is a conglomerate. I'm not ashamed of it. That's why I called it 'Corpcom'. I believe in profits accruing from the replacement of bad management by good management. That's what I know how to do. Look at Corpcom's history.' He showed his audience where to look by pointing to the long board at his left.

'In the last five years,' he continued, 'we have purchased over ten companies. Most of them were losing money and now they're making it. The result is that my shareholders make money along with my company. As far as I'm concerned,' he went on, 'that's my job as a manager.'

He paused. He picked up a glass of water and drank from it, but it was more for timing than because he was thirsty. He was gauging the reception.

'Armadale,' he continued, 'is a company with interests in three principal areas: computers, engineering and chemicals. In the last five years, it has barely managed to scramble a 5 per cent increase in profit. I believe that this is mainly due to bad management. Market share in the computer-technology sector has remained static for the last two years, engineering is losing money; only the chemical business is profitable, and it has to carry the losses of the other businesses. Attempts at expansion are minimal. I can do better than that. After I buy Armadale my objectives will be a return of capital of 15 per cent and an increase in profit of 15 per cent.'

Again Roger Andrews pointed at the board. 'The second graph will show you how my profits are forecast.'

He continued in this vein, denigrating Nick and his team, even though he never mentioned any of them by name, outlining his own strong financial standing, and presenting himself as a man who had planned this attack for a long time and who knew what he was talking about. He spoke like this for about fifteen minutes, irreverently and familiarly. At the end he offered to answer any questions, if they had any; he challenged them.

There was silence, as if the journalists were stunned by his performance.

Then someone asked him, 'Why Armadale?'

'I thought I had just told you,' Roger answered. 'But why not? It's a good company, badly managed. It's perfect for us.'

Julian was stung by this. He wanted to stand up and tell them that there had been a steady increase in earnings and dividends over the last five years; that 5 per cent was just a beginning.

'How do you know your offer will be refused?' asked the man at the front with the long overcoat. 'You said it wasn't official yet.'

'When the topic screen sends up a message advising shareholders to do nothing,' answered Roger Andrews, 'we all know what that means. I don't like to beat around the bush. If in two days my offer's accepted, I'll be delighted to be wrong.' He turned to Angela Truman, the TV journalist. 'Yes, Angela?'

'Do you expect to have the bid referred to the Monopolies and Mergers Commission?' she asked him.

Andrews smiled at her. 'I don't think so,' he said. 'We compete with Armadale in only one of their major activities, chemicals. We have a very small engineering arm and a few other small businesses that could be very usefully combined. That would be a service to the public good, not the other way around.'

'Combining businesses usually means losing jobs,' someone else said. 'How many redundancies are you planning?'

'I don't have the exact number. Very few,' Roger Andrews answered. 'The changes will be in administration mostly. In a year we will have created more jobs than we've lost.'

'Do you expect Armadale to argue that the bid should be referred?' Angela Truman went on. She wanted more of an answer.

'Of course. They're bound to try,' he said. He laughed, and then added, 'I don't think it'll work, that's all.'

At the end of the conference, while the journalists lingered in the hope of a personal interview, Julian and Rebecca left the building as quickly as possible.

'Interesting?' she asked as they walked out in the snow. It was still falling and beginning to settle.

'Not good at all,' Julian responded.

He stood in the street for a second, disorientated. Rebecca, meanwhile, was scooping up some snow, trying to make a snowball. All she managed was a loose handful of white fluff. Seeing Julian so worried, she shook the snow from her hands.

'Did you see how confident he was?' he said to her. He had not even noticed what she had been doing.

'Come on. I'll walk you to the office,' she said. She threaded her arm though his and led him away.

2

Howard slept late. He rang Nick around lunch time, knowing Nick rarely went out to lunch; that would be the best time to get him, even today.

Nick was in, listening to Julian's impressions of Roger's press conference. When he heard Howard was on the phone, he looked at the telephone, debating whether to take the call. Opposite him, Julian fell silent.

'I'll leave you, sir,' he said when he saw Nick looking towards him. 'We can go on with this afterwards.'

Nick nodded and gave a tight smile of appreciation at Julian's tact. He waited for him to leave the room before picking up the telephone.

At the other end, as he waited, the line crackling in his ear, Howard sensed Nick's indecision. He sat in the winged armchair in his study, with the telephone on a small round table by his elbow; through the windows, he could see the snow falling on the garden. He bit at his thumbnail. As soon as he had picked up the telephone, he had wanted to put it down again. Yet he had persevered. It was Nick, after all.

'Hallo.' Nick's voice was flat, with no apparent emotion.

'Nick,' Howard said. He paused. There was silence. 'Nick,' Howard said again. 'I'm sorry about yesterday.'

'I'm afraid it's still going on today,' Nick said.

'I didn't mean the bid,' Howard said. 'I'm sorry about that, too.' Again he paused, searching for his words. 'I meant . . . about your thinking I should have told you about it.' Howard sighed, and continued. 'I just didn't feel I could. Maybe I was wrong. I just want you to understand, I suppose.'

'I think I do understand,' Nick said. 'I think you made the wrong choice.' His voice was cold.

'I don't understand you,' Howard said, defending himself with growing passion despite his conciliatory intentions. 'I couldn't have told you. I still don't think I could. I would've expected you, of all people, to see that.'

'Somehow,' Nick said, 'everyone treats me as an arbiter of right and wrong. I'm accused of being rigid, morality personified, etc., etc., I don't know why. Because I don't believe in shoplifting or something.' He had picked up a pencil and was drawing lines that criss-crossed each other over and over again with no particular pattern. 'We're friends,' Nick continued. 'Close friends. I think that means something. I don't give a damn about what the Takeover Code says. I expect a close friend of mine to put me above a Code. It's an emotional demand. Not a moral one. I feel betrayed when my friendship is not put first.'

'I can't believe I'm hearing this from you,' Howard said, butting in.

'Since we're being open,' Nick went on, 'I think you put your own position, your own security, above our friendship. That's why I'm upset.'

'That's unfair,' Howard said. But there was not enough conviction in his protest. He knew that Nick was right.

'Perhaps,' said Nick. 'I'm sorry, Howard. I have a lot of work, as you can imagine.'

It was an end to the conversation. Howard just said, 'Of course. Let's talk again soon.'

They hung up. Nick took only a few seconds to consider what had happened. It was a confirmation of everything he had been thinking. Then he buzzed Sarah on his intercom and asked for Julian to come back in.

Howard put the telephone down on its little table. He thought back to the day their friendship had started. They were both waiting for their interview at Oxford. Although they had gone to the same boarding-school, there they had been acquaintances, not really friends. It was the nervous wait outside the interview room that had marked the beginning of twenty years of consciously shared experiences.

On that occasion, they had not said much to each other. Nick had stood in the dark wood-panelled anteroom, a space barely more than eight-foot square, with solid dark oak monastic chairs, austere with age and learning; even the windows were intimidating, ugly white-glassed mosaics. Nick's hands were in his pockets, his back was straight, and he remained silent, holding the tension in. Howard had been franker; he had sat biting his nails, his legs open, his body trying to sag into the hard chair. He looked with apprehension at the wooden door that led into the interview room, waiting for his turn which would come next.

'Mr Hicks,' had called a disembodied voice when the door finally opened to let out a timid teenager in an ugly grey suit and black tie, with the marks of acne all over his face. Howard had preceded Nick into the interview and, when he came out twenty minutes later, he was smiling with relief.

'Good luck,' he said to Nick, not considering that perhaps they were competing for a place. Nick was a familiar face, a school fellow. 'Thanks,' Nick had answered and had walked in, his head up, apparently unruffled. But, on the contrary, he had been very conscious of the competition.

Later, after both had been accepted, they sat in Nick's room. It had none of the romanticism of 'rooms', a simple rectangle with windows, iron bed, desk, cupboard and basin in the corner, in an ugly Victorian building. Howard told Nick how scared he had been while they waited for their interview.

'You seemed so cool,' he had said to Nick. 'I was amazed. You didn't even seem worried about it.'

'Didn't I?' Nick had laughed. 'I was nervous.'

Hearing this admission, Howard had realized that, unlike himself, Nick at no time had really considered the possibility of not getting in to the university of his choice. He had known all the minor emotions linked to exams, orals, interviews, but never the ultimate one of self-doubt. It was arrogance, but it revealed also a kind of virginal innocence, a lack of awareness that the world could have nasty surprises in store. And that was one of the principal reasons for Howard's affection for Nick; it was part of Nick's charm.

Howard found he had been staring at the telephone. He turned to look outside, watching the flakes come gently down from the sky. His thumbnail was back in his mouth. His foot tapped against the carpet. He was suddenly like a little boy again. Empty. Alone.

3

On Tuesday evening they de-bugged the top floor of the Armadale building.

Six men arrived at nine o'clock in the evening, each carrying a bag of equipment, and were met by Julian, who was to stay behind while they worked. Only four men in Armadale knew of the 'sweep': John, Richard, Julian and Nick. Julian and Nick were the only two left on the floor.

One of the six men had been there before. He was a tall, thin man who wore trainers: they still squeaked a little. He said little; he carried a long, sweeping machine, and had earphones which he would put on when he started work.

As Julian took them upstairs in the lift, he asked the head man how long they would be. The man was stocky, about thirty-five with a round balding head, a bushy moustache and very light blue-grey eyes; he walked as if he had been in the army, straight-backed, his feet out slightly.

'It depends, sir,' he said. 'Depends on how many rooms you have.'

'Two or three hours, do you think?' Julian hoped it would take no longer. He did not want to get home too late this evening.

They arrived at the seventh floor as he put the question. The man waited until the lift doors had opened and looked up and down the corridor. He could see at least ten doors on either side of the lift. He made a quick calculation: twenty offices at one, maybe one and a half hours each. That made anything from twenty to thirty man-hours.

He turned to Julian and said, 'We'll be here till well after one o'clock, I should think.' He saw Julian's face drop, but his own face showed no emotion at all. 'Might be here all night,' he added. He could not help enjoying Julian's disappointment. 'They don't have a clue,' he thought.

Julian went ahead of the men, and showed them the boardroom.

'The M D's still here.' Julian said. 'I'll tell him.'

As he left the room to try to move Nick, the head man delegated two men to start the search in the boardroom. He looked around him and saw the telephone.

'Start with the phone,' he said. He left the room with the other three, following behind Julian. The man with squeaky shoes went out with him.

They found Julian in Nick's office, helping Nick to gather up his papers. 'Hallo,' Nick said stiffly. 'I can't imagine you'll find much.'

'Probably won't,' the head man said matter-of-factly. 'Usually don't.' Then he added, 'Better be safe than sorry.' After all, this was his livelihood. He did not want to encourage clients not to use his services.

Nick nodded at him and followed Julian into Julian's own office. They could work there while the security people swept Nick's room.

In the boardroom, one of the men had a small black box and a large receiver, like a radio receiver. Placing them on the table, he turned a switch on the black box. A noise, a little like the loud ticking of a metronome, began to sound with regularity. The man put on earphones and began searching the various frequencies on the receiver. If there were a microphone in the room, it would pick up the sound of the metronome and transmit it. The receiver would eventually find the frequency and the man would hear the sounds he himself was creating.

The other man had begun to dismantle the telephone. He worked automatically; he did not think he would find anything. He opened the telephone and looked inside it. He checked every connection circuit. Then he saw it: a tiny electronic device, no bigger than a fly, and very much like the other connections. He pulled at it and it came out in his hand without difficulty.

'George,' he shouted, loud enough for his colleague to hear through his earphones. He held the infinity device in the palm of his hand, looking at it in amazement. This was the first time he had found anything on an official sweep.

George, the head man, came running in, followed by his colleagues. The tall thin man came a little more slowly.

'Jesus,' said George. 'This place *is* bugged.' He looked at his workmates. 'We'd better make this thorough, lads.' He nodded at them. 'I'd better go and tell them.' He left the room. He went to the door of Julian's office and knocked.

'Come in,' Nick's voice sounded irritated.

'We found something, sir,' George said with his hand still on the doorknob. His small moustache seemed to twitch from the import of his news.

'You found something?' Nick said, not quite sure what the man was talking about.

'Yes. We found an eavesdropping device, sir.' George himself was so taken aback that he was quoting his own brochure. He paraphrased: 'We found a bug in the boardroom.'

'In the boardroom.' Nick suddenly realized what he was being told. 'You mean someone's been listening in on our board meetings?'

'I'm afraid so, sir. Through the telephone.'

Nick was out of his chair and heading towards the boardroom.

'What's the range of this thing?' Nick asked when he was holding it in his hand.

'Well. They could hear everything in this room, once they activate it. They call this number, you see,' George explained. 'They punch in a code. The phone doesn't ring. But it becomes a transmitter. Simple.'

'It's incredible,' Nick said. He was so taken aback, he was not even outraged yet.

'That's why you should never have a phone in a boardroom,' George continued. 'No one ever uses it, really. It's a gift for the other side.'

'I cannot believe he had this done,' said Nick. 'It's incredible.' Still holding the tiny microphone, he left the room. He came back an instant later.

'You'd better tear the place up,' he said to George, who nodded solemnly. That's what he meant to do.

Nick went back to Julian's office, and Julian followed him. For a long time, they sat there, going over what they had discovered, as if they were talking about something outside their lives. They made no decisions, they did nothing but talk.

Meanwhile, George and his team moved from room to room. They found the microphone in Nick's office. Nick was no longer surprised. Together with Julian, he tried to reconstruct the last two days to calculate the damage. They felt somehow violated, as if someone had come in and burgled their home.

No more bugs were found that night. At one o'clock, by which time they were getting no real work done, Julian finally persuaded Nick that he should go home.

'I'll stay,' he said. 'There's nothing you can do. You'd better get some sleep.'

Julian did not get home at all.

He slept on the sofa in Nick's office until it was time to

show the men out. George and his crew were there till nearly dawn. Sometime before then, while Julian slept and the other men were hard at work, the tall thin man went back into the boardroom. In his hand he had what looked like an ordinary three-pronged adaptor. It was that, but it had been modified to act as a transmitter as well, working like a baby alarm. Using the building's electrical system, someone with access to the same circuit could pick up any sound made in the room. In the garage, there was an equally ordinary outlet. It would be a simple matter for the man with the basset-like eyes to plug a receiver in and listen.

'You should have another sweep soon, you know,' George said as he left the building just after seven o'clock. 'You never know when they'll try again.'

'I'll give you a ring,' said Julian. 'Thank you very much.'

Chapter Eleven

I

Wednesday was the third day of the bid. Armadale's share price stood at 247p, up 7p from the day before. Corpcom's was at 445p, down 8p.

'We want to keep the price as close to 250 as possible,' John reminded Nick at their morning meeting. 'Keep the pressure on. We'll keep an eye on it. You must monitor your share register. We want to know how much he's buying. And question every nominee holder. We have a right to know in whose name they're holding it.'

By the end of the day, Armadale's share price had risen 7p and fallen back 5p to close at 249p. Roger's optimism and aggressiveness at his press conference had been reported by the financial papers that morning. Corpcom's own shares had fallen a further 2p to 443p. Corpcom's offer was thus devalued since the day of the offer by some £15 million. This was a natural course of events: Armadale's price was going up because it was desirable, Corpcom's going down because there would be more shares on the market if the bid succeeded.

Roger was not worried about the share fluctuation.

Armadale's Monopolies and Mergers Lobby Group had drafted variants of a letter to Members of Parliament, advising them of the bid. The letter, for local managers to send to their MPs, carried two warnings about a Corpcom/Armadale merger: several hundred jobs were in danger of being lost in certain areas through consolidation of identical activities in these areas; and that such a merger would severely restrict competition in the engineering and chemicals fields.

According to the Armadale letter, Corpcom was essentially a diversified conglomerate, whose primary interest was in investment and not in the output of the individual businesses it was purchasing. Not only would the takeover bid therefore restrict competition in certain areas, there was no guarantee that Corpcom would remain interested in, and thus maintain, the businesses acquired. It was an opportunistic bid, which attempted to reap the benefits of the gradual organic growth Armadale had already achieved over the last few years.

Two days earlier, a letter from Roger, stating that the bid was in the public interest and should be allowed to go forward, had reached the desk of every single MP in the country.

Since then, he had spoken directly to several members of government about the bid. He knew them personally and the conversations had been informal, but each had been left with the feeling that Armadale should be allowed to fight the bid alone.

City analysts viewed the bid as more than fair.

One wrote that an effective defence might be difficult to produce in view of Armadale's sluggish trading record, even though recent performances had been substantially improved.

Another thought that Armadale was quite capable of producing encouraging forecasts, and this together with the major strategic moves of the last year would form the basis of the defence.

On the question of a possible referral to the Monopolies and Mergers Commission, according to many, there would be considerable sympathy with the government's tendency to let market forces rule such issues, unless a truly national interest were at stake.

There was universal consensus that Mr Andrews' timing was impeccable.

*

As both Roger and Julian had sensed at the press conference, the media favoured Corpcom's chances. It spread Roger's deliberately disparaging view that 'a fight was possible, despite Armadale's poor record'.

On Wednesday Alan spent the day huddled in an office with two members of the PR firm handling the press, describing Armadale's past successes to them. Alan's task, as the defence committee member in charge of liaison with the PR people, was to ensure that the perceptions of Armadale's record were changed. As Julian had said to Rebecca at the press conference, Armadale's record, even if not flamboyant, was anything but poor.

Jasper Thomas, member of the board of Armadale, rang a fellow member of his athletic club, a public affairs consultant, or more precisely a Parliamentary lobbyist. Thomas wanted help to get the bid referred.

'Can you set us up with a few people?' Jasper said.

'And whisper words of wisdom to the others,' said the lobbyist.

'That's it exactly. It's very important to us.'

2

Alan had chosen to have lunch with Annie Chinoise outside the City limits. London is vast but the City is a very small world. Too many people knew that Annie was an executive-search consultant, or, less euphemistically, a headhunter.

Annie was well-known for three reasons. The first was that she had spread her net wide; the second, even though this was not unusual among headhunters, that she was a woman; the third that she was very beautiful. For a man to be seen with her had a double edge: it meant conquest, either business or sexual. No observer would know for certain which it was.

Today, Alan did not want to be noticed by his colleagues. He was not looking for approval or for envy, but for a way out. He had chosen a restaurant in Covent Garden, not too far to be inconvenient, but far enough to avoid observation.

The Café des Ploutocrates had been started by its young French owner, Jean-Marc Scarron, with an unabashed eye to the better-paid young executives of London, whom, he knew, would not mind the gentle derision in his choice of name or in the quotation by the French nineteenth-century historian Renan that headed his menus. It was written in a delicate italic: '*J'appelle ploutocratie un état de société où la richesse est le nerf principal des choses.*' Below was a translation: 'What I call a plutocracy is the kind of society in which wealth is the prime mover.'

The restaurant was laid out on two floors, the larger room being downstairs. That was where Alan waited for Annie. He sat on a stool at the bar, facing a large mirror that reflected the room behind him. He hoped he would not see anyone he knew. He picked up his glass of wine, took a sip and tried to forget about it by thinking of Annie instead.

He had met her when he was in his teens. She had been a schoolfriend of his older sister and had often come back home with her. Fourteen years ago, he thought. He would be able to call on the past.

He waited impatiently, listening to the sounds of the street, just above him. He had been a few minutes early; he wanted to be sure that Annie did not wait for him. They were friends perhaps, but he was the supplicant; he would be paying for lunch today. He looked around again, turning away from the mirror this time. The restaurant was half full, filling up quickly, the young waiters with their long white aprons beginning to move more rapidly. The conversations made a background hum that killed almost all outside noise. Alan tried to stay alert. He was listening for the familiar quick coughing throb of a taxi. He heard several and each time he looked up the stairs for her.

He almost missed her entrance. He first knew she was there when he caught sight of slender legs coming down the spiral staircase. He turned rapidly, taken by surprise, and watched Annie arrive. She was dressed smartly in a wool-jersey dress under a short suede jacket. Her hand lightly held the rail as she descended to make sure her boots did not slip on the grille of the stairs. Alan stared as she approached him. He had had a crush on her ever since his sister's first introduction: 'The one with the spots is Alan.'

Even now, he felt his heart quicken. She had an oval face, with a well-defined chin and dark eyes, almost black. Her hair was thick, dark brown and fell in a natural wave down to her shoulders. Several people turned to watch her as, gracefully, she walked up to the bar and kissed Alan on the cheek. It did not matter this time, but he was already outplayed.

'Bonjour.' The slightly singsong greeting came from behind them. They both turned. Facing them, with a bright smile addressed specifically to Annie, was Jean-Marc Scarron. He was no more than five foot seven; his charm was discreet, but self-assured.

He leaned forward to give Annie a kiss, one on each cheek, his hand, which held two menus, casually touching her shoulder.

'Bonjour,' she returned; there was a very slight trace of an English accent. This form of camaraderie suited them both. For him, it was flattering to be on kissing terms with a beautiful woman; for her, to be friendly with the owner of a restaurant had its advantages, and set her apart from the ordinary customer. It was especially useful when she brought clients here.

He led them personally to a table for four in a secluded corner, quickly taking off the extra place settings. It was another act of favouritism.

'A kir royal?' Jean-Marc asked, again addressing himself to Annie.

'Not royal, please,' she answered. 'Just a kir.'

The Frenchman looked over to Alan, who nodded his agreement, and he was off. Alan and Annie were now on their own, and Alan relaxed; the intimacy between Annie and Jean-Marc had excluded him.

'So. How's Charlotte?' Annie asked after Alan's sister, who was expecting her third child.

'As big as a house,' he said. 'Thank God she loves having them.'

They ordered their meal and talked of many things, of Alan's parents, of the last time they had seen each other, which had been three years ago, at Alan's nephew's christening. Annie did not have a first course; she watched Alan eat his mussels. He slobbered slightly as he sucked the juice out, having to wipe his chin with his napkin to stop it from running down on to his tie. She saw him as he had been at sixteen, shy, skinny, with small spots on his forehead. She let him finish, then made a gently pointed remark at how rarely they saw each other.

He laughed nervously. 'Actually, I wanted to ask your advice.'

He was tentative, nervous about what he was doing. She said nothing, letting him find his pace.

'You know Armadale is being taken over,' he said. He poured some white wine into her glass as he spoke.

'I know it's being bid for. Aren't you fighting it?' Annie was amused. She knew now why Alan was taking her out for lunch. She would play the game then, and enjoy it. It would be like a flirtation, a flirtation between an older woman and a younger, inexperienced man.

Alan was not a subtle man. 'Armadale's going to lose.'

'Are you sure?' she asked.

'Pretty sure,' he said. 'It's a fair price and we're not up to a battle with someone like Andrews.'

'I heard Nick Bishop was a good man.' It was her business to hear about that. She was surprised at Alan's certainty.

'He's all right,' Alan growled at her. He thought for a minute. 'He's a man of peace. He's not a soldier.' He paused again. 'He can't – or won't – play dirty.'

'And Andrews has no trouble doing that,' she said.

There was a silence now. The first step had been taken. Alan was trying to find a way of making the next. He was allowed a break by the arrival of their roast chicken – the Café des Ploutocrates had the best roast chicken in town; the skin was crisp and the flesh juicy, and it was served with thin *frites* and a green salad. They both fell on it and said nothing for a few mouthfuls.

'This is good,' Annie said. 'Why are the French the only people who can really make a delicious roast chicken?'

'Because it's their national emblem,' Alan said, regaining a little of his natural combativeness. 'That ridiculous little cock.'

Annie laughed. Then she gently helped him along, returning the conversation to its real subject. Alan was vain and self-engrossed, but not without endearing traits – his straightforwardness, for example. He was honest in his own way too. He was one of those people who felt absolutely no remorse at stealing from or cheating a company, because he felt that was the game of life, a game that everyone knew. Individuals, though, people were different. Family loyalty, loyalty to friends was part of one's humanity. To that extent, Alan was reliable. Yet Annie knew that number one would always come first.

'I need to hedge my bets,' he said.

He looked at her directly now, trying to read the beautiful features, to see if she would help him. He could not. Her lips still carried that ironic smile. Annie was a very difficult person, he thought.

Alan went on, explaining why he felt that Corpcom would succeed in its bid for Armadale. He talked and she listened. Eventually, as they finished their meal, he popped the question.

'Can you help?' he said.

She was twirling her coffee spoon, concentrating, it seemed, on the circles she was making with it on the tablecloth. She was thinking about what he had told her now, not just playing with him. After all, Alan was a desirable prey. He was intelligent, hardworking, with all the right business values, love of property, love of money, love of self. He was a good catch.

'I think we should wait until it's decided,' she said, looking up and facing him. 'There's no real hurry. No one likes a rat . . .' she left the phrase hanging.

'What do you mean, a rat?' He was stung.

'I'm sorry,' she said. 'It may be wise on your part, but I don't think people will like it.'

He thought it over and he knew she was right. He was glad he had spoken to her.

'I'll keep my ears open,' she smiled at him reassuringly. 'And if you're wrong,' she added, 'and you still want to leave, let me know.' She was after all a businesswoman. She did not want to lose him to some other headhunter.

'Thanks.' Then he added, earnestly, 'I'm not a rat.'

She patted his hand. 'I know,' she said. And she brought the lunch to a close by looking around for a waiter. Alan called for the bill.

As they were leaving, Jean-Marc appeared and escorted them to the stairs.

'I hope everything was all right?' he asked, his French accent strong but not affected; the accent of a well-educated Frenchman who can still not quite get around the curves of English phonetics.

'Delicious,' Alan answered. But Jean-Marc was looking for approval from Annie and he waited for her to say something.

'Still the best chicken in town,' she said.

3

That same day, Julian was also having lunch outside the City. His reasons were similar in one respect. He did not want to be seen in public with his friend Dennis. Dennis Johnson was not a headhunter, but he worked for Corpcom. They were friends from boarding school and both of them had agreed to meet for lunch with the same motive. They had not seen each other for several months – perhaps they could discover something useful. What bothered Julian was that it showed an opportunism in himself which he could not hide from.

As Alan had with Annie, they played a game with each other, probing, and deflecting, throwing seemingly innocent questions such as, 'What's the mood like over at your place?' and being answered with the evasion of, 'Oh, you know how it is . . .' It was a strange, gentlemanly affair in which neither dared ask what he had come to ask, because the question might embarrass the other. They fed on scraps, hoping it would amount to a meal.

Lunch was a miserably ordinary Italian meal in Soho. The tablecloths were red-chequered and the wine bottles lined around the room were wrapped in straw, but the spaghetti was thick and overcooked and the bolognese sauce made with fatty mince; only the packaged bread-sticks were good. Toward the end of their meal, Julian was thinking that he had been foolish to have felt guilt about using friendship for ulterior motives. He would be returning to work empty-handed anyway. He changed the subject.

'Did you watch that new series on television a few nights ago?' he asked. 'The one about the Hungarian spy?'

'Based on a true story,' Dennis said. 'I read about it in the papers.'

And, because secrecy and surveillance had become every-day topics for them, they talked about it. There had been yet another attempt by the government to squash the publication of a former MI5 employee's memoirs, and, a week later, a diplomat had been involved in a sex/spy scandal, an almost embarrassingly familiar tale of a high-ranking civil servant being caught spanking a prostitute, who herself was known occasionally to spank an Eastern European official.

'It's a wonder they don't learn from experience,' Julian said. 'It's always the same story. "Diplomatic Sex",' he went on. 'There must be a book in it.'

They analysed the stories, compared fact with fiction, safe at their table, away from the reality, like academics analysing a text.

'It's like the TV thing,' Julian continued. 'How could he not realize somebody was following him? I can never believe these people don't ever notice,' he said. 'I mean, if I were doing what he was up to, I'd make sure I wasn't being followed.'

'You know Bishop's being followed.' It was a statement, not a question, but as soon as Dennis saw Julian's face, the utter surprise and shock, he knew he had made a mistake. Their private game had swung suddenly back into a public battle.

'*Nick* Bishop?' Julian was horrified. 'By whom?'

'Oh, you know, a detective,' Dennis answered as casually as he could. 'It's nothing really. Everybody does it. Somebody from your end is probably hot on Andrews' tail.'

'No, they're not.' Julian was adamant.

Dennis was embarrassed. He wanted desperately to change the subject, yet he did not know how.

Thoughts were pelting through Julian's head. He realized that he must calm down, remove the panic and the surprise from his voice lest he worry Dennis too much. What Julian had just found out must be put to some use, he thought.

He drank some more wine. He said, 'That's a pretty dirty trick, isn't it?' He managed a smile, as if he were beginning to see it as a game again.

'They probably don't even bother to look at the reports,' Dennis said with a shrug. 'Andrews must order that kind of thing automatically. He's the sort who would.' Dennis was still being careful.

'I wonder what we've got in our "dirt" file.' Julian changed the subject a little.

'You should take a look.'

The moment had passed. Both men knew that the other had not been fooled. They had changed the subject, washed over the real issue, knowing that they would not able to lunch like this again until it was all over.

Dennis tried to pay for lunch, as if to atone for his involvement, but they ended up sharing the price of the meal.

'It's better that way,' said Julian. 'In view of what's going on.'

They parted outside the restaurant, walking backwards from each other, Julian with his hands in his coat pockets, a little penguin-like, Dennis putting his gloves. When they were about twenty yards away from each other, they turned and went their separate ways.

Julian waited to turn the corner before hurrying. He grabbed a taxi in Old Compton Street. He sat holding on to the strap, seesawing backwards against the seat and forwards willing the traffic away.

Dennis turned after a few yards and saw that Julian had disappeared. He returned to the office more slowly, wishing this lunch had never taken place. He found that he kept looking back, to make sure that no one was following him. So long as no one had seen him with Julian, he did not have to worry about the repercussions of his slip.

4

Roger had not felt the need to go anywhere. At one o'clock, he had taken the lift up to the top floor of the Corpcom building. In the company kitchen, Sam was cooking lunch for three people. Roger was entertaining Simon Harner, Peter's journalist friend. Peter would also be there.

Roger felt cheerful. The bid had thrown them into disarray. They were concentrating their efforts on getting a referral to the Monopolies Commission, and he felt fairly sanguine that such an attempt would fail. Furthermore, he had just returned from an informal meeting with an acquaintance of his, a Conservative MP, whose wife was a close friend of his own wife, and with whom he had discussed the issue of the referral.

Roger felt sure that one of the issues raised by Armadale would be that, if a takeover were successful, Corpcom would close a small engineering parts factory in the West Country and that the resulting loss of jobs would be against the public interest. Roger had had no problem convincing the MP, whose constituency fell within the area in question, that the consolidation would enable him to create jobs within a year, and that the MP should write a strong letter to the Secretary of State arguing that a referral would definitely be against the national interest.

Roger was looking forward to lunch. He liked meeting the press. He did not feel that it was all-powerful. On the contrary he believed that it was remarkably easy to manipulate.

'They want a story,' he had said to Peter once, during another bid, soon after Peter had become his finance director. 'Above all they want a story. The truth comes later, if at all. I always give them a story. If possible a true story, favourable to me. But any story will do.'

'What's for lunch, Sam?' he said. 'I'm starving.'

'Mediterranean prawns in a spicy sauce, cold sesame noodles and fried green beans with garlic,' Sam answered as Roger went up to the plate of beans and tasted some. He waited for Andrews' reaction.

'Good,' Roger said, licking his fingers. 'Next?'

'General Sam's chicken, bean curd with chinese parsley, spicy eggplant with onion, and steamed rice,' Sam smiled at his employer.

'Nice and spicy?' asked Roger.

'Yes, sir.'

'You're priceless, Sam,' he said as he took another bean and left the kitchen.

He always had Sam make the food very hot when he entertained in the line of duty. It usually put his guests at an immediate disadvantage: even if they were wise enough to eat selectively, the first bite had usually done its damage and, while Roger, who thrived on hot food, was quite at ease, they were concentrating on how to cool their burning palates.

He walked into the dining-room just as the lift doors opened for Peter and Simon. Roger strode towards the journalist with his right hand extended.

'Simon,' he said. 'Good to see you. Drink?'

Roger poured the drinks himself. He put a strong dose of gin into Simon's glass and, as he was doing so, said, 'How's the market, then?'

'I'm sure you know that, sir,' Simon answered.

'Roger, please,' Roger said. 'Call me Roger.'

Simon nodded, but did not call him 'Roger'. He would avoid using 'sir', but he was not sure he had graduated to 'Roger' yet.

'You're right,' Roger said, 'I do know. Corpcom's price is holding.'

'And Armadale's going up,' added Simon.

'So we're going to talk about that, then?'

'It seems like a natural topic of conversation,' said the journalist.

'Let's talk over lunch.' Once they had sat down, he shouted, 'We're ready, Sam.'

Simon, who had spent two years in India and three in Hong Kong, relished every bite of his food, especially the prawns and the spicy chicken. Peter suffered in silence, downing glass after glass of water; he had tried hard to avoid the worst of the chilli and had failed. He could only watch as Roger dispensed and Simon gathered information.

'I love a takeover, Simon,' Roger said as Sam was bringing in the main course. The journalist looked questioningly at the businessman and he continued, 'I always do well out of them. If I lose the bid, I sell out my holdings and make money. And if I win the bid, I get what I wanted in the first place.'

'It's a no lose situation,' said Simon.

'That's right. And in this case, I'm going to win it.'

'Why so sure?' Simon asked.

'Off the record?' Roger asked conspiratorially.

'Does it have to be?'

'I'm afraid so.'

'Off the record, then,' Simon agreed.

'I'm going to have enough acceptances by the end of the month,' Roger said with a self-congratulatory air that Peter knew, even through his discomfort, to be a sham.

'Why can't you announce that?' Simon said.

'Because it's still only hearsay and instinct.'

The journalist did not look convinced. Roger dropped the

subject. He had spread his own rumour. It would be more effective with a soft sell. Even if Simon did not publish it, he would be tempted to believe it. That was what Roger wanted. If the press believed he would win, then that particular skirmish was won. It all made for a smoother road.

5

Nick's lunch was a dry ham sandwich and an apple. He did not really like apples, and he did not eat the whole sandwich. Nick rarely ate much at lunch, unless he was out on business; colleagues looked on his slim figure with envy.

He was working on the draft of the letter that was to be sent out to shareholders that afternoon. It was a short note asking shareholders not to do *anything* until Armadale's defence document had been published or, as the letter put it, until Nick wrote to them 'setting out the reasons why you should reject Corpcom's bid'.

Nick looked up from his draft as Julian stepped in.

Julian had first gone straight to his own office and closed the door, ignoring the messages that Sarah had handed him. He sat in his chair, tapping his desk with a pencil. Once he picked up the phone, and was about to try to reach Rebecca, but then he hung up again. As he sat behind his desk, the thought he had been avoiding ever since the restaurant returned even more strongly: what if there were something in Nick's life to be uncovered?

Nick waited for Julian to say something. Julian cleared his throat, coughed.

'Can I talk to you for a few minutes, sir?' he said.

'I thought you were about to,' Nick said. 'What is it?' he asked when he realized that Julian was still hesitant.

Still Julian did not answer. He did not know how to start this revelation.

'I had lunch with a friend of mine today,' Julian started.

'Yes . . .' Nick said.

'He works for Corpcom.' Julian paused again.

'Come on, then. Spit it out.' Indecision made him impatient.

Julian told him. Nick listened and said nothing. He was outwardly calm, but his very stillness indicated his growing anger. He, Nick Bishop, was being followed. By a private detective. Paid for by Roger Andrews. It was outrageous. He had never thought it possible. Even now that he knew, he still found it incredible that a businessman should stoop to such methods. It was seedy, sordid, the stuff of dark alleys and dirty raincoats.

Julian finished and then stood waiting for a reaction. He knew Nick would be furious, but how would he express it?

'Andrews is scum. I'm going to report it to the Takeover Panel.'

'We can't prove it, sir.' Julian said.

'Well, we'll find the bastard and then we'll report it.' Nick thought for a moment. 'I'm going to call Andrews right now,' he said.

'What for?' asked Julian.

'To call the bugger off,' Nick said.

'We could get more mileage out of reporting him.' said Julian.

'I don't want someone tailing me around the place. It's unacceptable.'

'Would you call him off if you were Andrews?'

'I wouldn't have hired him in the first place,' Nick said pompously.

Julian made no reply and Nick paused, realizing that he was not thinking well.

'All right,' he said. 'We need to find out who's following me.' He added, 'We'll organize it later.'

It was a dismissal, but Julian did not leave. If anything he now looked even more embarrassed than before.

'What is it now?' Nick asked him. 'What else are they up to?'

'I just wondered . . . I mean,' Julian was almost stuttering. 'I just thought that if there was anything, maybe I would need to know about it. To help, I mean.' He had spoken quickly.

Nick looked at his assistant, half knowing what he was saying. But he looked puzzled. 'What exactly are you saying?'

'If there is anything to hide, then maybe I can help you hide it. That's all.' Julian looked straight at Nick.

'Something to hide?' Nick's tone had hardened. He was even angrier than before.

'I don't know.' Julian was lost. 'Dirt, I suppose. You know what I mean.'

'No. I don't know what you mean.' Nick looked at Julian as Julian had never seen him. His eyes were cold and steady, holding their gaze with inexorable focus.

'I'm sorry,' Julian said. He was going to drop the subject. 'I just wanted to be able to help. Nothing more. I'm not judging or anything. I mean, things happen . . .' He trailed off.

'Not to me, they don't,' Nick said.

Chapter Twelve

I

That same evening, when Nick left the office, he walked down Cannon Street towards Bank. He took the emptier streets whenever possible. Since he left well after 8.30, the City was not crowded.

Julian waited in the shadows of the Armadale entrance, trying to spot anyone going after his boss. But, even in the limited pedestrian traffic, he saw no one. Luckily they had planned for that, not knowing how the tail would operate. Julian would wait three minutes and then leave the building himself, following the same route Nick had taken. Nick would be walking quite slowly, so Julian should have no trouble in coming up behind him and his follower.

What surprised them both was how easily it worked. Julian walked fast down the preordained route. He saw Nick's tall figure on Moorgate, as he was turning into Telegraph Street. Julian waited to see if anyone followed. And out of a doorway, a shadow he had not noticed darted across the road, and down the alley. Julian ran ahead to Telegraph Street. Half-way down was a man in a dark blue overcoat, a scarf tied around his neck.

Julian did not see Nick, but he knew he would not be far ahead. He put two fingers to his mouth and blew. A sharp, high whistle sounded. It was a trick he had learned at school. He was still proud of it.

The man whirled around at the sound and stared at Julian who was standing in the middle of the narrow street. The detective therefore did not see that, behind him, Nick had retraced his steps and walked right up to him.

'Good evening,' Nick said.

The man turned again, frightened, taken by surprise. He did not know what to expect. Nick was tall and looked powerful, Julian was a much younger man. Did they plan to attack him?

'What's going on?' he said. It was a London accent. The man was in his late forties, of medium size; he had a thick greying moustache and sad, basset-like eyes with deep pouches under them.

'What's your name, please?' Nick pursued, ignoring the detective's question.

'I don't have to give you my name,' the man said. He continued the pretence. 'Listen, I don't have any money . . .'

Nick smiled at him. 'Listen. Either you give me your name and your profession, or else my friend and I are going to take it from you.'

Nick moved just a little closer towards him and Julian did the same from the other side. It worked. The detective had not been paid for valour, and since the request seemed simple enough, he answered it.

'Jim Green. Investigations Limited.'

'Who's paying you?' said Nick.

'I'm afraid I'm not at liberty to tell you that, sir.' The man had sized up his opponents by now and realized that they were unlikely to attack him. Having admitted his work, he could now fall back on its status.

Nick said, 'Professional ethics, is that right?'

'That's right,' was the answer.

And without another word, Nick moved away and started back up Telegraph Street. 'Come on, Julian,' was all he said. They left the detective looking after them, not quite sure what had happened to him.

The following day, Nick discussed the matter with John. The merchant banker was delighted.

'At last something worth taking to the Panel,' he said.

They reported it, together with the bugging incident, to the

Takeover Panel who immediately asked both parties to refrain from harassment and unethical practices aimed at any one particular party, either in the offeror or offeree company. The spirit of the Takeover Code should be followed.

It was a moral victory.

That was how Julian described it when he told Rebecca of his adventure that evening. They were sitting in the small kitchen of his flat, in which a table and two chairs by the window, overlooking a small paved back garden, substituted for a dining-room. Rebecca had been waiting for him, sitting in the living-room watching television. Julian turned up after eleven, just before the end of a programme. He came into the room and sat heavily on one of the armchairs.

'You wouldn't believe what I did today,' he started.

'Ssh,' she said. 'I'm watching this.'

Julian looked at her with a hurt expression. He got up and went to the kitchen, poured himself a whisky, put in some ice, came back into the living-room and sat in the chair again, turning his attention to the television.

When the programme was over, Julian was wondering what else would be on, having forgotten that earlier he had wanted to talk to Rebecca.

'I hope this isn't developing into a habit,' she said. She got up and turned the television off.

'What?' Julian looked up at her from the comfort of his chair.

'Coming back from work at eleven o'clock every night,' Rebecca said. 'It could get boring.'

'I'm sorry,' he said. 'It's probably going to get worse.'

'You hungry?' she asked.

'Starving. What's for supper?'

'I don't know, yet,' she answered and went off to the kitchen.

Julian followed her, sipping his drink as he went. He watched her break eggs into a bowl for an omelette, and automatically he began making a salad dressing. As they worked he told her of the nabbing of the detective.

'Whose idea was it?' she asked.

'Nick's,' he answered. 'I can't believe it worked. It was so simple.'

'Some detective.' She chuckled at the thought of the slightly flabby man Julian had described caught between these two athletic-looking businessmen.

'I'm not sure what good it will do us,' Julian said as he threw the salad leaves into the bowl. 'It's got no practical effect. It's a ripple. Next week, it'll all be forgotten. It really depends on what the numbers are like. It's all about numbers, really. You can lie, cheat, and break all the rules of this game, and still come out ahead.'

'I have a feeling Andrews knows that full well,' Rebecca said. She took the pan off the flame and said, 'Get the plates. It's ready.'

She served the omelette and they ate rapidly. They were both hungry. There was little time left between mouthfuls for conversation.

2

Julian had been right. Controversy about the private detective died down.

The first week ended with Armadale's formal announcement that it was rejecting Corpcom's offer as unsolicited, unwelcome and inadequate. Armadale's board of directors urged its shareholders to turn down Corpcom's offer.

Armadale's shares closed on Friday down at 246p. Corpcom's share price remained the same, 443p. Roger's offer remained attractive.

Alan, Jim, Philip and Edward all worked on Saturday well into the evening. Most of those who sat on the seventh floor did.

Julian and Nick both came in on Sunday as well.

They were scurrying from task to task, protecting their territory from the invader.

*

Roger flew to New York on Sunday. On Monday, he spent all day in a board meeting of Corpcom USA. He did not return to London until Tuesday evening.

Business was very much as usual at Corpcom.

3

The second week of the bid opened with Jasper Thomas reporting that his friend the lobbyist had met with limited success. The mood of the times was against referrals.

In light trading, Armadale shares hit 250p on the Tuesday, whereas Corpcom remained stubbornly at 443p.

On Wednesday, nine days after Corpcom's announcement, Nick was in his office with several hours' more work ahead of him. It was eight o'clock. Sarah had left, and although Julian and several others were still there, the atmosphere was more peaceful than in the middle of the day, as if the cool of the night had come after stifling heat.

He was working on a section of the defence document entitled 'The Long-Term Value of Armadale'. He felt the danger in the last line of the draft, 'Armadale's future as an independent company now depends on you.' It was all too true.

The telephone rang.

He picked up the receiver as he continued to write.

'Nick Bishop,' he said.

'Mr Bishop,' it was a woman's voice. 'My name is Annie Chinoise.'

Nick's face showed his irritation. She had called several times this week and Sarah had put her off. Now there was no Sarah to protect him.

'You've called before,' he said. 'I've been very busy.'

'I can imagine,' Annie said. There was a pause and then she went on, firmly, 'I'll come to the point. No need to waste your time. I wondered if we could meet, chat . . .'

'What about?'

'You know what I do. I'm suggesting a business meeting.' Annie was used to people trying to avoid her.

'I'm perfectly happy with my job, Miss Chinoise. Or is it Mrs?'

'Miss, or Ms, whichever you prefer,' she answered and there was irony in her voice. Nick heard it. He could feel that she was smiling. Annie was silent for a moment, pondering the next move. Then she plunged. It was a risk.

'You might lose your job quite soon,' she said. 'Then you'll need another.'

Nick was taken aback by her remark, not only because it was blunt and unexpected, but because no one yet had put the truth in such exact words.

'I can always find myself another one then.' He rallied.

'Why waste the time?' she said, hanging on.

'I don't think it's appropriate,' he said. 'As you know we're in the middle of a takeover bid.'

'Are you afraid of me?' She took the tried and true feminine tactic. Most men fell for it. Attack their virility and you get a reaction.

Nick was too straightforward a man not to rise. 'Of course I'm not afraid of you.'

'Well, then?' she asked.

Again he heard the smile in her voice and he knew he was being manipulated. He laughed at his own gullibility.

'All right,' he said. 'I don't have my diary with me. Would you mind ringing my secretary in the morning and setting a time with her?'

'Will she do that?'

'Absolutely,' he said. 'We'll meet. For lunch.'

He hung up and found he was looking forward to meeting her.

4

Later that evening, a few minutes after 10.30, Nick looked at the clock and decided to go out for a walk and a drink in the

142

pub. He had been struggling with his description of the way Armadale intended to enhance profits by a renewed expansion into the ever-more accessible European markets. These days, he left the office in the evenings not because he was tired, but because he was beginning to go round in circles. Tonight he would go out and come back for a couple of hours' more work. A stiff drink could not hurt.

It was a cold, beautiful night. Last week's snow had gone and had not yet been replaced by rain. He took long strides down the road. His hands in his coat pockets, he inhaled the icy air. It felt good to be out of the office and its dry, centrally heated atmosphere. A car drove past him, noisier for the quietness that surrounded him. When the roar of its engine had died an even more potent stillness succeeded it. He became aware of the echo of his own footsteps, and it seemed to emphasize his isolation. That feeling of isolation warmed him, consoled him in the very knowledge of his pain.

He heard other footsteps then.

There is nothing extraordinary in hearing footsteps in London, but this was the City, and it was after 10.30. Even that was not necessarily odd. What was odd was that, when Nick turned round, he saw no one. He found it almost unbelievable that Roger should have placed someone else on his tail. The detective had been caught. Surely that was enough.

Nick walked on, trying to decipher other steps from his own. There was nothing. He relaxed a little. And then he heard them. The buildings could not help catching the sound and throwing it back into the night. He did not turn this time. He had made up his mind. He walked on, aiming for the next corner.

He turned it and saw a doorway a few yards in front of him. Running on tiptoe, he hurried into the doorway and hid in the gloom, waiting for his pursuer. He held in his breath, which was hurried from the running and the sudden excitement. He let it out, breathed in again more slowly.

From his hiding place, he heard the rush of feet, then the stop at the corner. The figure of a man turned casually into the street.

143

It was dark. It was a small street, not as well lit. Nick could not recognize the man, but he was not the detective he and Julian had caught. This man was broader and shorter, and was now scanning the darkness for sign of Nick. Not seeing him, he slowed. The detective's body tightened, suspicious, careful.

Nick lunged at him just before the man reached the doorway. But this private detective was alert. He must have caught a peripheral glimpse of Nick's arm striking at him and he stepped aside, avoiding the full impact of the blow. Nick's clenched fist barely scraped the man's shoulder.

Nick had been a boxer at boarding school, a graceful fighter who had once knocked out a much stockier, stronger-looking opponent with one punch. But this time his opponent was a professional. Before Nick could move again, a fist had hit him in the ribs and another in the stomach. He took a sharp intake of breath and saw the other moving away.

Instinctively, he made a grab for him and caught the man's overcoat, pulling him back. The shorter man swore and grunted. Nick had made him lose his balance. Nick punched out and again hit a shoulder, but harder. He punched again. This time, the impact was blocked and Nick felt a fist hitting him squarely on the chin. He slipped, one of his legs going out under him. He went down; his head hit the pavement as he landed. The shock dazed him.

Just as he was recovering, sitting up to get back into the fight, he heard running and saw his opponent turn the corner and disappear. Nick knew he would not catch him. He remained sitting for several minutes, catching his breath.

Tentatively, he got up, checking to see if all his bones would fit into place. They were sore, but there was nothing broken. His side hurt where he had been punched and now he felt a bruise on the knee that had hit the ground when he had fallen. He limped a little as he walked back towards his office.

He forsook his drink. But he felt better. Fighting had done him good.

Nick did not go back to work. He went home, driving with a sense of exhilaration. He slowed down as he was going through Bromley; the excitement had abated, and he felt growing weariness. By the time he reached the dark and narrow roads leading to Downe, his face and his ribs were hurting.

The house was dark, except for one light in the living-room. He headed straight for it, without switching on the hall light, and poured himself a drink. With it, he sat heavily into an armchair and went back over the incident, trying to remember every detail, relishing it. It was an extraordinary experience for him, even more so than the unmasking of the first man. That had been exciting, but simple. This latest meeting with a private investigator had introduced him to a dark side of life that he had never touched: a street fight, a man following him, himself using violence. It was so un-expected.

He was sitting slouched in the chair, taking a sip from his drink, when he heard Sophie coming down the stairs. Then she was in the doorway, in her nightdress, squinting at him because of the light.

'Nick!' she gasped. She had seen his face. 'What happened to you?'

'I got into a fight.'

'What do you mean, a fight?'

She went to him and knelt beside him. Gently she touched the bluish mark on his cheek. Nick started and moved away. He had not realized that it hurt.

'How did you get this?'

'I jumped on someone who was following me,' he said with almost drunken pride. 'Missed him mostly.' Then he added, 'Got him a couple of times, though.'

'Who was following you?' Sophie kept looking at his face as she spoke.

Nick was irritated by her apparent obtuseness. She seemed

stolid, unimaginative. In fact, she was just trying to make sense of Nick's thoroughly unusual behaviour. He seemed completely possessed by the act of violence. She wondered if he weren't seriously hurt.

'Where else were you hurt?' she said, looking worriedly at him.

Instead of answering her, he sat up, wincing from the pain on his side and put his arms around her. He drew her face to his and kissed her. She was so surprised by this that she did not respond. After the first contact, she tried to move away as if this were just a kiss, a banal peck on the lips. But it was not. Nick intended it as a full-blown kiss. He held her head to his, pushed his tongue into her lips, parting them for her. He kissed her deeply and for a long time, he ran his hand down her back to her buttocks, until finally she pushed him away, gasping for breath and for sanity.

'Are you all right?' she said. She saw his disappointed face then, and laughed feebly, trying to turn it into a joke.

'I'm fine,' he said angrily. 'Fine.'

'I'm sorry,' she said, knowing he was disappointed. 'It's a bit unexpected,' she added.

He was calling on a passion that they had known when they first met. It was as if the brawl in the street had thrown him back in time, as if he were a young man who had just had a punch up and was now swaggering home to his girl to get laid. There was also a yearning for something else, an undefined need that had been touched on by a simple and ridiculous punch-up. Nick was not just being childish; he was searching for vitality.

But Sophie felt none of this. Her day had been average, spent with children and meals, catering to what seemed like a constant list of demands on her attention and concentration. She had gone to sleep alone, as she had more times than she could count in the last twelve years, every night in the last nine days. Nick's unexpected desire was importune and unreasonable. She did not mind being woken up by someone who was hurt and needed her, but she had no time for a husband who was transmuting foolhardiness into sex. It was meaningless to her, as unemotional and unloving as an early-morning erection. Although she had apologized for not responding, she felt irritated by this new demand. It was like having a third child in the house.

'Come upstairs and I'll fix you up,' she said. Then she rose and left the room. She was beginning to feel as if this takeover bid was a manifestation of Nick's mid-life crisis.

Nick watched her go. He nursed his disappointment, then felt a wave of exhaustion sweep over him. He emptied his glass and got up painfully. He hobbled up the stairs to be patched up.

Sophie was in bed, sound asleep.

Chapter Thirteen

I

The North Sea oilfields lie on the 61st parallel, 150 miles north-east of Sumburgh in the Shetland Islands. Tracing the latitude along an atlas, one's finger wanders slightly below Iceland, on to Greenland, through the North-West Territories of Canada, across Alaska and Siberia. Four hundred miles to the north is the Arctic Circle. London is about 600 miles south.

It was on the first of February, on *Desis*, the most Northern of Usoco's oil platforms, that an explosion ripped through the room in which natural gas dehydration was carried out. High pressure built up in what was a low pressure system. In the space of thirty seconds the dehydration tower had blown and, with it, two large storage modules. The sound of the explosion was contained by the steel walls and echoed like a dull thud around the platform. A tremor ran through the structure, and an alarm screamed its high pitched screech. As the instruments in the control-room registered the wild imbalance, immediately the fail-safe devices went into operation. The flow of oil stopped. The system shut itself off. Production was closed. The platform was shut down.

The damage was contained. It did not take long, for survival depends on it. But when the crew clearing the damage finally reached the location, they found two men lying dead next to the valve, their bodies burned, mutilated and distorted, like cloth puppets tossed across the room by a petulant child.

It was the first time in seven years that men had died on a Usoco platform. The accident shocked and dazed those who worked on the platforms and rigs and all the staff back on the shore. Two members of a large family had just died, and the death accentuated the constant precariousness of all the oilmen stranded over a cold and hostile sea.

The national press came to Aberdeen. The two bodies flown back by helicopter were shown on television, shrouded in blankets and strapped on stretchers.

And then the rumours started. Apparently a valve had malfunctioned.

All valves are tested and tested again under rigid conditions before they are shipped out and installed. But no test can protect against a later malfunction, a fatigue that cannot be seen. As the shock of death began to be replaced by passion and anger, people sought something or someone to blame. There must be a cause, a reason for disaster and death.

It was Armadale Engineering who had manufactured the valve. Before anyone at Armadale even knew the company was involved, the finger was pointed at them.

An inquiry was called for.

2

The accident in the North Sea had taken place at tea-time. The evening news was full of it. Library footage of the platforms surrounded by the grey swell of the sea was intercut with shots of the shrouded corpses being unloaded from the large Chinook helicopter. There was an interview with one of the widows, weeping without shame as she responded to the questions.

Julian caught the ten o'clock news. He had left work earlier than usual that evening, but when he came home, the flat was empty. Rebecca had been staying at her own flat for the last few days; with Julian never home, there was little sense in sitting in his flat. Julian grabbed a beer from the fridge and turned the television on. It was his way of relaxing, the most passive occupation he could think of. These days he watched the news more often than usual, for it gave him the illusion of remaining a part of the real world, of not being sucked into the quicksand of the bid.

He watched the news of the explosion with mild interest. With a numbress that was due more to weariness than to insensitivity he watched the bodies of the two men being unloaded from the helicopter, an image that had now been repeated on every channel, in every newscast of the evening.

When the images of death had cleared and the newscaster faced the camera, holding his microphone in front of him, ignoring the wind that blew his hair into wild strands, Julian was about to turn off and go to bed. The mention of Armadale Engineering froze him. Suddenly he was concentrating. He turned the volume up and the small television loudspeaker vibrated, rattling inside the television.

In fact, little was said. It was thought that a malfunction had occurred in the natural-gas dehydration system, in which a chemical called glycol is used to remove water from gas. It was not yet clear what the specific malfunction was. The equipment was made by a company called Armadale Engineering and there had been no comment from the company as yet.

Julian did not wait to hear the homily spoken by the newscaster, his voice dropping into appropriately solemn tones. He was already on the phone. He rang the office, but there was no reply. Nick must have left already. He rang his home instead.

Sophie answered the telephone. No, Nick had not arrived. He must be on his way. 'He rarely gets home before eleven these days,' she added, and there was a trace of complaint in her voice.

'Did you see the news?' Julian said, ignoring what he had heard in her remark. He was about to confirm her opinion.

'The accident? Yes,' she said. 'Isn't it horrible?' There was genuine pain in her voice, reminding Julian of his own lack of feeling. So, television did not numb everyone's sensibilities, he thought.

'You should tell Nick, I think. When he arrives.'

'Nick?' she asked. 'Why? He hates that sort of thing.' She could not see that Nick would want to hear of a disaster in the North Sea.

'They mentioned Armadale,' Julian explained, embarrassed to have to bring it up. 'Nothing much yet, but we'll probably have to make a statement.'

'Armadale?' She had not heard the company mentioned. It was as if, even here, in death and misery, the company was competing for attention. 'What's Armadale got to do with this?' she asked sharply.

Julian told her apologetically. Her tone had made him realize the callousness that had come over him. Two men dying seemed to mean nothing to him, whereas the company's name being mentioned was serious. It was the inevitable result of the obsessiveness of the last two weeks.

Sophie waited up for Nick since he was going to be home before midnight. But when she told him about the accident and of what Julian had told her, she was infuriated to see exactly the same reaction in Nick as she had heard in Julian.

'That's all I know,' she said angrily when pressed for more details.

She went to bed, and Nick looked after her, wondering why she was so bad tempered. But he had no time to consider it. He returned to the problems that were more pressing to him at the moment.

That very afternoon, they had reviewed the press conference he was going to give the next day. Against what he regarded as his better judgement, his colleagues – Richard, who would be there with him, Harold and Tom Stillwood – had forced it upon him. It was, they had insisted, the appropriate response.

They had sat in Nick's office, around the coffee table, reviewing the contents of Nick's re-drafting of the 'Long-Term Value'.

'It's so bloody difficult to get across,' Tom said about the growth in profits. 'It's got to sound good and yet not over the top. I believe it, but why should they?'

'We're not addressing little old ladies in Scotland, you know,' said Richard. 'Most of our shareholders spend all their working lives looking at this kind of thing.'

'Yes, but if I don't understand it, how can they be expected to?'

It was out of this remark that the idea of the press conference came. All of them felt the need to be understood. Ever since Roger had announced his bid and had his own talk to the press, the newspapers had been looking at the takeover from his point of view. Armadale had been analysed according to his criticisms of the company, not according to Armadale's own points of reference.

'I think, Nick,' Harold said, 'it might be a good way of putting our own views across to a wider public.'

'The press sets the agenda,' said Richard. 'Fund managers read newspapers on their way to work. They're picking up the mood of the City.'

'It's playing Andrews' game,' Nick said, but there was already less conviction in his voice. 'And the press's. Why do they always get their own way?'

The three looked at him, waiting to hear what he would say next. He stood up, put his hands in his pockets, looked down at them. 'I'm the one who's going to have to do it?' he asked rhetorically.

'Who else?' Harold smiled up at Nick.

Now it was too late to cancel. The commitments had been made, and to cancel because of an accident on an oil rig, in which a valve manufactured by Armadale might be responsible, would be interpreted as a tacit sign of guilt. The press would eat it up. Nick had gone to bed that night cursing the freedom of the press. Its freedom was everyone else's prison. ' "Fourth Estate",' he muttered as he went up the stairs. ' "Usurpers of power", more like it.'

*

The next day, in the very same room that Roger had used, he faced the journalists with a shy aggressiveness that gave his face an unwitting arrogance. This did not endear him to his audience, who had not, in any case, come to like him. They had come to test him. Everyone in the room was aware of the two deaths in the North Sea. And although most of them were financial and business journalists, some reporters from the tabloids had come, smelling trouble, sniffing a possible story.

Three of them sat together near the front, chatting to each other, waiting for question time, looking forward to it. One of them wore a red bow-tie, and leaned back in his chair, one leg crossed over the other, smoking, a cigarette held gingerly between his thumb and index finger. His two companions were less flashy, if somewhat more untidy: rumpled suits and unironed shirts, with ties loose around the collar.

Nick stood up and touched the microphone. The thick sound played around the room. The journalists turned towards him. Voices quietened, but were not silenced.

'Would you mind not smoking, please,' Nick said into the microphone, leaning down slightly, approaching it tentatively, and his voice echoed around the room, bringing a sudden silence to the assembly. Explaining his request, Nick pointed to a 'No smoking' sign posted on the mantelpiece.

Most of the reporters looked at him with disbelief. The smokers, and there were not many of them, began stubbing their cigarettes out. The man with the bow-tie at the front stared at Nick angrily. He began looking around for an ashtray, found none and used the floor instead. He turned towards his neighbour and whispered, 'We've got an abolitionist here.'

'Thank you,' Nick said. He straightened himself to speak. Richard, who was sitting next to Nick, was shaking his head slightly, a hint of a smile on his lips. Later, Nick himself was unbelieving at his own behaviour: to find antagonism is one thing, but to seek it?

Nick cleared his throat, looked around the room one last time. Now there was silence. He had their attention.

'The board of Armadale International,' he began stiffly, 'wish to make a statement regarding the current offer by Corpcom for the shares of Armadale. Much has been written in the press,' Nick looked up for a second from his paper on which his speech was written. He hesitated, looked back down again. He was not an orator.

'We have no objection to the facts,' he went on, 'but to the selection of the facts and to the opinions that have accompanied them. We feel that they are biased in Roger Andrews' favour and, if you don't mind,' and here Nick attempted a smile, 'we would like to unbias them a little.'

Again he paused, but this time it was planned. He waited to see how this had been received. There was no comeback, little conversation. So he continued, turning to a large flip-chart that stood to his left.

'I'd like to take you through the last couple of years of Armadale and bring you up to date. I think you'll see that we can demonstrate a solid rate of growth and successful man –'

Nick never completed the word 'management'. He was interrupted by the slicing voice of the journalist with the bow-tie. The man did not stand up; he was still leaning back in his chair with his legs crossed, his hand now resting on his thigh since it held no cigarette.

'Mr Bishop,' he said, 'is your company accepting responsibility for the terrible explosion in the North Sea yesterday?'

There was a moment of silence, interrupted only by outside noises, cars and buses, the distant hum of a vacuum-cleaner. Then someone coughed. Nick turned away from the flip-chart and looked towards the man in the front row.

'Would you mind letting me finish, sir?' Nick said.

'Two men died,' the man continued, triumph in his voice, 'Is what you are about to tell us truly relevant in light of that?'

'Sir. I don't know who you are, but . . .'

'George Simmons of the *News*,' the man answered.

'Mr Simmons,' Nick said, facing him squarely. 'I have

come here to describe my company in view of the recent offer made by Mr Andrews, chairman of the Corpcom corporation. Although the death of two men in the North Sea is tragic, I do not think this is the appropriate moment to discuss it.'

'You were just talking about success. I don't call producing faulty valves successful management. I think it's irresponsible.' Simmons looked about him now. He was enjoying Nick's discomfort.

The business journalists had not come for this, but they looked on with interest. It was certainly more entertaining than what they had expected. After all, in front of them they already had the hand-out Armadale had produced. They knew the facts; this line of questioning would add spice to their column. They remained silent, resolved not to interfere.

'There is absolutely no proof that the valve we delivered was faulty.' Nick tried to fight back. 'That is something for the inquiry to discover. Not for us to speculate over.'

'So you won't accept responsibility,' Simmons' neighbour spoke now.

'There is no responsibility to accept,' Nick answered. 'I admit that a division of Armadale International is responsible for the manufacture of the part, not for its malfunction. No malfunction has been shown.'

'The bloody thing blew up,' Simmons said.

'There was an explosion,' Nick raised his voice. 'No one knows yet what caused it.'

'Will you pay compensation to the families of the dead?' Simmons went on, regardless of the point that was being made.

Nick glanced at Richard, who was looking uncomfortable, but was clearly going to be no help. Nick looked around the room, saw no support from there. What he did see was a man getting up from his chair towards the back of the room and leaving. Nick realized then that his press conference was at an end. He walked back to the table, picked up the papers that were in front of his chair, and said, 'I'm not willing to answer questions on this subject. This is not why we called you. Goodbye.'

He glanced over at Richard and, without another sign, he strode out of the room, walking past the journalists who turned to look after him, surprised by his action. Then the room burst into conversation, people stood up, scraping back their chairs. At the front, Simmons and his friends looked pleased with themselves.

'Listen to this,' Julian said to Rebecca from behind his newspaper.

They were in the kitchen having breakfast together. That morning Rebecca was going to Stratford for an article on the new Shakespearian stars she was preparing for an American magazine. She would be away several days and she had come the night before to be with Julian. She sat opposite him, in her dressing-gown, sipping her coffee, holding the cup in two hands, her elbows propped on the table.

Julian was wide awake. He sat at the table, one hand holding the paper, the other his cup, the plate in front of him littered with crumbs of toast. He was in his shirtsleeves, a red tie knotted tightly against the collar of his blue-and-white striped shirt. His hair was slicked back, still damp from his shower. His cheeks shone from his shave.

'"Mr Bishop was unlucky, to be sure,"' he read from the newspaper, '"but perhaps he should have been better prepared. A disaster in the North Sea is bound to attract more attention than figures from a balance sheet. That the managing director of Armadale International seemed aloof and antagonistic to the press from the beginning did not help his cause when he was questioned on the North Sea accident. No doubt he responded in the only way he could, yet he could have shown more sympathy towards the dead and their families. It is clear that Mr Bishop is no politician.

'"As far as his facts and figures were concerned, they do not differ a great deal from what we already knew," etc, etc.,' Julian added. 'Bastard.'

'He's just doing his job,' Rebecca said.

'Simon Harner likes Roger Andrews,' Julian countered. 'That much is obvious.'

'Perhaps he does. All I'm saying is that you've been telling me much the same thing over the last few days. One press conference doesn't change that.'

Julian returned to his newspaper. He checked the price of Armadale's shares. As he had feared, it had dropped – down to 240p. Infuriatingly, Corpcom's remained at 443p.

3

Morale at Armadale sank even lower than before. Beleaguered by preoccupations with Corpcom's bid, haunted by Andrews' shadow, the staff felt the blow of the link between Armadale and the North Sea accident. The comments of the press after their questioning of Nick did nothing to alleviate the sense that they were in a corner, attacked from all sides.

The malfunction had by now been clearly attributed to a control valve which had not closed and thus permitted a build-up of gas. Usoco, the oil company, pointedly confirmed that Armadale Engineering had sold them the equipment. Although reason said that the exact cause of the malfunction was difficult to ascertain, reason does not sell newspapers. Blame was firmly lodged with Armadale, where the feeling was that fate was selling them out and that Andrews was going to be the buyer.

Edward did not work for Armadale Engineering. But, being one of the members of the defence committee, he had struggled for days now with sales figures past, present and future, profit margins, net and gross income, including those of Engineering, knowing that these figures could affect his life. He returned every night more exhausted than the day before. His wife, Edna, watched him grow paler, seeing his system being weakened with every new anxiety.

One night, as she watched him eat yet another warmed-up meal, she dared speak of her worry. Watching her husband's condition worsen had broken the optimism of the first couple of days. They sat in the drawing-room, watching a late sports programme on television. At least Edward watched the television. Edna was watching him.

'It'll be over soon,' he said.

He knew she was right to worry. He could feel it in his chest. He had introduced her to the worry, speaking of his anxieties about his company, his job, about the fear of never getting another one. There were two children sleeping upstairs. Redundancy payments would not cope with that. But because she had raised the subject, he was going to ignore it tonight. When he spoke of trouble, he was expressing his own doubts and his own worries. When Edna expressed them, it was as if they had become a reality by being spoken elsewhere. They were no longer subjective impressions, but had become objective reality.

After the accident on the oil platform, Edward did not dare tell Edna even of his latest anxiety. He could not help but wonder if indeed all the rumours were right. Had there been a malfunction and was his company to blame for the death of two men? He began to carry this guilt along with his other burdens.

Edward spent less time with his friends for the same reasons that he would not allow his wife to address the issue of his health.

Jim and Philip worried about Edward's retreat into himself. Alan was more ghoulish.

'They're going to have to carry him out of here,' he said the day the inquiry on the accident in the North Sea was set up. He was having lunch with Philip and Jim in an Italian restaurant close to Armadale.

'You seem to like the idea,' Jim said to Alan, staring him straight in the eye, his mouth tight and angry.

Jim had been persuaded to come by Philip. Ever since the bid had been announced, Jim had found Alan's company an irritant. It was not the truth he objected to, it was Alan's unrelieved pleasure in its sordidness.

'I hope you're wrong,' Philip came in, trying to stop an argument. 'It's that North Sea accident. We're all on edge because of it.'

'You're bloody right we are,' Alan came back. 'Do you blame us?'

Jim turned to Alan with distaste. He could stand this no longer. He had been affected by the accident, perhaps more than any of them. He had been a volunteer in Africa. He had seen death, looked at corpses, not just at a body in a coffin or in a hospital bed, but the young and the old dying in the dirt of infested town streets. He knew what death was.

He could also clearly see the damage that accident had done to the company, whether Armadale Engineering was ultimately to blame or not. This was a blow it might not withstand during a takeover bid.

Seeing these things, feeling as if he had just witnessed the beginning of the end, Jim could not bear that when people were dead, when a company was being sold, Alan could still only concern himself with his mortgage payments. There was something indecent in this. He wondered how Philip, honest Philip, could bear to be with Alan so much.

Philip did not mind Alan. What he minded was how distasteful the takeover bid had made everyday life. The bid was to be blamed for his colleagues unusual behaviour. It had thrown people into turmoil and made them fear for their future. The bid had focused attention on Armadale; the bid, even, was to be blamed for the attention Armadale was receiving in the press after the North Sea explosion. And Philip resented the press. He had always thought that newspapers were allowed too much leeway, were permitted to print lies that masqueraded as stories. Their stories were worse than lies, they were half truths, and more pernicious because of it.

Jim had stood up. 'You don't give a damn about those two men,' he said to Alan.

He looked down at them, opposites at first glance; Philip, the older man, all generosity in body and in spirit, Alan a nest of tension and dissatisfaction. He no longer cared about

Alan, but he wanted to warn Philip, tell him what he thought. He was about to, when Philip looked up at him and smiled.

Jim dropped some money on the table. 'I have to get back,' he said. He left before they could say anything.

Chapter Fourteen

I

It was Friday. The second week of the bid was almost over. Armadale's share price had not recovered from the North Sea accident. It had dropped further, to 238p. John was anxiously waiting for the publication of the profit forecasts in the defence document. That would enable the banker legally to buy some shares and shore up the price.

'I don't want to do it before,' he had said to Nick and Richard. 'There's too much privileged information. Let's wait.'

Three days more. On the Monday, Armadale would be publishing its defence. On Nick's desk was a mock-up copy of the document.

He was flicking through it when his intercom sounded. It was Sarah, reminding him that he had a lunch appointment with Annie Chinoise.

'Damn,' he said. 'What time?' Nick had not even bothered to look at his diary.

'One o'clock, sir,' Sarah said apologetically. 'I did check with you.'

'I know you did,' he said. 'It's right there in my diary. Thank you.' He dreaded that lunch now, rued having accepted Annie's challenge.

He returned to the mock-up. He winced at a picture of himself. It was the official photograph: almost like a passport photo, his tie just visible at the bottom. He was smiling but his smile seemed more like a smirk, his eyes were puffy. He must have been tired that day. These things are always ignored when times are good, necessary annoyances that the public relations department force one to carry out. Nick remembered the session, fitted in between appointments. The photographer, he realized now, had probably felt rushed and the job showed it. He found himself wishing he had paid more attention to it. The next time, he would. 'The next time,' he thought, muttering it aloud. He wondered suddenly whether he would get the chance.

It was a cold winter's day, the sun having finally replaced the week's rain. He looked up at the sky. It was blue, and streaked with strands of clouds, like slightly unruly hair. Cheered by the sight, he strode out on to the street and briskly walked away from the City.

As he walked he tried to imagine what Annie would look like. He had heard that she was beautiful. He felt a thrill of anticipation, as if there were something a touch illicit about this meeting. The fact that Annie was a headhunter was perhaps illicit enough. Her being a woman had nothing to do with it – although, he had to admit, it added a dimension.

He went into the restaurant and looked around for an attractive woman who might be waiting for him. He spotted no one. He got rid of his coat and went up to where the headwaiter stood with the reservations book. A small man with thin hair that was combed back so that every strand seemed in focus, allowing glimpses of a shining, polished skull to pierce through, the headwaiter was poised over his book, and he turned as Nick approached him. Gently, he bowed his head.

'Miss Chinoise,' Nick said. 'Has she arrived?'

The headwaiter beamed at Nick and with a sweep of his arm he led him without another word to a table at the other end of the room. At last he saw her, seated with her back to the wall, watching him as he came towards her.

He was struck by her beauty, and immediately noticed that the irony he had heard in her voice was reflected in the hint of a smile with which she followed his approach. Her hand was poised on her glass of wine, and her dark suit jacket was thrown over her shoulders. Her thick hair was put up in a chignon.

'Mr Bishop,' she said. 'I'm glad you could come.' She did not get up, but extended her hand across the table.

Nick and Annie looked each other over without speaking. They were both accustomed to meeting strangers on business. This was different, though; especially for Nick. Nick's world was peopled principally by men and, in any case, this meeting had been made personal by Annie's challenge. From his point of view, it barely qualified as a business meeting; he knew what Annie's purpose was and he intended to refuse any offer she might have. He could think of no advantage he wanted from her. He smiled at her. She was very beautiful.

Annie was accustomed to meeting men under these circumstances and she had less to think about; most people were reluctant prey at first, some irritated by her advances, just as she was so often by their more blatant passes at her, others confident that they could withstand her allure. It was interesting to her how sexual the metaphor of her job was; she seemed, by being a woman in a headhunter's job, to turn into a certain female archetype men carry in their imaginations, and they feared her while desiring to fall prey to her. It was definitely something she liked about the job. It had a certain poetic justice to it.

'What shall we talk about?' Nick said to her, breaking the silence.

'You, of course,' she answered.

He laughed. 'I am happy at my job, Miss Chinoise,' he said. 'You cannot entice me away from it.'

'You must call me Annie,' she said to him. She was not above flirting with potential – whether candidate, client or source. Nick was attractive: tall, with a handsome forehead and deep brown eyes that gazed directly at her. Also, he seemed unaware of his good looks.

'Then you'd better call me Nick, hadn't you?' he said back at her with an engaging smile. He had not had this much fun for a long time, and it was only the beginning of a lunch with a woman whom he would probably not see again for a long time, if at all. Was it to be one of those conversations with a stranger when you bared your soul in the knowledge that it could not be used against you? Nick was not sure.

'I'm sure you are happy at your job,' she returned to the subject. 'But will it last for ever?'

She saw the flash of anger come into his eyes, and she marvelled at it. He was so open-hearted, so artless it seemed, and yet he was not unintelligent or unaware.

'That isn't the issue,' Nick was tight-lipped.

Annie wondered whether to pursue this. She paused and then went on, almost apologetically, 'Well. It is really, isn't it?' Nick did not answer that, so she went on. 'I mean, either you're going to keep your company or lose it very soon. Knowing Roger Andrews, he won't keep you on. And,' she continued so that he would not interrupt her, 'having met you I can't see you working for him.'

'Thank you,' Nick was stiff and formal. He had lost his sense of humour, as if it had been plucked from him. 'Though how you've come to that conclusion escapes me.' He added when she looked at him in question, as if to ask what conclusion he meant, 'That you cannot see me working for him. We have only just met.'

'You don't look the type,' she explained casually. 'Am I wrong?'

She looked him over. He had become as tense as he had been relaxed before. Again, she was taken aback by his lack of concealment. She decided she would try to relax him again, and wondered if it would be as rapid and easy as it had been to put him on the defensive.

'It was meant as a compliment, you know,' she said. 'The people who work for Andrews are not known for their charm.'

It worked, although not because of the flattery. Nick realized he had been put on the defensive and that she was trying to make it easier for him.

'I'm sorry,' he said and forced a smile. 'What do you know about Andrews?' Maybe there was an advantage to be got out of the meeting.

'I don't know him well. He's everything they say about him: aggressive, domineering, sometimes rude, but very effective. And very bright.'

'And you think he's going to win.'

'I don't know,' she was evasive.

'Of course you don't know. What do you think?' he looked her straight in the eyes.

She answered almost immediately, after just a hint of thought, 'I think it's pointless to speculate.' She had been about to tell him that she thought Roger would win, but she stopped herself. Nick only thought he could take the truth.

Yet, again, she saw the flash of anger in Nick's eyes, replaced quickly by an intense determination. 'Andrews won't win if I can help it.'

She made no reply, just a gesture with her hands. She could not help him. She also knew that she was not going to hunt Nick's head any more. At least not until he had finished with this bid. Then? Well, he was a good catch.

'Shall we order?' She changed the subject. She would draw him away from business and takeovers.

She watched him relax again as he read the menu.

'I rarely eat lunch,' he said to her. 'No more than half a sandwich.'

'I spend my time eating lunch,' she said. 'It's half the job.'

'How nice,' he said, and he meant it. 'I'm starving.' With that he closed the menu.

He ordered pasta to start with and then a veal dish, whereas she had a tomato salad and a grilled sole. He realized why she did not become overweight from all her lunches. She ate like a taster, carefully and with discrimination. It did not stop him from enjoying his food, which he swallowed wolfishly and with enthusiasm.

'Do you live in London?' she asked as he was engulfing a large mouthful of pasta.

He looked at her over his fork and shook his head. He swallowed rapidly and said, 'In Downe. Do you know it?'

'No.'

'Downe, in Kent,' he went on. 'The home of Charles Darwin.'

'Downe with an "e",' she said.

'That's right,' he answered. 'Down House, Darwin's home doesn't have an "e", though. I've never known why. In fact,' he added with an embarrassed laugh, 'I've never even visited the museum.'

'It was changed in the 1840s, I think,' she said. 'The government was afraid it would be confused with County Down. The Irish troubles, you know.' He looked at her in amazement, and she added, 'I read history at Oxford. It's the kind of useless knowledge I carry about with me. But I'd forgotten about Darwin.'

'You'd have to have read biology to remember that,' he said, 'And I didn't read either.'

It was a leisurely lunch. Nick felt at ease with Annie, as if he had known her at least as long as Alan had; longer in fact, and better. Eventually, he could not keep away from the subject that obsessed him at the moment and he talked to Annie as he no longer did to Sophie, perhaps because Sophie and he had so many other subjects to cover in their limited time together.

Her ironic smile pulled him up short: 'I'm sorry. I've been ranting.'

'It's all right,' she said. She liked his passion. There was innocence in it. 'But I have to go back to work. Hunting.'

They fought over who should pay the bill. She won that battle, and he gave in with a gentle bow of thanks.

They parted in the street, shaking hands. Nick had an urge to kiss her, but he resisted it. Annie sensed it and wished he had.

'Why did you ask me to lunch?' He threw a last question at her.

'I had a job for you,' she answered. 'But I don't think

you'd be right for it,' she smiled as she said it. 'Anyway, you're not available,' she added.'

'That's right,' he laughed.

They both walked away at the same time, and each one turned once to look at the other. They caught each other doing it and waved.

2

Nick had not considered that he was being followed when he had accepted Annie's invitation, nor even when he had left for lunch. He had certainly not thought of it during the meal. He was not used to having a shadow and, despite his fight several nights previously, he thought little about it. The initial indignation had been followed by anger, and then, after his punch-up, by disregard. Since he had nothing to hide, he stopped worrying about it. If Andrews was going to waste his money having him followed, he would ignore it.

The trouble was not with Nick's imagination, it was with his honesty. He thought that because he was innocent, he was untouchable. It never occurred to him that he could be made to look guilty, and that that would be enough.

Ray, the short, solid man who had bruised Nick in self-defence, had seen Nick and Annie lunch together and had enjoyed looking at Annie even more than Nick had, for he had not been distracted by words. He had enjoyed the meal as well; he rarely got to eat at a fancy restaurant at the client's expense. It was like a Christmas bonus.

Ray had plenty of imagination and, though he was reasonably honest, plenty of craftiness. He realized as soon as he discovered what Annie did for a living – from the young woman who sat in reception at Annie's offices – that this was the first titbit of any interest he had gathered since he had started on this job.

'Beautiful headhunter in tryst with beleaguered MD' was not a proven headline, but Ray would be more than happy to try to prove it. In fact, he wondered if it would be necessary.

He wrote his report in the most unemotional and factual

terms he could muster. He enjoyed writing it. He even laughed.

His typed report first went to Peter, who read it with amusement as well. The possibilities were interesting, he thought. He wondered if Roger would think it worthwhile. It was typical of Peter that, instead of going to see Roger with the information immediately, he should wait until he was scheduled to see him next.

At six-thirty, he went into Roger's office as usual. It was a daily ritual when both were in the country for them to meet at the end of the day and for each to brief the other.

Roger was at his desk, glancing through some documents. The tape-recorder had disappeared and the office was again open to all. Armadale had been debugged once more and this time Roger had not been able to secure the retention of an old microphone or the placing of a new one. He did not mind. The microphone had been useful at the beginning, to assess the adversary and his staff. He now received hard information from another source. He was looking at it as Peter entered, bearing his own brown envelope.

The two men bore a satisfied air. They said nothing about their prizes until Peter had sat down in the armchair opposite the desk.

'You've got something. What is it?' Peter spoke first.

'Armadale's profit forecasts. At least, the ones they're playing with,' Roger answered.

'We got a pretty good idea of what they'd be like from the press conference,' Peter said. 'If we can call it a press conference.' He laughed. 'Poor Mr Bishop.'

'This is the real thing, Peter,' Roger said, looking up at his assistant with a half smile. It irritated him when Peter gloated. 'The figures aren't bad,' he added, 'but they won't be good enough,' and he smiled with satisfaction.

He was even more delighted when he saw the effect of his scoop. The younger man was annoyed and could not help showing it.

'I still don't want to tell you who "our man" is. It's best if I'm the only one to know. Even with you, Peter. Elementary security, that's all it is.'

Peter shrugged his acceptance, but it had taken some of the pleasure of his own news away. He tossed the envelope he had been holding on to the desk. Andrews had to grab it or it would have slid right off the other end.

'Our other man,' Peter said. 'The agency sent it in a couple of hours ago.'

'What does it say? It's been very dull so far.'

'Read it. You should enjoy it,' Peter answered.

Roger began skimming the report. He looked up once. Then he went back over what he had glanced at and read it more carefully. Peter spent the time he was waiting picking at his nails.

When he had finished, Roger burst out laughing. 'This man Ray can't be as stupid as he makes himself sound.'

'Quite the contrary,' Peter said.

'Do you know Annie Chinoise?' Roger asked.

'No.' Peter shook his head. 'I hear she's quite something.'

'She's a knockout, is what she is.'

They both fell silent again. For a few minutes they were like writers, trying to find the best way to express something. They could see the story unfolding before them. It was just a matter of structure: it was going to be fiction, but it would have to be very credible.

'We'd better use it, I think,' Roger said. They looked at each other conspiratorially.

'It shouldn't be hard to do,' Peter said.

There was a kind of aesthetic objectivity to their discussion.

'Who are we going to leak it to?' Roger asked.

'I'll think of someone,' answered Peter.

'O K, I'll dictate, you write,' Roger announced. 'Or do you want to go first?'

'You do the first draft, and I'll do the second.'

Roger reached for a cigar. After lighting it, he leaned back in his chair, putting his feet up on the desk. His eyes moved towards the ceiling, following the cloud of smoke.

He considered the first sentence.

Chapter Fifteen

I

Sophie entered the quiet house and closed the door behind her with relief. It was ten o'clock on Monday morning. Nick had left more than three hours ago. The children were at school. She was home after doing the day's shopping. No one was coming today; no cleaning woman, no window cleaner, and the milkman had already been. The day was hers until mid-afternoon.

She took off her shoes in the hall and undid the waistband of her skirt. She relaxed a little more as the pressure on her stomach was eased. Sophie was not overweight, but she had allowed the slenderness of youth to pass unchecked.

She put away the shopping and stayed in the kitchen to have a cup of coffee and look at the paper. She did not read the newspapers on a regular basis; there was rarely time during the day and by evening she had lost interest. But she had started reading them again after the announcement of Corpcom's bid. It was a form of fidelity; she felt she should know what was going on in Nick's immediate and troubled world. As a result she read the business pages first.

Sitting cross-legged on the kitchen bench, she scanned the columns. It was on her second cup of coffee that she caught a small item in the financial pages: 'Armadale MD linked to Head Hunter'. She read it, wondering what it might be. She did not consciously think of Nick at first. The headline seemed so unlikely, so unrelated to the takeover and to her husband. Reading on, the report became more improbable. It was so charged with hidden meaning that it seemed too portentous. Annie was described as a 'renowned headhunter', and their lunch as an 'intimate tête-à-tête in a small restaurant'. The journalist had ended his two paragraphs by commenting on how unusual it was for a managing director to be meeting with a headhunter when he was fighting a hostile takeover by another company.

Sophie read the piece twice. She wondered if Nick had seen it. Immediately she rang the office.

Sarah answered the phone.

'He's in a meeting, Mrs Bishop,' she said. 'Can he ring you back?'

'Yes,' Sophie said, automatically.

She hung up and returned to the newspaper. She found nothing further, and so she went rummaging into the pile of old ones that were amassed next to the fireplace and used for kindling. But she found no other mention of Nick, or even of Annie.

She decided that she would go out again and buy the other papers to see what they said, if anything. Then she remembered that Nick was supposed to call her back. She waited five minutes more, and rang again.

'Sarah,' she said, 'can you interrupt him, please? It's quite important,' she added, sensing Sarah's reluctance.

When Nick came on the line, she was a little out of breath, panic in her voice.

'What's the matter?' Nick was brusque, but he did not sound worried. He sounded annoyed.

'There's a piece in the newspaper about you,' she said. 'I wondered if you'd seen it.'

'Of course I saw it,' he answered.

'You didn't tell me about it,' she said.

'No. I didn't think to. There's nothing to it.' There was no hidden guilt in his voice. He was angered by it, she could tell. He was indignant that his probity could be questioned.

'Is it true?' she asked.

'I had lunch with the woman.' Nick's voice had hardened and his temper was showing. Impatiently, he went on, 'I'm in the middle of something, Sophie.'

'I'm sorry,' she said, suddenly contrite. 'I'll see you this evening.'

He hung up immediately and she heard the phone go dead. She had not expected the call to reassure her, she realized.

Putting her shoes back on she hurried out of the house. When she returned, she had bought every newspaper she could find and several magazines. She began to look through them methodically.

Not all the papers mentioned it. Only one other of the so-called quality press carried the item. It was mentioned in the same vein, an implication rather than a statement.

In the tabloids, the story was addressed more blatantly. The news was still deep inside the paper, but the headlines were in larger print and cruder. 'MD FALLS PREY TO HEADHUNTER?' The sexual innuendo continued. It was noted that, although the 'scandal' that was developing over this meeting *à deux* had more to do with business ethics than morality, that Annie's profession and not her gender was the issue, the headhunter's renowned beauty could not be ignored. Falling prey to Annie Chinoise, it was said, could be nothing but pleasurable and was certainly very easy.

Sophie was kneeling on the living-room floor, with the papers open in front of her; she got up to ease the tension. She looked about her, then picked up a magazine in which there was a feature on Britain's bright new business stars. She turned the pages quickly, and her heart sank at finding a photograph of Annie: a full-length portrait, showing her perched on her desk, one long, beautiful leg touching the floor, the other left dangling. The face was confident, the smile beguiling. Sophie was surprised at how beautiful she was.

Just looking at the photograph made Sophie feel matronly, overweight and dull. The papers were right. How could Nick resist her? Then she began to wonder why they had met for lunch. The scandal might be about business ethics, but Sophie was sure Nick would never consider leaving Armadale; he had built the company up, he regarded it as his own, and he was far too honest to desert it.

Nick never read the morning papers at home. His time with Alistair and John, while Sophie made them breakfast, was often spent on the sofa in the drawing-room, a boy on each side of him listening as he read a story.

That morning, like every morning since Corpcom's bid, Nick had left too early to have that quarter-hour's communion before breakfast. A kiss on the cheek and a pat on the head was all the boys got.

Once in the car he had opened the newspaper to the financial pages without even a glance at the headlines. He saw the two paragraphs almost immediately. After reading them, a feeling of disbelief enveloped him.

He looked up from the newspaper and watched the grey landscape pass by. They had already reached the more built-up roads of outer London. As he glanced at the houses through the grey light of the fog, Nick wondered about what he had just read.

'This is Andrews ...' was his first thought. It was an automatic thought, a reflex. Then he became aware of his own stupidity. He remembered the private detective, the one he had tried to punch and missed, the one whom, he realized, he had forgotten about.

'Fool,' he muttered. He hit himself on the thigh, creasing the newspaper. The driver turned to look at him, but Nick was oblivious. He was trying to assess the damage. With childlike innocence, he decided there would be little. What was printed was a lie. It would blow over.

By the time he reached the office, he had decided to ignore it. It was not worth his concern. Yet his first act once at his desk, before anyone else had arrived, was to ring Annie. Rumour and scandal would not deter him from behaving properly. There was no answer and he tried every few minutes until there was.

Annie was surprised that Nick should phone her. She had seen the report herself, in more than one newspaper. To hear from Nick was the last thing she expected. She picked up the receiver, dreading the recriminations she thought were inevitable. Instead she got an apology and was even more astonished.

'I'll survive it. I think you should be careful,' she said. 'I'm not even sure you should be talking to me.'

'I doubt my phone's tapped. They haven't done that for several days,' he said, his tone filled with self-pitying irony.

'Still,' she insisted, 'I think perhaps we should leave it as a nice lunch for the moment. It would be wisest.'

'I hope this won't do you any damage.' His concern for her was honourable and somehow perverse. It was genuine, certainly, yet Nick was hamming it up as well, choosing to snub a world that could spread scandal about him.

'It'll be good publicity,' she joked. 'I love to see my name in the papers.'

'Ah . . . Good then,' Nick was a little stiff, not up to her humour.

Annie found his seriousness touching. They hung up and both felt equally rueful. Nick went back to work. Annie did not immediately. She felt sorry for him; he was playing his cards honestly and still losing the game.

Annie had not asked about Sophie. Yet, when she had seen the newspapers, Nick's wife had been one of her first thoughts. She wondered how Nick would alleviate her doubts and anxieties.

Annie did not worry about her own career. By the time Nick had called her, she decided that the damage would be slight: possibly a falling off of clients who would fear her, a slowing down, which would reverse in a short time, as Armadale and Nick Bishop faded into memory. What came after would probably do her good. This kind of publicity, though she did not seek it, always did her good. Her predominantly male clientèle would be excited by it all.

She moved out of Nick's life as easily as she had slipped into it.

During Nick's conversation with Annie, Sarah had arrived and Julian had put his head around the door to announce himself. Nick emerged to find Sarah waiting for him with a series of telephone messages. Journalists were after a statement. Sarah smiled at him sheepishly; she seemed embarrassed. It was obvious that she too had read her morning newspaper. Standing at her desk, people passed by, just getting in. He acknowledged them all by name, and again he noticed embarrassment. What was worse, he sensed hostility in some. He looked in on Julian and asked him to come in.

'I take it you saw the papers too.'

Julian nodded but said nothing. He did not know what to say. He was a little surprised by Nick's directness. He sat down on the hard-backed chair in front of the desk. He found the papers difficult to believe. He would have sworn that Nick was not looking for another job and he found it incredible that he could be having an affair. He was not a good liar, and an affair requires efficient concealment.

'Don't tell me you believe it too?' Nick had misunderstood Julian's silence.

'I don't. No.' Julian paused, then took the plunge. It was his job. 'I think a lot of other people do.'

'Other people?' Nick was getting up on his high horse automatically. He had sat upright, his head a little higher.

'Most people believe what they read in the papers.' Julian almost apologized. He carried on bravely. He was beginning to feel uncomfortably inappropriate. 'If you want my opinion, I don't think the main problem is whether you are having an affair or not. Most people don't care.'

'My wife cares,' Nick interrupted.

'I'm sorry, I'm sure she does,' Julian said. He was becoming embarrassed. 'I was just trying to tell you what people out there think. What I've heard. What is really upsetting people here is that you were seen with a headhunter.'

'Are you saying that people here actually believe I could be asking for another job?' Nick was incredulous. He had concentrated on the sexual issue and had barely considered the professional aspect.

'They're very worried. They're frightened.'

'Damn it,' he shouted and pounded his desk with his hand. 'Don't they know me? Would you do that?'

Julian did not know what to say. He sat in front of Nick uncomfortably, knowing the answer to the questions, knowing that people would believe both rumours about Nick because, especially under the pressure of the bid, most people would believe in Nick's corruption, in his lack of honesty. There was nothing to stop them believing it: men lied, cheated, stole for all sorts of reasons – power, money, sex. There was no reason for Nick to be any different. Julian knew that he was, but other people didn't. He probably would not have believed in Nick's innocence if he had not known him so well.

Nick saw Julian's discomfort and was grateful for it. He knew it to be sympathetic.

'I suppose I'm going to have to deny it,' he said, suddenly practical. 'I'll talk to those journalists. They're ringing Sarah up and giving her a hard time.'

'It would be best,' Julian said, relieved. Nick seemed to have moved on. Yet something compelled Julian to add, 'I'm afraid I don't think it'll make much difference.'

Before speaking to the journalists, Nick knew he would have to speak to the members of his board. They deserved an explanation, at least: if he did not hear disbelief, there would be a flicker of doubt. It was pain that he felt. He had been attacked in such a way that he could not defend himself. His standing had been hacked at, his self-esteem knifed.

He realized for the first time since the bid had been announced that he might lose. There was another thought lurking in his mind: he had been careless, he hated himself for it.

3

Howard read the item aloud to Norma over breakfast. They sat in the kitchen together at a square table. The windows, like the ones in Howard's study, gave a view of their garden.

A misty rain was falling, soaking the landscape without seeming to. Norma had placed a warm croissant in front of Howard, and sat opposite him; toast was all she ate for breakfast. She was just pouring the coffee when he said from behind the newspaper, 'Listen to this, Norma.' After he had finished, he dropped his paper on his lap, appearing before her with a look of utter astonishment on his face.

'Poor Sophie,' was all Norma said.

'What d'you mean, "poor Sophie"?' Howard said sharply. 'It's absurd. You can't believe this.'

'Why not?'

'Because Nick's incapable of doing something like that.'

'He's forty,' Norma said, as if that explained everything.

'Well, so am I,' he said, carried away by the shock of what he had read and forgetting about Sheilah for a moment. He remembered quickly, though, and hurriedly said, 'It doesn't have anything to do with anything. All this rubbish about a mid-life crisis.'

Norma shrugged her shoulders. She did not really mind Nick being in trouble. She felt that there was a certain justice to it. He was so smug, so sure of everything, so unyielding.

Howard said nothing further. He was thinking about Nick. Why did Nick meet Annie Chinoise? They did not know each other. He was almost certain of that.

Howard phoned Nick from the office. It was mid-morning. Sarah answered the phone.

'Hello, Sarah,' Howard said. His voice seemed cheerful.

'Hello, Mr Hicks,' she replied, recognizing his voice immediately. She liked Howard. He always joked with her, and treated her as an equal. 'He's in,' she added, not aware that the two friends had not spoken since the morning after the bid was announced.

'I miss you, Sarah,' he said, just before she put him on hold. She said nothing, but she had a broad smile on her face when she buzzed Nick on the intercom.

Nick picked up the telephone after a long moment of doubt. He spoke with evident reserve in his voice.

'Nick,' Howard plunged in, pretending not to have noticed, 'I read the papers. I'm terribly sorry. Of course, I don't believe a word of it.'

'Why not?' Nick asked perversely.

'Because you're too bloody honest,' Howard said, as if nothing had happened to their friendship. 'You wouldn't know how to go about an affair anyway.'

'The woman's a headhunter. Why does everyone assume I'm sleeping with her?' Nick said.

'That's exactly what I mean,' Howard said. 'You don't understand the first thing about it.'

There was a silence. Then Howard said, 'Nick. Why *did* you see her?'

'Because I'm an ass. I was being followed. I knew it.' He added. 'I didn't think.'

'Jesus,' Howard let out the word in a whisper. It was too much information all at once. 'I'd forgotten how dirty Andrews plays,' he said meditatively.

'That's right,' Nick said. There was accusation in his voice.

Again, there was silence.

'I'm sorry, Nick,' Howard repeated, 'I wish I could do something.' He let the sentence trail away.

They hung up and a sense of emptiness crept into the hearts of both men. Each sat still at his desk, saddened by it. Against hope, Nick had wanted Howard to return to the fold and leave Andrews, and Howard, although he had sensed a need from Nick, had not realized what it was.

4

Sophie spent the whole day with doubts about Nick's fidelity crowding her mind. She had no time to consider it at length, because she had to do other things.

For once she wished for a nanny or for someone to take the household burdens from her. She had to fetch the boys from school and they did not allow for relaxation from the moment they were picked up till they were asleep; they had to be talked to, fed, organized, fed again, played with, bathed, read to and scolded.

She lost her temper with both of them after supper. They were in their rooms. John was building a large space station with a construction kit and Alistair was reading.

'It's time for bed, children,' she called up to them from the kitchen. 'Go and brush your teeth, please.' There was no answer, and Sophie finished the washing up. A quarter of an hour later she went upstairs and found them engrossed in their occupations, as if nothing had been said.

She lost her temper and made them go to bed earlier than usual. John cried and shouted that she was unfair. Alistair sulked and did as he was told, every move performed more slowly than necessary, and with more meticulousness than usual.

When the lights were out she felt guilty. She realized that it was she who was unreasonable, she was bad-tempered and on edge. She had wanted them in bed and asleep, and had provoked their disobedience and bad behaviour. She went back into their darkened rooms.

'I'm sorry,' she said. She kissed them and hugged them, wiping away John's tears and tickling him until he was happy. Then she had to calm him down again. She turned on Alistair's light and said, 'You can read for ten minutes.'

After that, it was 9.30.

She went down to the living-room, and thought about what the morning had brought. She recalled conversations, mannerisms, unusual events, and felt uncertainty in their interpretation, or re-interpretation.

Everything can have a double meaning, and Sophie began to see each one of them, reading every gesture from a new perspective. When she considered her marriage, the tensions bred of fifteen years together, of having children, of

Nick's work, of exhaustion, of habit and of boredom, she began to believe that an affair was an inescapable, logical conclusion. She wondered if that, rather than the work demanded of him by the takeover, was what was really keeping him at the office, in the age-old excuse of the adulterous businessman. Just because it had been used so often before did not mean it could not serve again. She cried at the thought of it.

That night, Nick returned again just before midnight. Sophie was up, waiting for him. He showed his surprise and she interpreted that as further proof of what she feared most.

When he saw all the newspapers that she had deliberately left on the table in the living-room, he said ironically, 'Catching up on the news, eh?'

'I wish you wouldn't come back so late every night,' she snapped back. She was angry because he was deceiving her, lying to her.

'You know what's going on. I should probably not come back at all.'

'Is that what you want?' she stabbed at him.

He looked at her, noticing the tone in her voice. She looked like a trapped animal, on the attack because it is the only hope of escape.

'What's the matter, darling?' he said. He walked over to her, touched her, but she moved away.

'Why didn't you tell me about the piece in the paper?' she asked.

'I told you. It's nothing. It's not important.' Nick looked at the newspapers again now. He realized what the question had implied. He went over to the table and picked one up. 'What are they saying?' he asked.

'Page seven,' she said, and there was a sob caught in the back of her throat.

Nick found the report, read it carefully, looked over at Sophie who was looking back at him with sad eyes, her arms limp by her side. Quickly he glanced at another paper. He threw it down on the table after reading it.

'This is disgusting.' He stood up in frustration. He felt ashamed of his own stupidity.

'This is Andrews' doing. You can't believe this,' he said, and saw that she did. 'They've made it up. It's this private detective. He saw us having lunch and . . .' Nick trailed off. Sophie looked at him, still with unbelieving eyes.

'Is she as beautiful in real life?' she asked. 'There's a picture in there.' She pointed at the magazine. Nick answered without looking at it.

'Sophie. You are being ridiculous. This is exactly what they want to happen.'

'Look at it,' she insisted.

Nick was suddenly furious. He picked up the magazine, but couldn't find the picture. He threw the magazine on the floor in rage.

'I don't see what her beauty has to do with it.' He looked at Sophie. 'I'm your husband,' he said. 'Believe me, not the newspapers.'

He faced her, but she wanted more from him. He could not give it.

'I'm going to bed.' He turned and left the room.

Sophie watched him in despair. His every move, his every word seemed to reinforce her fears.

She could not forgive Nick for walking out on her. She did not believe in innocence so feebly defended. Even she, knowing Nick so well, could not understand his uncompromising attitude towards adversity, his obstinate ignorance of the world.

The following morning the children were getting dressed upstairs and Sophie was making them breakfast. She and Nick had not spoken since the night before. Each one carried an aura of righteous anger around the house, refusing to speak even when strangers would have said something. Nick was leaving and had opened the door, when suddenly he turned and went into the kitchen. He spoke to Sophie from the doorway.

'I have told you there is nothing to those articles in the papers,' he said. 'I expect you to believe me.' He paused and then added, 'I don't want to discuss it any more.'

She was about to speak, to fight him, but when she turned to face him he had gone. She heard the door bang shut a second later.

'I hate you,' she said to herself and went back to making the breakfast.

Chapter Sixteen

I

That Monday, the day the news broke about Nick's lunch with Annie, Armadale published its defence document, a thirty-page document with 'REJECT CORPCOM' printed on its dark-grey cover.

Despite its optimistic profit forecast and some urgent buying by John, the Armadale shares were trading at 233p by the end of the day.

Corpcom's price went up for the first time in the two weeks, settling at 449p.

Morale at Armadale dipped with the share price.

On Tuesday, Edward again turned down an offer to lunch with Alan and Philip. Edward had taken to bringing his lunch from home. He carried it in a plastic bag, a sandwich and an apple, which he took out of his briefcase once the others had gone out.

That Nick should abandon the company seemed impossible to him. He did not believe it. Nick was having an affair; of that he was certain. It surprised him because Nick did not seem the type. But then nor did he, and he had had an affair ten years ago with a secretary from the office. It had lasted three months. His wife had found out and had been so ravaged by his infidelity that he had stopped it immediately and had spent the rest of his life persuading her that he loved her, which he did.

'No thanks,' he had said to Alan, 'I've got too much work.' In fact, that morning Edward had had to stop working several times. He found he could hardly breathe. He wondered if he should not go home.

Alan had left Edward's office shaking his head. Edward was retreating into himself, he looked worse with every day.

'His face is grey,' he said at lunch. Philip was there, even Jim was there, and Julian was with them too, invited by Alan. He had gone principally to find out what they were saying. For him, this was a business lunch. They sat at a square table in the corner of an Italian restaurant, this one in a dark basement a few buildings away, which they frequented along with several Japanese from the neighbouring Bank of Tokyo.

'He refuses to take any time off,' Philip said.

'Good for him,' said Jim. He thought they were making too much of Edward's condition.

'Anyway,' Alan said. 'We didn't come here to talk about Edward.'

'I still can't believe it,' Philip was shaking his head.

'Nick Bishop doth protest too much,' Alan used the Shakespearean cliché with bitter conviction.

There was no doubt in his mind. Nick was both an adulterer and a traitor. It was not that he hated Nick. Alan knew that he would have done exactly what Nick was accused of doing. Indeed, he had approached Annie himself. He merely resented Nick's success. He had even gone as far as dialling Annie's number to confront her, but he had hung up before the phone could be answered, afraid that Annie would speak a truth he did not want to hear, some rejection he did not want to live with.

'He hasn't said a thing about it,' Philip said. 'I wish he would deny it.' Philip was the saddest man there. He found it difficult to envisage how Nick could have done what he had done. 'It's probably just the newspapers spreading more rumours.'

'It doesn't make any difference,' Jim said.

'I think it makes the world of difference,' Alan spoke

vehemently. 'If your managing director is deserting the ship, then you can be sure everybody else will.'

'The MD's deserting because the ship's abandoned. Or can't you tell?' Jim faced Alan belligerently. He despised him now, just as he was disappointed in Nick. Jim viewed the bid with distaste. In his own mind he had already left Armadale.

Julian got up. He had had enough. 'You're pathetic,' he said. 'You're willing to believe everything the newspapers say without even thinking about it. You know Bishop. He'd never do anything like this.' He picked up his coat from the next chair.

'What was he doing with the woman, then?' Jim asked, and then gave the answer. 'He's either cheating on his wife or his company. In my book, that doesn't inspire trust.'

Julian looked at the three of them, Jim sure of himself, Philip looking down at the table, Alan wondering whether Julian would respond, whether he had an answer to it. Julian decided to leave it. There was nothing he could say to change their minds. He left them to pay the bill.

Julian could not get away from them so easily. That afternoon he was chairing another meeting of the defence committee. With the defence document out, they were concentrating exclusively on Armadale's efforts to get the bid referred. Most of them now believed this was their last hope. There were only a few days left.

Alan and Julian sat next to each other in the boardroom. Everybody was there except Edward, and they waited for him. He was to bring in the final set of figures for their last meeting with the Office of Fair Trading before the decision on the referral was made.

'Did he have anything else on?' Julian asked Alan.

'Not as far as I know.'

'I'll try his secretary,' Julian said. He was about to pick up the phone when Alan got up.

'Don't bother,' he said. 'I'll go and look for him.'

Before anyone could say anything he was out of the room. He hurried towards Edward's office wondering if he was ill.

It was only when he stood outside the office that he hesitated. He wondered why he had volunteered to fetch Edward. He was suddenly afraid of what he might find behind the door. After all, he had predicted a heart attack for Edward often enough in the last two weeks. He stood holding on to the door handle, unable to turn it and open the door.

'What's the matter, Alan?' a man said as he walked past. 'You all right?'

'I'm fine,' Alan answered, shaken out of himself.

He opened the door.

'Oh, my God,' he said as soon as he had looked inside. Edward was there. His head was slumped on his desk, his sandwich, half eaten, next to it, his mouth wide open. He was dead.

'Oh my God,' Alan said again. Frightened, he yelled for help.

2

Edward Falcon's death was perceived as a direct result of the takeover. It was the pressure that killed him. People throughout Armadale saw it as a symbol of the end. Now it was only a question of time.

To emphasize the state of siege that enshrouded Armadale, the scandal of Nick's lunch with Annie did not die down. It could not feed on further facts, but it sparked off a discussion in the press about business ethics in general, and takeovers and headhunters in particular. Back and forth, commentators, then politicians, and, to complete the circle, journalists reporting what the politicians had said, discussed the issues that had been raised by one innocent meeting.

The whole of England seemed to Nick and Sophie and to Annie, to be discussing their lives. Annie watched it happen with detachment and even with interest. Nick and Sophie both felt shame. He was incapacitated in his work and his name, it seemed, had been turned into a synonym for corruption; she felt her private life had become a public spectacle.

Roger and Peter, on the other hand, watched the whole affair with unmitigated glee. They both read the newspapers as writers read reviews of their work, and, for the most part, they were delighted with the response. It was all very gratifying.

As far as Roger was concerned, the comic crescendo was reached when Nick rang him up and asked for a meeting.

'Maybe he's come to ask for the deal Howard offered him,' Roger said to Peter. They were waiting together for Nick.

'I don't think so,' Peter answered. It did not fit the profile. He still could not find a satisfactory reason for it.

'Perhaps it wasn't enough. You know what I say about first offers.'

'That was Twain, not you.'

'So it was. The fact is, my first offers are always low.'

Nick was shown in. He walked into the room and looked at Peter in surprise.

'I'd like to talk to you in private, please,' he said to Roger.

'Of course.' Roger looked at Peter, who was already on his way out. Nick saw the younger man smile as he left. His anger grew.

Roger pointed to the armchair, but did not sit in the other chair. Instead he walked around his desk and sat behind it.

'This is a little unusual,' he began. 'How can I help?'

Nick had acted on impulse and had not bothered to prepare what he was going to say. On a business errand, he always knew the way to start a conversation; he planned it and rehearsed it. Here, for a second, he was at a loss.

Roger was about to speak again, but Nick put his hand up to stop him. 'Please,' he said. 'I'm here because of the rumours that are circulating in the papers.'

Roger played his part well. He looked at Nick with an air of surprise and cocked his head to the side as if he had no idea of what Nick was talking about.

'Don't play with me, Andrews,' Nick said, his tone sharp and aggressive. 'You're spreading lies about me. I want them to stop.'

'You're making me out to be much more powerful than I am.' Roger said. He was amazed that Nick should have come to see him about this. It was so manifestly unprofessional, and childish. He was in complete control. 'I can't stop what the newspapers print.'

'It's not worth it,' Nick pleaded.

Roger was taken aback by that. He said, 'Of course it is. You deserve to lose if you think like that.'

'Would you let your wife be dragged into this?'

'No. But I wouldn't give it cause, either.'

'Cause . . .?' Nick was astounded at Roger's remark.

'It's out of my hands, if it ever was in them.' Roger stood up now. He was angry too, angry at Nick's innocence, at his idea that they were gentlemen playing a game. The sooner he went, the better for everyone.

Nick said nothing more. He was dismissed and he left. He was at the door when Roger spoke again.

'You should have been more careful.' Nick had made a mistake. He was now paying for that mistake. Roger had no regrets.

And so simply, with those few words, Nick's anger was turned into hatred.

3

Nick left Corpcom's offices deeply dejected. He knew he had played his cards wrong and that he had just made a quite pointless and humiliating visit. He began to wonder at his own gullibility. 'What was I trying to prove?' he thought.

They were heading back towards the City. He leaned forward to his driver and said, 'Don't take me back to the office right away.'

There was a pause.

'Drive around,' Nick said. 'Wherever you want.'

The driver looked back at him in his mirror. There was a query in his eyes, but he said nothing.

Nick had thought a takeover followed simple rules. After all there was a Code that spoke of 'general principles', of the 'spirit of the code', and of 'good faith'. He realized now that he had made many errors, not least of which was his refusal to worry about public opinion, and his determination to ignore the outside world. This had led to his meeting with Annie, to his estrangement from Sophie and his break with Howard. For a minute he wondered at Howard's and Sophie's fidelity. They allowed him to behave according to his whims and principles while he berated theirs. He remembered what Sophie had said once, after an evening out in London. They had taken an American client of Armadale's and his wife to the theatre and then to supper. Nick had not liked them much; he had been parochial, English about them, found fault in what he called their 'brashness', their materialism.

'You criticize too much,' she had said to him.

Howard had said much the same when they were in their early twenties, as he bemoaned the failure of others to match his utopian dreams.

They were right. He criticized still, and was intolerant of weakness in others.

He decided to go and visit Howard. Since their conversation on the phone, Nick had often thought about Howard. He missed him. In his present mood, he wondered if perhaps he had not overdone his outrage.

Howard had an office in the London headquarters of Hicks Breweries, the family company Corpcom had bought from him ten years ago. Howard was chairman of the brewery, but had no say in the running of the company. That was Roger's bailiwick, even though part of the unwritten agreement had been that Howard would continue to run the business. Howard was too malleable to be trusted, and so Roger had just ignored his commitment and upped Howard's salary by a few thousand pounds. It had been an easy way to by-pass the problem.

Howard had accepted the inevitable. He never forgave it, but he did not act on his resentment. Now, he used the office as his base. He made appearances, but did little actual work.

He stood up when Nick walked into the room.

'This is unexpected, Nick,' he said. He remained standing as Nick sat in the armchair in front of Howard's desk.

The office was a contrast to Howard. It was small, modern, and, above all, tidy. The walls were white, the light fluorescent, the filing cabinets grey. There was nothing of Howard there, not even a painting. Nick looked around it.

'I've always hated this place,' he said.

'It reminds me how much I hate work,' Howard said with a self-deprecating smile.

Howard was relieved that Nick seemed friendly and pensive. He was almost placid, chastened it seemed. Perhaps, Howard thought, he was ready to give in to the world Howard had known since he had been eight: a young boy who wanted to stay at home with his mother, but who had been persuaded that boarding school was where he belonged. He wanted to welcome Nick into the fold. And just as that thought crossed his mind, he was saddened. No, he did not want a different Nick. He wanted his idealistic friend to remain as he was, self-righteous, rigid, moralistic, critical, proud. After all, that is how he liked him; Howard did not want to stop admiring his friend.

'You've never worried about work, have you?' Nick said, looking up at Howard, who was still standing.

'Silly to worry about it,' Howard said. 'Do what you have to, so as not to have to do all of it.'

'We weren't ready for this takeover,' Nick said, letting his random thoughts control the conversation. 'It's my fault.'

'No one's ready for a takeover,' Howard said. 'Don't blame yourself. Believe me, Roger planned it well,' he added.

Nick looked up as Howard said that. It reminded him that Howard had known about the bid. Howard saw it immediately.

'Remember,' he said quickly, 'he did it to me.'

'I remember,' Nick said. He was already less deflated.

Howard wanted to help his old friend. But he mistook Nick's dejection for capitulation. It was not; it was a need to be rejuvenated. Howard obliged.

'Quit,' he said. 'Give Andrews Armadale.'

'I can't do that,' Nick said. 'I won't do it.'

'You'll survive,' Howard went on. 'Take the money. Find something else.'

Nick looked up at Howard. He shook his head.

'Never,' he said. 'If he wants it, he'll have to come and get it.'

When he left, Howard watched him walk down the long corridor and disappear down the stairs. Nick had not changed. He would insist on his pain.

Chapter Seventeen

I

Edward Falcon's simple funeral was a crowded affair. The little church in West Kensington was filled by an unexpectedly large contingent of Armadale's staff. Nick was there. Sophie had come, reluctantly, not for Nick so much as for Edward's wife and children. Julian, Alan and Jim were there. There were many others. It was as if they all acknowledged that he had died for the cause, in the performance of his duty.

Edna Falcon was surprised at the turn-out. She had not thought her husband had been so popular. She had loved him, but their lives had been insular and introspective. Later that night, when she sat in her living-room, her children having finally agreed to leave her alone, she wished that the funeral had been more private, more intimate, just as their lives together had been. She felt robbed of a final communion with her husband.

The members of Armadale were also pleased to see so many of themselves present. It was a show of strength and solidarity, a symbol of their cohesiveness at a time when all of them feared the separation that would come. The dissolution of their company loomed up before them now; there was little hope of averting it.

Towards Nick they felt ambivalence. Indirectly, they blamed him for Armadale's ills. Unquestioned fidelity and affection had been taken over by doubt and resentment. They had forgotten why they had always liked him: his straightforwardness, his lack of pomp, the trust they were able to place in his word. Now they doubted their own judgement and felt that Nick had led them astray, that he had never been anything but a boss, a member of the other side, just as the top brass always were, and that they, his employees, should have known it and not been fooled. The majority of those present, with the exception of the Falcons, wished he had not come, wished he had left grief to them alone.

He stood straight and tall, easy to see, towards the front of the church with Sophie beside him. He faced the altar with the same determination as he did the hostile world. His face was grim; he had sensed the distance between himself and those who worked for him. No one greeted him without being spoken to first. That was new, and he wondered whether, if they did fend off Corpcom's offer, he could ever regain their trust. If Armadale remained his, would he now have to leave anyway, three months, six months, a year from now because he had lost his ability to lead its staff.

Sophie noticed the coolness towards Nick as well. It was matched by unusual warmth accorded to her. It was as if she were one of them, betrayed in her affection, deserted for something better. This very warmth now made her wonder about Nick's relationship with Annie. Sophie knew that Nick would never have betrayed his company, yet many believed he had. Could the same be true of Nick's betrayal of her?

After the funeral, Sophie drove Nick into the City before going on back to Downe. She turned towards him; he was hard-faced. She could feel the sorrow and anger in him.

'Why don't you tell them it's all a lie?' she said to him.

'I have.' He looked at her. 'No one believes me.'

'I believe you,' she said.

'Do you?'

She thought for a moment, looking inside herself. 'I think I do,' she said. Then she smiled at him and added, 'I do now.'

'What about tomorrow morning? And the next time I come home after midnight? What about then?' He was asking for complete trust again, with no compromise.

She made no reply; the questions were more like accusations. She realized how out of tune with each other they seemed. When she made a move towards him, he edged away, as she did sometimes when he tried to embrace her. For the first time since they were married, she wondered if she was not fooling herself in calling their bond 'love'.

Twenty minutes later, as they were struggling through the traffic of Fleet Street, she said, 'Perhaps we should separate for a little while.'

He snapped his head towards her and his gaze was cold and hard. It was as if no further pain could surprise him. He was like a martyr, but without any gentleness; there was no forgiveness in his heart for his executioners.

'After this business is all over,' she went on. 'Just to see.'

'To see what?' he said.

'If we still want to be together.'

'It's absurd,' he said. She waited for him to say something else, but he did not.

When she dropped him off in front of the Armadale building, he had still not said a word. He did not even look at her when he got out of the car.

'Thank you,' he said. 'I'll see you this evening.'

He stepped around the car and on to the pavement. Sophie opened her window and called his name. He turned, looked at her. She looked imploringly at him, hoping for some understanding, but she did not know what to say.

He turned and walked into the building. She looked after him, but was distracted by someone hooting behind her. She cried as she drove home, the tears flowing freely, only the needs of the driving itself acting to stop her from sobbing. When she waited at a stop light other drivers would look at her and wonder why she was crying.

2

On the following Monday, three weeks exactly after the bid had been launched, Corpcom's offer lapsed. Roger declared that 5 per cent of Armadale's shareholders had accepted his offer. He was therefore extending it for another week to allow a little more time for the other investors to decide. It was usual to extend for longer than a week, but, after the North Sea disaster and the scandal surrounding Nick, Andrews felt confident. He did not want to give the shareholders time to wait, which he knew they would do. The institutions would only make their decision at the last moment. Better that it should be sooner.

For the past week, there had been very little movement in the price of both companies' shares. Investors had a lot to take in and were waiting for things to settle before committing themselves. Armadale remained at 224p and Corpcom at 449p.

On that afternoon, the Office of Fair Trading announced that Corpcom's takeover bid for Armadale would not be referred to the Monopolies and Mergers Commission. With that, Armadale's defence came apart. A referral would have officially forced the bid to lapse, and in effect dragged it into limbo for six months at least. It would have afforded Armadale precious time to reorganize and ready itself for a proper fight.

Now the market reacted. The price of Armadale's shares climbed in rapid trading back to 246p and Corpcom's dipped to 435p. People were expecting acceptance.

That evening there was another emergency board meeting at Armadale. It was held at seven and again all the members of the board had managed to be there except Bob Sands, the American, and Howard. It had not been such a difficult meeting to assemble. All the board-members had been aware that the Office of Fair Trading was about to make its report. They had made themselves available with a minimum of rearrangement.

It was a sombre gathering.

John was there. So was Tony Morris, Armadale's stockbroker, a medium-sized man with a square, polished and clean-shaven face. To him would come the responsibility of interpreting the mood of the pension funds, Armadale's largest shareholders.

Nick opened the meeting, but he had barely started talking when Sir Edward interrupted him.

'John,' he said to the banker, 'You told us we would lose if we didn't get a referral. What do you think now? Have we lost?'

'I didn't say that, Ted,' John said.

'But that's what you meant,' Sir Edward persisted.

John did not deny it. Instead, he handed the question over to Tony Morris.

'It doesn't look good, I'm afraid,' Tony said. 'I would have thought most of the large institutions would sell. Somebody's already selling. Look at the closing price.'

'Andrews is very sure of himself,' John said. 'Extending for only a week. He's bluffing, but at this stage . . .' He let the sentence trail away. At this stage, no one cared whether he was bluffing or not. The cards were his. 'Is there anything we can do?' asked Jasper.

'We could recommend the bid,' John said tentatively.

'Never,' said Nick. His voice was like acid. It burned through the atmosphere of the room, and now everyone turned towards him.

'I refuse to recommend this bid to our shareholders,' he continued. 'Roger Andrews cannot be good for this company.'

'Your shareholders won't be concerned with that once they sell,' John said. 'They won't own this company any longer.'

'It is a good price,' Tony repeated himself.

'It is the short term view,' Nick said. 'Our shareholders can do better. That's my honest opinion. That's what I think we should tell them.'

'It won't work,' Richard said. 'They're going to sell.'

'That's not the point,' Nick retorted. 'The point is, what do we recommend?'

'I agree with Nick,' Harold said. He had spent the last three years heading the chemical arm of the company and felt he had done it well. 'If they'd stick by us, they'd do just fine.'

'It's a waste of energy,' Richard said. 'We've been defeated.

Let's accept it.' Nick was staring at him in anger, and he added, 'I genuinely don't know what else to do to stop this bid from succeeding.'

'What about a White Knight?' Roger asked, but there was little hope in his voice.

'It's much too late to try to get another company to outbid Andrews,' John answered the question. 'To be absolutely blunt, I don't think anyone would want to try.'

'There may be nothing we can do physically,' said Nick. 'But I won't cave in. If shareholders want to sell, let them. I won't recommend it.'

'I don't think you have to,' John said. 'It was just a suggestion. But Tony is right. After all that's happened, it is a good price.' John knew that the ship had been scuttled. The North Sea explosion had damaged Armadale's credit and the newspaper stories had almost destroyed Nick's ability to manage the company.

'Let's vote on it, then,' Sir Edward said. 'Do we recommend or don't we?'

They voted not to recommend.

They all knew it was a meaningless gesture. Yet, whatever the board-members believed about Nick's private life, they did not believe he would be looking for another job. His position at the board meeting confirmed it. They all felt that the least he deserved was their support.

Richard voted to recommend the bid. He was the only one to do so. His breaking ranks surprised the rest of them. But pessimism was so strong that they attributed the choice to the realism of a financial man: if there was no hope, why pretend?

Only Nick, rightly as he was to discover, held the vote against him. It was yet another betrayal.

3

Two days later Andrews issued an announcement that 41 per cent of shareholders had agreed to sell at Corpcom's price.

With their own 10 per cent ownership, built up over the last twelve months, Corpcom now controlled Armadale.

That day at Armadale, no work was done. People stood in clusters, talking in low tones, interspersed occasionally with raised voices. The tiny room with the topic screen, announcing the results of the selling of Armadale, had been thronged all day, smoke filling the air, people spilling out on to the hall, as if they were waiting for the result of the Grand National.

In his office, Alan held a kind of court. He would speak to anyone who cared to listen. A morbid, masochistic pessimism emanated from his room.

'I'm starting a sweepstake,' he had said to Julian in mid-afternoon. 'Who's going to be the first to be sacked? I'll take any bets.'

'Nick, I'd say,' answered Julian. They were all tired of Alan's ranting, yet they all came for more.

'The M D's not a contender,' Alan said, his voice loud with his own disappointment. 'No one on the board's in the running. I'm afraid they've gone already.'

'I'll bet on me then,' he said. 'Whoever takes over from Nick won't want me around.'

'Now you're making sense. How much?'

Alan seemed drunk, though his speech was not slurred. Julian shrugged his shoulders and left the room without giving him an answer. On his way back to his office, he walked past Jim Ferrar's office.

Jim was at his desk. Across from him sat Philip Porter, and he seemed to be in a dream. Jim was looking at him with sympathy. He made a note of something, the only one on the floor who was still working, apparently unconcerned by the day's news. Julian appeared in the doorway and remained standing there. Jim gave him a little wave, but Philip did not notice him.

Philip was clearly distressed. His twenty-year-old world had just been shattered. Nick Bishop, a man whom he respected, had been thrown out – or would be, it was obvious. And, just as bad, Philip's own job was on the line.

'How many do you think will have to go?' he said to Jim Ferrar. Philip had gone looking for Jim. Alan, in his present mood, was more than he could face. It was like talking to a gargoyle. Jim, on the other hand, remained friendly.

'You don't care, do you?' Philip asked.

'Not any more,' Jim said. 'I'm going to leave whatever happens. I don't like it around here any more.' He looked towards Julian and shrugged his shoulders helplessly.

Nick was the only man who did not take off his jacket and undo his tie. He sat in his office all day, going through papers, organizing his office.

Sarah came to say goodbye when she left for the day.

'I'm so sorry, sir,' she said.

'I won't be back, Sarah,' he said. 'This is it.'

She said nothing. She started crying on the spot, as if Nick had turned on a tap. She stood there and cried. He went up to her and put his hand on her shoulder.

'I'm sorry,' she said and this time she was apologizing for her tears. She wiped her eyes with the palm of her hand. Then, suddenly she stood on tiptoe and kissed him on the cheek. Before he could react, she turned and left the room.

He let her go.

He spent a long time with Julian, giving him instructions about the company as if he were handing over power, making a last will and testament. Nick had been adamant that he, Julian, should remain with the company.

'What if they won't have me?' he had said.

'They'll need you, if you want to stay.'

'I don't,' Julian had said.

'Please do. They won't expect you to. But I'd like you to.' Nick looked at Julian; a father looking at a son. 'Armadale is a good company. Help it along for a while.'

So Julian went home early, leaving Nick alone in his office. Nick had urged him to leave and, finally, Julian had, walking through the empty office building, abandoned as if there had been a bomb scare. Everyone had gone home.

*

Julian arrived home forty-five minutes after leaving the office. It was the rush-hour, something he usually avoided. It had taken him almost twenty-five minutes longer than usual and he was furious when he walked into his flat. He found Rebecca cooking a meal.

'Fucking traffic,' he yelled at the top of his voice as he came in, and then walked into the kitchen. 'I want to go out. I don't want to stay in.'

'No problem,' she said. She turned all the burners off. 'Where shall we go?'

Midway through the meal, in a local French brasserie, Rebecca reached out her hand to touch his.

'We could have stayed home, you know,' she said.

'I'm sorry,' he said and he managed a smile. 'I was thinking of Nick. He wants me to stay on.'

'Why not?' she asked. 'It's a job. You've worked hard there.'

'I worked for him.'

'So you'll work for somebody else. It's not the end of the world.' Again she reached out her hand.

'Andrews snapped us up just as we were on the cusp,' he continued, emphasizing his words with a curve of his hand in the air. 'He grabbed us before we could do too well. After years of low dividends and a sluggish share price, Andrews offered the shareholders a quick way out with a decent profit. They couldn't resist it.'

'It's hard to resist,' Rebecca said. Then she wondered why she always played the realist in these conversations.

Nick waited for Julian to leave before emptying his desk and packing the contents into cardboard boxes. He was not taking much with him, only what was his; what was Armadale's he had no desire for. It was part of what he was leaving behind.

He had drafted his letter of resignation, and it sat prominently in the middle of his desk, addressed to the Board of Directors of Armadale International. It was short and addressed none of the issues that burned in his heart. He made no apologies, gave no explanations. He just expressed his regret and offered his resignation.

He carried the boxes to the lift, then walked around the floor one last time, turning out the lights as he went. The only light now came from the corridor. He stopped at Edward Falcon's office, looking inside but not entering. By the light from a pale gleam that shimmered through the window, he noticed that there was still a picture of Edna and the children on the desk. He turned and walked briskly away towards the other end.

It was over.

4

Roger had called a special meeting of the Armadale board of directors for his final dramatic touch. It was one of the things he enjoyed most, the climax of several months' work.

Like a monarch, he made them wait. They all sat in the boardroom, brought in for the second time in a week, feeling uncomfortable and angered by the position in which they had been placed. The only member of the board who was absent was Nick Bishop. He had stayed away, refusing Andrews' call, and the others wished they had done the same.

Howard was there, in the Armadale building for the first time in over a month. He looked around him with embarrassment, sensing disapprobation, more in fact than there really was. Every one knew that he had been put in the middle. But Howard had further reason for discomfort. He felt that he was likely to be the only member of the board to remain, and he could then be accused of taking sides. Yet his presence was required.

Sir Edward Reald stayed apart from the others, standing at the far end of the room, beside the large still life, in its heavy gilt frame, that dominated the room. Howard talked to George Freeman, while the others formed a cluster together. One other man remained apart. Richard sat at the table, making notes on a pad; he seemed to be working.

Sir Edward looked at his watch. 'I've waited long enough.' He was walking towards the door when it opened and Roger stood in the doorway, Peter at his side.

'Gentlemen,' Roger said, and he sat down at the head of the table next to Richard.

Peter sat on his other side. With exaggerated civility, Roger waited for them all to sit. Then he opened the folder he had brought with him and took out several pieces of paper. He handed them out, calling each man by name. Howard did not receive one, nor did Richard.

'That's a letter of resignation,' Roger Andrews started. 'I'd be grateful if you would sign it.'

'I think I won't sign this,' Sir Edward said in the silence, replacing the letter in front of him and sitting back in his chair.

Roger looked at him with curiosity, and Sir Edward added as he stood up, 'I don't like its tone.'

'Rewrite it.' Roger was dismissive. 'Pick any tone you want.'

'I'm afraid I'm not prepared to resign.'

The others were looking at him in surprise, wondering what game he was playing.

'I'm going to have to fire you, then.' Roger was a little harsher.

'I'd rather be fired. It is truer to what is going on.'

'Well, you're fired.' Roger immediately turned away from him, back to the others.

'Please put it on the record, won't you, and confirm it in writing,' Sir Edward said before leaving the room.

The others watched him go.

'Any more games?' Roger said.

'This is a game, isn't it?' Harold said. He stood up. 'I think I'd rather be fired too. My contract isn't up.'

'Quite understandable,' Roger said. 'So long as the settlement isn't exorbitant. There are no golden handshakes out of my companies. A deal is a deal, but I'm not handing out any parachutes.' He faced Harold firmly, waiting for his agreement.

'Our contracts were always fair,' he said.

The other non-executive board members signed their letter. George Freeman handed his back to Roger. The others, Jasper

Thomas among them, left it in front of them. They rose to follow Sir Edward.

Harold looked towards Roger, who had also stood up without signing the letter. 'I'm with Harold,' he said. 'I'd rather not resign.'

'Fine.'

Both men glanced at Richard, who had not moved. Harold spoke first. 'What kind of arrangement have you made, Richard?' he said, with venom in his voice.

'Richard is going to be Managing Director.' It was Roger who answered.

'Really?' said Harold. 'How very convenient.'

Roger waited till the door was closed. There were just four of them now in the room, he, Peter, Richard and Howard.

'Not too bad,' he said, 'as these things go. Reald was a variant I haven't come across. Interesting.'

Howard was looking at Richard in astonishment. A mole. Roger had had a mole in the camp; with a simple carrot, the top job.

'Surprised, hey, Howard?' Roger said. He was intolerably pleased with himself. 'Richard's been a great help.' He added, 'And, of course, of great value to Armadale.'

'Of course,' Howard came back. 'A selfless servant of the public good.'

'Come off it,' Richard spoke for the first time. 'No hypocrisies, please.'

'Even I am capable of disliking certain actions,' Howard said with a self-deprecating smile.

Richard glanced quickly at Roger, who nodded.

'Howard,' Richard said. 'I think,' he spoke his lines carefully, slowly, like an actor enjoying his moment, 'I think, in view of your close relationship with Nick, you'd probably agree there might be a conflict of interest . . .'

Howard could not believe it. He laughed, 'Draw up the letter of resignation and send it to me. I'll sign it.'

He left the room, too amused to be angry. Anger and shame would come later.

Roger Andrews looked at the two men at either side of him. They, literally, had the floor. And Roger liked it like that.

'Very good,' he said.

5

There had been a granite-like hardness about Sophie when Nick had returned bearing his boxes. She knew what it meant to Nick, but having made her mind up to leave once the bid was finished, she had steeled herself to carry it out.

She made plans to move out immediately, taking the two boys with her. She was not going to sugar the pill. She did not know how to.

The following day she collected them from school. They were walking home through the small village. She waited till they had passed the church.

'I want to tell you something,' she went on. She paused. Then she took the plunge. 'Your father' – she did not use the usual 'Daddy' – 'Your father and I have decided to live apart for a little while. You're going to live with me,' she continued for fear of interruptions, 'but you can see Daddy whenever you want, of course. In fact,' she added, 'I think he's going to have more time these days. You should be able to see him much more than usual.'

Both children understood that their parents were quarrelling. That much was simple. Alistair perhaps grasped some of the idea of separation; after all, friends of his had parents who were divorced. Separation and divorce meant about the same to him. John, only seven, did not see why they should live apart from their father, especially if he was going to have more spare time.

'Why?' he said.

'Well,' Sophie started. It was the question she had dreaded. She had known it would come. 'Daddy and I just need to live apart for a little while,' she said. 'We're always arguing. Getting angry with each other. It's not good for anyone.'

'Where are we going to go?' Alistair asked.

'We'll stay with Granny and Grandad,' she answered. Sophie's parents lived in London, in Hampstead, and the flat would be large enough.

They pondered this.

'Are we going to have to leave school?' Alistair asked.

'Yes,' she said. She wished this had never happened. She wondered if she would weaken. But she forced herself not to.

'Why can't we stay here?' John said. 'I want to stay at home. With Daddy.'

'Because we can't,' she said.

Nothing explained anything. She had the wisdom to realize it. It became just another of the *faits accomplis* that riddle the lives of children. The answer to the question 'why' was 'because'.

Nick helped them to get ready. The children asked him why they had to go and live with their grandparents.

'It won't be for long,' he said. That was all he said. He did not talk about it again, and just added, 'We'll talk about it another time.'

He was tired. Losing the children because he and Sophie could not get along pained and shamed him. He knew he would miss them. Yet he wanted to be alone, and he was honest enough to admit it to himself.

When they finally left, at the weekend, he embraced both of them. John clung to him speechlessly, like a little monkey, not wanting to leave.

'It'll be all right,' Nick said and placed him in the back seat. He watched the car disappear around the tall trees of the driveway. As soon as it had, he turned and strode inside.

That night, well after midnight, Nick stood in the living-room, looking out at the night through the undrawn curtains. He listened to his empty house. Alone, as he had never been before, he sobbed, his face contorted with a child's agony, tears dropping down his cheeks, their saltiness a forgotten sensation. He could not remember the last time he had cried, but it was so unusual and painful that he wept for a long time, his sobs renewed by the force of the moment.

PART II

<u>Divergence of Character</u>

The Code has not, and does not seek to have, the force of law, but those who wish to take advantage of the facilities of the securities markets in the United Kingdom should conduct themselves in matters relating to takeovers according to the Code. Those who do not so conduct themselves cannot expect to enjoy those facilities and may find that they are withheld.

From the Introduction to *The City Code on Take-overs and Mergers*

Chapter Eighteen

I

During the first week of his exile, Nick kept the telephone off the hook. He turned his back on the world – on Sophie, on Howard, on all his acquaintances and friends, as well as on Armadale. He wanted nothing to do with any of them. He roamed around the empty house, littering it as he went. He dropped clothes, papers, left dirty plates when he no longer needed them. It was a period of regression, of emotion rather than thought. He found he could not break the pattern of rage, disillusion and self-hatred that locked his mind into stupor.

On Saturday he heard a key in the front door. He had not noticed a car pulling up to the house. It was just after three in the afternoon and Nick was sitting in the drawing-room, watching a rugby match on the television. He stood up, furious at the disturbance.

'Who is that?' he shouted, not even considering that whoever it was had keys.

It was Sophie. She was standing in the doorway as he came out into the hall.

'My God,' she exclaimed as she saw him.

Nick had a week's beard on him, his hair was uncombed, and he wore a pair of dirty jeans beneath a pyjama top and a sweater. His feet were bare. Despite the cold February weather, the house was hot and airless from the central heating.

'What do you want?' Nick said. He was abrupt. 'Did you forget something?' He never considered that she might have come for his sake. He wanted her to be gone again.

'I've been trying to reach you for days,' she answered. She was clipped, antagonized by his questions.

'Why?' he asked.

Sophie gave him no answer. She closed the door and went in. She went no further than the kitchen door. She looked in and saw dishes, glasses, empty cartons of food stacked haphazardly around every surface of her once tidy, clean kitchen. She turned away in horror.

'This is disgusting,' she said to Nick. 'How can you live like this?'

Automatically, without thinking, she picked up an empty tin and threw it in the bin.

'Leave it!' he shouted.

Sophie stopped, reminded of her reason for being there. She had been trying to ring him for three days without any success and on the fourth day had not been able to control the anguish she felt. Was Nick all right? Might he be ill, or dead? Had a burglar come into the house and hurt him? Had he killed himself? These questions had gnawed at her until she had been unable to control them. As she drove through the traffic of South London, different images of what she might find darted through her mind. She saw herself walking around the house, turning familiar corners in fear of what she might discover. By the time she had turned off the main road and was winding her way on the last stretch to Downe, she was opening the bathroom door and finding Nick's body in a pool of blood in the bath.

When she saw Nick, dishevelled but alive, heard him ask her what she wanted, when she looked at the mess that had once been her house, all her fears and anxieties turned to fury.

'I'm not going to clean this pig-sty,' she said, turning on him. She noticed the telephone in the hall, lying off its cradle, silencing all communication with the outside world. She walked over to it and replaced it. 'How dare you do this? I've been trying to ring you for days . . . .' It was like talking to a child.

She was about to go on, but the ringing of the telephone stopped her. The noise surprised Nick; he had forgotten how loud it was. Sophie picked it up.

'It's for you.'

He did not move. For a moment she remained motionless too, her hand out towards Nick. 'I'm sorry, he's not in,' she said eventually, and hung up. Her rage had been distracted. She went on, 'I couldn't get through. I thought something might have happened.'

'Everything's fine. I just didn't want to talk to anyone, that's all.'

He seemed to be genuinely unaware of her anxiety, even that she might have cause to be anxious.

She said, 'I thought you might be dead.'

It was then that he realized what he had wrought. Had he wanted this all the time? Was this a way of bringing Sophie, or Howard, or someone to him? But no, he genuinely did not want anyone's anxiety or care at the moment. He wanted their rejection, he wanted to be deserted. He could just as easily have left the phone on the hook and enjoyed the fact that it did not ring, thus confirming his sense of isolation.

'I'm sorry,' he said to Sophie. 'I didn't think.'

'You certainly didn't,' she said. 'Are you all right?' she added, knowing that he was not. She looked again at her house and her first instinct was to clean it all up. She stopped herself, thought she would compromise.

'Do you want me to help you clean the house?'

'No.' It was a sharp refusal. Then he added, 'Thank you.'

'But you can't live like this, Nick.'

'Yes, I can,' he said. 'This is how I want to live.'

'You never used to.'

'I do now.'

He was still hard, unyielding. She looked at him standing before her; tall, handsome, but with his body as stiff as his will. She turned around and walked out of the front door.

She stopped in front of the car, turned to see Nick in the doorway.

'Are you punishing me?' she said. 'Is this what this is all about?'

'That's absurd,' he said. 'If you hadn't come down, you would never have known.'

She merely looked at him in silence, as if she did not believe him.

So he added, 'I did not bring you down from Hampstead with a phone off the hook. You came of your own free will.'

She climbed into the car and closed the door. He came out to it in his bare feet. She opened the window, thinking he might soften.

But he said, 'I will keep it on the hook from now on. You won't have to come down again.'

He was an unforgiving man. She had always known it, but never felt it quite as intensely. She started the car and drove out. She looked back in the rear-view mirror and saw Nick already walking back towards the house.

Nick stayed in Downe for the next two months, speaking only to shopkeepers, local pub landlords, the odd telephone caller. It was as if, with his silence, he was shouting his anger at the outside world. The only break to his solitary life was a weekly journey to London to see Alistair and John. After his second week in Downe, Sophie had rung him and insisted he see his sons.

'They're asking after you,' she said. 'Don't you want to see them?'

'Of course I do,' he answered. It was only a half-truth. He could have coped just as easily without seeing them.

'Well then, see them,' she said.

She arranged the weekly visit. She would drop them off at Nick's club in the West End and watch them go into the Georgian building from the car. They disappeared inside without her ever seeing Nick. She picked them up in the evening, and they rushed out and jumped in. Again, she would not see Nick. It was only from the boys that she knew he had indeed met them and taken them out to do something.

The first time, he met them in the small entrance hall. John rushed up to him and hugged him as hard as he could. Alistair was a little more reserved. They kissed, but there was no overflowing emotion between them.

'When can we come home, Daddy?' John said almost immediately.

'Soon, I think,' Nick answered. He looked over at Alistair and smiled, but he saw that he did not believe him.

'Come on,' he said to them. 'We're going to Madame Tussaud's.'

The children were delighted and seemed to forget the separation.

Every week, he would take them to some special place. He spoiled them as a means of making them forget that they lived apart and to make their time together less difficult. They looked forward to their visit and missed him less. But, on each return, Sophie was handed two indulged and maddening children: overfed, overtired and overindulged

She spoke to Nick about it, but every time the same thing happened. She gave up in the end, and decided that this was yet one more thing she would have to learn to handle. At least the children enjoyed it; that was a consolation. But Nick's carelessness saddened her; this was not the man she had married.

After Sophie's visit, Nick had kept the telephone on the hook, and he answered it when it rang. But his conversations were perfunctory and the calls never lasted long. He was so discouraging that his callers tired of monosyllabic responses, just as he tired of the same concern for his state of mind and recommendations for its improvement.

Julian was the only person he did not mind speaking to. Julian rang soon after Sophie's first visit to Downe. He had not tried earlier, so had no idea that Nick had been unreachable. After the first call, he rang regularly.

Julian still worked for Armadale. Already, his initial interest in the repercussions of the bid had gone; it had been replaced by an ever-increasing sense of discomfort, and of betrayal. Julian did not quite understand how he could work for Richard just as he had done for Nick. Although Nick had urged him to stay on after his overthrow, Julian had never expected to be retained; after all, he had worked closely with Nick for eighteen months. Surely he would be regarded as untrustworthy. The reverse happened.

Richard had not only asked him to stay, but to remain in the same position.

'This is not America,' Richard said smugly. 'A staff doesn't have to leave with its chief. I prefer continuity.'

So Julian had stayed, adapting to a new personality and to new quirks. His routine was the same, but for a few variants.

'I rarely stay on past six these days,' he said to Nick and laughed. 'No lunches in your office either. I go out more.'

'You always liked a proper lunch,' Nick said.

'I'm putting on weight.'

The conversations were tentative at first, but, with each one, they relaxed more, forgetting the ghost of January. Nick liked to speak to Julian. Julian was the only one who joked, and spoke of Armadale without taking a mortician's tone; he spoke of it naturally, funnily, giving a report on it as he would have done had Nick merely been a retired chairman. The report was perhaps painful, but it was alive like nothing else that was put before him.

Julian rang just before Easter. It was two months since Roger had taken over the company.

'So. What's new?' Nick said, waiting for his news report. 'Who else has gone?'

Over the last two months, with every call, Julian announced another redundancy. Almost the entire top floor had left. Jim had resigned as soon as the new management took over. They did not try to keep him. Philip, as he had feared, had been made redundant. All about him, Julian watched them fall. Only he was left. Even Sarah had gone. She had been moved downstairs to another office, demoted back into anonymity.

'You remember Alan Turner,' said Julian.

'Of course I do,' said Nick. 'He was good. One always knew about it, though.'

'This is an interesting twist,' Julian said. 'He's gone.'

'Why?' Nick asked. 'I thought Richard liked him.'

'He's moved into Corpcom itself,' Julian said. 'Head of Marketing South. I don't know how he managed it,' Julian added. 'The flow has been all the other way so far. Corpcom people taking over here.'

'Ask Richard about it,' Nick said.

'Fat chance.'

Julian was rarely as privy to Armadale's new practices as he had been previously. Richard did not trust anyone and did not confide in his assistant the way Nick had.

Initially, Julian had resented Frye's secretiveness. By now he was glad of it. To be kept apart enabled him to think of himself as apart, and so to feel uncommitted to the new management. He need not owe them anything and could abandon them whenever it became too difficult to remain.

At the end of two months, it was clear that Andrews was building a hierarchic company, moving away from the much more democratic system that Nick had created. In corporate terms, it did not really matter. Roger was a good demagogue. He had imposed his form of dictatorship without hypocrisy, making changes in the company on the basis of 'supply and reward'; there were cash incentives in following Andrews' law. If anyone found this distasteful, he or she was welcome to leave the company within one week, receive two months' pay, and the equivalent of an honourable discharge.

It worked. The new boss – and everyone knew it was Roger, not Richard – was perceived as tough, but fair. It paid off as a gamble as well. No one took him up on his offer. He could now do what he wished. If he had not earned their fidelity, he had earned their respect, the kind a dog pays his master.

'Are you looking around for something else?' Nick asked Julian, sensing his lack of commitment.

'Not really,' Julian answered. 'I'm going with the flow at the moment.'

'That's not a bad way to go.'

The only flow in Nick's life was inert. He was marking time. That Julian was in the same position made their conversations more easy to bear. Nick was not conducting his life vicariously through Julian; they could be just two disappointed friends together. The difference was that Julian was younger and he had Rebecca. His life had just changed in focus. Nick's was empty. He needed change, yet he did not know where to find it. So he was lucky that it came to him.

One morning in April, at about eleven o'clock, as Nick was making himself breakfast, the bell rang. He was still in a dressing-gown. His beard, full-grown now, touched with grey, unlike his hair, which was still dark, gave him a strangely Victorian air. In addition, the weeks of solitude and reflection had given him a semblance of priestly composure and thoughtfulness. He was an imposing figure.

He opened his front door. Howard took a step back, as if he were afraid, surprised by Nick's appearance.

For Nick, seeing Howard on his doorstep brought back all the passions that had been forced out in the open months ago. The two men stood in the doorway in silence.

'Hallo, Nick.' Howard gave an embarrassed laugh.

'What do you want?'

'May I come in?'

'I don't know.' Nick looked straight at Howard as he said it.

'I've been to see Sophie,' Howard said.

'Did she ask you to come down to see me?'

'We talked about it.'

'Come in, then,' he said, and he moved aside to let Howard past, although why Howard's visiting Sophie should make a difference, neither really knew.

In the hall, he glanced about him. He wondered in what state he would find the house. Sophie had described what she had seen. That had been almost three months ago, and Howard felt a morbid curiosity about what had happened since.

Nick took his coat and, as Howard was making his way to

the living-room, said, 'Let's go into the kitchen. I'm having breakfast.'

Howard stopped. He managed to snatch a look at the living-room, but had found the room as he had always known it. Perhaps it was a little less neat, the cushions on the sofa had not been fluffed up, the ash from the fireplace had not been swept, but there were no empty tins of food on the floor, no plates encrusted with cold leftovers, no chicken wings thrown idly on to the nearest chair.

The house was back to normal. Nick had soon grown tired of living in squalor. Sophie's visit had made him see its destructiveness and he had tidied the house and kept it in reasonable order since then. He channelled his energy into domestic chores.

Still Howard stepped into the kitchen carefully, just in case. When he found it reasonably tidy, he relaxed. He sighed audibly as he sat down at the kitchen table. Automatically he had looked at his watch to see the time: breakfast at eleven o'clock; it was a forgotten luxury.

'Do you want some?'

Howard was tempted, but he said, 'No thanks.' When Nick returned to his cooking and said no more, Howard added, 'Wouldn't mind a drink.'

'Help yourself,' Nick said. 'You know where it is.'

When Howard returned with a large whisky and soda, Nick was at the table; the yolk had run over the plate and he was scooping it up into his mouth with a piece of bread. Howard sat down opposite him and for a second looked hungrily at the food. He took a sip of his drink.

'So. What did Sophie have to say for herself?' Nick said, leaning over the plate, with his mouth full. It was a challenge, not an invitation to a confidence.

'She's all right,' Howard said. But that was not what he wanted to talk about. He went on, 'How are you? You look all right. The beard's a bit odd.'

Howard was being jovial, but Nick said nothing. Howard was not really asking him how he was. He was preparing to say something. Nick waited for it.

Howard decided to address the issue. 'I think you're taking it all excessively seriously,' he said.

'How so?'

'You're behaving as if the world was caving in. It's only a business deal. One among many.' Nick said nothing, so Howard went on, 'It's a game, Nick. It has rules, a code. There's a winner and a loser. It's nothing more than that.'

'The takeover code is more than just a rule book,' Nick said sharply. 'It's a standard of ethics.'

'The standard wasn't broken, for heaven's sake,' Howard said, 'it was just bent a little. Haven't you ever broken a rule?'

'Andrews did more than break a rule. You know that. Business is a way of life, like politics, or medicine, or the law.' Nick spoke with passion. 'You can't lie, commit perjury, malpractice. There are people involved here. People and principles. A thief in a suit and tie is still a thief.'

Nick looked at Howard and saw there the look that a father gives to a thoughtful, adolescent child, understanding and tolerant, but condescending. It infuriated him. He took a deep breath, forcing himself to stay calm.

'You mentioned Sophie,' he said. 'Isn't that what you came to see me about?'

'Yes, I did. Aren't you being a bit rough on her?' Howard said, unusually aggressive. He knew that Sophie was frightened by her sudden and unfamiliar independence. Even though they had never been friends, he admired her courage at leaving Nick; in any event, it had always been Sophie who had disliked him, rather than the other way around.

'What are you talking about?' Nick spoke carefully, enunciating every word. 'She left me.'

'Well, yes,' Howard said, and he added, not realizing that he was falling into quicksand, 'but not without some cause . . .?'

Nick looked up from his plate. Howard was left speechless by the sudden animosity he saw on his friend's face.

'I thought you believed I didn't do anything,' Nick said bitterly. 'At least, that's what you said.'

'I did.'

'So what changed your mind?'

There was a pause. 'Sophie leaving you,' Howard answered, sucking in air as he spoke the words. It was true. Howard believed in Nick's affair with Annie because Sophie had left him.

'You're a fool, Howard,' Nick said. 'You actually believe I had an affair with Annie Chinoise? For Christ's sake, don't you realize how absurd that is? I had lunch with her. Once.' His anger changed to exasperation at the stupidity of it all, 'Sophie believes it too. You, Sophie, you all believe something that was made up one day by an unscrupulous man.' He was shaking his head now, 'I don't understand. Don't you know me?'

'It's because we do know you . . .' Howard paused, then went on. 'It's so easy to have an affair, Nick. You would never have abandoned Armadale, been looking for another job. Everyone knows that. But sex . . .'

'My commitment to my wife was certainly the equal to my commitment to my company.' Nick stood up, taking his empty plate to the sink. 'I don't see why everyone finds that so difficult to understand.'

Howard stood up. 'The world may be evil,' he said, 'But you are not a saint.'

'That's a stupid thing to say.'

'You're being stupid. You're behaving as if all that's gone on in the last few months has given you a kind of divine right to sit back and judge.'

'You betrayed me.' Nick was indignant. He stood facing Howard squarely. His hands were fists. He had never made the accusation so blatantly before.

'That's melodramatic rubbish. No one betrayed you. I was caught in the middle.' Howard was impassioned too. 'You seem to have all the answers. What would you have had me do?' he shouted.

'Make a choice.'

'I did. I chose my family and my life.'

'Your family. That's a joke.' Nick thought of Sheilah, Howard's bird-like mistress.

'We're still together.' Howard wished he had not said that. It hurt Nick. 'I'm sorry,' he added quickly. He began to whine again. 'I would have done you no good by telling you. Can't you see that? Andrews had planned it for ages before I knew about it. I just would have done myself a lot of harm.'

'For once in your life, Howard,' Nick said, 'you could have stood up for something.'

Howard was stung by that. 'I did,' he replied. 'Myself. And you would have done the same.'

'I would have resigned,' Nick said.

'Then you're a fool.' And he added, 'I wouldn't have expected you to.'

There was nothing more to say. Howard could not stand Nick's unconcealed contempt. It angered him. He doubted himself enough to feel guilty, and yet he knew that Nick was being unjust.

They faced each other in silence for a few seconds. Howard headed towards the front door, Nick right behind him. By the entrance, Howard turned back towards Nick, who already had his hand on the open door. They stared at each other, and still said nothing. Howard turned away, shaking his head.

Nick slammed the door shut. He was alone again.

Chapter Nineteen

I

If Sophie's visit had put an end to Nick's inertia, Howard's ended his reflective period. It was as if each visit precipitated him into the next phase of recovery. But, as with a man who is heavily bandaged after an accident, it was not clear what Nick would be like once his wounds had healed.

As he sat moodily in the country, Nick had blamed himself for having trusted so much, for having slept while the world he knew was being eroded. Armadale circled around his mind like a satellite; he continued stubbornly to regard Armadale as his company and, although he would never have used the image consciously, he saw himself as a deposed monarch, and Roger as a usurper. He, Nick, was the legitimate leader of Armadale, and he could not believe that he had not been overcome by subterfuge and corruption.

The story about Annie, Richard's connivance, the microphones, Howard, all these factors were such evident treachery that Nick wondered what other betrayals he remained ignorant of, wondered even at times if Annie herself had not been a plant, willing to put herself on the line for Andrews and act as his Judas – betraying him with a kiss. Whenever that thought cast its shadow over him, he resisted it with every fibre of optimism left in him. That lunch had been the only moment of peace during the nightmare, and he clung to the image of Annie looking at him over her glass of wine.

Nick analysed the bid from every angle. If he admitted now that Armadale had been vulnerable to attack, that he had almost deliberately turned his back on the possibility of a takeover at a time when takeovers were more fashionable than BMWs, he was still convinced that he might have been able to fend Roger off. Too many circumstances had conspired to undo him.

It had begun with the accident in the North Sea. Excluding Richard's treachery, the bid had been lost with that explosion and with the death of those two men. The scandal surrounding his meeting with Annie had been the finishing touch that no one could have predicted, but which he could have avoided.

It was the timing of that explosion that struck him as having been too precise to have been purely coincidental. It was a problem that kept nagging at him, demanding an explanation. If that was the beginning of the end, he wanted to know more about it. Eagerly he awaited the outcome of the inquiry set up by the Department of Energy.

Propelled therefore by this nagging question and by Howard's visit, Nick began to re-enter the world. He telephoned friends, and former colleagues at Armadale. But having turned away offers of help, having isolated himself in his own accusatory world, Nick now found himself shunned. For the most part his old friends had been business associates; they had become hard to reach. Messages were not returned. When he managed to catch someone on the telephone, there was always, he found, a reason to avoid a meeting or even a protracted conversation on the phone. No invitation for lunch was accepted, and certainly none was offered in return. There was always an embarrassed moment, a clearing of the throat, a hesitant stutter.

He spoke to Jasper one day.

'I'm sorry, Nick.' Then came the stutter. 'I can't this week.'

'How about next week?' Nick said.

The throat was cleared. 'I'm afraid I'm off to America next week.' There followed a silence. 'Why don't I give you a ring sometime after I get back?'

'Fine,' Nick said. 'I'll wait to hear from you.'

They both knew what that meant. That 'sometime' was the telltale word that meant nothing. There was an almost audible relief at the other end.

'Good. I'll see you soon. Goodbye,' and the phone was hung up.

Sir Edward remained friendly. He took Nick's call immediately, and spoke in his usual direct and slightly brusque manner.

'Where the hell have you been?' he said. 'Underground?'

'Been spending some quiet time,' Nick answered. It was almost an apology. Nick had always had the sensation, when talking to Sir Edward, that he was talking to his father. He reverted to being a son, if not a child. The feeling was even more pronounced now.

'Not good for you, you know,' the older man said. His words came in rapid bursts. 'Got to get on with life. Get a job.'

'It's not that easy,' Nick said. He had not tried, but he could tell from the reaction to his calls that it would be hard. He found himself ostracized. It was as if he was contaminated by being out of work.

'You're wasting your time, Nick,' Sir Edward said. 'Get back to work,' he advised again.

'I will soon,' Nick said. In an abstract way, he meant it.

'Keep in touch. Always good to hear from you,' Sir Edward said. 'Let me know if I can do anything.'

Nick's standing with his peers was more truly reflected in Richard's attitude. He and Julian spoke of Nick on the day the Department of Energy report of the inquiry into the explosion landed on Richard's desk.

They were in Nick's old office – Julian still thought of the corner office on the seventh floor as 'Nick's office'. Richard was at the desk, Julian on a chair opposite him. Behind them, the sitting area had been changed. The tweedy sofa and armchairs had been removed and their replacements were heavier, more ostentatious, in dark brown vinyl, simulating a rich leather.

'An accident,' Richard said as he patted the report. 'We all expected it, of course. But it's always nice to have it official.'

'Should I distribute it to the heads of department?' Julian asked.

'Yes. But no further. Not everyone has to see it,' Richard said. 'Should be kept reasonably confidential, you know.' He spoke with exaggerated self-importance. He added, 'You should take a look. You'll find it interesting.'

'I'd like to,' Julian said, playing the role of pupil to Richard's mentor. It seemed to be what Richard liked, and it was the path of least resistance, even if Julian was finding it more and more intolerable. He stood up and reached over to pick up the report. He remained standing, wanting to bring this meeting to an end.

'Get a copy over to Engineering,' Richard said. 'They should see it a.s.a.p. Boost their morale.' He took up something on his desk, dismissing Julian without saying anything. It was another sign of the way Richard liked to wield his new power: he confused its trappings for the thing itself.

Julian walked away. At the door he stopped, wondered if he should ask the next question, then decided that he might as well.

'Do you think it'd be all right if I sent a copy to Nick Bishop?' he said. He tried to sound as unconcerned as he could.

'Nick Bishop?' Richard asked, looking up in surprise despite Julian's air of nonchalance. 'Do you see him?' It was clear from his tone that he did not consider it appropriate for Julian to see Nick.

'Haven't seen him since the takeover,' Julian said. He did not have to lie. He paused, then went on, knowing that this would have the right effect. 'I have seen his wife. She's living in London, you know.'

'I heard they were separated,' Richard could not conceal the smugness in his voice. Julian had played him right. 'I hear Nick's in pretty bad shape,' he went on.

'Oh, really?'

'So I've heard. He's completely obsessed with what happened. On the verge of a breakdown, apparently. Lives alone, his house is completely filthy. Talks of nothing but the takeover.' Richard paused, shaking his head. 'Tragic.'

'It might do him good to know that the whole thing was an accident,' Julian said. 'I know he took the death of those two men up there quite hard.'

'He drinks, you know.' Richard seemed not to have heard Julian. He wanted to get all the dirt out. But Julian stood in silence, waiting for him to run out of steam, and Richard, seeing Julian impassive, seemingly uninterested in his gossip, did stop. It did not matter. He had given all the gory details; he was willing to forgo a discussion of them.

'You think he'd want to see it?' he asked Julian.

'He was managing director at the time,' Julian said. 'Perhaps it's only right he should see it.'

Richard pondered it for a moment. He decided to be magnanimous, and with a wide sweeping gesture, he said, 'You're right. Send it to him.'

As Julian was opening the door, Richard added, 'With my compliments.' With that, he bent his head down over the papers on his desk.

2

The explosion that had killed the two men on the North Sea platform was deemed by the investigators from the Department of Energy to have been caused by a faulty control valve, situated at the base of the natural-gas dehydration tower. The control valve maintains the level of pressure of gas going to a flash drum. There is a relief valve also, an ordinary back-up system. Each valve is made up of a 'seat' and a 'stem', in which the seat is removable if necessary.

The inspectors of the Department of Energy, having visited the site, spoken to managers, foremen and workmen on the platform, to Usoco officials and to Armadale's engineers, had determined that the seat of the control valve had become loose; then, when the valve had opened, the seat had moved off its location and the valve had not been able to close. The orifice had become wider than usual and the flash drum had continued to receive gas. The relief valve had not then been able to cope because it was receiving up to ten times the normal amount of gas. The explosion that had occurred had thus been a direct result of this abnormal build-up of pressure.

The inspectors' conclusion was that the explosion had been accidental. They blamed no one, neither Armadale's Engineering branch, who had supplied the valve, nor Usoco, the oil company that had been in charge of the maintenance. Since the valve had been tested several times under extreme conditions before being sent out to the platform, and since maintenance checks had been carried out with regularity and had not detected a fault, the malfunction was assumed to have been accidental, a tragic and freak accident for which no one could be blamed.

Nick kept returning to the report, searching it for a fault, reading through the evidence as if it contained a secret somewhere, sure that the accident was other than the inspectors held it to be.

There was one short paragraph that Nick read many times, as if by reading it, he could decipher the message held by the words. It came in the section of the report dealing with maintenance. The inspectors placed no blame on the maintenance of the dehydration system, but they noted that 'although the last official check on the control valve had been carried out three days before the explosion, it was difficult from the evidence given by several members of the maintenance crew to determine when exactly the control valve had actually been physically examined for the last time.' What Nick was able to gather was that one of the maintenance men had believed that his supervisor had looked at the valve on the day of the explosion itself, whereas the supervisor had not been able to remember exactly when his last visit had taken place. Since it would have been an informal check, it was not logged. Exact timing was even more uncertain, inevitably it was thought, because of the turmoil brought about by the explosion. The inspectors noted that, on a second interview, the maintenance crew-member had, been much vaguer and questioned his own memory.

The whole incident nagged at Nick, even though he knew that he was not an objective observer, that he was looking for discrepancy and uncertainty.

Needing to discuss his obsession, he rang Julian at home. Rebecca answered the telephone. She had met Nick only once, a couple of years before, when she and Julian had gone down to the country for lunch one Sunday. She had liked him, but she had also liked Sophie. Instinctively, she sided with Sophie now. As far as she was concerned, Nick had been having an affair and Julian was naïve to think he had not. Her greeting was cool.

'Is Julian there?' Nick asked.

'He went out to get some beer,' she answered. 'He should be back any minute. I'll get him to call you.'

'Please.' Nick added, 'I wanted to talk to him. I was going to suggest lunch on Sunday, if you were free. Perhaps you could both come?'

'I don't know if he's doing anything,' Rebecca said, giving herself the 'out'. She was not sure she wanted to go to Downe for lunch.

'Why don't you talk it over with him,' Nick said, aware of what she was doing. 'Julian can give me a ring and let me know. There's no rush.'

Rebecca relayed the message to Julian with little enthusiasm.

'You don't have to come,' Julian said to her.

'He invited me,' she said.

'Well, come then.'

It was a beautiful spring day. For Julian, the visit was filled with nostalgia. He remembered the Sundays he had driven down for lunch with the whole family. He had always been welcomed by all of them. He felt awkward that Sophie and the boys should be absent.

Nick greeted them warmly, embracing Rebecca, which surprised her. She had not remembered him as so expansive, and she enjoyed the feel of his generous beard on her cheek. Nick gave them a lot to drink and had made a coq au vin. He had stood over the stove for hours that morning, following the recipe with painstaking fidelity.

'I'm proud of myself,' he said at the end of the meal, after they both complimented him.

They had eaten in the kitchen, so that he could watch over the meal and talk to them. Julian marvelled at how different he was from the boss he remembered. He seemed so relaxed, so carefree. It seemed to belie all the memories he had, as well as all the rumours he had heard.

It was, of course, only partly the case. Nick was the same, as obsessed, as intransigent as ever. Three times already, he had talked about the paragraph that bothered him in the Department of Energy's report. Yet he had never been a formal man. Without the restrictions of a company to perform for and a family to be responsible for, he could afford to be more generous with himself. Julian was lulled by this, even though the conversation about the explosion bothered him. Nick seemed to be going in a direction that would do him no good.

After lunch, they walked in the garden. Although the grass had been mown recently by Nick, there were few flowers; Sophie had always looked after the garden, and now that she was gone, Nick had neither the skill, nor the interest. They were at the farthest end of the lawn, skirting the fence that separated them from a field in which cows grazed. Back towards the house, they could see Rebecca who had abandoned them to lie in the sun. She lay back in a deckchair, her eyes closed, her arms dangling down. Her legs were spread out, and her skirt pulled up to bare her thighs to the sun.

Both men looked back at her. She did not see them watching her.

'How long have you know Rebecca?' Nick asked.

'Two years.'

Nick nodded. It was obviously approval. He liked Rebecca, but he was shy of telling Julian, not wanting to make it sound like a stamp of approval.

'I want to talk to you again about that explosion,' he started in again.

Julian turned towards him with reluctance. He let a little sigh escape.

'I know,' Nick said. 'I'm going on about it. But I've read that part of it over and over again. It looks to me as if that hard-hat changed his testimony.'

'He could have made a mistake, Nick.'

Julian could not conceal the exasperation in his voice, and Nick noticed the change in tone.

'If I can't talk to you about it, Julian . . .' Nick had raised his voice a little, finding his temper.

'It's not that,' Julian started. 'It's . . .'

'You think I should stop worrying about it,' Nick interrupted him. 'That's what everyone says.' He turned away from his view of Rebecca. 'You might be right,' he said, and he forced a laugh; he shrugged his shoulders. 'I'm sorry,' he went on, 'I don't seem to be able to shrug it off.'

Julian was about to explain himself, but Nick put up his hands. 'Case closed,' he said. 'Come on, let's get back to Rebecca. She's much better value than all this anyway.'

They walked back towards the house. Julian was tense, worried about his rebuff; but Nick was cheerful again. He put his arm around the younger man's shoulder and they joked about Richard. It was their favourite pastime since Nick no longer worked at Armadale.

Nick did not press Julian, fearing to lose his only remaining friend, and becoming more careful as he felt closer to a breakthrough. Julian's anxiety was lulled, and Nick was pleased to have managed it. He dropped the subject and they spent the rest of the day almost as they might have done in the past. They both knew it was different. Yet they enjoyed it.

Rebecca helped. She was an outsider. Both men were delighted to be with her and she enjoyed their attention. As they sat in the sun, with drinks in their hands, laughing at their own jokes, it seemed almost as if they were courting her. She flirted with them and the air tingled with sex.

When they left, well into the evening, Nick kissed Rebecca on the cheek. It was a gentle kiss, and lingered for just a second.

'Thank you for coming,' he said to her. 'I'd forgotten how nice it was.'

She did not ask him what had been nice, but she knew that, among all the things that Nick had missed in the last few months, a woman was one of them.

'I enjoyed it too,' she said simply.

Nick shook Julian by the hand. His grip was strong.

'Thanks,' he said. 'And there's one thing I want to ask you to do for me.'

Julian looked at him apprehensively.

'It's not that bad,' Nick said. 'Please. Get in touch with someone at Armadale Engineering? Find out about these control valves?'

Julian's face openly reflected the sinking feeling that had come over him. He got inside the car. Rebecca, who was standing by the open door on the driver's side, got in herself.

'Just academic interest,' Nick said quickly. He gave a little laugh. 'I just want to know how often it's happened in the past. That's all.'

Julian hesitated. 'All right,' he said finally.

'Thanks,' Nick said and closed the car door.

'I wish you'd forget about it,' Julian said through the open window.

'I know. Everyone does.'

Rebecca waved as she drove away, putting her arm out of the window, looking at him in her rear-view mirror.

Nick stood in front of the house, watching them go. He waved back at Rebecca and waited until they had disappeared before turning and striding back into the house.

Julian did not wave. He was torn in his feelings towards Nick. On the one hand, he had not found his former boss so untroubled and energetic since before the takeover bid was announced. Yet, his single-minded focus on Armadale and on the accident in the North Sea worried him. It seemed to Julian that it could only lead to failure and recrimination.

'I wish he'd give up on Armadale,' he said to Rebecca as they drove back into London. 'It's crazy.'

'He will,' she said. 'Give him time. He's lost everything.'

'That's why I wish he'd give it up.'

'Maybe he's right,' she said. 'Maybe something isn't right with that accident.'

'You Americans, you can always be trusted to find a conspiracy.'

'We're usually right, too,' she retorted. 'You guys pretend there aren't any. Official Secrets Act, stiff upper lip and all that shit. You repress everything over here, even conspiracies.'

'Since when did you start agreeing with him?' Julian asked. He looked over to her as she drove, and she smiled, lighting up her face.

'He's very attractive,' she said. It was true. Rebecca's allegiance had shifted again. She had fallen for Nick's charm and liked him all over again. Now she did not believe in this affair with Annie. Or perhaps she did not care.

'It always comes down to that,' he said, shaking his head in jest. 'Sex.'

'It's an important motivator. You know your problem?' she added. 'You're becoming too much of a company man. It's time you left Armadale and got yourself a decent job.'

'I will,' he said. After a moment, he added, 'Soon.'

Chapter Twenty

One evening, quite early, soon after Julian and Rebecca's visit, Nick was reading when the telephone rang. He was in the garden, sitting outside the open windows of the living-room, and he hurried to get the phone. He had begun to feel oppressed by his isolation and to welcome contact with the outside world. It was not just the panic of unemployment, although he was feeling it, it was more simply a need for human contact.

'Nick Bishop?' It was a woman's voice. For just an instant he searched his memory, and then he placed it.

'Annie?' he said.

'That's pretty good,' she said. She was flattered. 'I didn't think you'd recognize me so quickly.'

'How could I forget?' he said jokingly.

'I suppose it would be difficult,' she responded. 'I caused you a lot of trouble.'

'It was my doing,' he said. 'But I think we've had this conversation before. How are you? How nice to hear your voice.'

There was great charm in his enthusiastic honesty. Annie was glad she had called. She had been meaning to ring for several weeks, but she had put it off, unusually nervous about doing so.

'I saw your name in the paper,' she said.

'*My* name? Not again. What did it say?'

'Not much,' she laughed. 'The inquiry on that explosion in the North Sea. They just said you were Armadale's MD at the time.'

'I only get one paper these days. I didn't see it,' Nick said.

He wondered if the report would be published; it would be unusual.

'It was just a small thing.' There was silence. 'I wondered if we could have lunch,' she said finally. The memory echoed in both their minds.

'I'm not sure anyone's going to want to employ me,' he said. 'I'm not exactly in people's good books.'

'Oh, I don't know. You'd be surprised.' She had not rung him as a headhunter, but the mistake was natural.

'Let's have lunch, anyway.' Nick was already looking forward to it. 'You pick the time. I'm free every day.'

'How about tomorrow?'

He had not expected it so soon and he agreed immediately.

'Let's make it a public occasion, shall we?' he said. 'You don't mind?'

'Of course not. On the contrary.'

'Poetic justice, I think,' he said.

'Why not same time, same place then?'

There was a small mirror in the hall, just above the narrow table on which sat the telephone. Nick hung up and saw himself in it. He looked at his long, full beard, noticed the touches of grey.

Immediately he went upstairs, and began searching for a pair of scissors. Eventually, he found them in Sophie's dressing-table, next to a necklace of white beads that he had given her for Christmas several years before. She had never worn it much. She must have forgotten it in the drawer. Seeing the necklace, abandoned in the empty dressing-table, which still emitted the familiar smell of Sophie's perfume, made Nick pause in his rush to tidy himself up. He picked up the necklace and let its beads slide through his hands as if they were water. He thought about his eagerness to see Annie, was aware of his excitement. Was this an act of betrayal? He remembered how Sophie had sat at this mirror, completely naked, making herself up. From the other side of the room, he would watch her, enjoying it, his eye occasionally catching hers in the mirror; they would look at each other for a moment in communion and then return to what they were doing.

Nick shrugged his shoulders. He was doing nothing wrong. He dropped the necklace back into the drawer, picked up the scissors and strode into the bathroom. He began hacking at his beard.

He cut himself several times, his skin unaccustomed to the razor. But he was immaculate the following day as he made his way into London. He had dressed in his best dark-blue suit, the one he had always worn for annual general meetings, or for going out with Sophie on special occasions. His white shirt felt clean against his chest.

He drove into the City. He could have been going to work. Indeed, he parked the car in the Armadale car park. The guard looked at him in surprise when he saw Nick stop at the barrier.

'Got a place for me, Joe?' Nick asked.

'Take your pick, sir,' Joe answered, and waved him in. He watched Nick drive down into the darkness. He shrugged his shoulders. He liked Nick; the antagonisms of the takeover bid had not been explained to him.

Nick parked his car in a spot marked 'Visitors', then walked by the front of the Armadale building. He did not stop, but he noticed a couple of his former employees coming out as he went by. James Lamb and Julie Towers, he remembered their names. They had both worked in Richard's office in corporate finance. He saw them looking after him, in the way passers-by look at a film star they have recognized. Nick knew his presence would be reported. He found it amusing. There was some consolation to being a free agent, with no responsibilities other than getting to lunch on time.

Yet by the time he reached the restaurant, his mood had changed. He no longer felt as sprightly as he had; the re-run of that previous day had brought back memories which distilled bitterness even now. He looked serious and thoughtful when he approached the headwaiter, the same small, neat Italian with the polished skull who had greeted him last time.

At first, Annie thought he seemed as preoccupied as he had the first time. She sat waiting for him at the same table, her back to the wall. He was slightly thinner; yet he looked more robust too. His face was rugged from the fresh air, a little paler where the beard had been. His hair was longer, less under control. He did not look like the tired and troubled businessman she had first seen, his eyes bloodshot from lack of sleep.

She smiled at him as he followed the headwaiter towards her, and when Nick saw her, his face brightened. He leaned across the table and kissed her on both cheeks.

'You look very beautiful,' he said.

'And you look very healthy,' she answered. 'Where's the beard?'

'How did you know I had a beard?' he asked back, surprised.

'Word gets around,' she answered. 'I think someone called Alan Turner told me,' she added.

'Alan Turner,' Nick said with a smile. 'I wonder how he knew.' He paused, then said, 'I shaved it off.'

Gently, she reached her hands up to his face and touched one of the cuts on his chin with her finger. 'A pity.'

'Not really,' he said. 'I looked like a Victorian madman.'

'Like Charles Darwin,' she said with a smile.

He laughed. 'You remember,' he said. 'Since we met, I've visited his house. And read his books. But he wasn't mad at all.'

'But then, neither are you.' She said it looking him straight in the eyes. There was no coyness in her.

Now that they were together, they both knew why they had met. The pretence of a business meeting had disappeared. He held her gaze, but it was he who looked at the menu first. He was aroused and felt embarrassed by it.

'I'm hungry,' he said. 'Let's spend some money, shall we?' He looked up at her, composed again, game.

'Oysters and champagne, you mean?' she said and laughed. She had a dimple in her left cheek when she smiled.

'We're in May, I'm afraid,' he answered, infatuated with her. 'No "r" in May.'

'Caviare and lobster?' she responded.

'Vodka with the caviare, Chablis with the lobster and we can have champagne at the end instead of the beginning.' He turned to look for the headwaiter, who had miraculously appeared by Nick's shoulder, with his pad and pen poised for the order.

Thirty seconds he left them, beaming at the order, and they were alone again.

'Don't tell me you've got a job for me,' he said. 'I'm not sure I want a job.'

'Actually, I wasn't going to suggest a job.' She looked at him and smiled.

It was the way she said it, as much as the words, that excited him. Instinctively, he sat up.

'Well,' he said, clearing his throat, 'I'm glad that's dealt with.'

She looked at him more earnestly. 'How are you? Really,' she asked. 'People have been talking about you,' she added.

'What people?' He did not seem troubled by it, just faintly amused.

'A lot of different kinds, I don't remember all of them.' She paused. 'It's funny,' she went on. 'I'm afraid that whole affair did me a lot of good.'

'Why afraid?' he asked.

'I hate to flourish on your poison,' she said. 'But you know, being a headhunter and a woman, and now a femme fatale, I've become irresistible.'

'I can imagine,' he said.

'You men are such boys, really,' she said. 'So predictable. Everything's on the surface.'

'We're very simple and straightforward,' he said.

'Well, as far as I'm concerned,' she said, 'the rumour-mongers have got it wrong. You look all right to me.'

The caviare came. They ate with pleasure, relishing every mouthful, enjoying their recklessness.

'I've been living the life of a monk,' he said as he layered a thin piece of toast with the small shiny eggs. 'I'd forgotten about all this.' He proceeded to describe the period of his isolation, omitting nothing, with a mild self-deprecating humour.

At the end of the meal, over the champagne, she said to him, 'Are you sure you don't want a job?'

'Why? Have you got one?' he asked.

'No,' she answered. 'But I might be able to find one.'

He thought it over. 'Not yet, thank you,' he said.

They separated on the street, as they had done the first time. They had agreed to meet again the following week. Nick kissed her this time, he did not shake her hand.

'I wonder if anyone's watching me now,' he said to her.

'They're probably watching me,' she answered with a smile.

'Next week, then,' Nick said. 'I can't wait.'

When she had turned the corner, he turned away. He ambled back to his car, taking his time. He browsed in shops, went into St Paul's Cathedral and sat in a pew for a while. Eventually, he collected his car and drove home. He was suddenly aware that he had not made love for four months.

The morning of that second meeting, Nick woke early. He got out of bed immediately and dressed. By eight o'clock, he had had breakfast. He waited another half-hour, then rang Annie's office. She was not there, and he tried again every five minutes. Finally, on the fourth try, she answered.

'Can you take the afternoon off?' he asked her. The idea had only occurred to him late the night before. He was worried that she would not be able to.

'Yes,' she said and spent the next two hours cancelling her appointments. Her last appointment that day was with a new client and she did not want to cancel without due cause. There was only one reason that would do, so she asked her secretary to ring up in mid-afternoon and say that Annie had been taken ill and had had to go straight home.

'For Christ's sake, don't forget to make that call,' she had said again as she left for the day.

'I won't,' Mary, her secretary, said. She could not avoid a smile. She added, 'What if he rings you at home?'

'By then,' Annie said, 'who knows? I might be in hospital.'

They were lucky. It was another sunny day, the third in a row. After lunch, they walked from Covent Garden to St James's Park and mingled with the tourists who crowded the gardens. Children ran up and down the paths with their parents calling after them, trying to get them to look at the swans, or to stop bumping into people.

Nick and Annie walked in step; her arm held his, and, occasionally, as they swayed a little, they bumped against each other. They spoke only intermittently, concentrating on each other, on the proximity of their bodies, on their slight shortness of breath, on the acceleration of their heart beat. It was there, on the path that led to the Mall, that Annie suggested to Nick that they do what everyone had assumed they had done long ago.

'Let's go home,' she said.

He looked down at her.

'Let's,' he said.

As soon as they had closed the door of Annie's flat behind them, they leaned against it and kissed. She put her arms around his head as he bent towards her. Her body pressed against his and he could feel her small breasts on his chest as he held her. What happened next seemed to take place in one flowing, uninterrupted movement, from the door to the bedroom, to the bed. They separated and almost carried each other along to the bedroom. She led the way, moving backwards, undoing his tie as she went. She laughed as she pulled it off and lurched back a step. He reached for her, caught her. Again they kissed.

They were both smiling broadly as they reached the bedroom, conscious of the sexual exhilaration. They were bursting with it, unable to hold it back. Their arms bumped into each other, entwined as they undressed themselves and each other at the same time. He reached for her blouse and was undoing it from the top at the same time as she undid the bottom buttons. She pulled it off, let it drop on to the floor and had unclipped her bra before he could even reach it. He stood still for a second when her breasts were uncovered. He looked at them and, with his hands flirting by them, held her against him again and kissed her. She began to unhook his trousers, but then he took over. She was stepping out of her skirt in an instant. She was naked before he was, and was kissing his chest while he took his trousers off, bending down while trying not to bump into her. They laughed again. They did not bother to get into the bed, they lay on top of it and he was all over her, unable to contain himself any more. She moaned slightly as his mouth ran over her body. And then it was her turn. When he was on top of her, their faces were so close they could feel their breath. They moved slowly and made love oblivious to anything else.

Nick rediscovered love with breathlessness, and the passion was even more intense for the memories it brought back. He had forgotten; yet, being reminded of how it had been many years ago made it poignant as well. The last time he had felt this way had been with Sophie. He had never thought he would experience this again. Love was coming back to him with all the force of a dream.

Next day, Annie left Nick in bed as she went off to work late. She was tired; they had slept little that night. She showered and dressed in a hurry, then kissed him as she left. He put his arms around her and kept her near him, but she edged out of his hold and rushed off. He looked after her, and then went back to sleep.

Mary looked at Annie as she hurried in; it was clear enough what she had been doing for the last twelve hours. She felt a twinge of envy as she watched the effects of love on her boss.

'How was hospital?' she said as Annie was going into her office.

'You know how it is,' Annie said, looking back at Mary.

'Not much sleep. There are so many things going on. They wake you up every few hours to check on you. Feel you all over. Pump you full of stuff. Still, I feel much better.'

'You look much better,' Mary said.

'Well, thank you.' Annie went into her office and closed the door.

Nick woke up again two hours later. He got up and roamed around the flat, looking it over, nosing out as much as he could without actually prying. It was a large flat in Holland Park, and as he gazed out of the window of the drawing-room, which overlooked the back of the park itself, he wondered how close he was to Howard's Sheilah. He wondered what Howard would think now if he knew.

'Who cares?' he said aloud. He returned to his examination of the flat.

There were three large rooms, and a smaller one which Annie used as an office; a cluttered room, crowded with books and papers, and a small kneehole desk.

The desk had been Annie's mother's, and the only thing she had wanted to keep, apart from some jewellery, when her mother had died. She had asked for the desk when she and her two brothers had divided the inheritance. It was the last of the legacy. Their father had died a few years back and now that her mother had gone too, all that was left was being dispersed. It had been a friendly division, and her brothers had pressed more things on her. But she had wanted no more than the one piece of furniture. She placed it in her office, beneath a portrait of her father in his military uniform. That way she had one thing that reminded her of each of them. Their memory was uncluttered and fresh in her heart.

By contrast, the other rooms were sparely furnished. Each had one powerful element, with smaller details. So the bedroom was dominated by the bed, and behind it a painting of two people in a bed, only their heads visible under the sheets. The middle room, used primarily as a dining-room, had a simple black table in the centre of the room. Finally the drawing-room had a large comfortable sofa with a standing lamp at one end of it. There were other furnishings too, but they were secondary. A visitor needed to spend time looking at them carefully.

Over the next few days, while Annie was at work, Nick was to enjoy finding out about her through this cache of objects positioned around the rooms: photographs, scattered among prints, books that had spilled out of the small office into the bedroom, records in the drawing-room. There was enough there to occupy his time, when it was not taken up by Annie herself, who had needed no pressing to take some time off from work.

They had two weeks. It was a honeymoon.

They stayed indoors. Even though they were capable of enveloping themselves with privacy when they went out, closing out the world altogether, it was easier to do so by remaining in the flat. They had thought of flying off somewhere and leaving England behind, but then they decided against it. They preferred to lose themselves here, in London, for the moment. A trip abroad was for later, when life was being lived less intensely. Now it was unnecessary.

Annie had never married, although she had often been asked. She had resisted the early urge to settle down and have children, and now she found it difficult to find a man whom she might want to marry.

She had been in love before, but there was a freshness in her relationship with Nick. She wondered if it was because he was such an unusually passionate man, despite his formal exterior. The affairs that she had had before had been sexually charged and intense, but she had never felt this kind of seriousness and honesty before. She enjoyed being swept up in their embrace.

Nick savoured the joy of love with abandon. He occasionally stopped to wonder whether it was just sex, a new partner, a fresh spice, but he recognized enough of the symptoms of what he had felt fifteen years ago with Sophie. The memories brought pain along with them and he hated those moments. It was not just that they interfered with his present happiness, they reminded him that he was being unfaithful to Sophie. He felt ashamed of the emotions he was having, because they were not new. He recognized them and he had always believed and wanted to feel them only for Sophie. He exorcized them by remembering that he had been left, and left when he was innocent. Then he could throw himself back into Annie's arms with pleasure, which had the force of revenge added to it.

At the end of the two weeks, they felt like doomed lovers, forced by circumstances to part. That last Sunday seemed like the last day of a leave in wartime. It was only on the Monday, when Annie kissed him on her way out, that they realized that the world had not changed. They felt foolish.

'We're too old for this kind of thing,' she said to him.

'What do you mean?' he joked. 'This is my mid-life crisis. Bang on time.'

'Thanks a lot,' she said. 'I can think of better things to do than be the manifestation of your crisis.'

He put arms around her and kissed her.

'I can't,' he said.

Chapter Twenty-One

I

The affair with Annie was as much a cause of change as a sign of it. The day she returned to work, Nick went back to Downe. He had just settled to another quiet, idle day in Holland Park when suddenly he decided to pursue his own investigation of the accident on the oil platform. He would go to Scotland and see for himself.

He gathered the few things he had fetched from the country for his stay in London, and left. As soon as he got to Downe, he was on the phone to Scotland. He wanted to make sure he would be expected and that a trip off-shore could be arranged. He did not admit to the real purpose of his trip, which was to see for himself and in as much detail as possible what had happened to that control valve in the dehydration system. He knew that he would never have been allowed to go, if for no other reason than that the inquiry was over, that the men were buried, the platform was working again. The last thing Usoco wanted was a former managing director of one of their suppliers dredging up old disasters. In the North Sea oilfields, enough time was spent preventing new disasters.

Nick had therefore told Stephen Dayton, the head of public relations at Usoco, that he had decided to write a book about his experience as a managing director. He was at the moment doing a little memory-refreshing research and, since he had once visited an oil platform many years earlier, he had hoped he would be able to visit the platform again.

Stephen Dayton had no reason to doubt Nick. He knew he

was out of work, and therefore had time to write a book, if that was what he wanted to do. The trip was approved.

Nick rang Annie just before leaving. He was in the bedroom, his suitcase on the bed, packed.

'I'm going to Scotland,' he said.

'When?'

'Now.'

'Now,' she repeated. 'When did you decide this?'

'This morning,' he said. It was natural for him to act on his decisions. He did not feel it to be abrupt. He had done so little for so long that a positive action was revitalizing.

'Where are you going to stay?' she asked.

'Aberdeen.'

'Be careful,' she said.

'I'll ring you as soon as I get back.' He signed off, eager to get going.

That evening he landed in Aberdeen and took a room in an airport hotel. On previous visits to the city, he had stayed either in private homes or in the more comfortable country hotels on the Dee a few miles outside Aberdeen. For this trip, he had decided that the anonymity of an airport hotel was preferable either to the hospitality of friends, or even the more clubby country hotels. He did not know how long he would end up staying and he wanted to be alone to try and find out as much as he could before word got around that he was in town, and he was forced into calling on his acquaintances.

Nick's friends in Aberdeen were actually business acquaintances from his time at Armadale. But, unlike his Southern contacts, they lived far enough away from London not to have heard the more alarming rumours about Nick's state of mind. It was unlikely that they would have paid much attention to them anyway. The oil business is all-engrossing and up in Aberdeen, amidst the grey granite buildings, with oil rigs as familiar a part of the horizon as the green golf courses, they cared little for the cutthroat atmosphere of the City of London.

Nick did not stay in Aberdeen long enough for any of his precautions to prove important. The evening of his arrival, he got a call from Stephen Dayton who offered him a chance for a visit to the platform the following morning.

'We've got a place available,' Stephen said. 'And I have to go anyway. I'll escort you.'

Nick accepted immediately. His trip seemed to start well.

'Six thirty at the airport,' Stephen said. He laughed and added, 'I hope it's not too early for you. Plane leaves at seven. If it leaves on time. If it leaves at all.'

It left late. It was a beautiful June day. The aeroplane took off from Aberdeen's Dyce Airport and flew over the still waters of the North Sea. Conditions were completely different from what they had been at the time of the explosion. There was no wind, no rain; it was even warm.

Apart from Stephen, who was to accompany him during the whole of his visit, the plane was filled with workmen for the platforms: a new shift, a temporary maintenance man, an official visitor, a helicopter pilot. Nick sensed that he had entered a different existence, austere, teetotal, celibate, and purposeful. There was an intensity about life on the platform that he had noticed at every turn and which impressed him anew with its force. Nick sat by the window and looked down at the sea, across which flitted shadows and little bursts of foam. He said little during the hour-long trip. Stephen, a tall, thin man with curly reddish-brown hair, fell asleep early in the journey with his knees protruding slightly into the aisle. He woke only as they were making their descent on the Shetlands.

They landed at Sumburgh airport, on the southern tip of the islands. There was a simple power to the land. Surrounded by miles of water, and today by a cloud-free sky, it was marred only by the ugly, flat buildings of the airport. The light was particularly clear, sharpening the contours. When the engines died, everything was still with the soundlessness of the countryside. There was no hum surrounding it; on the contrary, there was an ambient silence. Life here seemed more intense and time had lost its urgency. The elements ruled.

The travellers had a long wait. They were placed in a bus and taken to a hotel on a rise beside the airport. After breakfast, he and Stephen went outside to wait for the bus to take them back. Nick looked out over a cove and then the expanse of blue water and thought that this might be a peaceful place to live.

'It's beautiful,' he said.

'It is today,' Stephen said. 'It can get pretty rough. I know what you're thinking,' he added, seeing Nick's yearning look. 'But you have to be an islander to live here.'

Nick imagined the map he had examined before coming and he thought that perhaps Stephen was right. This was in the middle of nowhere.

After a few more minutes, they piled back inside the bus and were returned to the airport to wait for the helicopter. Nick wondered who organized all this. Then he remembered that all these people were Usoco employees. This was a managed journey, part of an operation working to instructions and schedules, however loose these might be.

Finally their flight was announced. For the trip, Nick heaved himself into an orange wet-suit. It covered every part of his body and fit so snugly that he had to take off his shoes and wear them over the suit itself. He had to give his weight and, at last, they climbed into a small helicopter. The pilot, who was one of the passengers on the earlier aeroplane – or fixed-wing as a plane was more precisely named out in the field – prepared himself, examined his instruments and went over his checklist before taking off.

It was a dull and deafening flight. They reached the platform after an hour and a half. Nick saw it in the distance with its flag of flame licking at the sky from the gas-flare tower. They hovered down onto the roof. As soon as they disembarked, Stephen took Nick to the manager's room.

Once Nick had got his breath back, had relaxed after the

tensions of the journey, he realized the hopelessness of his quest. He had come hoping to discover facts that others, empowered to question, with knowledge of how to question, had failed to discover. Sitting in the manager's narrow office, listening to tales from off-shore, he felt lost and foolish. He said little as Stephen and the platform manager exchanged news. He would act like a writer, he thought. He would ask as many questions as he could, be as much a journalist as he could. It was the only way to make the journey valuable.

Once again they donned protective suits, red this time, and thick boots and went out to the working platform. The smell of crude oil, thick black and sickly, pervaded the atmosphere. Nick listened to the explanations of the mechanics of the platform. Occasionally he would ask a question which was somehow related to his own concern. He started gently enough. He asked how the platform had re-adapted to life after the explosion, how often there had been fatal accidents. He was answered with patient urbanity, by people accustomed to fielding the more morbid questions always asked of those who live in constant danger. Stephen told him that the explosion was the only fatality in seven years, since the opening of the platform in fact. He changed the subject with practised ease to the safety measures on the platform.

Nick's curiosity, of course, was not to be deterred. He was looking for answers. Eventually, circling the issue of general safety, of accidents as an abstract concept, was no longer enough. He had to become more specific.

In the module that housed the dehydration tower, Nick had to shout his questions, for there was a constant loud roar inside the module. They did not wear the ear protectors that they carried around their necks as they had earlier in the turbine modules, and Nick could guess at the fatigue of working with this constant noise.

He asked about the control valve, how it worked, what had caused the explosion. With each question, the answers became more guarded. The platform engineer, a red-cheeked, broad-shouldered man, obviously resented them.

'At the time of the explosion,' Nick asked, 'who last inspected the valve?'

There was no immediate answer. The platform engineer looked over to Stephen. Nick did not know how to interpret the look; certainly, the engineer was irritated. Nick looked at Stephen, unable to decipher the silent answer that had been given.

The platform engineer never did answer Nick's question. He stood up and suddenly shouted over the din, 'I have to check something, I'll meet you outside.' He was gone in an instant. Stephen led Nick back outside.

At this level, the module floor, the platform was circled by a narrow grilled gangway. Above them was the drilling floor and, above that, the accommodation floor. Yet they were still three hundred feet above the water. Nick looked down and saw through the metal grille the dark waves lapping at the platform legs. He held on tightly to the railing, which reached his waist, fighting the dizziness that he knew was not far from the surface.

'What are you doing here, Nick?' asked Stephen.

Nick could not help but wonder if Stephen was being menacing. The two men stood facing each other. The sun shone brightly, was even warm. Nick looked out to the distance, where he could see other platforms not too far away. He felt so precariously poised over the void beneath him that to be questioned about his real intentions brought a moment of panic. He decided not to hide what he wanted. There was no point in dissimulation.

'I wanted to find out about the explosion,' he said.

'That's not what you told me,' Stephen said. He spoke sharply, not attempting to conceal his anger.

'You wouldn't have let me come,' Nick said, looking straight at him now, standing tall, almost defiant.

'You're absolutely right,' Stephen said. 'And it's over. As of now. This trip is cancelled.'

'Are you afraid I might find something out?' Nick said. He regretted it almost immediately. He saw the hurt pride and the indignation in Stephen's face.

'I don't know what gives you the right to come out here and slander me,' he said. 'We've always treated you right. I've got nothing to hide. Be sure of it.'

'I'm sorry,' Nick said. 'I didn't mean that.'

'Then what did you mean?' Stephen said, but did not wait for the reply. 'Come on, we're going.'

He led Nick away, hurrying up the metal stairway. They climbed to the top floor of the platform, and Nick saw himself being distanced by the more experienced man. Stephen did not even bother to hold on; he almost ran up the stairs. Nick tried it a couple of times, but could not do it.

When he reached the floor that housed the living quarters, Stephen had already taken his protective gear off, and was waiting impassively for Nick to do the same. His whole countenance warned Nick not to speak, and it was in silence that they donned their safety suits, climbed back on to the landing square, got back into the helicopter and flew off the platform.

Five hours later they were back in Aberdeen. Stephen had only spoken to give instructions. He carried his indignation with him through the trip like a valuable suitcase.

At the airport in Aberdeen, the two men walked through the arrival gate, and Stephen was about to walk off without saying anything. Nick called him back.

'Stephen,' he called.

Stephen turned and faced him. Nick walked over to him.

'I'm sorry I deceived you,' he said.

Stephen was about to reply, but Nick put his hand up to stop him.

'Please,' he said. 'Let me explain myself. Two men were killed in that explosion. You know those valves are rigorously checked. People were vague about who checked the valve last. And when. That explosion took place just when my company, who happened to supply that particular piece of equipment, was itself in trouble. That's a lot of coincidences. I just wanted to check them.'

'You are out of line,' Stephen said.

'That explosion cost me my company.'

'Your sex life cost you your company, Nick Bishop,' Stephen said with an even, controlled anger, then turned and left.

Nick had learned nothing, nothing specific. But he had got his doubts in some sort of order, something he had not achieved before. By being placed into the real context of the platform, he had made them more concrete. Now he knew what he was talking about. But he left Aberdeen embarrassed by what had happened, wishing he had been able to avoid the confrontation. And he had lost another friend; he had few left. Yet he was single-minded enough to feel that a little further isolation was a price worth paying for information.

On the plane home, he thought about Stephen's parting words. To have someone believe that Andrews' rumour had been true no longer enraged him as it had in the past. Perhaps it was because he and Annie now made it true. Something else nagged at him, though. He had lied to get on to that platform, lied without hesitation. Yet, when it came to his meeting with Annie, he had expected and demanded of people that they believe his version of the facts, however incredible it seemed to them. Could he demand that people believe him if he could lie to them so easily? Had he changed? Or were some lies justifiable? Was the posing of that question itself a sign of change? Nick did not attempt to answer those questions yet.

He returned to Downe, wondering about the present state of his life. He lived alone in a small village just outside London, seeing his children rarely, his wife not at all. He had no work, and no prospect of work. He had not looked for any, and that worried him. As he examined himself, he seemed to have become a man of obsessions. Only two things ruled his life at the moment. Annie, a recent obsession, and with whom he found himself as infatuated as a schoolboy, and Armadale, which he still regarded as rightfully his. Try as he might, and he had begun to think that he should try harder, he found it difficult to be interested in anything else.

As soon as he came in the door, he rang Annie. She was at work.

'Can I ring you back?' she said.

'Can I see you tonight?' he had to ask.

'Yes,' she said. 'I'll ring you back.'

They had hung up, elated at their own passion. It was something they had both assumed would never happen again.

Nick rang Julian next. Since leaving Armadale, he had never rung Julian at work. Now he thought nothing of it as he dialled the number. Only when a woman's voice answered Julian's phone with 'Mr Campbell's office,' did he think of being circumspect.

'Is Julian Campbell in, please?' he said.

'He's in a meeting,' she answered. 'Would you like to leave your name, please?'

'Could you just tell him Nick called. Thank you.' And he hung up before she could ask for his surname.

Nick unpacked and waited for Julian to call back.

'Where have you been?' said Julian when he rang back forty minutes later. 'I've been ringing you for more than two weeks. I was getting worried about you.'

'Seems to be the story of my life at the moment,' Nick said. 'I've been busy,' he went on. 'Been to Scotland. Which is why I rang.'

He told him of his trip and of the way he had been bounced off the platform by Stephen Dayton.

Julian said little. He could not understand Nick's persistence but he could not help admiring it. He recognized that old fire in Nick's voice which he had missed over the last half-year. Nick's energy was back. He even managed to be light-hearted as he narrated his Scottish excursion.

'To be found out 300 feet above sea level is pretty unsettling, I can tell you,' he said. 'Especially when you're staring down at the water. I wondered if you'd found out anything from Engineering?' he added without a pause.

'Not much,' answered Julian. 'They did say there'd never

'Never?' Nick said.

'No, never,' said Julian. 'But they also said it could happen. Just when it did too. About six to nine months after leaving the factory. If there was a fault, that's when it would surface. Because of all the checks,' Julian added. And he went on, since Nick said nothing, 'I'm afraid that's it.'

'It's never happened, but it's not impossible.' Nick repeated it for himself.

'That's right.'

'Do you still see Jim Ferrar?' Nick asked. It seemed like a tangent, but it was not.

'Jim? Not much. Once or twice.'

'Still living in Barnes?'

'As far as I know,' answered Julian.

Jim had got a new job right after leaving Armadale, as everyone had foretold, with the company that had been offering him a slightly higher salary to leave Armadale before it had been lost to Corpcom.

Nick was about to sign off, when Julian said, 'Nick. Jim was pretty unhappy when he left.'

'Thanks for telling me,' Nick said. 'I'll be in touch.'

Nick knew what Julian meant. At the end of Nick's tenure at Armadale, Jim, usually friendly to Nick, had been cold and distant. Nick knew that he too had believed Andrews' smear.

He rang Jim at home. At first, Jim remained distant and Nick kept to the point. He briefly described the facts of the accident as it had been described in the inquiry report, and what he had just learned from Julian.

'How can I help you?' Jim asked, as if he were not interested in helping.

'I want to know how likely such an accident is,' Nick said.

'I'm not an engineer,' Jim said. 'I know about computers.'

'You started as an engineer. You know a lot about everything.'

Jim was not impressed by the compliment. But he had always liked Nick's directness, which was like his own. Nick spoke rapidly, not wasting time on niceties, the manner Jim remembered from the good days at Armadale. He was not a man who held a grudge for long, and he had no real grudge anyway. He softened.

'It's not impossible, but it's not very likely,' he said.

There was a silence. And then Nick said, 'What does that mean, then?'

'I suppose somebody could have tampered with it.' Jim said this without any joy. He was suggesting that the death of those two men could have been manslaughter. Even murder.

'On the platform?' Nick asked.

'Or in the factory. That's the significance of the six to nine months. It could have happened either place. If it did,' Jim added.

'Thank you,' said Nick. 'How's the new job?' he said as an afterthought.

'I'm getting used to it. Same thing really.'

There was a pause. Neither man hung up.

'One thing, Jim,' Nick said, and then he did not know how to say that he had been innocent. He suddenly felt self-serving. So he said, 'It doesn't matter. Nothing.'

Jim had had time to consider what had happened. It had softened his rigidity; he knew the loss of Armadale had embittered his reactions. Nick, like all of them, had been a victim.

'I know,' he said to Nick.

Nick believed him.

He hung up and the word 'sabotage' echoed in his mind. It frightened him. He had not actually been looking for this, even though it justified his sense that there had been wrongdoing. He had never dreamed it would be something like this.

'Would Andrews really resort to it?' he asked himself.

2

Roger was furious when he heard of Nick's visit to the oil platform.

Peter had been told of it by Richard, who had mentioned it

in passing one day. Stephen Dayton, outraged by Nick's visit when he had discovered its real purpose, had alerted Richard. As far as Stephen was concerned, Armadale was no longer any of Nick Bishop's business. That Nick should be snooping around behind people's backs seemed wrong to him. He rang Richard as the new managing director of Armadale.

Richard did not fear Nick. What he actually thought was that Nick had abused the privilege of being given the report to read.

'That's what happens when you do someone a favour,' he said to Julian, tacitly reproving him for having suggested giving the report to Nick. 'Did you know he was going to Scotland?' he asked.

'No, sir,' Julian answered. Again he was not lying. Julian was amazed that it never occurred to Richard that his own behaviour during the takeover had been reprehensible. It seemed that he found it easy to justify his own actions and did not spend time worrying what others thought of him. He was blessed with a wonderfully thick skin, so that he had seen no reason to conceal the fact that it was he who had authorized giving a copy of the inquiry to Nick.

'The man's a complete idiot,' Roger was raging. 'What the hell's he doing giving out that report?'

'It did say it was accidental,' said Peter, always calm when Roger had lost his temper.

They were in Roger's office. Peter sat in one of the armchairs, his eyes following Roger as he paced restlessly around the office.

'So what?' he said. 'It's elementary business sense. You don't give out documents like that unless you have to. What if the inspectors were wrong and Bishop found out about it?' Roger stopped his marching to stare down at Peter.

Peter said nothing at first. Then very softly, he spoke, 'Of course. The inspectors are wrong.'

Roger looked at Peter, just as enraged to hear that from him. 'Don't act stupid,' he said. 'I didn't mean that and you know it.'

Peter shrugged. He realized that Roger was more angry at Richard than anything else. Nick had discovered nothing, and had been thrown off the platform. They could not have asked for more.

'How dangerous is he?' Roger became practical again.

'Not very.'

'Well, could he become dangerous then?' Roger asked. Peter's nonchalance annoyed him. It smacked of carelessness.

'For heaven's sake, Roger,' Peter rose now. He had had enough of this game. 'Of course he could *become* dangerous. Anybody could. Two men died in that explosion.'

'Good,' Roger said; he had heard what he needed to hear. 'Then, let's make sure we keep an eye on the problem.'

'I'll make sure we know if he goes back to Aberdeen,' said Peter. 'That should be enough.'

They abandoned the subject, shrugging off the problem for the moment.

Chapter Twenty-Two

I

Soon after his return from Scotland, Nick began looking for a new job. Annie kept an eye out for him and would return home with suggestions. It was the cause of their first row. Having taken on the task, it became important to Annie that she find Nick a job. It suddenly mattered to her that Nick should have a job; she began to feel that he had been on an extended holiday and that it was time he put an end to it. It irritated her when he rejected some of her suggestions. It was a personal and professional affront. She wondered whether Nick really wanted to work.

'You can't sit around here for the rest of your life,' she said to him one evening in mid-July after he had just declared another position unsuitable.

They were in Annie's drawing-room, before supper. Nick was sitting on the sofa, leaning forward over the coffee table, looking down at the descriptive sheet that lay on it. Annie was sitting on the arm of the sofa, holding a glass of white wine across her lap; she had been watching him look over the paper with eager anticipation.

'This is a very small company in the Midlands, for heaven's sake,' Nick replied heatedly. 'I'm not "sitting around".'

'You could have fooled me,' she responded. She stood up suddenly and spilt some of the wine on her dress. 'Shit,' she exclaimed and urgently began wiping the liquid with her hand.

He looked up at her; her movements were brisk, angry. Suddenly she glared at him and said, 'What's wrong with the Midlands?'

'For one thing, you don't live there,' he said after a pause.

She faced him, ready for a fight. But he was smiling affectionately at her. He had intended the remark to defuse the situation; looking up to find her battling spilled wine had made him aware of the brewing quarrel. He had not wanted a fight; certainly the job did not merit it.

'What are you laughing at?' she said in a fury.

'It's just a job, Annie. I'll look for another one.'

'Are you sure?' she asked, still angry.

'I promise.'

He stood up and put his hands on her shoulders. 'I promise,' he repeated.

'Sometimes I think you've just given up,' she said, looking up at him.

'I've just started looking. I haven't given up.'

'You haven't worked in seven months. It's not going to look good.' She was concerned for him, afraid that he was aiming too high.

He knew what he wanted though. He had not told her all that he was looking for; he did not want to upset her.

'Another month isn't going to hurt,' he said. 'I'm not a hot property, let's face it. Let me make the right choice, then. I'm still all right for money.'

She seemed unconvinced, but she did not argue any more.

'Perhaps you should recommend a headhunter for me to see,' he said with no emotion, as if he meant it, and waited for her reaction. He could not help smiling when it came.

'Are you saying I can't find you a job?' She was outraged.

He laughed. 'I'm sure you can,' he said. 'I just don't want you to any more. Ever since we started looking, we've done nothing but quarrel. I don't want to spend our time together fighting over whether I should take this or that job.'

'You mean I'm "personally involved"?' she asked and leaned against him. She slipped her hand inside his shirt, running it over his chest. She kissed his lips. Then she stood on tiptoe and put her mouth to his ear.

'Let's go to bed,' she whispered.

He put his arms around her and lifted her up. He swung her around to grab her under the legs. She was heavier than he thought and he faltered.

He lost his balance and fell, bringing her down with him. They laughed as they landed on the floor. He kissed her and she put her arms around his neck and held him. They made love there instead.

Annie stopped looking for work for him. Occasionally, the cloud of her doubt hung over them and still Nick kept his intention secret. But it was better that way. They had fun again.

They spent most of their time together at Annie's flat, with an occasional excursion to Downe at the weekend. During the week, Annie often worked till eight or 8.30. Nick would cook the evening meal. Cooking was a new skill he had acquired since Sophie had left. Forced on him by necessity, he had grown to enjoy it. As for Annie, she loved coming back and eating a meal she had not had to cook.

'It's such a luxury,' she said one evening to Mary.

'What does he cook?' she asked, laughing. 'Pasta, I bet. All men love to cook pasta. It's so easy.'

'Not Nick,' Annie said. 'He cooks all sorts of complicated things.' She smiled and added, 'He's found this wonderful cookbook and he follows every direction to the letter. It's rather sweet. Last night, he made *canard aux cérises*. It was delicious.'

'You're making me jealous,' Mary said. 'That's what I need. A wife.'

Annie laughed, but it reminded her that Nick had nothing better to do.

One evening, they were at home eating another of Nick's meals: another coq au vin; he was trying to perfect it. He had found the sauce for the one he had made for Julian and Rebecca not rich and dark enough.

'I think it's almost right,' he was saying after a few mouthfuls.

The telephone rang. Annie got up from the table to answer it. A man's voice asked for Nick. She hesitated, surprised. This was the first time Nick had received a telephone call at her house.

'I'm sorry,' the man said. 'Nick Bishop. Is he there?' Annie did not recognize the voice.

'Who's speaking, please?'

'Howard Hicks. I'm a friend of his.'

Annie knew of Howard. Nick had told her of his friend, and of his behaviour – his betrayal – during the takeover. Like Sophie, Annie was not sure that Nick had been as betrayed as he felt, but she had said nothing. It was not her fight.

'Hold on,' she put the phone down and went into the dining-room. 'It's for you,' she said to Nick.

'Who is it?' he asked. No one knew of his presence here.

'Howard,' she said.

'Howard,' he repeated. 'Howard Hicks?'

She nodded. He got up, dropping his napkin on the table.

'How did he know I was here?' he muttered as he went to the phone.

'Nick. I'm sorry to bother you.'

'What is it?' There was a trace of worry in Nick's voice. He wondered for a moment if something had happened to Sophie. If something had happened to the boys, Sophie herself would have rung.

'I've been trying to reach you for about a week,' Howard sounded embarrassed to have had to call him at Annie's. 'You haven't been home.'

'Not much.'

'I'd like to talk to you about something,' Howard said.

'Go ahead.' Nick was guarded.

There was a pause. 'I think maybe it would be better in person,' Howard said hesitantly.

'What's the matter? Can't you tell me over the phone?' Nick would prefer not to have to meet Howard. It would only be an awkward get-together, with Howard trying to pick up the pieces and Nick unable to oblige.

'I could, I suppose,' Howard stuttered, 'I'd rather not. It's not that secret but it's . . .' he hesitated. 'It's just complicated. It's about a job, actually.'

'A job?' Nick could not resist being interested. 'For whom?'

'Well, for you, of course,' Howard was pleased not to be rebuffed. 'Are you interested?'

'We can meet at the club,' said Nick.

'At the club,' Howard said. 'Yes, yes. That would be nice.' He was delighted.

They arranged to meet the following day. Nick wondered what Howard had come up with. He hung up and went back to the dining-room. Annie had been picking at her food, listening to the conversation, trying to figure out what was being said. She looked up at him, the questions evident on her face.

'Howard's got a job for me,' Nick told Annie. 'Comic, isn't it?'

They met in the usual place, in the small room upstairs, by the fireplace. Nick, this time, was not standing at the mantel. He was in one of the armchairs, reading a newspaper, waiting for Howard. As Howard came up to him, Nick welcomed him perfunctorily.

'I'm sorry we can't have lunch,' he said. 'I've got to be at Downe by about two.'

'No matter,' Howard said, not believing him.

Nick was not a good liar. He had been unconvincingly abrupt about his statement. Howard knew all about lying. He could tell a lie from anybody but a master. Yet Howard knew he should not expect immediate forgiveness from Nick. They could not return to normal as if nothing had happened.

'Next time, perhaps,' he said and sat down.

'Drink?' Nick asked.

'Bloody Mary,' Howard said. 'Haven't had one of Harry's Bloody Marys for a long time.'

Nick looked around for someone, then decided to order himself. He went out and returned in a few seconds.

'On its way,' he said.

For a moment, they sat in silence, each wondering how to start. They had not met like this for almost nine months.

'How did you know where to find me?' Nick asked.

Howard laughed awkwardly. 'It wasn't very difficult, I'm afraid,' he said. 'It's not exactly a secret.'

'Does Sophie know?' Nick asked anxiously.

Howard wanted to avoid this subject. He remembered their last conversation. 'I don't know,' he said. 'I doubt it.'

There was another pause, and again Nick broke the silence with a direct question. 'What did you want to see me about?' he asked.

It was Howard who had come with the offer of a job; yet, oddly, it was he who found himself in the position of supplicant.

'It would mean a move,' he started at the end. 'To Edinburgh.'

Nick shrugged and said, 'Go on.'

It was an odd sales pitch. With an apologetic air, Howard described an ailing Scottish company, a large, diversified company, but with too many investments in oil. The company had suffered badly from the drop in the price of oil; management had been slow to react to the crisis.

'Essentially, they're looking for a new MD,' he said in conclusion.

'What's the name of it?' Nick asked.

'Faulkner. Faulkner Industries,' Howard answered. 'Have you heard of it?'

Nick shook his head. 'It's not private, is it?' he asked.

'No, no,' Howard said, 'plc.'

Nick considered what he had been told, looking into his drink absent-mindedly. Howard watched him in silence, hoping Nick would not reject the job out of hand.

Nick looked up. 'Are you offering me the job?' he said to Howard.

'Not exactly,' Howard laughed awkwardly. 'I can't do

that. But I think the board would hire you if we put your name to them.'

'Desperate, are they?'

'I wouldn't say that.' There was another gurgle from Howard. 'I'm sorry. I didn't make it sound very attractive, did I? But they're in Scotland, you know. London isn't the be all and end all up there.' He paused, hesitated almost, 'You've got a pretty good reputation.'

'Oh, thank you,' Nick said with bitter sarcasm.

'You're a difficult bastard,' Howard said. 'You know what I mean.'

'I know what you mean,' said Nick. He added, 'Tell me. How come you're telling me about this. What's your connection?'

There was mistrust in Nick's voice. Howard wondered if he would always hear that tone from now on.

'I know the company pretty well,' he said. 'I used to be on the board. Until Corpcom took me over.' He paused, as if he had mentioned a dead relative, and continued, with a twisted smile, 'I had to resign, you see. A conflict of interest.'

'Really,' Nick could not resist the sarcasm.

'After the takeover, not before it,' Howard said forcefully, unwilling to accept the blame Nick was placing onto him. They looked at each other, locked in antagonism.

'When would it start?' Nick asked, breaking the tension.

'When could you move?' Howard said.

'Immediately.'

'It won't be that quick,' Howard apologized again. 'I'll get it moving.'

'Great.' Nick drained his drink.

Howard saw it as the moment to leave. He placed his empty glass on the low table next to him and pulled himself out of the seat. He looked down at Nick, who was still seated. Nick looked well: fit, energetic. Howard wondered what Annie was like. He had never met her. Maybe he would soon.

'It's not the best job in the world,' he said. 'But it's a challenge, I think.'

'Thank you,' Nick had finally said it, a reluctant expression of gratitude, polite, not warm.

'I'm glad you agreed to get together,' Howard said. Still he did not move away. He was waiting for something, a hand-shake perhaps.

Nick saw it and rose. He made an effort, patted Howard's elbow. 'I need the work,' he said. 'Let me know.'

Howard left. After he had turned the corner and disappeared, Nick sat down again. He felt sorry for Howard. He knew he could not give him the old affection again. It was as if the one breach of trust had released all the nettles that Nick felt pricked by when he saw or thought of Howard and which affection had been able to disregard. He realized that, even as he felt sorry for Howard, he despised him also.

Howard stood outside the club for a few moments. He was considering where to go for lunch. He decided against his club; the food was not good enough. There was an Italian restaurant nearby, but he did not want pasta; and he could not go into an Italian restaurant and not have a pasta dish. Japanese was too austere, Indian too spicy and both were too marginal for today.

He hesitated, changed his mind and chose the Italian restaurant. It was nearby and he could just have a little *linguini con le vongole* as a starter, which would satisfy him. As he walked the few hundred yards, he decided on the rest of his meal: sautéed sweetbreads with mushrooms, an escarole salad, and, because his meeting with Nick had gone well, a zabaglione to finish. A bottle of Orvieto and an espresso would round it off nicely. He walked a little faster. He was hungry.

In the restaurant, decorated in sickly cream-coloured wall-paper and maroon carpets, with waiters in mustard-yellow tail coats, he sat on his own, watching the clientele: a very wealthy group of people, businessmen, women with pearl necklaces and hats, a father with his six-year-old son, who did not want to eat the food he had been given.

A waiter opened the bottle of wine and poured a little of it in Howard's glass. Howard tasted the wine and approved it. His glass was filled. He took a large gulp and savoured it.

He was very pleased. Nick had agreed to take the job. He could have been friendlier about it, but he was a serious bastard; he would relax eventually.

Howard had another reason to be pleased. A few days ago, he had had a telephone conversation with Roger. It was after Nick's trip to Aberdeen.

'He's been snooping around, Howard,' Roger had said. 'I don't like it.'

'I'm very sorry, Roger,' Howard had responded, quite unmoved by Roger's state of mind. 'But I don't see what I can do about it. I'm not his nanny.'

'I just wondered if you could ask him about it,' Roger said, already regretting the conversation. 'You know, check up on him.'

'I can't do that,' Howard had said, astounded that Andrews would ask him to. 'I'm not a spy.'

From Roger's point of view, Howard had taken sides already. After all, Howard had worked for him.

'I'm not asking you to spy on him,' he had said, irritated by Howard's show of sensitivity. 'Ask him straight out if that'll make you feel better.'

'And then tell you?' asked Howard.

'Yes.'

'That would be the same thing,' Howard enjoyed being so upright with Andrews.

'I hadn't noticed that you were so particular in the past.'

'I'm sorry. Even I have standards.'

Roger had hung up, furious at being defied. He wondered if Howard would prove a problem. When he had calmed down, he remembered what he himself had told Peter: Howard would do the moral thing if given the opportunity. Roger had just given him that opportunity. He kicked himself for it.

To Howard, therefore, this little lunch was a celebration, a pat on the back for success on two fronts. Not only had he thwarted Roger but he had carried out a back-handed strike at him. He felt a personal sense of justice in his being able to offer Nick the job at Faulkner Industries. What Howard had not told Nick, was that he had been happy to resign from Faulkner's board, to give up the position and the money. Roger had promised him an executive position within Corpcom itself, including financial compensation for any loss of income. Howard had obliged, he remembered with embarrassment, and had helped build a trap designed for himself, for Roger had never stuck to his side of the bargain. He had wanted control of Howard and had got it. When Roger had seen that he need not give more away, he had not. Howard had been powerless and had had to accept the inevitable. It was gratifying for him now that he could be subversive in a small way.

Howard also hoped that, by his action, by giving Nick a new opportunity, he was redeeming himself for his past lack of action. Nick had told Howard that there had been betrayal. He hoped, naïvely, that this would lead to forgiveness.

2

The board of Faulkner Industries appointed Nick to be the new managing director within a month. Although it had depended on an interview, Howard had not expected any difficulty. He had made sure that they wanted Nick before approaching him. He would not have done it otherwise.

The interview took place in London. Nick was taken out to lunch by Michael Hyde, the non-executive chairman of the board of Faulkner. Michael Hyde was a retired managing director himself. He had run a company that made prefabricated housing modules for the North Sea oil-platforms and which had been bought a few years back by Faulkner, when the price of oil was more than $20 a barrel. He was a handsome man of sixty-seven, with white hair and hazel eyes that shone brightly at Nick as they talked. He had a slight Scottish lilt to his public-school accent.

The two men liked each other. They were both straight-forward and they recognized like-minded souls.

Nick made one condition only: he wanted to be chairman and chief executive. Nick addressed the issue at the end of the meal, when they had already discussed Nick's trip up to Edinburgh.

'That's my job you're after,' Michael Hyde said. He did not seem upset.

'I'm afraid I am,' Nick said. 'I prefer to be my own boss.'

'You would be. I wouldn't interfere.'

'It's what I'm used to,' Nick went on. He felt he was being tested, not fought. 'A psychological necessity. And, from what you've been telling me, I don't see that Faulkner needs a figure-head.'

'We'll put it to the board, then,' Michael Hyde said. 'I agree with you. I've always felt the same.'

A week after that meeting Nick visited Edinburgh and met with the full board. The discussions were perfunctory and everybody knew it. Since Michael Hyde himself saw no reason not to step down and become just a board-member, the others saw little cause for opposition.

A month later Nick would be in Edinburgh.

Nick knew that his life had changed again.

Back in Downe, as he prepared to leave for Scotland, packing everything he owned – his personal belongings, not what he regarded as communal property, which he was leaving to Sophie – he was aware of his own impatience and re-discovered optimism. It was as unconditional as it used to be, even if not as all-embracing; it was optimism limited to the immediate future and to the opportunity that had presented itself. That was all, but he marvelled at his own life over the last eight months; expressed on a graph, it could have represented currency fluctuations as readily as his own emotional ones.

His standing in the outside world also changed as soon as

his appointment to Faulkner was announced. It was no more than the normal line in the *Financial Times* appointments box, but it was read. His telephone began to ring again. The voices at the other end were friendly, conciliatory, enthusiastic and a lot of them were relieved.

'Nick Bishop had come back to the fold,' they expressed. 'All is forgotten and forgiven.'

His favourite message of congratulations was from Richard, who sent him a short note. It ended with the words: 'Good luck. And no hard feelings, I hope.'

Nick laughed aloud when he read that. He wondered why so many people could believe that there would be no 'hard feelings', sometimes after the worst of occurrences. He remembered, at school, having to shake hands with his headmaster, who had just beaten him with a cane.

'The gentleman is a masochist,' Nick thought. 'It's absurd.'

Before leaving for Scotland he had two immediate problems to deal with. Annie and Sophie. And with Sophie came the children. Emotionally they were a different problem, but he knew that they could not come with him to Scotland. Nick would not receive custody when he and Sophie were divorced. In his mind, divorce was an inevitable fact. And, in truth, he did not want custody; so he never really considered Alistair and John separately from Sophie.

He saw Sophie first. The met in Regent's Park, by the open-air theatre. To met in the house in Downe might have been logical, but neither Nick or Sophie had wanted to do that. Sophie had vetoed organizing the household in Hampstead so that they could be alone.

He drove in to the Inner Circle just as drops of rain began misting the windshield. He parked the car just outside the tall iron gates of Queen Mary's gardens and walked quickly towards the theatre. They had chosen it without thinking, because they knew it from twenty years ago. Their first summer together, before they were married, they had gone to watch Shakespeare there.

It was raining hard by the time they met, sheets of water

which, under normal circumstances, might have postponed a get-together in Regent's Park. Neither of them had wanted to delay this meeting. They met under umbrellas and rushed to the shelter of a small shed with an overhanging roof which would keep them dry. They stood there listening to the rain and looking out on to the deserted park.

'We should have been able to find *somewhere* to talk,' Sophie said. It was almost unbearable to her that they had had nowhere to go. There was no neutral ground. Everyone had taken sides.

'At least it's private,' he said.

She turned abruptly to face him. She wondered what he needed to say that was so private, and feared what that might be.

Nick had changed again since the last time she had seen him. He had shaved his beard. He was leaner than when they had lived together, healthier-looking, more robust. She also noticed that his energy had returned. He had always been full of energy. It was, of course, as simple as that he was no longer depressed. It showed. She thought that perhaps he looked harder, but she could not be certain.

'Do you remember coming to see *Titus Andronicus*?' he said.

'Yes,' she said sullenly. 'I didn't like it.'

'Not many people do.'

They said nothing for a while. Both were remembering their happiness.

'What did you want to say that's so private?' Sophie spoke first once again.

He told her about the job in Scotland. Instinctively, without thinking of what its implications might be, she was glad for him. 'So that was why he's emerged,' she thought. Before she could focus on his moving north, he spoke again.

'I think we should get a divorce,' he said. He did not look at her, but faced straight out, towards the rain.

She stared at him. The move might have been a confirmation of their separation, but a divorce was something else. As far as she was concerned, it confirmed his affair with Annie. Of that she was certain.

'You are sleeping with that woman,' she said. It was unbearable. He said nothing, and she was quick to continue, 'You lied to me.'

'I didn't.' He faced her now, adamant in his denial.

'What do you call it then?' She hated feeling so powerless, so much at his mercy.

'This thing with Annie started months after you left. In May.'

'Well, it was announced in January,' she said. Her head was down; she was trying as hard as possible to avoid tears.

'That was a lie, Sophie.'

In the very emotion of the moment, Nick realized how incredible it all sounded. He would not have believed it himself had he heard it.

'Sophie,' he tried to explain, 'in January, I had seen Annie once in my life. I was not having an affair with her. I saw her again in May. That's when it started.'

She was crying, shaken by months of despair and loneliness, watching her whole life discarded, smashed, like an empty glass, with a throwaway gesture. It was too much for her to understand or to bear. She felt cheated, lied to, betrayed. She could not believe that this affair had not started when it had been announced. She walked out of the shelter.

'Sophie,' he called after her, trying to stop her.

She waved him away with her arm, not turning back, 'Stay away from me,' she shouted at him and walked on in the pouring rain, heading home.

That was their sad, bitter farewell. Sophie refused to see him again. She spoke to him on the telephone to make the necessary practical arrangements, but she would not meet him in person.

Nick saw Alistair and John before he went to Edinburgh. He went back to seeing them once a week, something they had not done after he and Annie had started spending so much time together. They came to Downe. He was ashamed at the missed opportunities of the last several months, of all the days they might have spent together and had not.

'We don't see you very often,' Alistair said. 'Why not?'

'I don't know,' he answered, and he felt pathetic for not knowing and for having done it. 'I don't know,' he said again and he embraced both boys together.

They hugged him back with passion. Later, he wondered if it was not a measure of the distance that had grown between them, or indeed that he had allowed to be built up over the years, that they did not question him further.

They were happy to be in their own house again. They played with abandon. They were still young enough to be insatiable playmates, and satiated with play. At the end of the day, as he was driving them back to Hampstead, he broached the subject of the divorce. His craving for honesty required telling them the truth. He wanted no euphemisms.

'I'm not going to be living with you any more,' he said eventually.

'Why not, Daddy?' John, the youngest, asked unsuspectingly.

'I've got a new job. In Scotland,' he answered. Avoiding the truth with children was so easy, almost natural, he thought. He was lying to them, after all.

'Why can't we come with you?' Alastair asked this time.

'You're going to be staying here. You're going back to Downe.' That had been Nick's idea. Since he was going, they should return to their own house. Back home.

'But why can't we go to Scotland?' John asked.

It was not going to be easy. He was going to have to tell the whole truth, he realized, or most of it at least. He did not know how to.

'Mummy and I have been fighting a lot,' he started. It was feeble.

'Are you getting a divorce?' Alistair had pierced through the murkiness of Nick's answers. He might not know the full meaning of his question, but he knew the right words.

'Yes. We are,' Nick said, and he knew he was relieved that Alistair had taken the burden of using the words off him.

'What's a divorce?' asked John.

In the rear-view mirror, Nick saw Alistair put his hand on John's arm and shake his head. It was such a poignant sight, he felt a constriction in his chest. His two blond boys, the oldest not even ten years old, sitting upright, each contained by his seatbelt, protecting each other, and protecting him too. He was grateful he did not have to explain any more, but he felt a terrible sadness that it had come to this. He wished he could say more, but he felt that more would just confuse, not make clearer.

The rest of the journey was spent mostly in silence, except for the occasional remark about something noticed out of the window. When he dropped them off in Hampstead, he did not go up, but said goodbye to them in the street.

They hugged each other in a parody of separation, holding on to each other for a long time. John did not want to let go. He kept his arms firmly around Nick's neck, and Nick did not dare force him.

'I have to go,' he said weakly.

Finally, it was Alistair who stopped it. 'Come on, John,' he said. 'We're going to miss the programme.'

'I'll see you soon,' Nick said to them. He saw that they wanted to believe him, but were not convinced. He watched as they gloomily went up the stairs to their grandparents' flat.

He drove down to Annie's flat, knowing that he had just committed an injustice.

Later that night he sat in the living-room, unable to sleep, guilty that Annie was capable of making him forget all those problems. With her, he could look forward. He dropped his past like scales. People receded into the background. He thought of what he could achieve out of Edinburgh. It was a new town, a new job. It was a new life.

With Annie, the distance seemed no problem. They talked a lot about it, about how difficult it would be, but they both knew they would survive the separation, such as it would be. Perhaps they were old enough not to be frightened by time.

Annie was looking forward to the separation. She wanted time alone, apart from Nick. She was enough of a bachelor to prize her independence, and sometimes she felt that this passionate affair engulfed too much of her life. A little distance would return her to sanity. She could always go to Edinburgh to see Nick, if she needed to. There was no need to have him in London all the time. In fact, she believed that the job was essential for him. They might not have survived together if he had not got it. She missed him immediately before he left, but there was relief in his departure.

Nick had a purpose, a purpose he had kept completely to himself. He was going to Scotland full of it, and had decided he would tell Annie before he left. He told her on the station platform as they embraced before he took the train. The guard was already walking down the platform, closing the doors. Their loud banging echoed in the station with a regular beat.

'Do you know what I'm going to do?' he asked her. It could have referred to anything.

'No,' she said, pressing herself against him. She smiled up at him, 'What are you going to do?'

'I'm going to take Corpcom over,' he said in the same matter-of-fact tone and smiled down at her.

He kissed her and climbed on to the train. Stunned by his revelation, she followed him as he went down the train to find his sleeper. He opened the window and leaned down to her. He reached out his hand to touch hers.

The train was edging out and she had still not said anything. She ran a few steps after the train.

'Good luck!' she called after him.

He smiled. He waved at her from the window as she watched him from the platform, still dazed by what he had said.

PART III

Natural Selection

'The Panel deprecates anything which amounts to a confrontation between representatives of offeror and offeree companies or between competing offerors or which leads to any kind of gladiatorial combat . . .'

From *The City Code on Take-overs and Mergers*

Chapter Twenty-Three

Julian was on the night train from London to Edinburgh. Sitting on the berth, with his bed made up, a glass of whisky in his hand and no further responsibilities for seven hours was comfort and relaxation. He had just returned from a two-week trip abroad – Singapore, Hong Kong, Tokyo and, finally, New York. He had taken the night flight from New York, spending the whole day in the City, and finally meeting up with Rebecca in the evening. They had had dinner in a restaurant on Upper Street, and now, at midnight, he was on a train to Edinburgh. Julian knew that he was more likely to sleep on the train than if he had taken a late flight and walked into the cold and empty flat.

He sat back on the bed, exhausted but still unable to fall easily asleep. Before this new job, he had had no trouble at all sleeping. Now he was working harder, the task was more demanding, and sleep was more elusive.

Two years had passed since that September night when Nick had himself taken the night train to Edinburgh. More than two years, Julian thought, since it was now December.

Almost Christmas. New York had been ablaze with lights and shopping, with men and women in heavy overcoats and overshoes, crunching through the snow, going into the stores and coming out more laden with each visit. He loved New York in December. It was always so festive. London had been seasonal as well, but, instead of the cold, cruel air, it had been raining and the crowds had had to shelter beneath their umbrellas, wrapping themselves up against the damp.

That he was even able to make the comparison reminded Julian of how much time he had spent abroad during these last two years. For it was also just over two years since Julian had left Armadale and joined Nick at Faulkner Industries.

Nick had got in touch with Julian in late September, one week after he had started at Faulkner. At the end of a long, dull day at Richard's side, Julian had gone home and found a letter waiting for him. At first he had thought of Rebecca, who was still away in the States. Every year she visited her parents in Concord, and this year she was not due back till October. When he picked the letter off the floor, he had recognized Faulkner's logo on the envelope. It was from Nick.

Julian wondered if it would be one of Nick's quick notes, like the ones he used to write when he had been at Armadale, short, informative letters, almost like memos, asking for something, passing on a piece of information, often with a newspaper clipping inside. He had never received a long letter from Nick.

The letter was short indeed. Julian took it with him to the kitchen, where he poured himself a large drink, and, with a sense of liberation coming over him, he read it again.

'Dear Julian,' it said, 'I have a job for you. I hope you will come up and take it. Yours, Nick.'

Julian went to the telephone. He was going to ring immediately. Then, he stopped. For once, he was going to be a little more flamboyant, honour the occasion. He picked up the phone book and searched through it. At last he found the number, and dialled.

'I'd like to send a telegram,' he said when the operator answered.

Without considering it further, without discussing it with anyone, he gave his message: 'Have kilt. Will travel. Julian.'

Nick had rung him early the following morning, as soon as he had received the telegram.

'Julian. Nick,' he said. 'I'm delighted.'

'So am I,' answered Julian. 'I'm giving in my notice today.'

'Come up as soon as you can,' Nick said. He was talking

rapidly, as if he had too much to do already. 'We'll talk then.'

'What am I going to be doing?' Julian asked. He laughed.

'I'll tell you when I see you,' Nick answered. 'Quite a lot of travelling, by the way. Is that all right?'

'Fine.' Julian was even more pleased.

'Let's talk later,' Nick had said and rang off, leaving Julian dazed but elated.

He had hurried into the office and immediately went in to speak to Richard who had looked at him in surprise.

'Found something better?' he asked, slightly piqued.

'I just need a change, I think.' Julian tried to evade the question. 'There'll be quite a lot of travelling in the new job,' he added.

Richard's curiosity was aroused by Julian's reluctance to elaborate. He did not expect Julian to be garrulous, but in his experience most people volunteered excuses if they had them.

'Do I know the company?' Richard said.

'I don't know,' Julian responded, trying to be as innocent as possible. 'A Scottish company.' Trying to head the questions off he added, 'I'll be able to work on my golf,' and swung at an imaginary ball.

He looked at Richard and knew it had not worked. Frye was purposefully not going to get the message. He was going to have to tell him where he was going.

'Faulkner Industries,' he said. 'In Edinburgh.'

Richard smiled at Julian. 'Going back to Nick Bishop, hey, Julian?' he said with an edge of scorn, and enjoyed watching Julian blush. Nick, in Richard's estimation, was finished. He had peaked. And immediately he added, 'I'll waive the month's notice, if you want.'

'There's no need.'

'Wouldn't you prefer a clean break?' Richard insisted. 'It's perfectly all right, you know.'

'Maybe you'd prefer it, sir?' Julian said.

'Why don't we compromise, then. Two weeks.'

'It'll give me time to break someone in,' Julian said, jumping at the opportunity.

It had been easy, a polite fencing match, in which no one had been hurt.

The following weekend, Julian had flown to Edinburgh. He found Nick back on top, full of confident energy, light-hearted and, if anything, he thought, sharper than before.

'So, when can you come?' he had said to Julian as they sat in the comfortable, slightly anonymous flat that had been provided for Nick by the company. It was luxurious but it was pre-fab luxury, tasteful but heavy-handed, and lacking in spirit. The furniture came from a warehouse providing innumerable companies around the United Kingdom with sofas, dining-room tables, coffee tables and bookcases. Nick had put a few personal touches to it. It was supposed to be a temporary measure but, with only himself to consider, it was unlikely that Nick would bother to find the time to look for anything more homely. Home was not what he was after these days; he had left most of his life behind, just as he had his family.

'In about two weeks,' Julian had replied. 'Unless I have time for a holiday?' Knowing his man, Julian had put it as a question and as he had expected Nick shook his head.

'I'd rather you didn't,' he said. 'The sooner you get here, the quicker we can get started.'

'I thought you'd say that,' Julian said. 'I've got another week at Armadale.' He thought, then went on, 'Then another week to get ready. All right?'

'Fine,' said Nick. 'Better than I thought. So Richard let you off after only two weeks, eh?' Nick asked.

'We bargained,' said Julian.

'How did he take it?'

Julian hesitated.

'He thought you were making a mistake, didn't he?' Nick said before Julian could answer him.

'He didn't say that.'

'That would have been rude.' Nick found it comic. They

had all dismissed him. Coming to Scotland, he thought, had been the perfect touch. So far away, so out of the mainstream.

'Don't worry about me, Julian,' he said. 'It doesn't bother me any more. At least, not half as much,' he added with a self-deprecating laugh.

They were silent for a moment. Nick looked down at his glass of whisky. They were both drinking malt.

'You're going to be working for me, Julian,' he said finally. 'Directly for me, that is,' he added. 'I'm going to tell you everything now so that you know what you're getting in to.'

'That sounds very ominous,' Julian said light-heartedly, but with a thrill of anticipation. 'Maybe you should have told me before I resigned.'

'Perhaps I should have,' Nick said. 'I hadn't thought of it.' And, almost to himself, he continued, 'I didn't think you might not have the taste for it.'

'For Christ's sake, Nick, will you please tell me what's going on?' Julian said, wondering what Nick could be referring to. 'What am I going to be doing for you?'

'Don't rush me.' He wanted to prepare Julian.

'I took this job for two reasons,' he said. 'One, I needed it and I know I can do it well. We can build this company back up to what it was. And more. Just the way we were doing at Armadale,' he could not resist adding. Nick spoke with absolute confidence, as if his success was in no doubt, merely a question of time.

'Second,' he continued, 'and I've only told this to one person,' he looked over at Julian with great intensity, 'and that's how it's going to stay for a long time.' He paused and faced Julian, as if he were asking for a confirmation of trust. Automatically, Julian nodded his assent.

'I'm going to take Corpcom away from Andrews.'

The dramatic revelation had the required effect. Speechless, Julian looked at Nick. It was far-fetched, but now that it was out, it felt inevitable, like a well-plotted book; looking back on the conversation, he could almost feel as if he had seen it coming. The symmetry was there.

'What do you think?' Nick said.

There was no denying it, Julian was excited. It was like a call to adventure.

'I think it's bloody amazing,' he said. 'Unbelievable. But bloody amazing.'

'I can do it,' Nick said.

'I'm sure you can,' Julian agreed in a soft, pensive voice.

He believed it then, although later he wondered whether it was not a completely mad scheme. It was at that moment, though, that Julian realized what was different in Nick. His boss had acquired the restless energy of the adventurer. Working for him had become exciting.

Over the next two years, Nick had re-hired many of the people who had worked for him at Armadale. It had been a slow migration north, and he had created a family feeling in Faulkner. It was like the gathering of an old team that had not played together for a long time and which was being regrouped for one last match. They had come from all over England, bearing their gear, ready to be fitted back together and, this time, to play so that they would win the trophy.

Nick had left most of the round-up to Julian, who had found it a gratifying task, like going shopping with someone else's money. He had almost invariably met with an enthusiastic and grateful response, and, as it was done slowly, by the time he was on his fifth recruit, he found that the rumours of his hiring had preceded him and that when he arrived they knew why he was coming.

The most pleasant mission was his call to Philip Porter. Philip was in hiding when Julian reached him. His wife had gone back to work, but he was still looking. He was bitter at having been thrown onto the pile of rejects. At fifty-three he had been told he was too old. He was being retired when some people reached the top of their profession. Philip saw no one who could remind him of his past with Armadale, he felt too ashamed to face them.

At first, Philip did not recognize Julian's voice on the telephone. He had put Armadale out of his mind and had never expected to hear from anyone connected with his old company again.

'Philip?' Julian had said. 'It's Julian.'

'Hallo,' said Philip with no recognition in his voice.

'Julian Campbell,' he added. 'Armadale. D'you remember? We used to work together.'

'Julian,' Philip said, and Julian could not tell if he was pleased or not. 'Julian. How are you? What a surprise.'

'How are you?' Julian asked.

He knew that Philip had no job, and that his affirmation that he was well, fine, enjoying life, was a lie.

'I'm ringing about a job,' Julian said. 'You interested?'

They met at an Indian restaurant on the Finchley Road. It was raining again, and Julian arrived a little late, having had to battle especially bad traffic.

It was dark and stuffy in the restaurant. They had a beer and they both ordered a chicken curry for the sake of simplicity.

Philip looked older than Julian remembered him. He had put on weight and his face was puffy and pale. He greeted Julian with loud enthusiasm.

'It's good to see you,' he said. 'Tell me about the job.' Embarrassed at his own keenness, he went on, 'I'm sorry, Julian. Have a beer. Sit down.'

Julian felt sorry for him. He was glad he could offer him work.

'It's in Scotland,' he said. 'There'll be lots of friendly faces,' he added, sensing hesitation. 'We're trying to get Jim to come up. Harry and Bill have already moved. We're talking to a lot of others.'

'Jim, eh?' Philip said. He sounded pleased at the thought of seeing him again. 'Haven't seen him since he left. How about Alan?' he asked after a moment.

'Alan Turner?' Julian said. He smiled. 'No. I don't think so. Alan's with Corpcom anyway.'

'Just as well,' Philip said. 'He made me nervous.' He laughed. 'Wait till I tell Susan.' He fell silent.

Back home, Philip waited eagerly for his wife, his only reservation being the move to Scotland. When he told Susan neither of them knew how to react. The unexpected boon of work was coupled with the wrench of a move. It meant leaving everything they had known in twenty-seven years of marriage. They had always lived in London; Philip had been raised in Kilburn, where they lived. Their children had gone to school there and their youngest still did. It meant leaving friends, the neighbourhood, habits. They debated the issue well into the night, each one alternatively opting to take the job and then finding reasons for refusing it. And then just as Philip had thought he had decided he would not take it and his heart had grown leaden with loss, it was Susan who made the final decision to leave London behind.

'Let's do it,' she said. 'It's been awful ever since you left Armadale. You know how much you want this job. I'm sick of this place anyway. I'm sick of the people. I'm sick of the place.'

She was voicing all the anger they both felt at what had befallen them in the last year; at the rejections and the desperate loneliness they had both experienced, the sense of worthlessness which had escorted their lives since Philip had been dismissed from Armadale. The move to Scotland represented a break from that, a break from the past and its failures. And once having made up their minds, from feeling that their lives had ended prematurely, they now experienced unusual optimism. They were getting a second chance after all.

Nick himself visited Harold Clemens. But Harold refused his offer. He had moved on and left Armadale behind. He now ran a department in a chemical engineering firm ten minutes from his house, and he preferred to stay put. Even though he had no idea what it might be, he sensed trouble in Nick, and did not think the job worth it.

Nick also went to meet Jim Ferrar. Something had remained unsaid during the loss of Armadale and had only been touched on in the telephone conversation they had had six months later. It was now more than a year after the takeover battle, and Nick wanted to deal with it himself. It mattered to Nick what Jim thought about the rumours Roger had started.

Jim worked on the outskirts of London, in Chiswick, not far from the M4, in a sprawling mass of reddish buildings, built after the Second World War. Nick waited for Jim in the reception. Through the narrow, rectangular windows of the compulsory fire-doors that appeared at regular intervals, Nick saw him coming down the long corridor. He recognized Jim's purposeful stride from afar, then noticed the familiar sports jacket with the brown elbow patches, and he almost felt at Armadale again.

Their handshake was firm.

'It's not far away. We can walk,' Jim said to Nick and he led his former boss to the restaurant.

It was a Chinese restaurant. It appeared suddenly without warning, amid a cluster of shops that serviced the residential neighbourhood. The restaurant was evidently designed for the wealthier, executive clientele of the companies that were headquartered in the area, a stark modern Chinese restaurant, in grey and black. They drank wine with their meal, not tea, and allowed the headwaiter to select their meal for them while they talked business.

'So. What's this about a job?' Jim started in immediately.

'I thought you might want to come and work among familiar faces.'

'I heard you were putting a lot of us back together.'

'We could use you up there, Jim,' Nick said.

'Scotland's pretty far away.'

'So is this place,' Nick looked around him as he spoke.

Jim laughed. 'It's a bit like no man's land isn't it?' he said. Then he added, 'I've never been up to Scotland. Is it very cold?'

'Cold enough. And wet.'

'And what about the women. Are they cold too?' Jim said.

Nick shrugged. After all, he did not know. But he said, 'It's the way they speak that strikes you first. And then, you see them, and there's no turning back . . .'

'Ah, well,' Jim said. 'If you put it that way.'

They talked on in this vein, as if the deal had been done. They spoke of Nick's plans for Faulkner, but never of his ultimate aim; they spoke of Jim's role in the company. Jim waited till the end of the meal to discuss money.

'How much are you paying?' he said.

'How much are you getting now?' Nick asked, and when Jim told him, he said, 'I can't offer you any more.'

'But not less?'

'No. Not less,' Nick said.

'That's good enough for me, then,' said Jim.

After the meal, they walked back to Nick's car together. They both felt satisfied with themselves; it was an arrangement they both wanted. They looked at each other for a moment, each one thinking he would speak. Finally, it was Jim who spoke.

'I'm sorry about what happened,' he said.

'It's over now,' Nick said in return.

Driving away, Nick thought about what else might have been said, and realized it did not matter any more. He considered his plans for Faulkner and he wondered how Jim would feel if he knew about Corpcom. By bringing in former employees, Nick was not only creating a team he knew to be successful, he was building an army of faithful and trusted soldiers, people he felt would follow him and encourage him in his battle against Corpcom. This vendetta was not so alien to them. He trusted they would approve when they found out about it. Of Jim, he was less sure; Jim was less predictable.

Julian knew of Nick's ultimate plans and he found it remarkable that Nick had been able to aim towards Corpcom and, at the same time, bring Faulkner out of loss and into profit with such ease. For, in two and a half years, Nick had put a stop to the decline of Faulkner Industries, and had reversed its fortunes. When Nick had been asked to take charge of

Faulkner, the company had reported a trading loss for five consecutive quarters, each one slightly larger than the last. Under Nick's management, the trend had been literally reversed, and, after six quarters, Faulkner had posted a small profit.

Historically Faulkner, like much of British industry, had sheltered in the relatively safe United Kingdom market and the equally familiar countries of the Commonwealth. It was initially a precision engineering company engaged in the design and manufacture of drilling machinery. With the coming of off-shore oil to Scotland, its inward-looking tendencies had been accentuated. Faulkner had expanded with the oil industry. It was typical of its insularity, however, that, although it set up a subsidiary office in Aberdeen, it insisted on remaining in Edinburgh.

Thus Nick, with Faulkner based in Edinburgh, was able to remain within the other major financial centre in the UK and change the perspective of the company without moving location. He began to export the knowledge and expertise that Faulkner had acquired in what were the toughest conditions known to the oil industry. Working systematically, he further diversified, geographically and in the kinds of business Faulkner became involved in. From precision engineering, he moved into electronics, and from electronics into computers, from pre-fabricated modules for the North Sea, he soon included home improvements and the lucrative DIY market. With every year, Faulkner was looking more like an octopus, its tentacles stretching out in every direction.

Julian watched this strategic development with surprised admiration. Nothing he and Nick had done together at Armadale had revealed the scope of Nick's imagination. None of what was being done out of Scotland had ever been attempted from Cannon Street and Julian wondered if these were the bitter fruits of Nick's loss.

Yet, this did not seem to account for it. At Armadale, Nick had run the company as if it were a village store, efficiently, economically, with steady but limited ambitions. This had resulted in regular and unexplosive profits. Armadale, in the last five years under Nick's management, had become like a profitable, well-managed farm, for which there was no more available land. Now Nick revealed a capacity for aggressive and adventurous decision that Julian did not recognize.

He had rationalized Faulkner – 2,000 redundancies over the whole of the companies Faulkner controlled. This did not include the stripping that Nick had carried out. He had raised cash by selling off assets directly linked to the North Sea operations, and then financed acquisitions selected by Julian.

Julian sensed an uncompromising single-mindedness to these actions, these wise business decisions. And he had become the executor of Nick's plan, a man without a title, a roving ambassador. On average, he spent two weeks out of every month travelling. He covered the world in search of Corpcom and its subsidiaries, in the United States, in South-East Asia. He visited Kuala Lumpur, went to the stock exchanges of Singapore and Hong Kong. Slowly, in small, patient amounts, he built up Faulkner's holdings in Corpcom.

He did it, like a good spy, without revealing himself as an agent of Faulkner's. Anonymity was essential. For as long as possible, Nick and Julian did not want observers, Roger Andrews in particular, noticing the actions of a single buyer. They had formed a subsidiary corporation in Bermuda to act as the principal holding company for Julian's activities, an off-the-shelf company with no apparent link to Faulkner. A further series of small companies was created around the world, most of them in countries where impertinent questions were rarely asked. The companies, which did not trade in anything, had as their corporate addresses firms of lawyers, a different firm for each city and each country. The names of Faulkner and of Nick Bishop never appeared.

From his board, Nick had requested what he had called an 'acquisition fund'. A cash fund which would be filled by taking a percentage from each branch of Faulkner, as well as from the sale of assets, and which would be used to buy on the outside. It was essential to the company's growth, Nick had argued; acquisition, not just consolidation, was an important way to achieve it.

Officially, Julian was out looking for properties to buy, and part of his job was indeed to fulfil this assignment. To take Corpcom on, Faulkner had to strengthen itself. While Nick concentrated on organic growth, Julian focused on growth through acquisition. What remained hidden as much as possible was the slow accumulation of Corpcom stock.

Chapter Twenty-Four

I

In two years, Faulkner had bought five small companies, all of which had been selected as targets by Julian. On this last trip, he had chosen a sixth, a very small firm making electronic components that could be applied to the more sophisticated instruments that were used for off-shore drilling. Oil was still one of Faulkner Industries' important activities, if no longer its principal business.

All this activity had transformed Julian into an experienced predator himself, and his experience showed. It was not just that the travelling, with its accompanying exhaustion, had added lines to his face or that he had put on a few pounds. He had lost some of his bright-skinned innocence, and left the safe and one-toned world of north London and the City, graduating to a real international existence. He had grown to feel comfortable in many different countries and accustomed to their individual quirks, so much so that he was no longer sure what 'home' meant.

He and Rebecca were married, the decision to marry nudged on them by Julian's departure for Scotland. Marriage had seemed like the formality necessary to justify their both leaving London and going up to Edinburgh.

They kept Julian's flat in London and rented a pied-à-terre in Edinburgh. Ironically, with Julian away so much, Rebecca spent most of her time in London. It made no sense to stay in Edinburgh on her own. Even if the rationale for getting married had evaporated, they did not regret having done it.

*

Nick was divorced, but he and Annie had not married. She flew up on most Friday evenings, and that day Nick was invariably more cheerful than usual, working at a restless pace, bursting into people's offices, making a few comments, a joke and then leaving.

They acted like young lovers, their sexual need for each other intensified by separation. Nick usually returned home after Annie let herself in, and always called her name immediately. She, waiting for him, smiled as she heard his voice and went to meet him.

'I'm sorry I'm so late,' he said as soon as he saw her and he took long strides towards her.

'Hallo,' she managed before being swept up in his embrace.

They kissed. He held her then and said, 'God, I missed you.' And without another word, they led each other to the bedroom.

Monday mornings, Nick drove her to the airport to catch the first plane out. He arrived in the office as revitalized as he had been excited on Friday.

Julian could sense their physical attraction whenever he spent an evening with them. Annie, he felt, had a completely different effect on Nick from Sophie. Annie was a challenge, whereas Sophie had always seemed more passive. He admitted that Sophie had had a different role, wife and mother, and that he had met her well after the formation of habits. With Annie, he was a witness to fresh love.

Julian's relationship with Nick had changed. They were now co-conspirators, Nick no longer like a father to Julian, but more like an older brother. They held many meetings in Annie's flat out of convenience, but also out of secrecy. Nick wanted no leaks or eavesdropping this time. This secrecy and Annie's part in it, for she was still the only person other than Julian who knew what Nick was planning, added romanticism to her and to Nick in Julian's eyes, just as it added dash to his own job.

Julian had quickly found that getting thoroughly involved

in Nick's fight was unavoidable. Even as Nick's head of operations, he had thought that he could remain detached, watch Nick from the outside and pretend that the job did not require full commitment. But, no longer an assistant, he had too much responsibility to hold back and still do the job well. In the end, the simple truth was that Nick's single-mindedness was an obsession with which Julian sympathized too much to remain detached.

He realized he was hooked one evening when he and Rebecca had dinner with Nick and Annie. It was unusual that both couples were in Edinburgh at the same time. It was at Nick's flat, a late supper that Nick cooked himself at the end of a long day. He had not lost the habit after his long period of unemployment; he cooked now as a form of relaxation. They drank champagne for no other reason than that they were together.

Nick and Julian were in the kitchen, talking over the day's business, while Nick cooked the meal, wearing a chef's white apron. Every now and then, he dipped a finger into the sauce to check its flavour and consistency.

In the sitting-room, Annie was with Rebecca. Rebecca liked Annie, and noted with satisfaction that Annie sat while Nick cooked. This, she often complained to Julian, was a rare event in England, even these days. Annie was relaxed; self-assured, she seemed a benign presence, sitting very still on the sofa, holding her glass of champagne, that ironic smile that Nick had first noticed lighting up her face.

'Does Julian cook?' Annie asked. They were thinking of the same thing.

'Not much,' Rebecca answered. 'I'm trying to encourage him to. But he's away too much of the time. It gives him an excuse for not trying.'

'Keep at it,' Annie said. 'Once he starts, he'll never stop. Men can be so thorough.'

'They always treat everything as a challenge,' Rebecca said.

'That's right,' Annie laughed. 'It's all to do with their drive.'

'When the flag's up, the ship can't be far behind.'

They were both laughing now, pleased with themselves, confident of their superiority. Julian appeared in the doorway, and fed their laughter when he asked, 'What's the joke?'

When he heard the renewed laughter, Nick called from his pots, 'It's bound to be about us. Leave them alone and come and help me. It's almost ready.'

A few minutes later, they appeared from the kitchen, carrying steaming dishes towards the dining-room table. They wore thick oven mitts to carry them and Nick, with his apron against his pin-striped trousers and a dishcloth slung over his shoulder, was an incongruous sight. Rebecca smiled as she watched him place the food on the table; he reminded her of a *New Yorker* cartoon. Even Annie seemed amused as she sat down to eat.

'Looks good, Nick,' she said, unfolding her napkin and reaching for the food.

'Tuck in,' he said. And, a few seconds later, as Rebecca and Julian were waiting for him to sit down, he cried, 'For Christ's sake, don't wait. Eat while it's hot!'

Later, when they had finished eating and were sitting back, sipping their wine, Rebecca looked around the room at the contented faces.

'I didn't think business could be this much fun,' she said.

'Absolutely,' Nick said. He looked over at Julian who was smiling slightly drunkenly into his glass. 'How much fun can you stand?'

Annie flashed a look at him, but Julian was oblivious to his intention. He just smiled more broadly.

'What do you have in mind?' Rebecca said with a sexy smile.

'I'm going to let you in on a little secret, Rebecca,' he said.

This time, Julian caught it. He awoke from his comfortable slouch and looked over at Nick. He felt a mixture of worry and relief. He had not told Rebecca of Nick's final target – that had been the agreement; no one was to know. He would be relieved if Rebecca were told for he had found it difficult, even unfair, not telling her. He hoped she would not resent his secrecy.

'Can you keep a secret?' Nick continued.

'So long as it's legal,' Rebecca answered carefully. She looked over at Julian, who just smiled sheepishly back at her. Rebecca did not like secrets.

'Oh, it's legal. The letter of the law,' Nick said, 'but not one stroke more than necessary.'

'Go on.'

The atmosphere had changed. Only Nick was confident now; even Annie was uncertain and on edge. Rebecca was afraid she was going to hear something that she did not want to know. Julian kept his eyes on her, checking her every reaction.

'I am . . .' he started, then he corrected himself. 'We are . . . Faulkner Industries are going to take Corpcom over.' He paused. 'Roger Andrews will soon be out on his ear.'

Rebecca's immediate reaction was relief; it was only a business deal; it was not so serious.

'It's not to go beyond this room, Rebecca,' Nick said, serious now and he stared at her. She looked away, finally, intimidated by his intensity.

'It won't,' she said firmly, offended by Nick's insistence.

But the confidence had broken the spell. Instead of increasing their unity, it spoiled their fun. Soon after, Rebecca and Julian left.

As she cleared the table after they had gone, Annie said, 'Perhaps you shouldn't have told Rebecca.'

'She'll be all right,' Nick said.

'I was always told you should never trust a journalist with a story.'

'You're very cynical,' he said. 'Don't you trust her?'

'I do. I like her,' Annie said. 'But didn't you notice the change in mood?'

'That's what comes with revelations,' Nick said. He did not seem worried. 'Julian would want her to know. I think she should.'

Annie dropped the subject. She had said her piece and saw no purpose in discussing it further. There was no agreement or disagreement to be had. She had just wanted to voice a sentiment.

Rebecca did not mention it until they were inside their flat. Julian was silent, not sure what to make of Rebecca's solemnity, himself sobered by the incident. They stood in the hall as Julian locked the door.

'You're crazy,' she said to him. She had turned to face him and stood a few feet away, her head tilted to one side, even more serious.

'What? Why?' he asked.

'Trying to take over Andrews. You're crazy,' she said again.

'It's going to feel really good. I promise you,' Julian said. And that was when he knew he was hooked.

'I'm sure it will,' she said. After a pause, she added, 'If you make it.'

Rebecca did not know enough about the practical aspects of such a move, but she was sensitive enough to realize that, whatever the feasibility of the plan, it was a wild act of revenge. And that was what worried her: its motive.

'Just don't tell me you're doing it because it makes sound business sense,' she said. 'Because I won't believe that.'

'All right. I won't.' Julian said.

2

After almost two years at Faulkner Industries, with Julian well under way in his acquisition of Corpcom stock, with Faulkner's books reflecting a profit and the crew in place, Nick had turned to the one thing he had put aside but not forgotten, the North Sea accident. Knowing he had to proceed cautiously, unnoticed, he had looked for a professional, to take up the scent he had so unsuccessfully followed. He found Willie Banks.

Nick had not known how to go about choosing a private detective. Out of curiosity he had looked up the category in the yellow pages. He found it between 'dispatch riders' and 'detergent manufacturers and suppliers'. There was something appropriate about that sandwich, he thought.

'William Banks. Private Investigator. Knowledge of Criminal Law. Not too proud for any task,' was the advertisement.

Willie spoke three languages, all with an unremitting Scottish accent. Many years ago he had begun studies in criminal law, but had not lasted. He had planned on joining the police, then thought better of it. Finally he became a private investigator. A girlfriend had once told him he was a typical Aries: he started a lot of things but did not finish them. Willie thought she was probably right, because she did not last either.

They met in Nick's flat. Annie was in London, Julian was in America. Nick had kept the first meeting as private as possible. Hiring a private detective felt somehow dishonest. He had waited nervously, sipping a drink, and then gulped it down when the bell rang. He relaxed somewhat when he opened the door to a short, wiry man with untidy, thinning grey-brown hair, who looked seedy but not intimidating. Nick had not expected any particular type, but his imagination had veered to a rather more physically imposing man, somebody more 'hard-boiled'.

Nick showed Banks into the drawing-room. It had remained as undecorated as when Julian had first seen it; it was a little more rumpled and in the air hung the rich, slightly sweet smell of Mitsouko, Annie's perfume.

'Care for a drink?' Nick asked.

Banks looked over at the drinks, laid out on a trolley against the wall, a little as it had been in Downe.

'A wee malt, please sir,' he said.

Nick smiled at the use of 'wee', as he poured Banks a large whisky. Banks watched Nick with sharp eyes in an angular face; he was thin, and strong cheekbones aged him.

Nick handed him the drink and sat down. There was silence. He did not know how to start.

'D'you mind if I smoke, sir?' Banks asked.

'Not at all. Go ahead.' Nick waved him on.

Banks took out a packet of ten cigarettes, and picked one out. He examined it, then broke the filter off it and placed the yellow stub into the ashtray.

'Bought the wrong kind,' he explained to Nick with a crooked smile that revealed teeth discoloured from the tobacco.

Eventually Nick began, as usual not wasting time on a long-winded approach.

'I want you to investigate an accident that happened on an oil platform two years ago,' he said. 'Almost two and a half,' he corrected himself. 'I think we should talk about it. We can go from there.'

'That sounds all right to me,' Banks said. There was a slight dart of his eyes towards Nick at the mention of two and a half years. The trail would be cold.

'I suppose it's rather a long time ago.' Nick apologized.

'Gives things a chance to settle,' Banks said.

He had a way of looking at things positively. He knew people preferred hope, and indeed he believed that things could be found out if you gave it enough time. In Banks' experience, people ran out of money, or patience, or time; that was why cases did not get solved. There were no mysteries, just puzzles of varying difficulty, things hidden better or worse.

Later, when Nick had finished explaining, Banks took a puff of his cigarette, holding the quarter-inch stub in the tip of his fingers and inhaling for the last time before reluctantly stubbing the cigarette out.

'What am I trying to find out?' he asked.

'What happened, of course,' Nick said, surprised by the directness of the question, but not misunderstanding it as much as he seemed to.

'I know that, sir,' Banks said. 'Let me put it another way.

What would you *like* me to find out?'

Nick had never asked himself the question quite so nakedly. He thought about it now. What he wanted to find out was that Roger had somehow been responsible for the death of two men. But he was not sure that it would be wise to admit it to Banks.

'I'm not quite sure I know what you mean,' he said, hoping that perhaps Banks would back down.

Banks did not, but he played along.

'Let me try to explain,' he said. 'Most people who hire me to do something – follow somebody, find something or somebody, solve a puzzle of some kind . . . anything really – well, most people are looking for a particular answer. They may not get it. But they are looking for it. So, what I'm asking you, I suppose, is this. This accident, which was formally declared an accident. Are you hoping it was not?'

Nick said nothing, still wondering whether to tell the truth or not.

'I don't *need* to know,' Banks continued, seeing Nick's hesitation, 'but I always think it helps to know exactly what the client wants. It helps me to dig in the right direction, you see. For example, if I find there was something not right, will you be satisfied if I find out who did the actual fiddling? Or do you want to know if this person was mad, malicious, jealous, greedy or just paid? Do I dig up, down or sideways?'

Nick liked Banks for his directness: to him it was a sign of honesty. He decided to trust him; and knowing what Nick wanted to discover did not reveal why he wanted it discovered. So Nick explained about the takeover of Armadale, the accident that took place during it and the effect it had had. He talked of Roger, he even mentioned the business about Annie. Having decided to let Banks know what he had asked for, he saw no reason in holding back. The purpose was efficiency.

'Does that answer your question?' he asked at the end of it all.

'Very generously,' said Banks. 'Thank you.'

'Anything else?'

'I know what you want. I don't need to know why,' Banks looked at Nick with a smile. He went on, 'How much money are you willing to spend?'

'I don't know,' said Nick.

'Do you want me full time? Do you want me indefinitely? It could take a long time.'

'I see.' Nick paused for barely an instant. 'I want you on the job full time. Do whatever you have to. Go wherever you need. You can have expenses, but I expect you to account for them. You don't have to get my permission for any item, but I'll hold you responsible. Spend up to £50,000. Then come back and we'll review it.'

He paused again. 'You can reach me anytime you need me. Here or at the office. Speak only to me or to a man called Julian Campbell about this. I'll give you his numbers too. This is confidential,' he said finally, 'but, believe me, if you try to cheat me, I'll make it public. I won't be afraid to do that.'

'It's nice to know where I stand,' Banks said. He also liked frankness.

Banks left delighted. This was a big job and the client was willing to put money behind it. He had a cheque for £1,000 in his pocket right then, as he left Nick's flat. That felt good. It felt even better to know that he might not have to scramble for another job all year.

3

Julian slept well on the train, lulled like a baby by its rhythmic beat. He woke at six, shaved with an electric razor, something he had picked up in Japan, had breakfast on the train and went straight to work. He would be in before Nick. In the taxi from the station, he wondered if there had been any news of Willie Banks.

It was still dark when Julian went up in the lift to his office.

He was right, he was there before Nick; but only by a few minutes. He had barely unpacked the papers from his briefcase when he heard the lift doors open and he knew Nick had arrived. He was always the first, just as he had been at Armadale.

The offices, taking up the whole of the third floor of the building, were laid out to open off a long corridor, painted off-white, that went right round the floor in a square. On either side, each office door had a frosted glass panel at its centre.

Nick's corner office overlooked the Royal Botanic Garden. Julian's office, two doors down, also had a view of the gardens. When he returned from a trip he liked to stand by his windows and look over the Garden and the park across the road next to it. This brought him back to home base.

Julian walked out of his office when he heard the lift and stood in the corridor, waiting for Nick.

'Julian. You're back,' Nick said as soon as he saw him. 'Come on in.'

He went into his office, leading the way. 'What have you got for me?' he asked as soon as Julian had shut the door.

'Small US company. Electronics. Based out of San Francisco,' Julian reported. 'Good price, I think. And they're looking for a buyer, which is even better.'

'You're getting quite good at this,' Nick said.

'Perhaps. But this is all small stuff,' Julian said. 'I'm still not convinced we can take on the big fish.'

They never mentioned Roger or Corpcom by name, even when they were alone together. This was another precaution Nick had insisted on at the very outset. He feared slips of the tongue and he never again wanted to expose himself to an unseen listener.

'That's not what you said when you first came here,' Nick said, reminding Julian of his optimism.

'I didn't know any better then.'

This was a familiar exchange, a formal ceremony in which Julian expressed doubt, voicing their anxieties, while Nick remained optimistic.

'Anything new?' Julian asked.

'Nothing. I'm still waiting.'

They both waited for news from Banks. They needed to know Andrews' weaknesses, and Nick had been so drawn to the North Sea that they hoped his instinct would prove right. In the meantime, they knew they would have to be ready to move, regardless of what Banks came up with. Yet they both felt that if the piranha was to eat the shark, it should have as many sharp teeth as possible.

Chapter Twenty-Five

I

Willie Banks was staying in a small hotel in Aberdeen, on a narrow cobbled street between the railway station and the river Dee. Like almost everything else in the town, the undistinguished five-storey building was built of granite. The hotel exuded a sad, dark dampness. Banks' room was on the third floor, almost at the top, a narrow room with a basin that had a ring of rust around the drain, a bed with nylon sheets, a worn carpet, a gas fire and a single murky window that overlooked the street and, beyond, the railway tracks. If Nick Bishop could have seen him now, he would have known that his money was being well-spent.

Banks had grown used to his new existence. He knew how to live with little. Bread, cheese and cigarettes and a pint of beer had often served as a meal; at times that was what he preferred. Saving money was as much fun for him as spending it, and in any case, this time the job called for it.

He had become a familiar sight as he hovered around the landmarks of the off-shore oil industry. With his little note-book in front of him, he would be sitting at seven o'clock in the morning in the coffee shop of Dyce airport, sipping at his cup of coffee, which he drank as sweet as a honeycomb. The broad-shouldered riggers coming on for their shift would see him, recognizing his short, wiry body, and hail him from afar, having forgiven him his unlikely presence, his questions, his small terrier-like strangeness. Banks was masquerading as a writer researching a book on off-shore life, and he played the part plausibly enough. He was scruffy, always making notes; he smoked and drank too much; he had a ready wit and an unusual turn of phrase. To the oilmen, all these traits seemed appropriate to a writer. He was small and unprepossessing – what else would he be good for but writing?

Banks' method was one of attrition. He repeated his movements and his questions enough times that he became a habit.

When he had first arrived in Aberdeen and introduced himself to the oil companies, Usoco among them, he had been met with friendliness but no great welcome. Writers had come before him, and if that made him just another one in a sequence, it also made him less special. When his questions had begun circling around the accident of two years ago, he had met with polite but firm coldness. He had pulled back then, and decided to take it more slowly, to make himself as unthreatening as possible.

He had set up a routine, spending a great part of his time at the airport, or flying on the airplanes and helicopters that took crews from Aberdeen to the Shetlands and back. He talked to the men on board about their lives, their families, their homes that were scattered around the world. There was a diver who came all the way from Texas and spent four out of every seven weeks off-shore; the man spent three weeks in a pressurized cabin the size of a box room, one week being de-pressurized and three weeks in Texas; then he repeated the cycle. There were men who lived in Aberdeen, others in Glasgow; there was a man who had a farm in Devon and needed money to maintain it.

There were weeks when Banks spent more time in the air than on the ground.

His questions became more probing when he took the flights back to Aberdeen. Going out, the men would dismiss him when he became too specific. Coming home, they fought him a little less. He would look into their exhausted faces, with their features drawn and stretched from their twelve-hour shifts and trapped existence, with their eyes dazed and grey, like old glazed doughnuts, and his questions would become less circumspect. Yet, despite their weariness, their defences would come up again as soon as he asked about trouble, trouble of any kind. Whatever Banks was doing or writing, he became suspect when he asked about things none of them wanted to think about. It was the other side of the equation: even though they were more tired coming back, they also felt less like talking.

It was hard. Banks could no longer count the helicopter trips he had taken crammed in with forty people all dressed in orange wet-suits, all reading tabloid newspapers, and handing them back and forth from row to row, the newspapers crisscrossing the craft in silence, until every passenger had read and re-read each page and looked at those bare, heavy breasts on page three until they could stand them no more. Banks would have to snatch moments of conversation, knowing that talk would eventually become too much of a battle against the roar of the engines.

At every turn, Banks met with hostility. He knew that some of the men he spoke to worked on the platform on which the accident had occurred, and from them he sensed even greater hostility. Banks wondered whether this sprang from the natural antagonism of people who liked their privacy and disliked dwelling on an unpleasant past, or whether there was something they were hiding. The hostility was obvious and not hidden. It came over them quickly, a flare of anger at being probed. They did not want to answer him.

He pried at their reluctance as one fights to open an oyster. Eventually, his method began to work. He had been in Aberdeen almost six months without leaving. He had flown an average of fifteen to twenty hours a week, he had been on a platform more than once, and even on the square floating maintenance ship that patrolled the oilfields. Yet he had never visited the platform on which the accident had occurred; that had remained off limits. Eventually he managed to persuade people that they could speak to him of the accident, if only because they were tired of not doing it.

Banks was coming out of one of these flights one evening. It had been a long helicopter flight, delayed by the fog and it was late. The men were irritable, having been forced to spend the night in Aberdeen because they had missed their connecting flights and trains out of town. Several of them decided to go into town and to the pub. A drink, a whole load of drinks, would help.

'Want a lift in?' a short, square man called Fred Ormond asked Banks.

'Sure,' he said. 'Be great. Won't have to wait for the bus.'

Banks never took a taxi unless he had to. He had never offered anyone a lift. He offered a pint now and then, but he was careful not to be seen to want anything. It was much better for them to ask him; it was a sign of his good intentions.

In the car, there were four of them and the driver. Banks sat in the back, in the middle, squeezed like a rugby union hooker between two prop forwards. Fred Ormond was in the front passenger seat. He turned around to speak to Banks.

'Why are you always asking about that accident, Willie?' he asked. He spoke with a Glaswegian accent.

Banks knew that Ormond worked on the platform he was interested in. He would have to be careful. He felt especially vulnerable, sandwiched between the two other men.

'Why does no one want to talk about it?' he replied. The men tensed up. There was an unnatural silence in the car, and he could feel the bodies beside him shifting. He went on, quickly, giving a chuckle of false innocence, 'That's what we people feed on, Fred. Drama, scandal, accident. It's unusual, but it's what makes a story.'

They accepted that. They had watched enough television to know that death and disaster were as natural to those stories as flying was to them; even the news fed on it whenever they could.

Banks saw his advantage and continued, eager to make all he could of it. 'That accident is the only one out here in the last eight or nine years. Of course I want to know about it,' he said.

'There's been a couple of helicopters crashing,' said the

man to Banks' right. He had a deep voice, and he said it quietly, as if he had not meant to speak at all. 'Eleven people died in the last one.'

'That's not the same thing,' Banks said. 'Helicopters are dangerous. And anyway people talk about that. I don't even know why there was an explosion. How? Why? Where? Nobody's saying.'

'It was in the dehydration tower,' Ormond said.

'What the hell's the dehydration tower?' Banks said.

'That's no secret. You can find that out in books,' Ormond said again.

'So why does no one want to tell me what it is?' he said.

He was going to have to push. He did not know when he would next get an opportunity like this.

'As a writer, I need an angle,' he said, explaining himself. 'You know what I mean?' He did not wait for them to answer. 'People are always a good angle. Who was in charge? Who didn't do what they had to do?'

'Everybody did what they had to do,' Ormond was quick to rise to the defence of his mates. 'It was an accident.'

'Usually, accidents happen because somebody fucked up,' Banks said.

'Hey, nobody fucked up!' Ormond said angrily.

'That's not what I heard,' said the man on the other side of Banks. Ted Carter. His voice was not so quiet. He was more aggressive, he spoke like someone who had been holding back from saying something.

'So what did you hear?' Ormond challenged him.

'That there was no way that control valve could go,' he said defiantly. 'It'd just been checked a few days back.'

'That doesn't mean a bloody thing,' Ormond retorted. 'It could've gone at any time.'

They were quarrelling. Banks said nothing. He tried to make the men forget he was with them. If he was going to learn something, this was the one way he would learn it. He tried to breathe more quietly, tried not to move. He wondered why Ormond was so defensive.

'It didn't though, did it?' said Carter. 'It went just after it had been checked.'

'Always thought that was funny,' said the man with the quiet, deep voice. It sounded like an echo.

There was a silence, the three riggers thinking back two years. It was Ormond who spoke next.

'Bloody funny, if you ask me,' he said, his position apparently reversed. Again there was silence, as if all had been said.

'What was so funny about it?' Banks said. He risked breaking the confessional mood. And he did: Ormond looked at him and Banks could see the oyster closing. The men next to him shifted again. The mood was gone.

'Just the seat of a control valve coming off just after it was checked,' Ormond said. 'I mean, what's the point of checking them if they're going to go anyway?'

Banks said no more. He had got something. He knew it, and he must persevere along that line. But not now.

They reached the pub and he had a beer with the men. Half an hour later, he left them and walked back to his hotel. He would have to try again.

He walked into the hotel lobby, the hall light throwing such a dim light that it seemed to make it harder to see. Banks walked up to the hotel desk. Behind the desk, there were little cubbyholes for letters and messages. A nail hung from each slot, beneath a number.

'Any messages?' he asked as the man behind the desk handed him his key.

'There was a man who was asking for you, Mr Banks,' said the hotel clerk. He was a tall, skinny man who curved at the stomach and he wore braces to hold up his trousers.

'Who was that?' said Banks. As far as he knew, nobody except Nick Bishop and Julian Campbell knew where he was staying.

'He didn't leave a name,' said the clerk. 'Said he'd call back. Didn't say much.'

Banks shrugged his shoulders as he took his keys. From the stairs, he said, 'Was he a local boy?'

'Who knows?' was the answer. 'Not born here, that's for sure. A lot of people live in Aberdeen who weren't born in Aberdeen.'

'Thanks, then.' Banks went up the stairs.

Something was stirring. After all this time, it was as if everything was happening at once.

2

Peter McNeal had thought he was rid of Nick Bishop. Despite his name coming up occasionally at Armadale, for two years Nick had been a thing of the past, a fading memory. But then Willie Banks came into the picture and suddenly Nick was back with him.

Peter was at a dinner party given by Usoco, which, since Roger's takeover of Armadale, had remained Armadale Engineering's client. The dinner was given in the Tolbooth in Aberdeen, and was a lavish, if slightly indigestible feast. The main hall was crowded with large round tables and filled with the loud rumblings of many voices. Peter sat at the same table as Stephen Dayton, the man who had thrown Nick off the North Sea platform.

On Peter's left sat Stephen's wife, and on his right between him and Stephen, an attractive auburn-haired Aberdonian, who worked for Dayton and with whom Peter was discussing 'insider dealing'.

It was comic, Peter thought, how most people associated big companies like Corpcom, who were so often involved in mergers and takeovers, as part of the 'City', when in fact they were not. The City was a financial, not an industrial, centre; they were linked but not the same thing. He was condescending.

'Perhaps,' the Aberdonian retorted, 'but you people are blurring the distinctions between what's financial and what's industrial.'

'Us people?' Peter queried.

'Roger Andrews and you. Yes,' she went on, undeterred, 'all this buying and selling of companies. It's transforming industry and manufacture into just another pawn in the financial game.'

'I think you're exaggerating our importance,' he said. 'A company has to make a profit. That's its mandate. That's what people like us,' he emphasized the words, 'do best. We make money. Now insider dealing is something else. That's theft.' He smiled at her.

'It is, you're right,' she said. 'It's like a modern gold rush. Sacrificing long term wealth for short term profit.'

Stephen had begun to hear snippets of the conversation and thought he would defuse the passion he heard in his subordinate. He waited for a natural pause in the conversation, then he broke in.

'Peter, I think it's about time you paid us another visit,' he said jovially as if he were just turning away from one conversation to another.

'I'm here, Steve,' Peter answered.

'Off-shore, lad. Not here.'

'I've been off-shore,' Peter said. 'Has it changed?'

Stephen laughed, 'Not much. But then, how well do you remember it?'

'I'll never forget it,' Peter responded.

Stephen turned to the dark-haired Aberdonian and included her, 'He didn't care too much for all that helicopter flying,' he said.

'I don't blame him,' she said, playing along. She glanced at Peter and smiled, even though she did not like him. Her face was a flash of beauty.

Peter glanced at the name tag in front of her plate. He had forgotten her name: *Jean Craig*, he read.

'Can't say the same about that fellow Banks,' Stephen continued. 'Can we now? He's been coming and going for months now.'

Peter took a bite of food, paying only the kind of attention one pays to small talk, using one's diplomatic overdrive, allowing for polite repartee at the appropriate time without complete concentration on what is being said.

'Writers are supposed to suffer, aren't they?' Jean Craig said.

'That's a hell of a lot of research, if you ask me,' Stephen said. He turned to Peter again. 'They always ask the same questions, these people,' he continued. 'Very interested in that accident a couple of years ago is Banks. Keeps coming back to it.'

Peter concentrated now. 'What's this Banks doing?' he asked.

'Research for a book,' answered Stephen.

'What kind of book?'

'Dunno. Didn't say. D'you mean a novel or what?'

'How long has he been here?' Peter pressed on.

'Six months at least,' Stephen answered. 'Persistent little bugger, that's for sure.' Stephen turned to Jean, 'Excuse my French, Jean.'

Peter changed the subject away from Banks. There was no certainty in the connection, but coincidence. Yet does anyone with something to hide, or something to find, believe in coincidence? Peter did not. The problem was, what should he do about it?

At first, he did not bother Roger with Willie Banks. But a month later, after he had heard from his own man, hired out of Aberdeen, that Banks was a private detective out of Edinburgh who was definitely after information about the accident, and furthermore who seemed set to stay until he got what he wanted, Peter had decided to tell Roger. As far as he was concerned, there was no longer any doubt that Banks and Bishop were connected.

Again, he waited until their evening meeting. It was the last thing Peter raised, delaying the inevitable, knowing that Roger hated the mosquitoes of life – and Banks at the moment qualified.

Roger had just reached for a cigar; he always started one at the end of these meetings. He bit off the end.

'Before you light that,' Peter said, 'we have a little problem I want to discuss with you.'

Roger looked over at Peter. He did not like his deputy's 'little problems'.

'Can't I smoke and listen at the same time?' he said.

'You might prefer not to.'

'I don't like the sound of this,' he said as he put the unlit cigar in his mouth.

'There's a private detective from Edinburgh who's been asking questions about that North Sea explosion,' Peter said.

'You mean, the Armadale takeover?'

'That's what I mean.'

'That was two years ago,' Roger said with disbelief. 'Why would he want to do that?'

'He's been in Aberdeen for at least six months,' Peter continued, disregarding Roger's interjection.

'That's a long time to be in Aberdeen,' said Roger, but there was no telling from his tone whether it was a joke or not.

'That's what I think.'

'Isn't Bishop in Edinburgh?' Roger asked. Peter nodded. 'So you think Bishop hired this detective?' Roger said.

'I can't be sure,' Peter answered.

Roger thought about it and Peter let him. There was silence. Roger chewed on the end of his unlit cigar.

'What could Bishop want?' Roger said, to himself as much as to Peter. 'He could want to sue us, I suppose.' He thought some more. 'He can't want the company back after all this time.' He shook his head. 'No, that's absurd.'

'He wants to prove that we're responsible,' said Peter.

'I know that.' Roger was getting irritated. 'But why?'

'Revenge?' Peter said it almost as if he did not believe it. It was, after all, such an unbusinesslike motive.

'Revenge . . .' Roger repeated the word. 'Bishop's an ornery bastard. He's sure capable of it.'

Peter could always tell irritation in Roger; he became more North American the angrier he got.

'Can he prove we were involved?' Roger asked.

'I doubt it,' Peter replied. 'We paid people very well.' He paused. 'He could spread rumours, I suppose. That would make it a little uncomfortable.'

'We taught him all about that,' Roger said. Again he shook his head. 'Nah, he's not the type,' he added. 'He's looking for proof.'

'I can't see him getting it.'

'Fine. Then let's forget about it,' Roger said. He was already dismissing the problem.

'What should we do about the detective?' Peter insisted.

'I don't know,' Roger said with a trace of irritation. It was no longer his problem. 'Just make sure he doesn't get on to the platform.'

'That's not very helpful,' Peter McNeal said. His tone was petulant.

'Listen,' Roger came back at Peter, facing him straight on, 'you told me the deaths were an accident, right? No one was supposed to be there when the thing blew. So, let's not panic.'

'Do nothing?' Peter said.

'Do whatever you think. It's your territory.'

Roger picked up a match and began the elaborate ritual of lighting his cigar. Peter watched him, and as the thick clouds of brown smoke poured out of Roger like steam from a kettle, he got up to leave.

That was singularly unhelpful, Peter thought. He would have to do something.

3

Since that conversation in the car, sandwiched between the two oilmen, information had come more easily to Banks. It was like learning a new word, which suddenly appears in everything one reads. Banks now found information on the accident wherever he turned. The months of waiting were finally paying off.

This evening Banks was in a pub, not far from the station.

Over the last couple of weeks he had found that seats on the airplanes and helicopters were harder to get, and he had been told that he would not be considered for a visit to the platforms any longer: there were a lot of people waiting for such trips and Banks had been on several; it was hoped that this would not affect his research.

So he had been grounded, Banks thought. He must be getting close for that to happen. Banks, like Peter, did not believe in coincidence.

He had had to spend more time hanging around since then, from the outskirts of the action as it were, moving in on groups of people. It had cramped his style, because he had become a more obvious parasite, waiting for people to appear, rather than living according to similar rhythms. Luckily for him, the groundwork had been done and he was accepted.

In the pub with him was a short, solid-looking Frenchman. He had thick black hair and a black moustache, he smoked Gauloises and would have looked perfect with a beret stuck on his head. Even his name fit the part: Jean-Marie Chavel. Banks called him John. John-Mary stuck in his throat. It was an impossible name.

Chavel was a diver with the maintenance ship that patrolled the North Sea platforms and the miles of pipeline that sat on the seabed and reached all the way to the refineries of the Shetlands and Scotland itself, pumping oil into them. Chavel had learned to dive with the French navy. He loved diving and, in his exuberance and enthusiasm, could not really understand the fear that non-divers showed about his profession and the conditions he lived under. Chavel thought it was perfectly normal to spend eight hours at a time beneath 500 feet of water, with just a couple of cables attached to him as lifelines.

Banks felt a chill run through him when Chavel lovingly described what he did. They had met on a helicopter flight back from off-shore. Chavel had been on his way home to

Toulon. He would return in three weeks and go back under water or in his pressurized cabin.

They talked freely. There was no suspicion in Chavel. It was perhaps that his loyalties were different. He was a diver, a sailor who travelled on a ship, even if only a square maintenance ship; he did not spend his time in a construction that was 'earthed'. He saw no reason to hold back from this interesting, angular Scotsman who smoked as much as he did.

It was three weeks later now, and Chavel had returned. The next day he would fly off-shore. In the noisy pub, Banks carried his pint of beer and a whisky for the Frenchman back to the table. Chavel drank no beer; if he could not have wine, he preferred whisky.

Chavel offered Banks a Gauloise. Banks took it and patted the filterless cigarette on the table. They inhaled deeply, both of them, and then they went back to their conversation.

'What was so strange about it?' Banks asked.

Chavel laughed. 'No one talked about it very much.' He thought about what he was saying. Then he went on, analytically, speaking as if he were explicating a text. 'It was not that they did not speak about it, it was how they did not speak about it. Do you understand what I am saying?' He was pleased with his distinction.

Banks did, but he said, 'Could you be more precise?'

'No one off-shore likes to speak of accidents. It is too,' he searched for the word, 'traumatic'. Chavel pronounced it instinctively as a Frenchman would. 'This explosion. People spoke about it as if they should not. Like schoolboys whispering in the corridors. That was strange.'

'What were they saying?' Banks asked, wondering how much Chavel would tell him.

'I'm a diver,' Chavel explained. 'You know that. But what I do is maintenance. I get to speak to maintenance people. There were many rumours about the maintenance on the platform.' He paused, like a good story-teller, and took a sip of his whisky. 'I heard that there was a disagreement between the platform engineer and a maintenance worker. Someone had been seen near the control valve the day of the explosion. Then, after the disagreement, there was no one seen any more.' He laughed, and added, 'If you see what I mean?'

'You mean somebody fiddled with the control valve.' Banks was trying to get facts.

'More or less.' Chavel shrugged his shoulders.

'Do you happen to know the name of the maintenance worker?' Banks asked Chavel. They were both playing a game and they knew it.

'He was German, I think,' Chavel said. After a brief pause, he added, 'Helmut Jurgens.' There was no hesitation. And then he went on, 'He's gone back to Germany, I was told.'

Banks had got what he wanted, but he saw the evening out. He liked Chavel anyway. You can't always treat people like means to an end, he thought, even if that's what the job says they are.

At closing time, they shook hands. A firm, friendly handshake.

'I hope I have been helpful,' Chavel said. 'Good luck.'

'Thanks, John,' Banks said. 'Take care of yourself down under.'

They left the pub together and met a wall of damp and foggy darkness. A misty rain spat at their faces. Chavel swore at the English weather.

'This is Scottish weather,' Banks said in mock indignation.

Chavel laughed, and hurried away. Banks buried his head inside his coat and walked back towards his hotel.

The street was dark. There was a streetlight at the other end, but the ones in between were out. Banks got off the narrow pavement, on to the street and hurried on. He knew that by the time he reached the hotel he would be soaked. This kind of rain went right through, even though it seemed like mist.

Towards him, out of the only light and into the shadows, a car wove down the street. It did not follow a straight line, but swerved, as if the driver were drunk. Banks heard the car before he saw it, when the accelerator pumped power into it. Banks looked up and, through the wet, saw the car's headlights coming at him.

He ran for the pavement and jumped onto it. But still the car drove menacingly onwards in his direction. It was ten yards away when it leaped up onto the pavement and kept its pace towards him. It was too dark for Banks to see anyone at the wheel and, just like a fighter plane, the car was coming out of the light.

Banks turned and saw a doorway a few feet away. He ran towards it. The squealing of the tyres that strained against the curb was in his ears. Just as he squeezed into the doorway he felt the edge of the car hit the side of his coat, which flapped in the wind.

Banks stepped out to look after the car. With the light behind him now, he could see the shadow of a man in the driver's seat. The car drove away, this time in a straighter line, and took the corner very fast.

Was it a drunk? Or perhaps a killer? It was another coincidence. They were cropping up again and again. Banks had no doubts what that driver was trying to do. He would have to be much more careful now. He had almost finished his work here. Just a few more days.

Chapter Twenty-Six

I

Banks hurried back to the hotel and straight up to his room. There he reached for his only luxury, the pint of whisky that sat on his chest of drawers. He went to the basin, took his toothbrush out of the glass mug and poured himself a large measure. The gurgling sound as the whisky came out of the bottle warmed him before he even took a sip. Then he sat at the rickety table by the window and began to put order in his papers, as if he were drawing up a will. He made extensive notes, writing down as much as he could: names, conversations, random thoughts. He brought his accounts up to date, checked on how much he owed and was owed, wrote it all down. It was two o'clock in the morning when he finished. He gulped down the last sip of whisky from his glass, which he had been saving for this moment, and went to bed.

The alarm woke him early. His head ached from a short night of worried sleep. He felt as if he had not slept at all. He got up anyway. He wanted to ring Nick at home.

Nick could not keep the expectation out of his voice when he heard Banks.

'I hope I didn't wake you,' Banks said.

'No. Of course not.' Nick had been shaving. He was now in the bedroom, bare-chested, his towel slung on his shoulder, shaving cream around the ears. 'What have you got?' he said.

'I found what you wanted me to find,' Banks said.

'You did?'

'I don't have any proof,' Banks said, automatically qualifying his earlier statement. 'Not yet. It's just rumour.'

'Can you get proof?' Nick asked.

'I don't know,' Banks said. 'Something better than I've got, I should think.'

His voice was faint, growing fainter with every exchange, as if he were getting further away each time he spoke.

'Do you need more money?' Nick asked, speaking a little more loudly.

'No.' Banks was saying little. He had just wanted to let Nick know that he had been right. That if he, Banks, should die, then somebody else could be sent without wasting any money.

'I'm sending you my notes and my accounts,' he said.

'You do need money,' Nick did not understand why else Banks would be sending him his accounts. He had no practice at this.

'I don't need money.' Banks spoke emphatically. His voice had suddenly become normal again. 'I would like you to keep my notes.' His voice dropped again as he added, 'Keep them safe. You never know.' He paused. 'I think somebody tried to run me over last night,' he said.

In the hall of the hotel, Banks was crouched over the telephone, a call-box in the corner under the staircase. He held his lips close to the mouthpiece, his hand covering it. He looked around him every few seconds. He had whispered the last sentence, and Nick had not heard it well.

'Somebody did what to you?' Nick asked, shouting into the phone because Banks was speaking so softly, as if by increasing his own volume, he could make Banks' voice louder.

Hearing Nick shout down the phone made Banks feel foolish. He was safe. Nothing was going to happen. At least not right now. He straightened out and spoke up.

'Run me over,' he said clearly. He took a packet of cigarettes out of his pocket and lit up.

'Somebody tried to run you over?' Nick said in disbelief. 'Do you mean someone tried to kill you last night?'

'Yes.'

'You'd better come back to Edinburgh, then,' Nick said firmly. 'I won't have you getting killed over this. If they're trying to kill, we know why and we know who,' trying to add logic to what he was saying.

'You can't prove it,' said Banks, being more practical.

Nick had never actually considered the need for proof. He had assumed that finding out the truth would be enough. Standing there by the bed, with his razor in his hand, he realized that the truth would indeed be enough. He did not need proof.

'I don't need to prove it,' he said.

'Believe me, sir,' Banks was adamant. 'Whatever you want to do, you need more than I've got. I know you do.'

Nick could not tell without seeing what Banks was sending him. He had faith in the detective, and he did not want to discuss things on the telephone in too much detail. He distrusted phones. He did not insist.

'I'll wait for the package,' he said. 'Be careful,' he added.

'I will be that, sir,' Banks said. 'Thank you very much. It may be nothing at all,' he added. He hung up and went back upstairs to prepare his parcel for Nick.

Nick put the phone down and stood still, feeling a mounting thrill. He sensed the moment of battle. He would have to be careful. He would have to ensure they made no mistakes. The closer he got to the moment of attack, the more dangerous mistakes became.

The thought of danger brought back what Banks had said. He wondered if Banks had been right. Nick could not easily grasp the concept of murder. He was too far away from it to understand the reality of the threat.

On reading Banks' package, Nick realized the extent and thoroughness of his work. He had indeed been like a ferret and he was digging out the rats. From it, Nick felt even more hopeful that Banks would provide him with the ammunition he needed. But when? For Nick agreed with Banks; there still was not quite enough.

A few days later, Faulkner published its quarterly report, its largest trading profit in ten years. Two days after that, Nick left for London. In the next few months, he knew that he would have to spend more time in the capital. With the announcement of Faulkner's profits would come a buzz on the stock market, and with that, potential danger. A re-emerging company is attractive prey to the stalking predator. Catch them on the way up, not on the way down, was the practice. Nick had to protect his supply lines and shield himself from another bid.

The City was where his shareholders lived, the institutions that controlled the nation's public companies and its wealth. The future of Armadale had been in the hands of a few portfolio managers, he knew. He had ignored them in the past, thinking that minding the store was enough. So now he would court. He would woo them with his recent high profits, his increased earnings per share and his forecasts of more success. The City likes to be courted.

Nick did not like doing it. He felt demeaned by it, as if he were a flatterer. It irritated him that it should be necessary. He would have preferred dealing with thousands of small shareholders, each one questioning him at the Annual General Meeting, writing him letters when they disapproved of the way he was handling their investment. There was always a utopia hidden in Nick's heart, and now it was as if he, Nick, was born free, and the portfolio manager was one of the people who kept him in chains.

It was a complex business. He could not give out information that his shareholders did not have, yet he had to keep his investors, the financial analysts, the journalists up to date about what Faulkner was doing and how well it was doing. It was often more a question of innuendo than of hard fact.

Over the last two years, Nick had had to build these relationships from scratch. By now he knew which people could be trusted to read accurately the information he handed out or leaked, and which people felt could trust him. He spent two days a week in London, coming down from Edinburgh early one day and returning late the following. Working for him in London was Mike Jones, a principal of the Brogan Thomas PR firm, who was helping him build up a repertoire of City men and women with whom he would make contact regularly.

That is how Nick met Simon Harner, the journalist whom Roger had courted so successfully during the Armadale take-over. Mike introduced them at an early December party. Nick and Julian were there, several journalists, Annie had come too, principally in her capacity as headhunter, but also because she was a friend of Nick's. There were many others from the City. It was a clever mix, designed by Mike to promote his clients.

Mike, a trim, fair-haired man with a barely discernible Welsh lilt to his accent, grabbed Nick away from a young woman analyst who had just returned from an organized visit to Faulkner's recent San Francisco purchase, the company Julian had found.

'Sorry, Barbara,' Mike said, 'I've got to take him away from you. Otherwise people will start to talk.'

Nick smiled his apology and followed Mike, who led him across the room where Simon was in conversation with another journalist.

'You haven't met Simon Harner, yet,' Mike Jones said. 'I think it's time.'

Nick looked towards the journalist. He was above average height, a little shorter than Nick, slender, with short, wavy, dark hair. He wore round, gold-rimmed glasses, and like most of the financial journalists, he looked like a businessman.

Mike moved on to make another introduction or to check that a match was going well. A party was hard work for him.

'I've read your stuff,' said Nick affably. 'You're very reliable.'

'Thank you,' Simon said.

'Most of the time,' Nick added with a smile. 'I wasn't so impressed a couple of years ago.'

'Ah, Armadale,' Simon said. 'You didn't like what I said. But was I wrong?'

'Not exactly wrong, perhaps,' Nick said. 'Just looking at it from one perspective only.'

'You may be right,' Simon said. 'Nothing much has changed.'

'It might have done if the outcome had been different,' Nick persisted.

'Still worried about it?' Simon questioned Nick.

'No,' Nick laughed. He seemed not to care. 'I've got other cares now.'

'Yes. You're doing very well out of Scotland.'

'You should come up and see us,' Nick said. 'I'll show you around.'

'You've become quite a predator yourself,' Simon said. He let the sentence hang. It was half a question.

'Small acquisitions,' Nick said. 'Consolidating the changes we're making. All of them friendly,' he added.

'It makes a difference,' Simon said.

Their every sentence seemed to make a veiled reference to Roger and his takeover of Armadale. Or so it seemed to Nick. To Simon it was just chat. He liked Nick. He felt he could rely on him to be fairly straight. Only in that way could a comparison with Roger be made. Roger was a manipulator. One had to be extra careful when he told you something. Simon had learned that over the years.

'You down in London a lot?' the journalist asked.

'About once a week these days,' Nick said.

'Something happening?' Simon said.

'Not yet,' Nick said. He smiled.

'Let's have lunch some day,' Simon suggested.

'Love to. On me,' Nick said.

'All right.'

They moved on. It had gone smoothly. Of such meetings, successful relations were made. This was one of the reasons Nick came down to London.

He spent the night with Annie. Despite Nick's more

frequent visits to London, they had seen less of each other in the last few months. They had both been busy in the autumn; it was a hectic season for Annie. Nick's focus was changing. He knew that his attack on Corpcom was approaching. There had been more work, and with it, he had become more mono-maniacal.

His love-making revealed his obsession. It was not just that his need for Annie was less intense. He seemed somehow less subtle about it, less emotional and more physical. Annie understood perhaps, but there was little charm in it for her.

After Mike's party, they had gone out to a restaurant, during which Nick had reported to her on his progress, more especially on the report from Banks. For the first time, she had not cared and she wondered why. This should have been important news. Was she less interested in Nick? Perhaps we're settling down, she thought, like dust in a room. She smiled at her own analogy and Nick caught her doing it.

'Why are you smiling?' he asked.

'Nothing,' she said.

And he did not bother to wonder any further.

That night, in bed, they made love. There was nothing satisfying about it for her. It angered her, especially since Nick seemed not to care much.

'You're rutting these days, Nick,' she said sharply.

He had already lain down, his head on the pillow, ready for sleep.

'What do you mean?' he said, sitting up.

'Guess,' she said.

'I'm sorry,' he said. It was a matter-of-fact apology. He realized she was right, but it was as if he were saying that he could do nothing about it.

'That makes me feel much better,' she pursued, even more annoyed by his tone. 'I'm glad you're so concerned about it.'

'I apologized,' he said. 'What more do you want?'

'I want you to mean it,' she said angrily. 'I want you to stop acting like someone who would screw anything with a hole in it.'

'I'm sorry you don't like the way I make love,' he said. His male pride had been hurt.

She laughed at seeing it.

Annie hated to fight with Nick. She was far more venomous than he. His back would straighten, his mouth would tighten and he would fill with outrage and reasoned anger. She was a better fighter. There were no rules in battle, and she wounded him more easily and then hated herself for it. Afterwards, she would remember the way he looked, hurt, his eyes wide with surprise at the blow, sad and helpless, the way he looked now. That was when she understood how Sophie could have left him. Nick did not know how to fight and he refused to. This refusal did not make him more innocent; on the contrary, it made his guilt seem even greater. Annie could imagine Nick's cold dismissal of the charges of adultery and could see how Sophie might have disbelieved in Nick's fidelity.

'You're unyielding,' she said to him.

'That's what Sophie used to say,' Nick meant it as an insult. He was not devoid of all spite.

'I don't blame her. She sounds like an intelligent woman.' Annie knew the insult had been intended, but did not feel it.

'She is,' he said.

'Then you're a fool to have left her.'

'She left me.'

'Don't you believe it,' Annie said. 'You are guilty, as much as she is.'

'Rubbish,' he said.

He was being pompous, and it angered her.

'Ask your children, then,' she threw at him. Immediately, she regretted it for she saw that childish look of hurt. She turned over as if to go to sleep. Nick was left to do the same.

In the morning, they would make up. They both knew that. They were lucky; they still could afford to leave it like that.

Annie was strong. She was patient and independent. But she wondered if Nick would ever be able to look after his private life at the same time as his professional one. He did not know how to reconcile the two.

Annie knew that his behaviour with his children was the worst manifestation of this dark side. She wished he would look after them more.

Nick wished it too, but did not know how to go about it. He usually saw his children once a month, when Alistair and John came to Edinburgh for the weekend. It was another benefit of his having learned to cook that he could have them at his flat and it could almost be home. But his concerns were so far removed from children at the moment that he could not manage to forget them long enough to enjoy his boys. His mind was always itching to be elsewhere, when it should have been with them.

Now that he was in London more often, he saw them there. In London, even more than in Edinburgh, each visit left them all with a dissatisfied feeling. He had become a visitor in Alistair's and John's lives, sharing moments more as a distant relative than as a father. Their lives moved on more rapidly than he could keep up with them.

Coming upon them now was the third Christmas they would have spent apart. Alistair was twelve and John ten. The closeness that comes from constant, even sometimes stifling, physical contact was gone. They had to make up for it every time they saw each other, and, because he had no place of his own in London other than Annie's flat, which, owing to a kind of strict puritanism, he did not like to use, he felt homeless, wandering aimlessly through London, lacking any solidity, which he knew to be the very thing he should be providing.

Then he wished he was back in Edinburgh. He was always looking for activities to do because he could not just *be* with his children any more; they had to do things or else be lost again. He did not enjoy these days much and began to force himself to spend time with them.

He fell back on gifts, and then bought the wrong things. One day he picked them up from the station, with a gift for each boy; they came up by train to meet him and he would drive them back at the end of the day. He had bought Alistair *Treasure Island*, and John a set of colouring books. He met them at the train and watched them walk down the platform towards him. They did not run, the way they had two years earlier; they walked. They were both wearing track suits and trainers. It was their uniform, and Nick could not avoid the irritation at seeing them always wear the same things. It was irrational, but he felt it.

They kissed. At least, he kissed them. Even that was a fight these days. They would both recoil a little as he put his lips to their cheek.

When he gave them their presents in the car, there was a silence as both of the boys opened them.

'I've got this book, Dad,' Alistair said. His tone was bored, condescending, slightly superior.

'What do you mean, you've read *Treasure Island*?' Nick said. 'You're twelve. I hadn't read *Treasure Island* when I was twelve,' he added as if this made sense.

'I didn't like it,' Alistair responded. 'It's boring.'

'Boring,' Nick retorted. 'How can you say it's boring? That's a silly thing to say.'

He looked back at him and saw Alistair's face set into silence. Nick felt powerless; he knew he was being unreasonable.

'Give it back to me, then,' he said. 'I'll exchange it. What do you like?'

'There's a new Stephen King,' Alistair said.

Nick's reaction was instinctive. 'I'm not getting you Stephen King. Don't tell me your mother lets you read Stephen King?'

'Yes, she does,' Alastair spat at him.

Nick was taken aback. He stopped himself, looked over at

324

John, hoping to defuse the moment from there. But John had discarded the colouring books; they were on the floor of the car, and he was glancing at the copy of *Treasure Island*.

Nick decided to give up and drive away. They would go to the cinema. The film and the ice-cream would put them in better humour. But he felt defeated.

The final blow, the coat of shame layered over the one of guilt, came when he took them back to Sophie. She would greet him at the door of the house in Downe, her mouth set in silent, constant recrimination. She was embittered and did not hide it. On the contrary, she felt like a woman abandoned and she held up her loneliness like a banner that proclaimed an enforced widowhood.

This was the price of his stubbornness. He returned to Scotland to re-immerse himself into the work, allowing it to wash away his sins. There he could begin again to feel that his revenge was justified.

3

In the latter part of that year Julian travelled less. It coincided with Nick's more frequent trips to London. It suited both of them for Julian to be in Edinburgh. Julian had been made a member of the board a year and half after joining the company, and although he was not the titular second-in-command, it was he who Nick depended on.

They managed an interesting juggling act, the two of them. They led double lives, two-timing their company in a way, yet being faithful to its future at the same time. By preparing Faulkner Industries for taking over Corpcom, Nick was necessarily creating a strong, healthy company; it was the only way his plan would work. In his position as travelling buyer, Julian had a clearly defined job, which allowed him considerable independence and easy access to Nick himself. Because he was unassuming and easily liked, Julian was able to perform on his own without causing internecine jealousies. Both Nick and he underplayed their relationship, and since the core of it was secret, they had decided early on to keep the things that related to Corpcom to private moments. Those, because of Nick's insistence on security, were often held at home. They were then able to carry on at the office 'as usual', with secrecy a part of the thrill of the chase, an added aphrodisiac.

This relatively settled period gave Julian and Rebecca time to see what official marriage was like. Since Julian was to be in Edinburgh for a while, she had chosen this period to come up. She had been commissioned to write an article on Edinburgh for an American airline magazine. Since they were going to spend Christmas in Concord, now was a good time to write the article. She would deliver it in person, on her way.

They finally lived in their rented flat in Bellevue, a few minutes away from the office. Rebecca worked all day in the living-room, the table set up next to the window overlooking the street. It was a restful period for her also, away from the constant hustle of London; she enjoyed the more sedentary activity of writing in what was, for her, an unusually quiet environment.

Julian looked for Corpcom's weaknesses.

'Andrews relies too much on takeovers for growth,' he said to Rebecca one evening, using her as a sounding board. They were sitting in the living-room, she at her desk, revising some of the day's work, he on the sofa, with his papers spread out over the low coffee table, considering the information he had been collecting over the last several months.

She half-turned in her chair to face him.

'His victims are on to him,' Julian continued. 'That's his problem. The battles are expensive.'

'You're running around the world buying,' she said. 'Why's that not a problem?'

'We don't do hostile takeovers,' he said. 'Every company we've ever bought has wanted us to. That's a big difference.'

'At the moment,' she said. 'That's about to change, isn't

it?' Rebecca was still worried about what they were going to attempt. More than ever, she questioned whether there could be business sense to an action whose motive was so transparently personal and dangerous.

'For the first time,' he said. Rebecca's point of view was well-known to him and he tried not to let it worry him. She used it more as a thorn in his conscience than a bludgeon. 'Andrews is spending a lot of money these days,' he went on, 'especially in the States. They've come up with some interesting defences over there. Stripping assets isn't always enough to keep him with 15 per cent margin.'

Julian knew that Andrews was cash poor at the moment and would be hard pressed to defend himself adequately, even if he could attack with impunity. Attacking brought its own momentum and, although it did not always work, a predator raised cash on the very fact of his attack, whereas the defender had to prove himself worthy of defence, the burden of proof falling on the target rather than on the attacker. That people clamoured for its change did not alter the reality, and Julian doubted that it was possible to legislate that kind of justice. The market has its own laws and governments could only alter them if they were willing to counter its basic principle of natural selection.

Rebecca had gone back to her work, for her attention span for this kind of conversation was limited.

They both fell silent. A little later, Rebecca turned off the word processor she worked on, rubbed her eyes and turned back to face Julian again. He was still deep in his papers. He had a calculator out and was working with figures. She stood up and walked over to stand behind him.

'I wish you'd take the bastard over,' she said. 'This kind of life is not worth the suspense.'

Julian finished his sums. 'We've got almost 15 per cent secured as of now,' he said, 'and nobody knows it.'

'I thought you have to declare a holding once you get to 5 per cent,' she said, hoping Julian was not breaking the law.

'You do,' he answered. 'We've only got 4.9 per cent. But

I've been discussing the other 10 per cent. And we should be able to buy it as soon as we announce the bid.' He sat back in triumph, enjoying the fact of Corpcom's cash problems.

'Are you sure that's legal? Doesn't sound it to me.'

'Just about,' he said, smiling. 'Soon. Very soon.' He reached up behind her, put his arms around her neck and brought her face down to his. He kissed her.

'I've finished,' he said. 'Shall we begin?'

Gently, she pushed him away. She wished she could back him whole-heartedly, without reservation. His smile faded and was replaced by an innocent, wounded look.

'I'm not doing anything wrong, Rebecca. I promise you.'

'I know,' she said with a sad smile and she leaned down towards him again and put her arms around his neck. Her hair brushed his head.

Chapter Twenty-Seven

I

It was December when Julian next travelled to New York. Rebecca went with him. Nick would spend Christmas with Annie and Boxing Day with his children and then return to Edinburgh for the New Year. Julian and Rebecca would spend the holiday in Concord with her parents. It was like a last furlough.

Julian's trip was, ostensibly, an ordinary business trip to New York. Julian sat on the board of one of Faulkner's subsidiaries and the last meeting of the year was being held in the New York headquarters. But he had another reason for going. Julian was going to 'bump into' an old friend: Alan Turner now worked for Corpcom's American arm and lived in New York.

Alan's career had been a success. As Howard had tried to explain to Nick, fidelity to a company was for sale to the highest bidder. After his move from Armadale to Corpcom, Alan had done increasingly well, almost as if Armadale had been holding him back. He had moved from marketing to corporate PR; he was then put in charge of corporate communications and liaison between Corpcom US and Corpcom UK.

He and Fanny lived on East 83rd Street in Manhattan, in a modern two-bedroom apartment, with a small bathroom and a narrow kitchen, on the twenty-seventh floor of a high-rise building. The apartment was rented for them by Corpcom while they looked for a 'co-op' to buy.

Alan loved New York. He would look down upon it at

night from his balcony, which faced downtown, and with a drink in his hand gaze at it lovingly. Manhattan was his island indeed. London, he had realized after being in the States for only a month, had been like a corset to his ambitions. London is a family town, but New York is for the young, the single and the childless. In London he had had to hide his ambition, here he could flaunt it: people paid for it.

So Alan represented a potential source of information for Julian, and even though he did not know what he might get, he was hoping the fishing trip would yield something. It was a gamble. The time for their move on Corpcom was approaching and Nick and Julian were trying to muster all possible information before they moved. The visit to Alan could provide a piece of data.

'Don't you ever get sick of being devious?' Rebecca had asked Julian on the airplane over. They were in business class, which was a luxury for her, if not for him any longer. The plane was making its approach into New York and as she looked out of the window, she could see the skyscrapers in the distance. They were going to follow the Hudson River and then turn back into the airport.

She was looking forward to spending some time in the States. She missed home after a few months away – pizzas that didn't take twenty minutes to prepare, telephones that worked, American accents, her parents, the sun – and was pleased she could get a refill every now and then.

Yet this trip, she felt an unusual sense of discomfort. The closer the launching of the bid, the more she disliked it. She looked on Julian's role in Nick's revenge with considerable ambivalence. She would be happy if Roger were to lose Corpcom; he had caused great suffering to close friends of hers and, if Julian was right, had been responsible for the death of at least two men. She wasted no sympathy on him.

On the other hand, she did not like what learning all these tricks of the trade, and indeed mastering them with such proficiency, did to Julian. When she had met him, when he had been working for Armadale, his commitment to his work had been no more than from moment to moment. His sense of adventure was youthful and undirected. Now it seemed to have found a home. Julian enjoyed stalking his prey and Rebecca showed a good liberal arts distrust of those who found their vocation in the very practical world of finance and business. To her it was an unromantic choice, and possibly not a very moral one. The world of business was one in which the means were always justified by the ends.

'You're going to lie to your old friend Alan Turner.' She spoke the words 'old friend' mockingly.

'I suppose I am.' Julian thought about it. 'I'm going to pretend. Its not quite the same. It's all part of the game,' he added with a little less conviction.

They arrived in New York in the late afternoon on a Friday and could look forward to a weekend alone. They stayed at the Westbury on Madison Avenue. On Saturday morning Rebecca forced Julian out of bed to walk with her. It was a clear December day. The sun shone brightly through the cold air and was reflected brilliantly in the tall glass buildings of mid-town. Walking down Madison Avenue late on a Saturday morning, even in December, was something Rebecca had enjoyed doing ever since the month she had spent in New York after leaving university. She had stayed further uptown with a friend of her mother's. She remembered the romantic, slightly nostalgic feeling of walking down Madison, watching couples idling from shop to shop, arms entwined, their hands wandering over each other's backs, stopping occasionally for a kiss, all this ballet so clearly, it seemed to her, the relaxed aftermath of Saturday morning's love-making. She wanted to walk like that with Julian.

They had lunch at a deli because Rebecca wanted a real New York sandwich, and then went to the Frick Museum. They went to see a film, had dinner, and then went to another film. Sunday was equally languid. A lazy weekend.

On Monday, Julian staged his coincidental meeting with Alan.

It was lunch-time. He was alone. Rebecca had had no desire to see Alan; nor had she wanted to take part in the subterfuge of waiting for him to come out of his office building and then simulating a chance meeting. She stayed away, and did some Christmas shopping instead.

Julian saw Alan come out on to Sixth Avenue with a couple of colleagues, just as he used to in London. Alan looked fuller and much more prosperous; the edginess of impatient expectation had been replaced by a boisterous satisfaction at having arrived. Julian smiled as he watched him; it was against that self-confidence that he would be playing. He saw Alan and his friends walk down the avenue, and he followed them. When he was a few yards away, he called out to him.

Alan turned when he heard his name. Julian was hurrying towards him.

'Julian,' he called out in surprise, and with delight. 'Julian, what are you doing in New York?'

Alan introduced his colleagues. When he heard that Julian was free for lunch, he abandoned them and took his old friend from London to a favourite restaurant.

'What a coincidence,' he said as he and Julian walked on downtown together. He looked forward to reviewing the last few years with Julian; there was so much in his own life to be pleased with.

They went to a French restaurant on 44th Street. It was a large open room with banquettes and mirrors – a reminder of France, but definitely a New York restaurant, if only because the customers were not bent over their plates in quite the same way, and the seriousness was in the conversations and not in the eating.

Alan ordered a Bloody Mary.

'I'll just have some wine with the meal,' Julian said. He wanted to stay sober.

'So what are you doing in New York?' Alan asked.

'I'm here for a board meeting,' he answered.

'You're a board-member, eh?' asked Alan. 'Very impressive.'

'It's a subsidiary of Faulkner,' Julian said, trying to put it down. 'I'm still based in Edinburgh,' he went on. The last time they had met in London, Julian was just on his way to join Nick.

'Nick Bishop, eh?' There was a hint of condescension in Alan's voice. 'How's he doing then?'

'Very well. We've just announced a very good profit, actually.' Julian spoke the truth, but his tone of voice was gentle and unassuming. He was simulating a lack of ambition, a contentment with a small success, which he knew Alan, with his own sense of achievement and his new found American, ism, would interpret as being a typically English contentment and parochialism. He fuelled that transparent side of Alan.

'I heard you'd joined the fold, if you can call it that,' Julian said with what he hoped would seem like jealous irony.

'Not the fold, friend. Joined the wolf,' he said and laughed. 'No, it was just a good career move.' Alan had no shame about looking after himself. 'And guess who suggested I do it?'

'Who?' Julian knew exactly who had done it.

Annie had heard of the job and had told Alan. After all, he was an old friend. Later, enjoying the incestuousness of it, she had told Nick and Julian with delight. Nick had remembered it and it had been his suggestion that Julian make this trip. Nick had come a long way.

'The gorgeous Annie Chinoise,' Alan said. 'I'm an old friend of hers, you know.'

'That's where I heard you were in New York,' Julian said, as if Alan's mention of her name had just reminded him, 'from Annie.'

'She and Bishop still an item?' Alan asked.

Julian nodded. 'I see them quite a lot, actually.'

'Amazing what happened,' Alan said, shaking his head. 'Couldn't believe it at the time.'

Julian said nothing. He let Alan speak. There was no point in explaining how Nick and Annie came to be together.

'Tell her I said hallo, would you?' Alan said.

The conversation continued in this vein. They talked of Armadale, of Scotland, but especially of New York. Alan showed off his life, just as a shopkeeper displays his goods, and Julian kept asking to see more. They talked of Corpcom, of Alan's job in New York. Julian checked his facts and his impressions.

They had finished a bottle of wine, they had eaten well. Alan was pleased to see Julian's familiar, friendly face. He leant forward toward Julian.

'It's all very hush-hush,' he said in a stage whisper, 'Andrews is going for a very big fish. One of the biggest deals he's done in a long time.'

'Who is it?' asked Julian.

'Oh, I can't tell you that,' Alan said with a little chuckle of reproof. 'I told you. It's a big secret.'

'That's right,' Julian said. 'Of course you can't. Don't worry about it,' he added. 'I understand.'

He had what he wanted. The fishing trip had been worth it.

They met for supper two days later. Rebecca and Fanny were there. This time Julian paid for the meal. They went to an Italian restaurant in the Village that Fanny suggested. It was more relaxed, more like old times. Alan did not bother to wear a tie and Julian felt a little stuffy in his suit.

Fanny was happy to see them, but there was no nostalgia in her for London. She, just like Alan, loved New York.

'New York never shuts down,' she said. 'That's what I love most about it, I think.'

Rebecca smiled back. She knew what she meant. Rebecca, though, liked London exactly because it did shut down and, like its inhabitants, slept at night.

'Even at two o'clock in the morning,' Fanny continued, 'on a deserted street, with no one about, you can still hear this city breathe.' She paused, and then added, almost out of breath, 'It's so exciting.'

'We love it here,' Alan said, as if Fanny had not made it obvious.

They both seemed genuinely happy. It struck Rebecca with force. She had always found them, especially Alan, dissatisfied with their lot. Yet they had not been aware of it.

Now their lives were changed. They were new immigrants.

Seeing their contentment made her resentful of Julian's manipulation of their reunion. That evening, in the hotel room, she sat on the bed combing her hair. Julian was already in bed.

'Has your trip been a success?' she asked. She was very sarcastic.

Julian ignored her tone. She disapproved of what he had done. 'So what?' he thought defiantly.

'Even better than I had hoped,' he said and he smiled at her smugly.

She looked at him in silence for a while. She had stopped combing her hair. She wished he would not look like that.

'Alan won't get blamed for it, will he?' she asked.

'Since when are you so worried about him?' Julian said. 'I thought you didn't like him.'

'Alan's all right.' Unconsciously, she echoed the words Julian had used many years ago. 'I like Fanny anyway. She deserves everything she's got.'

'Well, I'm sure she'll get to keep it,' Julian said. 'Alan will be all right. He's very tough. He'll survive.'

Julian felt no guilt. No one would know what Alan had given him. It had just been friendly gossip, gossip which happened to have been invaluable to Julian.

The evening of his first meeting with Alan, he had called Nick. With Corpcom buying again, it would be stretched. Nick and Julian had agreed. Faulkner would have to be ready to move early in the New Year.

2

But where was Willie Banks? The New Year came and Nick had still not heard from him. The long days and nights of drinking were over and, as usual, the year had started with a hangover. Julian was still in America. Annie was in London. Nick stood in his office, looking out of his windows.

It was snowing. The sky was an even, thick grey and the flakes of rapidly falling snow obscured most of the Botanic

Garden from view. With the snow, an enforced silence was falling on the town. The cars were quietened and the thickening whiteness absorbed sound and seemed to hurl it back with the shriek of reflected light.

Nick stood still, watching the snow fall. But he was restless. Ever since Julian's telephone call from New York, announcing Corpcom's next takeover attempt, he had stayed in Edinburgh with growing impatience. He wanted to be completely ready to attack Roger. Now he was worried that his most valuable weapon would not arrive in time, that he would be forced either to delay and miss the opportune moment, or to attack without the necessary ammunition. After the lull of Christmas and, especially here in Scotland, of the New Year celebrations, life was returning to normal and Nick's desire to act was inflamed by the apparent quiet of a routine renewed.

He remembered how three years ago, almost to the day, his telephone had rung and Roger had announced his takeover bid for Armadale. He could imagine Roger and Peter preparing themselves over long months for that telephone call and the few weeks of battle that followed it. Nick had been doing it himself, with Julian, for over two years. And according to Julian's information, Roger and Peter were doing it again. He wondered what their thoughts were now. They were old hands. They had prepared more takeovers than Nick would ever attempt. Did they feel his restless need to pounce, to attack and get it over with? What if he had had a bug in Roger's office? The idea had not even occurred to him. But, in any event, the discovery of a bug might give something away; this was going to be a surprise attack, a surprise that not even the stock market would be able to read.

Nick thought of Howard. He had not seen Howard for almost a year; they had not spoken in private since they had met in the club and his taking over at Faulkner had been discussed. Nick had avoided meeting him. Howard had made overtures, but had followed them up only half-heartedly. Slowly, they had drifted apart, and finally Howard had accepted it, the way he accepted everything that happened. Howard was sad about his lost friendship, but he did not think it served a purpose to fight reality; it was a current one could not swim against.

Nick, on the contrary, had accepted nothing. He had surfaced out of his sense of failure and solitude, renewed by his love of Annie, which was still passionately intense. There was no doubt that he had been regenerated by his work at Faulkner's too, and even if he did not regard Faulkner the way he had Armadale, he was proud of his achievement there. Yet he had forgotten nothing, and forgiven nothing. Amazingly, the sense that injustice had been committed was still as strong in his dark, lonely moments as it had ever been.

There was a knock at the door and Sarah walked in.

Sarah had been another of his team he had gone in quest of. It had been easy. He had called her at her demoted post in Armadale soon after Julian had agreed to come. She had been so happy at the offer that she had screeched with joy the minute she put the phone down, startling the other people in the room. The next moment, she was crying, too moved to do anything else.

Sarah loved Edinburgh. She had a sister who lived there. It was as if she had come home, even though she had spent all her life in the south.

'Mr Banks is here,' she said to Nick.

Sarah did not know who Banks was, but she knew that Nick wanted to speak to him, whatever he was doing at the time.

'Here?' Nick said in surprise.

'In reception.'

'Show him in,' he said.

Nick could hardly contain his excitement. Willie Banks. Banks was not expected. Nick had not heard from the detective since before Christmas.

He went to the door and opened it. He stood in the doorway, waiting for Banks. He watched the private detective walk down the corridor towards him. The angular face looked weary and even greyer than Nick remembered it. His walk was slightly pigeon-toed, but he came towards Nick with a look of confidence. Under his arm was a worn satchel, brown with age and dirt. Banks was wearing a clean white shirt and a tie under his cheap grey suit. He looked like a tax collector.

'Willie,' Nick said as he threw out his hand at Banks. 'How nice to see you.'

They shook hands, and Nick enveloped his arm around the smaller man and led him into his office. He closed the door behind him.

'Sit down,' Nick said. 'Do you want a cup of coffee? A drink maybe?'

'I wouldn't mind a wee bit of whisky,' Banks said. He was pleased too. He had come with the right news.

Now that Banks had arrived, they both took it slowly. It was like getting a long-awaited letter; having arrived, it can be kept unopened, to prolong the anticipation. Nick knew that Banks would not have come so theatrically, without warning, if he had not had good news. Banks had a good sense of drama. Both men could wait a little longer.

Nick poured himself a drink as well and after he had given Banks his glass, he raised his own and said, 'Welcome back.'

'Thank you very much, sir,' Banks said. 'It's about time.'

Nick sat down opposite Banks and spoke to the point, 'So. What have you got for me?'

'I think I know what happened three years ago,' the detective answered. 'A deed of dreadful note,' he quoted.

Nick looked at Banks without speaking. Then, 'You mean, those men were murdered.'

Banks shook his head, 'Manslaughter,' he said. 'They didn't mean to kill them. But they meant to blow up the dehydration tower.' He paused. 'They sabotaged the control valve,' he went on. 'Do you know what that is?'

'Yes.' Nick remembered his own trip to the platform. He remembered now the look the platform engineer had given Stephen when he had questioned them about the valve. Had they been involved?

'Who are "they"?' he asked Banks.

'That's quite a long story.' He took a sip of his whisky. He paused, lit a cigarette. 'I've just come back from Germany,' he continued after this ritual. 'A little town called Schwarmstedt. I doubt whether you know it. I can't think what you'd remember it by.'

Banks had gone to find Helmut Jurgens, the man who, according to the diver Chavel, had left his job on the platform soon after the explosion. It was after his visit to Jurgens that everything had fallen into place with remarkable ease. Banks had marvelled at how he had spent months in Aberdeen trying to find things out, and it had all amounted to one name, the name of a man who lived in Germany.

From Jurgens, Banks had learned that the control valve in the dehydration tower had been sabotaged on the platform. The seat of the valve had been moved two days after the last official, logged check.

'I saw him do it,' Jurgens said. 'I was taking a short-cut through the dehydration module. And there he was fiddling with the valve.'

They were sitting over a beer in Jurgens' simple kitchen. It was a small, claustrophobic cottage. Jurgens lived there alone. He was unmarried. His parents lived a few streets away. Banks could well understand why Jurgens had tried to get away, even if it meant going to the North Sea. If being off-shore did not liberate him, perhaps the money would. Jurgens had had to leave before collecting enough of it.

'Who did you see?' Banks asked.

'The platform engineer,' was the answer. 'I didn't know what he was doing.' He shrugged his shoulders. 'I knew after the explosion,' he said. 'I didn't know why, but I knew what had happened.'

'That was when you had the argument?'

Jurgens had not bothered to deny the argument. He and the platform engineer had been seen arguing.

'The stupid bastard. Fooling around with a control valve,' Jurgens said. 'He thought, because he was the platform engineer, he could control who went in and out. You can't control people's movements on a platform. There are too many ins and outs.'

'Did he threaten you?' Banks asked. And when Jurgens looked insulted, Banks added, 'You changed your testimony.' He let the implication hang there, without repeating the question.

'He did threaten me,' Jurgens admitted, 'but that is not why I changed my mind. I decided I did not want to get involved. It was done. It was not my business.' He was sullen, unhappy.

'So why did you leave?' Banks asked. He had not come all the way to a little town north of Hanover just to be nice to a man who would not testify.

Jurgens thought about it for a second. Then, shrugging his shoulders in a hopeless gesture, 'I could not stand staying there,' he said.

'Not a happy man,' Banks said to Nick. 'He went back to a place he wanted to get away from.'

'Would he testify now?' Nick asked. 'If he were asked to?'

'He might have to now, if we could get him back to England.' Banks did not seem to think there was any point in it.

Now that he knew for certain that the explosion of the dehydration tower had been a planned accident, timed to coincide with the bid on Armadale, to add pressure on the beleaguered company, Nick still found it inconceivable that Roger would do such a thing. With all his experience, Roger could not have believed the accident would have done much more than put pressure on Armadale. Nick was astounded at such ruthlessness, that people should die for such a petty aim.

'Go on,' he said. 'I assume that's not all of it.' He was solemn. Perhaps he had expected elation, but there was no fun to be had with this news. He was not even able to gloat at what he would do with the information.

'Most of it,' Banks said. 'Not quite all.'

He went back to his narrative. Having discovered who was responsible for the actual sabotage, it was relatively easy to trace the line back to the purse strings. It was a matter of leg work. Knowing what questions to ask was half the battle. The platform engineer had been seen a great deal with a senior employee of a Corpcom subsidiary in Aberdeen. After the explosion there had been one other meeting, then none at all. The Corpcom employee was directly linked to Peter. They had been seen together more than usual around the time of the accident – before and after it.

'According to what I've heard,' said Banks, 'what McNeal knows, Andrews knows. And what McNeal does, Andrews pays for.'

Nick just nodded his agreement. People had been bribed, silences bought. Two men were dead.

'Casualties of war,' Nick said.

'I'm afraid so,' Banks agreed. 'In a way that's the worst of it.'

He paused to light another cigarette. He had been talking for a little over two hours now. Nick had topped up his drink three times already. This was his tenth cigarette. The air in the office was poisonous with smoke, but neither man had thought of opening the window.

'It's a cynical ending,' Banks said. 'There was a very large settlement for the families of the two dead workmen. It was Andrews who set that up.'

'Andrews himself?' Nick asked.

'He didn't do it in his name,' said the detective, 'but he did it through Armadale. Once he'd got rid of you. A very generous settlement. Very clever. A handsome pay-off. And it looks like generosity from the new boss.' He added, 'What could be better?'

'And it worked like a charm.'

'Absolutely.'

Nick reached for the bottle once more. He poured them each another drink.

'How much of this can you prove in court?' he asked Banks.

'At the moment, very little,' Banks said. 'Eventually you

341

could. Once it was broken.' Banks shrugged. 'You can be the judge of that better than I can. I didn't think that was quite as important to you, sir.'

'No. You're right,' Nick said. 'It isn't. This will be fine.'

So this was proof, circumstantial perhaps, but proof all the same, that Corpcom, and Roger, were directly linked to the manslaughter of two men. Two men sacrificed so that one company could take another over. Aware of all that he, Nick, had done over the last three years to organize a takeover, he still could not fathom it.

'You've done a wonderful job, Willie,' Nick said. 'Wonderful.'

'Thank you very much, sir.' Banks smiled a slightly crooked smile. He was pleased.

Chapter Twenty-Eight

I

A month after Banks' visit to Nick, Roger gave a press conference. It was an even more theatrical event than the one Julian had attended. The chairman of Corpcom had never been so photographed or sought out for interviews. He was announcing Corpcom's bid for one of the United Kingdom's largest and most visible printing and publishing companies, RIP, whose chairman, Rupert Ingram Parker, was as flamboyant as Roger, and equally pegged as a 'predator'. The press were on to them like flies to a corpse.

Nick had called Julian back from the States immediately after Banks had come in. Prepared, all they had to do was wait for Roger to make his move. They could not have wished for something more advantageous to them. With all the publicity that Roger had created around himself and his new attack, Faulkner's approach would be less noticed.

The evening of Roger's announcement, they were in Julian's flat, still being cautious, avoiding discussions in the office. Rebecca was back in London. They were alone.

'As soon as we declare, we can buy like hell,' Julian said. 'We should be able to get to at least 15 per cent in the first couple of days. People will wonder what's going on, but I don't think anyone's going to think we're coming in as Parker's white knight.'

'We're not,' Nick said. 'I'm just going to be Roger's black knight.'

'Carrying your scythe,' Julian said. He laughed, meaning it as a light-hearted remark.

'You're bloody right I am.' There was no laughter in Nick's voice.

A week later, Nick chaired a full board meeting. He had called it early, in advance of the monthly meeting. That was not due for another ten days. They sat in the panelled boardroom of Faulkner, which could have doubled as a dining-room, with its heavy mahogany sideboards and central chandelier. The windows were draped with thin net curtains that filtered out the light and darkened the room even more, so that whenever it was in use, the lights had to be on.

It was a small board, and Nick was thankful for that. He expected some trouble, knowing he would not be able to hide the personal side of what he was about to propose. The fewer board-members, the fewer problems there would be.

Julian was a member, of course. The former chairman, Michael Hyde, was still there, as vice-chairman. There were three others, Iain Matthews, Charles Grieve and Anthony Liddell; the latter the only non-Scot among them. Liddell and Hyde were the only two non-executive board members.

There was one other man present. Thomas McGregor was the representative of Faulkner's investment bankers. His presence alone would not tip off those who did not know why they were meeting. It had been kept so secret it would inevitably come as a surprise.

It was from the non-executives that Nick expected censure. They could afford to look at the long term, at the abstract, at the ethical. Like parents who have to discipline their children, they could be difficult; and, like parents, they could forget that they were once unruly themselves.

Michael Hyde had resigned his post as chairman for Nick. They had both been on very good terms since Nick's appointment, but Michael Hyde was an honourable man. Nick wondered how Hyde would take his particular brand of revenge. Liddell, Nick knew, would attack the vendetta. As far as the other two were concerned, Matthews and Grieve were both directors of Faulkner subsidiaries and would be profiting by Nick's move, if it worked. They would come around, he felt;

few people want to exclude themselves from successful enterprises.

Charles Grieve was Nick's finance director; it was unlikely that he had spotted something, or he would have talked to Nick about it. But, once told, he would find it less difficult to believe. Nick had been buying Corpcom's shares through Julian's web of subsidiary companies and with assets of some of the companies he had bought over the last two years, and the transactions would have been recorded. Grieve would know that Nick had by now bought almost 5 per cent of Corpcom's shares. Nick had argued that he wanted Faulkner cash rich as part of the regeneration; this explained the stripping of company assets, his own as well as those they bought; to a certain extent, it also explained the purchase of so many shares in another company.

What Nick had relied on to stop people from guessing his purpose was that they would not readily conceive of the kind of revenge it implied; a vendetta of that scale and calibre was difficult for most people to imagine. At this meeting, it would be the major stumbling block. He knew that; it would be disapproved of, just as Rebecca disapproved of it, because of its motive. He had therefore decided to try and turn this potential disadvantage into an asset. He would admit and tackle the problem straight on.

'I've called this extraordinary meeting,' he started when everyone was seated around the table, 'because I'm going to put a rather extraordinary plan to you. Some of you may cry scandal and outrage at first, some may think me mad. I assure you I am not, and that Faulkner Industries can only gain from it.' He looked around the room, making sure he had them. They would be wondering what he was talking about. 'There is risk involved,' he went on, 'but what successful company doesn't take risks?'

He paused. He had warned them. Perhaps that would defuse the initial shock and reproof. He had also challenged them. He looked over at Julian. Julian was waiting, just like the others. He betrayed no emotion. He was very still, tense.

Nick got up from the table, and walked over to the sideboard on which there were seven black ring binders, thick with paper. Julian stood up then.

'I can manage,' Nick said. He picked up all the binders and Julian sat down again.

As Nick, with careful ceremony, placed a binder in front of Michael Hyde, he said, 'This is a dossier on Faulkner's offer for a company called Corpcom.'

Nick went around each board member, handing over the binder. They looked at him now in utter surprise. There was no doubting that. When he sat down again, nobody had yet spoken. They had all looked inside the binder to make sure that they had heard him correctly. Every one of them knew Corpcom, knew its size, knew that Roger Andrews was its chairman and knew his reputation. Nick opened his own binder. He spoke again.

'This has been very carefully, and, obviously,' he looked up at them, 'very secretively prepared. I'll answer any questions you have, but I want to say a couple of things first.'

There was still nothing said, and Nick went on, 'The first is that I want a decision on this issue today.'

'Today . . .' said Liddell. Nick heard the anger in his voice.

'Nick . . .' It was Grieve, but he got no further, for Nick cut in immediately.

'Please, I want to say what I have to say first,' he said. 'I want you to know what I want before you start telling me it's impossible. Or that it's madness. Or whatever you'll say.'

Nick looked them over, every muscle of his face tense; he was as hard as he could be. They said nothing, once more. Nick could tell that Liddell, a red-cheeked, carefully groomed man of about sixty-five, was restraining himself with difficulty. He had obviously decided to hear everything so that his disapproval could encompass it all.

'I want a decision today,' Nick repeated. 'It's the reason for this meeting and for the amount of secrecy that's gone into the whole business. Secondly, I want a decision today because I want to make an offer for Corpcom tomorrow.

And third,' again he hurried on to avoid the objections, 'most of you won't know this. It won't come as that much of a surprise to Charlie,' Nick turned to Charles Grieve and smiled at him. 'At the moment, Faulkner indirectly owns about just under 5 per cent of Corpcom. By next week, I expect us to own over 15 per cent.'

He paused because, like an actor being applauded, he had to. The extent of their ownership of Corpcom was a shock to the board members. Grieve, contrary to Nick's flattery, was more surprised than the others. For a finance director to hold 4.9 per cent of another company's stock with the expectation of buying another 10 per cent and not to have known it was extraordinary. He was a young man, round-faced, with unruly curly hair playing around a receding hair-line. He alternately looked at Nick and at the open figures in front of him. Then he looked around the room at the others. He was smiling in disbelief.

'We own it indirectly, of course,' Nick went on in the same, almost monotonous, tone of voice, 'because we have been buying through a network of small companies that we've built up over the last couple of years. Today, I am having Julian,' he nodded towards him, 'who as you've probably guessed by now, has been working with me on this; I'm having Julian consolidate all these holdings into Faulkner Industries proper and tomorrow we start buying again.

'That means that tomorrow we'll have to declare our more than 5 per cent holding. I want to make my offer for Corpcom tomorrow evening.

'I apologize for springing this on you at the last moment. I don't apologize for having done it. I wanted complete secrecy for this venture. No leaks at all, from any source. Julian and I have been the only people working on this for two years. The file in front of you and the activities it reports have taken that amount of time to prepare.

'The offer document is ready, Julian has prepared it and typed it. We can amend it and have it ready for printing overnight. We've found a small printer who's expecting to do that this evening and whom we think we can trust.

'That covers it, I think. It's really very simple. I think, after I've answered your initial questions, that you should spend the rest of the morning going over the document. After lunch, we'll amend it if it needs amending. And then we can vote on it.'

There was a moment's silence after this speech. Nick's confidence, with its underlying, almost violent, purpose was intimidating and astonishing. They all felt its influence.

Michael spoke first. It was typical of his matter-of-factness, and showed his willingness to trust Nick. Although he knew that this could not be anything but principally an act of revenge, he accepted the terms Nick had stated.

'Nick doesn't seem to have left us much choice, I think,' he said in slight reproof. 'We need to do some reading.'

'Why Corpcom, Nick?' was Liddell's first question. It came out rapidly, compressed with anger and outrage.

Nick looked back at Liddell and saw the challenge there, but he was prepared for it.

'For two reasons,' he said. 'Faulkner has grown over the last two years and we've tried to expand out of the UK market alone and out of the oil industry alone. That's what I found when I came here – a company limited to the UK and to the oil industry. We agreed then that our aim was to turn this company into a truly international, diversified company. We agreed that was the best way we would survive in today's world. I believe we can achieve that aim by buying Corpcom and selling off some of what we buy – and it's all in there. Julian's done a lot of work. After that, not only will we be cash rich, but we'll be sitting on a vast empire.'

Again, he paused. But before he could be asked what his second reason was, he offered it, 'The second reason is much more personal. I want my revenge. Andrews took a company I'd built up. A good company. I intend to take Corpcom away from him.'

'I'd say that was your first reason,' said Liddell. Nick had hardly finished his sentence before Liddell had pounced.

'First or second, does it matter?' Nick answered. 'I'm here, in front of you, asking for your permission to carry it out. I may have been free with my executive powers, but I am now asking you to look at my justification. You may not like my motives. Frankly, so what?'

'It's a question of trust,' Liddell said.

'The only question is whether what I do is good for the company and its shareholders. I have broken no laws.'

'It just happens,' Michael said, 'that what in your opinion is good for the company coincides exactly with your desires for revenge. Is that right?'

'Absolutely,' Nick allowed himself a smile. 'It had to be dared. And I think if we have the boldness to move quickly, we'll be rewarded.'

Nick stood up now. 'Julian and I are going to let you get down to your reading. You can grill us after lunch. And turn us down too, if that's what you want to do.'

Julian had got up. He moved around the table towards the door. Nick remained by the table for a moment longer. He wanted to give them the chance to challenge him again before leaving. But they did not. He nodded at Julian and they left the room.

They walked down the corridor, feeling the weight of silence. They said nothing to each other until they were inside Nick's office and the door was closed behind them.

'Was I too antagonistic?' Nick asked Julian.

'You were all right,' said Julian.

It was Iain Matthews, red-haired, freckled, with bright intelligent blue eyes, who said, 'Did anyone have any idea what was going on?' There was admiration in his voice. It was quite a coup. He was impressed.

'No,' Michael said. He was already reading. If anything, although intellectually he could appreciate it, he was irritated by the theatrics of this meeting.

'Charlie. Didn't you know what he was doing?' Liddell turned to Grieve, who, of all of them, stood most to lose in terms of prestige and position. He was the finance director;

all this buying of Corpcom had taken place and was not picked up by him.

'I knew he was buying into Corpcom,' he answered. 'I never thought he'd do this.' Grieve was awed as well. He did not seem put out or humiliated. The boldness of the move was exciting. 'Who else would be prepared to take a company like Corpcom over and not tell his board?' he asked the room. 'Would you?'

'I most certainly would not,' Liddell said.

'Let's read this stuff over,' Michael said. 'I think it's pointless spending all morning being outraged or impressed, or whatever we are, at the way Nick has carried on. Let's have a look at it and then judge. If he's made a mess of it, I suggest we fire him this afternoon.'

He looked around the room, then he added firmly, 'Agreed?'

Before returning to the papers in front of him, he waited till all of them, bar McGregor, who was already considering the document and who, not being a member of the board, would have no vote, had nodded their agreement.

They had all begun reading, when they were interrupted. McGregor spoke, looking up from the document, into which he had been delving throughout most of Nick's speech.

'I just think you should know . . .' he started, and they all snapped around to look at him.

'Don't tell me you've got a surprise for us,' Michael Hyde said.

'A very minor piece of news,' McGregor said, 'compared to what you've just heard. I just wanted to tell you that I met with Nick and Julian three days ago. I was warned this was going to come up.'

'What's your opinion of this?' Liddell challenged him.

'Obviously, it's rather unusual,' he said. He did not want to commit himself yet. 'I'd like to get another look at it. I haven't had much time with it,' he continued. He patted the documents. 'It sounds very bold.'

He smiled at them, picked up the binder and moved with it to a corner of the room for a little privacy.

*

It took all day and most of the evening.

Nick and Julian had returned to the boardroom at lunch-time. Lunch was catered for them in the boardroom itself. Two white-coated men laid a tablecloth over the table. They then wheeled in a long buffet with several covered dishes on it, which they placed against the wall. It had been planned like that so that the discussion would not have to be interrupted each time a waiter entered the room.

The interrogation started immediately the two men had left the room and the door was closed behind them.

Michael and Liddell took the lead in it, while McGregor, and occasionally Grieve, acted as punctuation, asking questions that often summarized or cut to the heart of a problem. Matthews said little. He had a good lunch, then sat back and enjoyed the show. He knew that the others would hack the plan to pieces without his help and he wanted to hear what was being said. He was behind the idea anyway; he thought it was wonderful.

Liddell again raised the issue of Nick's revenge, but was interrupted by Michael, sharply this time.

'Nick's been very thorough,' he said. 'I think he's done it in such a way that his personal motives coincide with practical ones. Let's examine the document and judge it on its merits.' He added, 'It doesn't mean I approve of the motives or the emotion. All I'm saying is that I think it's irrelevant.'

'Up to a point,' said Liddell. He was not easily intimidated. 'I see the plan includes keeping Armadale in its entirety. Not selling off any of the company.' He paused, and Nick nodded his agreement. 'Is that for purely sound business reasons or is it more sentimental?'

'Armadale has not changed much since Andrews took it over,' Nick answered. 'It's been consolidated, if anything, into its three principal businesses. Chemicals, engineering and computer technology. It's a strong company. If we feel something should be sold off, I would suggest the chemicals. Computers and engineering would fit in very well with Faulkner as it stands.

'It's true,' Nick continued, 'that for sentimental reasons, I'd like to see it kept as one. But that's all it is. We wouldn't lose money either way. Keep chemicals or sell it, we'll do well out of it.'

Again, he had defused the animosity by making an asset out of his personal interest. He was brutally honest and it was keeping them off balance.

Nick finally sensed the turn he had been waiting for all day, when McGregor was running out of questions and his attitude began assuming the reality of the bid. His questions related to timing, to the practical aspects of the bid itself. Nick knew that, in the long run, it was what McGregor said that would matter the most.

By eight o'clock, Nick and Julian knew they had won, although the vote of approval would not come until 10.30.

They were discussing the financing of the bid. It implied a considerable amount of borrowing on Faulkner's part. Nick had followed Roger's principle. His main source of collateral would be Corpcom's own assets.

'Can we handle this kind of debt?' Liddell said.

'It depends how long we have to keep paying the interest,' Grieve said. 'This could get referred to the Monopolies and Mergers.'

'I don't think it will,' Nick said. He was firm and sure of himself.

'How can you be so sure, Nick?' Hyde asked. 'This certainly could be referred.' He was suspicious. He knew Nick was holding something back.

Julian looked worriedly at Nick. He wondered how Nick would get out of this one. They had anticipated the question, and had decided not to reveal what they held over Roger unless it were absolutely unavoidable.

'Let's worry about that one when it comes,' Nick had said to Julian.

Now it had come.

Nick remained silent for several seconds, holding the floor

as it were. Then he just said, 'It's a hunch.' He smiled broadly at them.

'It could be an expensive hunch,' Hyde said.

'If the bid is referred,' Nick said, 'if the whole thing falls apart, we can sell our Corpcom holdings. We'll still make money, even after repaying the interest.'

He looked over to McGregor. Nick wanted him to commit himself. He would have to arrange the financing.

'It is a risk.' McGregor said. 'But I think we could probably put the money together.'

It was a vote of approval. The rest of the discussion was technical and dealt with the particulars. The bid for Corpcom was about to start.

2

Nick was determined there would be no false civility this time. He would not follow the formal, polite, diplomatic route. No waiting till morning, no courtesy calls. He was adamant about that at the board meeting.

'This is a cutthroat affair. Let's treat it that way,' he had said.

So they attacked at night.

The City of London is quiet at night. No one lives there. In the darkness, the curve of its narrow streets and the usually comforting wealth of its buildings spread deep shadows, and with them uncertainty. Only twenty-four hours after McGregor's assertion that he could probably put the money together, Julian drove Rebecca's Mini down Threadneedle Street and stopped in front of the Stock Exchange. He felt the threat of the City's darkness.

He jumped out of the car, a manila envelope in his hand. He walked up the steps to the Stock Exchange. It was just after 8.30 on Tuesday evening. In contrast to the rich and ancient stone faces of the City, the Stock Exchange belies its aristocracy and the age of its institution by being a modern building of grey and glass, which at every turn, both inside and out, reminds one of a plastic diamond.

Julian went over to the postal slot in the wall, like a night safe at a bank. He stopped in front of the slot, looked at the envelope in his hand, checking it, making sure that it was the right one, in the same way he always hesitated before posting a letter. It was such a definite, definitive, action.

Finally he pushed it through the slot and it was gone. Faulkner's bid for Corpcom would be official in twelve hours; the commitment had just been made.

He got back into the car and drove away quickly. He felt as if he were driving away from a bank job.

At about the same time, Rebecca was on the telephone in Annie's flat. She sat in Annie's small room, at her desk, beneath the portrait of her father. She was calling her friends in the press, giving the news of Faulkner's bid. Faulkner was about to try to swallow a company four times its own size: the piranha was indeed going to eat the shark. She rang the newspapers and the BBC. They would do the rest. Andrews had always been good copy, especially at the moment, with his own fight on for RIP. The journalists were going to have fun.

In the next room, Annie sat while Nick moved restlessly about the room. He was as tense and restless as a big caged cat at the zoo. From the radio on the hi-fi, a programme on the Oxford English Dictionary was explaining how the editors had selected their illustrative texts. Nick was waiting for Rebecca's work to be announced on the news.

'It won't be till much later,' Annie said. She wished he would turn the radio off. It made her more nervous than Nick's pacing.

'I don't want to miss it,' he said.

'You won't miss it,' she said. 'We'll turn it back on. Anyway, you know what it's going to say.'

'Not all of it.' It was as if he wanted to hear his own performance. 'I want to know how he'll hear it,' Nick added.

'He might not know till tomorrow. On television.' Annie was persistent, against all common sense and against her own practice, a reflection of how tense she herself was.

'He'll know tonight.' He was sure of it. He went to the window and looked out, parting the curtains as he did so. 'Julian must be on his way back,' he said.

Rebecca came out of Annie's office. She was nervous as well, although her role had been very small. She sensed the enormity of the occasion.

'I reached everyone. Or everyone's assistant,' she said. Nick looked over at her, but said nothing. So she added, 'I've done all I can, I'm afraid.'

'Thanks. Thanks a lot,' Nick said, reminded by her own apology that he should acknowledge her efforts.

Julian came into the flat at about nine o'clock. They were all three sitting in the drawing-room, barely able to speak, as if they had never met and were shy guests at a party.

'I put it into the wrong slot,' he said.

Nick turned towards him in complete shock. Annie and Rebecca both looked at him anxiously. Julian immediately put his hands up before him.

'I'm sorry, I was only joking,' he said quickly. 'It's like walking into a morgue in here.'

Annie got up immediately. 'Time for a drink,' she said.

But it was Julian's remark, which had stolen their stomachs from them, like a sudden fall, that had cleared the air.

Roger did find out about the bid that night.

He was going home, late because he had worked on details of his own bid for RIP after an early supper at the office. He was sitting back in his Rolls-Royce, owned and paid for by Corpcom, smoking the last of his cigar, watching the darkness of Regents Park out of the window.

The radio was on. Roger had always liked radio. It was more relaxing than reading or watching television. Both those activities hurt his eyes. Listening to the radio was like opera; you could sit back, close your eyes and still enjoy it. He was listening with unfocused attention to the news programme that was on at this time of night. It was eleven o'clock. Margaret would be asleep by the time he got home.

London was quiet and unobtrusive. They were driving by the gate of the American ambassador's residence, on their way towards Hampstead, when he heard the announcement. The even, well-trained tones of the newscaster announced that 'one of the most spectacular takeover bids in recent months had just been announced. An Edinburgh-based company, Faulkner Industries plc, had announced a takeover bid for Corpcom, a company four times its size and one of the largest diversified companies in the UK. The offer was rumoured to add up to a total of £3.2 billion. The Chairman of Corpcom, Mr Roger Andrews, himself a well-known takeover specialist and predator, was unavailable for comment.'

The news continued, but was drowned out by Roger's reaction.

'Son-of-a-bitch!' he exclaimed. 'What the fuck's going on?' He reached across to the partition and ordered his driver, 'Go back to the office. Now.'

The driver said nothing. He began a U-turn in the park. But the car was large and did not make the turn in one go. Roger sat back as the driver went into reverse.

'No,' he said, 'what's the point. Go home.'

The driver stopped the car in the middle of the dark road. There was no traffic. He looked back at Roger.

'Go back,' Roger said, waving his hand at him. 'Go home. Hampstead.'

The driver turned the car again and headed back towards north London.

When Roger got home he went upstairs immediately and burst into his bedroom. His wife was asleep, but he sat on the bed beside her and shook her awake.

'That bastard Bishop is trying to take me over!' he said to her.

'What?' she said, in the frightened tones of someone who has just been roughly awakened from a peaceful sleep.

'I am being taken over,' Roger repeated. He got off the bed. He said it again, shouting it across his bedroom. 'Nick Bishop is trying to take me over.'

By then Margaret was quite awake.

Chapter Twenty-Nine

I

When the announcement of his bid had come over the radio, Nick had listened to it with rapt attention, as if he did not know what it would say. At the end of the bulletin, Julian and Rebecca had been in each other's arms, but the release in Nick had been more internal. He had not turned to Annie first, but away from the group, moving towards the other side of the room, towards the windows. His fists were clenched and he strode away with an energetic dance-like step, muttering to himself. Then, almost as if it had not happened, he turned, a broad, boyish smile on his face and put out his arms towards Annie.

They opened a bottle of champagne and had a party. Even though the fight had only just started, they celebrated the culmination of three years of work. The great excitement was making the first move. Losing would not be as terrible as not having had the chance to fight.

Both couples made love passionately that night, drawn together by love and the champagne and the thrill of battle. They slept only a couple of hours and before first light, like soldiers going to war, Nick and Julian had crept out of bed and left behind the women who had done so much in their preparations. They flew in a small chartered plane, leaving Heathrow with the coming of dawn and arrived at their office in Edinburgh at 8.30, a little later than usual.

Michael was there before them. He was waiting in Nick's office reading the papers. The door was open, his view of the long corridor unimpeded. There was a thick pile of newspapers on the floor next to his chair. When he saw Nick and Julian walk towards him from the lift, he did not get up, but looked at them from behind his newspaper.

'I heard it last night,' he said as they walked into the office. 'Sounded very impressive.'

There was a sense of adventure in all of them. They were like schoolboys starting in on a grand new project. The three men sat down and savoured the calm of the next few minutes. As people came to work and as the outside world began to clamour for attention, there would be no more of it for a long time. Both Nick and Julian were astonished at how much easier it was to be on this side of the fight. To have attacked removed the toxic waste of anxiety which they had felt so keenly when under attack themselves at Armadale.

Many of Faulkner's employees came in a little earlier that day. They had heard what their company was up to on the news. It was confirmed in the newspapers, as they had rushed to get them, feeling the need to read what they had heard, ensuring, by seeing it in print that it was indeed true.

There was a sense of triumph, of justice, as those men and women of Faulkner who had once worked with Nick at Armadale read about the takeover. There seemed to be no doubt in their minds that the bid would be successful, despite the enormity of its ambition. It was in fact the grandeur of the scheme that fed their optimism and they came into the office, chattering in unison like flocks of starlings at twilight.

Nick kept the door to his office open most of the morning. Just as they had done at Armadale, they used the boardroom as the war room. That was manned by Julian, who coordinated what at the moment was basically an informative task. He had to bring his own people up to date.

There was a radio turned on in the boardroom so that they could catch any new items; there was television, specially hooked up for this same reason, also on continuously, although the sound was turned down. Julian, wandering about in this room, handing out copies of the offer document, answering questions that were put to him at every turn, seemed like a media general in a newsroom. There was a cacophony of sound on Faulkner's floor which only the euphoria of attack made tolerable.

Philip Porter came into the room and the first thing he said was, 'Good show, Julian.' He expressed what everyone felt.

'Philip,' Julian welcomed him in, 'come in. So,' he asked, 'how does it feel?'

'It's the best thing that's happened in years.' Philip sat down in one of the armchairs. 'I feel like I did when I was a boy.'

'I know,' Julian did know what he meant. He wondered at the fact that the emotions he had felt over the past few months were the ones he remembered from childhood. Did adults then behave and feel just as children do? That was not supposed to happen; one was supposed to grow up.

'A bit risky, though. Isn't it?' Philip did not really think the bid was manageable. One did not buck the system and get away with it. 'A bit hard to pull off . . .'

'There's no reason we shouldn't,' Julian said. 'No one's invulnerable. That's one thing I've discovered in the last two years of running around the world. No company is untouchable, however big it is. None.'

Jim knocked on Nick's door. Jim had gone by the boardroom and seen Julian manning it like a ship's platform. He walked on towards Nick's office. He might have expected to feel equally unmoved by the elation that was electric in the air at Faulkner's as he had been by the gloom that had struck Armadale. But he was not. Jim was as high as everybody else. His familiar stride seemed almost to have become a glide, and there was extra bounce in his walk. He was not above a little revenge himself.

So Nick had been right to gather his forces from Armadale. Everyone was behind him. Nick and Faulkner were the little guys, the underdogs and clearly the favourites, even if the bookies would not have put them there. There was little thought given to business ethics any more. No one questioned whether a public company should be used in this fashion. All their private aspirations were being put into this new chance to fight Goliath.

'This is a very unexpected turn of events,' Jim said to Nick. He waved the newspaper he had folded in his hand.

'Pleasant surprise, I hope,' Nick answered.

'Very. I especially like the outrage in Mr Andrews' rejection of our offer.'

Nick laughed. His own turndown had been very much the same. 'Do you mean the outrage or the rejection?' he asked.

'Oh, the sense of outrage of course,' Jim answered. 'It's nice to know Andrews feels it too.'

'Pure rage, I would have thought,' Nick said. 'The moral tone is there for the press.'

There was a pause of satisfaction between them.

'You must be busy,' Jim said. 'Go get 'em,' he added, 'we're all behind you.'

'Thanks.'

Jim left and Nick followed his progress down the corridor, remembering their estrangement and Jim's mistrust.

2

As festive as was the atmosphere at Faulkner's, as frenetic was it in Corpcom's London headquarters.

Roger had woken Peter after midnight the night before and barked the news of Nick's infamy at him.

'I don't believe you,' Peter had said automatically, without thinking.

'You'd better believe it,' Roger said and made it sound like a threat. 'I want everyone at work at eight o'clock tomorrow. Eight o'clock sharp,' he went on.

Peter looked at his watch. 'It's almost one o'clock in the morning, Roger,' he said.

'I don't give a shit. Wake 'em up.' Roger had hung up.

At eight o'clock the next morning, the Corpcom building in Knightsbridge was busy, the panicked activity of the moment made even worse by Roger's loud rage. It enveloped the building like smog. He had already shouted at every person on the top floor; his bad temper affected everyone, much as his phone call of the night before had.

In his office, at the moment, while they waited for Corpcom's board to be gathered, Roger's other managing directors were trying to make sense of Nick's move. Even Peter was ruffled and felt out of his depth.

'I thought you were keeping an eye on the bastard,' Roger turned on Peter.

'Not for that reason,' Peter said. 'I wasn't expecting him to do this.'

'How come he can get 7 per cent of our stock without us knowing about it?' Roger yelled.

'He must have bought the last two per cent yesterday,' Richard said. He had been summoned at six o'clock that morning. Being the managing director of Armadale, and therefore Nick's titular usurper, he was even more anxious than the others. He could not help but feel that Nick's poisoned arrows were pointed directly at him.

'How can you do that?' asked Roger. 'Is that legal?' he turned to Peter again.

'I don't know,' Peter answered. 'He can't have bought it all in one day. It's not possible. We'll have to find out how he did it.'

Roger's mood fluctuated like a weathervane in a storm. At one moment, he was in a state of almost uncontrolled rage, and then something somebody said, or something he himself thought of, would calm him. He would then be able to think rationally, tackle the problem as if it were any other task. But with each reminder of what had happened, and how it had happened, his temper would flare again, an inflamed sore that had not healed.

'He's got a long way to go yet,' Roger said to the room, steadied by Peter's practicality. 'And a helluva lot of sweet-talking to do if he's going to take us over. We'll just go on as usual,' he added. 'Corpcom isn't the *Titanic*.'

'What about the RIP bid?' Peter said. 'Shouldn't we drop it?'

'No.' Roger's temper was up again. Nick's bid for Corpcom was frustrating him at every turn.

'It's spreading us very thin, you know.'

'Not yet,' said Roger. 'Not yet. We can always drop it later.' He looked at his staff. 'What you people need to do is some homework. I want to know everything there is to know about that mouldy piece of haggis, Faulkner Industries.'

Roger clapped his hands together as if they were a bunch of schoolchildren.

'OK, off you go,' he said, whisking them away. 'I'm going to blow the bastard out of the water,' he shouted after them.

3

Alan and Fanny Turner had been woken up at 6 a.m., New York time. They had been out late the night before, at the theatre and a late supper afterwards.

Blindly, Alan reached for the phone on the bedside table. 'Hallo,' he mumbled with a gravelly voice. He listened.

'My God!' he said, turning over and sitting up. Beside him, Fanny stirred. She looked at the clock beside the phone, then worriedly at Alan. 'Jesus bloody Christ!' he exclaimed. 'All right. I'll come in as soon as I can.' He slammed the phone down on to its cradle. 'Shit!' he shouted.

'What's the matter?' she asked.

'Armadale,' Alan said. 'No, not Armadale. Faulkner. Faulkner Industries. Jesus. Nick Bishop. We're being taken over.'

'Darling,' Fanny said. She reached out to him. She had no idea what Alan was talking about. 'Who's being taken over?'

'Corpcom,' he snapped at her, furious that she did not understand his jabbering. 'Nick Bishop has made a bid for Corpcom.'

'Nick Bishop?'

'Yes. For Christ's sake, Fanny,' he said, 'stop being so dense.' He pulled the cover off him and stood up.

'I don't believe it,' he said. 'It's unbelievable.' He sat back down on the edge of the bed, his arms hanging limp between his legs.

'It's amazing,' Fanny said. 'Who was that on the phone?'

'Oh someone from the office,' he answered gruffly. 'They couldn't reach us last night. I wish they'd never reached us.' He paused. 'I should never have joined this fucking company. I should've gone somewhere else. Away from it all.' He reconsidered. 'Ah, one of them would have taken me over somewhere else.'

'It's unbelievable,' Fanny said. 'Do you think he's been planning it all along?'

'Nick Bishop. A guy like him.' He thought, then he said, 'Yes, he's probably been planning it for three years. Bloody lunatic.'

Fanny decided to keep what she thought to herself. She would not make it worse. In fact, she was pleased, happy that Nick was having his own back. She had always liked Nick and found Roger rude and unattractive. Alan would land on his feet. And anyway, the battle really was far away. Fanny and Alan would never go back to England.

As if Alan were having the same thoughts, he said, 'We might have to go back to England.'

'Why?' she asked and now there was panic in her voice.

'We're here with Corpcom,' he answered. 'If I lose my job, we can't stay here. Green card, you know. Can't work without a green card around here.'

'Well, we'll get a green card, then,' she said. The thought of returning to England filled her with dread. With the new year had come the confirmation that she was pregnant. She loved New York. She wanted her child to be born there. Nothing else seemed to matter quite as much.

4

After lunch, amid the still shocked activity that rang around Corpcom like an alarm, amid a panic that was very familiar to him, Nick walked into Roger's headquarters in Knightsbridge. He had flown back down to London after lunch, and he was breaking another rule of the code of behaviour: he was visiting his opponent.

He walked so confidently into the building, not bothering to stop at the security desk, that he was in the lift before being challenged.

'Fifth floor,' he said jovially to the security man, and he pressed the button.

He was unrecognized as he walked towards Roger's office, people hurrying by him, rushing from task to task. Nick could feel the tension and, there was no doubt about it, it felt good.

Outside Roger's office, he stopped in front of a secretary He glanced at the name plate on her desk: 'Mrs Carey'.

'Yes,' she said, looking up at him.

'Roger Andrews, please,' he said. 'Nick Bishop to see him.' He gave his name in a clear, amused voice. There was a cluster of three young women a few yards away, around some filing cabinets. They turned to look at him at the sound of his name. Everybody on the fifth floor knew it. They stared at him with unabashed surprise.

Mrs Carey stared at him too. Then, meekly, she picked up the telephone and buzzed Roger Andrews. Suddenly, she thought better of it, hung up the telephone precipitately.

'Would you take a seat, please?' she said to Nick. She stood up, sidled around her desk, and went into Roger's office after a quick rap on the door.

Nick smiled as he watched her edge into the room. He walked over to a chair by the window overlooking the street. He sat down and waited with his briefcase on his knees.

He did not have to wait long. He had hardly sat down, when he heard a cry of rage. The office was obviously well-insulated, for he could not make out the words. He imagined the conversation from the sounds that escaped through to him. Mrs Carey's voice was very timid indeed.

Then the door opened and Roger came out swearing.

'Where is that bastard? Where are you, Bishop? I'm going to break your bloody neck.' He was shouting.

Nick stood up. The smile had left his face. He looked serious again. He held his ground before Roger with every inch of his height and every ounce of his anger seemingly untouched since their last meeting. The only difference this time was that he was in control.

'Get out of here,' Roger continued his tirade. 'Get out of my building. What the fuck are you doing here?'

Roger grabbed Nick by his jacket and tried to move him. He could not do it. He realized the absurdity of the situation, saw himself, a short, stocky man trying to attack the tall man who stood in front of him, still carrying his briefcase. From the doorway of his office, Peter, Richard and the others who had been in the meeting were staring at them.

Roger let go of Nick, straightened himself up, and said again, 'What do you want here?'

'I think we should have a little chat,' Nick answered.

'You do, do you?' But Roger was stalling for time, regaining his dignity. His opponent's confidence, his coolness, his self-assurance impressed him. It was as if Roger had suddenly become aware of Nick's presence. He turned and walked back towards his office, saying, 'Follow me.'

Nick went into the office, and the men who had been with Roger stayed, too shocked to realize they should go.

'What do you want?' Roger asked yet again. He had turned around to face Nick and seemed quite oblivious to the presence of his subordinates.

'I think this would be best done in private,' Nick repeated himself too.

And at last the others woke up. They began to file out of the office. Richard was the first to leave. He glanced quickly at Nick as he left, catching his eye, but Nick remained unmoved, as if he had not noticed him and Richard hurried out.

Last of all, Peter moved; he remembered the last time Nick had asked for privacy with Roger.

'He can stay,' Nick said to Roger. He did not speak to Peter. 'It concerns him too.'

Peter stopped, but Roger said. 'Go, Peter. I'll talk to him alone.'

Peter hesitated.

'I said go,' Roger said again. He was firm.

Peter left. He closed the door and the two men were left alone.

His arms akimbo, Roger faced Nick; he was ready for a fight.

'What've you got to say to me?' he said.

Nick raised his briefcase a shade, then gently put it down on a chair.

'In here,' he said, 'I've got evidence that could put you in jail.'

'Why don't you use it, then?' Roger said defiantly. He did not believe Nick. 'You've been wanting to do it for ages.'

'It would take a long time,' Nick answered him, 'and I don't want to spend long over this. I want your board of directors to recommend the sale of Corpcom to Faulkner Industries within two days.'

Roger heard what Nick said, but it took a few seconds for him to process his reaction. The request was so unexpected, and so patently absurd that Roger did not know what to do with the information.

'This is crazy,' he said. 'You know I'm not going to do that. What is this?'

'It's an ultimatum.' Nick spoke with a gentle, even voice. 'If you don't do as I ask, I shall make every scrap of information I have in that briefcase public.'

Roger looked directly at Nick, trying to intimidate him, stare him out. It did not work. He could see that Nick meant everything he was saying. He sensed the danger and he calmed down. He turned and went to sit behind his desk.

'You'd better tell me what it is, then,' he said and he sat down. He reached for a cigar. 'Sit down,' he said to Nick.

He found a match and lit the cigar. He blew a large billow of smoke up into the air. By now, he had a fairly good idea what Nick might have in the briefcase.

'It won't take that long,' Nick said, and remained standing. 'Three years ago, at about this time, two men died in an explosion on a North Sea platform,' he started.

Nick went on to tell the story Banks had told him, in perhaps a little less detail, but as thoroughly as he could remember it. He wanted Roger to be sure that he, Nick, had what he said he had.

Roger listened with care. He knew the story, of course, but even he did not know all that Nick told him. He had always remained aloof from the whole business. He had asked for something to embarrass Armadale, had approved the idea that Peter had presented to him, and let his people get on with it. The two deaths had been unexpected and he had tried to deal with them by giving money to the families. He could do nothing else. It never occurred to him that he might have avoided their deaths; he had not thought about it.

Even now, when Nick presented him with the facts, with Roger's own responsibility, 'criminal responsibility', Nick called it, Roger felt no guilt. In his mind, the deaths had been accidental. He was not responsible.

'It all seems very circumstantial to me,' Roger said. 'You'd have a hard time proving it.'

'I don't think I have to.' Nick was confident. 'You know how it's done. A leak. A story to the press. They'd eat this up.'

Roger said nothing.

'You've got a pretty high profile, at the moment, I'd say.' Nick could sense his victory. 'A planned accident. Two men dead. Murdered perhaps.'

'That's not true. You know that.'

'Manslaughter, I was told,' Nick said, undeterred. 'That's called "criminal homicide".'

'Without malice aforethought,' Roger interrupted.

'Very good,' Nick said. 'It's also defined as the "slaughter-ing" of human beings.'

'You've made your point, Bishop,' Roger said.

'One of my points,' said Nick with passion. His anger had surged suddenly. 'I didn't have to make this up,' he said pointedly. 'This particular scandal is true. Every disgusting little part of it.'

'Bully for you. Is that it?' Roger asked.

'I'll give you two days,' Nick said. 'By then I'll own 15 per cent of this company. Don't try to stop me.' He went to pick up the briefcase.

'I want that.' Roger pointed at the briefcase.

'You can have it,' Nick said. 'All of it. I have lots of copies.' Nick opened the briefcase, took out a large folder and tossed it on to Roger's desk. It landed with a thud.

Nick walked out of the office, past Peter, who was standing outside the door, and past the cluster of other staff who were all waiting to find out what would happen, surprised that whatever was happening was so quiet and subdued. Nick walked to the lift, looking straight ahead of him. He pushed the button and the lift opened immediately. He turned to face his public and saw them staring after him. The doors closed and he went down.

Peter was inside Roger's office before Nick had disappeared. He closed the door behind him.

Roger looked at him, but said nothing. He was thinking. Finally, Peter said, 'What did he want?'

Still Roger did not speak immediately. Then he said, 'The prig's got us by the balls.' He went on to tell Peter what Nick had said. At the end of it, he said to Peter, 'You fucked up.'

Peter ignored the accusation. He had been responsible for the operation, and it was pointless arguing with Roger over who was to take the blame.

'He couldn't prove it in court,' he said.

'He doesn't have to,' said Roger. 'We showed him how to work with a rumour.'

'He doesn't have the stamina to fight us,' Peter said.

He was younger than Roger, as ruthless and hard, but not as experienced. He did not want to lose what he had. It made him blind to the fact that he had already lost.

Roger would have loved to take Nick on. He hated men like Nick. Men who walked the straight and narrow path and looked down on those who did not, men who thought they were better than other people, men who were willing to sacrifice everything for their principles. In Roger Andrews' book, that made them hypocrites; worse, dangerous hypocrites. Roger would willingly have taken that kind of man on.

Yet Roger had sensed a change in Nick. Nick had learned. He had not lost his sense of mission, but he was tougher now. This bid had been carefully planned. Roger was sure that Nick had waited until he had the information he had wanted. In the end, the truth behind Nick's allegations was too dangerous. The fight was not worth it.

'You've got to face facts,' Roger said to Peter.

Peter was looking at Roger in disbelief.

'You're going to give up, aren't you?' he said.

'Survival's the name of the game,' Roger said, 'not pride.'

'You don't have to give in.' Peter did not want to give in to Nick. He was desperately trying to hold on.

Roger stood up, shaking his head. 'Sell out, Peter. Our shares have just gone up. We'll make a killing.' He looked at the younger man and smiled, 'We'll buy another company, for Christ's sake.'

Chapter Thirty

I

The doorman of Nick's club welcomed Howard out of the rain with a cheerful laugh.

'Good evening, sir,' he said. 'Haven't seen you in ages.'

'Good evening, George,' Howard replied. He sighed out the greeting.

A short, grey-haired man helped him off with his coat, chatting to Howard's back about the weather while Howard thought how strange it was that most people greeted you, even if they hadn't seen you in years, as if life were the same, always identical in its cheerfulness. Howard did not feel cheerful. This get-together with Nick worried him. Nick had sounded defiant on the telephone, and Howard did not like confrontation.

He reached the landing and cursed his weight; he had grown heavier in the last couple of years. Quickly he glanced around the room: a few men reading the newspaper in low armchairs, some playing backgammon, all fairly familiar faces. But he didn't stop today. Instead, he stepped briskly on through the double doors and into the next room. He wondered if Nick would be waiting at the bar. At the far end, men stood waiting for their drinks but Nick was not there. Harry, the barman, was pouring champagne. He looked up for an instant as Howard came into the room, then returned to his task.

The room was crowded; it always was. Men talked in clusters, fanning out from the bar. A fire burned in the fireplace. A tall man with a moustache turned as Howard headed for the bar.

'Howard. Where have you been hiding?'

'Hallo, Gerald,' Howard answered. He went on.

Harry was now making him a whisky and soda. Harry prided himself on his memory: he boasted that, from across the room, he could always put a drink and a face together. Modestly now, he said, 'The usual, sir?'

'Yes.' Howard sighed. 'I suppose so.'

'Haven't seen you for a while, sir. Everything been all right?'

'Absolutely, Harry.' Howard paused, and then, with a weak smile, 'Thank you.' He took his drink and looked around. Barmen can always smell trouble, he thought.

'Mr Bishop's in the next room, sir.'

'Ah. Thank you.' Howard took a sip from his drink, and went slowly out into the next room.

Soft, low sofas lined the walls, with armchairs facing them. The room, in the shape of a fat L, was like a series of small sitting-rooms and, in each section, small groups talked over drinks and club menus. Howard made a note of the women. He liked the fact that women were only allowed in at night. It made it seem a touch illicit, more exciting to his thoroughly English, masculine mind. He noticed also that Nick was not immediately visible, and with every face he scanned his heart raced and his stomach tightened. All this anxiety irritated him. Then he realized that he and Nick always met at the other end of the L. Why should tonight be any different? He hurried through and turned the corner.

Nick was the first person he saw. As Howard remembered him, slightly aloof, with his easy elegance, he stood by the fireplace. There was a glass of champagne on the mantelpiece beside him. Nick saw Howard turn the corner. He stood his ground, facing Howard, waiting for him. Howard hurried towards him, a smile on his face, reflecting the usual Hicks joviality, belying his nervousness.

'Nick, it's been ages,' he said, 'it's good to see you here again.'

'Have a seat, Howard,' Nick said with a wave of his hand. 'I see Harry's looked after you.' It was a formal greeting.

Howard chose one end of the sofa. Nick brought up an armchair and sat opposite him.

'It's been two years,' Howard said, 'and Harry still remembers.'

'There's a barman at the Ritz who's said to have remembered a drink over twenty years.'

'I hope Harry won't have to do that with me.'

'You should become a member,' Nick said. And he smiled, but his smile was an automatic one; it came with the remark.

'I should, I suppose,' Howard said.

Nick picked up one of the two menus on the table in front of him.

'Why don't we choose,' he said, 'then we can forget about it.'

He turned his attention to the menu. Howard forced himself out of his seat a little to grab at the leather-covered menu, sat back, opened it, feeling his stomach tighten a little further. He wondered if he would want to eat by the time he reached the table. In the next five minutes they went through the motions of selecting their meal, picking the wine, discussing it all as they had on many similar occasions over the last twenty years, except for the fact that a new formality had crept in. Everything was so damn formal this evening.

Nick, never one to spend a long time over choosing his food, looked at his old friend: the heavy body sitting sideways on the sofa, one leg slightly up on the cushion, the menu resting on the belly, the tie and collar tight around the neck, the mouth ajar like a door kept open by the wind, the eyes small and restless as they ran over the choices. Howard could never resist food, even if he was not hungry.

Nick realized, as he watched Howard's discomfort and nervousness, that he was enjoying it. Just for an instant, he wondered if inflicting physical pain could be this pleasurable. Was this the instinct that turned a man into a torturer? How much he, Nick, had changed over the past four years. He had believed he could travel through life using familiar truths and ideals to buttress his existence. Instead he had found that he was being forced to re-examine his whole adult life. Having lived the last twenty-five years under the supposition that 'coming of age' was something you did in your late teens and early twenties, Nick had discovered that he had had to undergo another rite of passage – not puberty, not growing up and not growing old, but growing older. It had been a spiritual much more than any physical ordeal, and one which was not adequately covered by the term mid-life crisis. He had been thoroughly unprepared for it, and now he was not sure that he was glad of its coming. He had matured, perhaps; he was a little wiser, but the price was innocence, another layer of innocence peeled away by experience and Nick feared that he would be left with nothing but cynicism.

He waited for the waitress to take their order. They both ordered mechanically, even Howard. The meal was not important. Nick chose the house claret, handed over the menu, watched as Howard did the same, watched as he took a long gulp from his drink. He said nothing as Howard sat back, settled into the corner of the sofa, looked back at him.

'How's Norma?' Nick asked.

'Oh, all right,' Howard answered. 'The same.'

'What about the other one?' Nick said.

Howard was surprised by the question. They had rarely discussed Sheilah before, and the question itself had been rude. Nick had always carried his heart in his open hand, free for all to take. Howard was not so sure any more.

'Sheilah?' Howard asked nonchalantly. He would ignore Nick's tone. 'About the same.' He smiled. 'How's yours?'

He had not been able to resist; Nick had asked for it.

'Fine,' Nick said, but it was barely a response. He placed his empty glass on the table and got up. 'Let's go and eat.'

He waited for Howard to edge out of the sofa.

They sat at a corner table in the dark-panelled dining-room. Nick had his back to a window and Howard sat to his left, so that they both faced the rest of the room. It was full. In the centre, at the long narrow members' table, a few youngish men had formed a group at one end, whereas in the centre an elderly man ate alone, forbidding in his solitude, daring anyone to speak to him. He was eating his soup and made a loud slurping sound as he put the spoon to his mouth. A couple of women turned at the sound, but the men seemed not to hear it.

Nick looked straight ahead, uninterested in the other diners, whereas Howard surveyed the room and took them in. He knew most of the members, and often, through the evening, as someone would come in to take his seat, he would exchange a wave with Howard. It was strange that it was Howard they greeted, whereas it was Nick's club. But Howard liked the club. It was reassuring and comfortable.

He turned back towards Nick. They had barely spoken since Howard had arrived. He decided he would address the issue for once. It hung about them, like a balloon waiting to be popped.

'Revenge was sweet, then?' Howard said. He knew that it must have been.

Two days after Nick's visit to Roger, Corpcom's board of directors had recommended Faulkner's offer to its shareholders. Roger had been quoted as saying that he was 'happy to make such a wonderful deal for his investors', and that he doubted he would stay on under the new management.

It had been a victory for Nick and his camp. Faulkner Industries had been jubilant. Revenge had indeed been sweet.

Nick remembered it well. After leaving Corpcom, he had gone to Annie's flat and whisked her away. She had been ready, her bag packed, waiting for him a little anxiously. He had ventured into the enemy camp. Would he be safe?

'Was it all right?' she asked as he came in.

'Went like a charm,' he responded. He was pleased, and she felt relieved.

They had flown to Edinburgh to wait for the result of his mission. Nick had decided not to stay in London. He would remain inaccessible to the press for those two days, making himself more interesting by consciously staying out of the limelight rather than hogging it.

The night of Roger's capitulation, after the celebration at Faulkner's itself, where the night had ended up like another New Year's Eve party, Nick and Annie had left early with Julian and Rebecca and they had brought the day to a close together.

They had been the four horsemen, and they celebrated their victory at Nick's flat, where so much of the plotting had started. This time, Nick did not cook. They drank champagne and ate smoked salmon until they could eat and drink no more.

At the end of the evening, just before Julian and Rebecca got up to leave, Nick turned to Julian.

'How would you like to rule the empire we've just conquered?' he said. It was a question, not an offer.

'Rule it?' Julian had asked. He thought for a moment. 'I don't know. I think I might like it.'

'Let's drink to ruling an empire, then,' and he had raised his glass towards Julian.

They had drunk one last drink.

Later, before going to bed, Annie questioned Nick about his toast.

'What did you mean earlier?' she asked. 'About ruling an empire.'

He told her.

Nick looked at Howard without any warmth, 'Yes,' he said, 'revenge was very sweet.'

Howard looked at his friend and shook his head. He could understand disliking a man like Roger. Howard disliked Roger. He could understand little acts of sabotage, but not the kind of terrorism Nick had carried out.

'You risked everything just for revenge?' Howard asked.

'Andrews took Armadale from me,' Nick said. 'It was wrong. I wanted it back. And I wanted to show him he couldn't get away with it.'

It was so simple. To Howard it showed a frightening, a dangerous passion. He wondered how Nick would excuse his use of Faulkner for such private purposes. After all Nick was a man of honour, an honest man.

'Don't you have any doubts?' he asked, unable this time not to dig deeper.

'Doubts?' Nick asked. 'About what I did? Why should I? Andrews is an unscrupulous criminal. People died because of what he did. Why should I have doubts?'

'Oh, Andrews,' Howard said. 'No. I didn't mean that. Andrews can't ask for sympathy.'

Howard paused. He wondered whether he should go on. Nick had become difficult to read. Yet Nick was so sure of himself, of his motives and justifications, that it irritated him. The world was not so easy.

'I meant,' he continued, 'your using a public company for this little revenge of yours.'

'Faulkner has done very well out of it,' Nick said. His response was clipped.

'That's all there is to it, then?'

'I beg your pardon?' Nick said. He turned on Howard, waiting for what he was really going to say.

'You've told me how much I betrayed you, Nick.' Howard suddenly was being franker than he thought he would ever be. 'You don't call this a betrayal? Of public trust? Of my own trust? I got you the job.'

'Stop right there,' Nick said. His hand was up, like a policeman's stopping traffic.

'What if it hadn't worked?' Howard said, surprisingly insistent.

'It did,' Nick said. '"What if" doesn't arise in this case.'

'That's very "practical" reasoning,' Howard said, undeterred.

'I learned it from you,' Nick said; it was bitter, 'among other people.'

'Ah,' Howard sighed dramatically, 'but you didn't learn humility.'

They were swiping like two swordsmen in a duel over a woman they both loved, as if their friendship were that woman.

'You taught me revenge,' Nick said. 'You taught me about survival. Survival of the fittest, Howard.'

Nick blamed Howard for his loss of innocence; it was out in the open now. Howard realized it and felt sorry for his friend. Howard was corrupt, but he was not degenerate. He got no kicks from corrupting the innocent. Nick had managed finally to make him feel guilty again.

'And Sophie?' Howard said.

'I thought you two didn't get on.'

'We understand each other better now,' Howard explained. He fidgeted with his empty glass, playing with the words he wanted to say, fighting the years of indoctrination he had received, and which made him almost physically incapable of expressing his emotions. He managed to conquer it – eventually.

'We have lost someone we love,' he said, looking away from Nick, looking down at the floor, beyond the table.

'Please,' Nick said. 'Don't trivialize it.'

Nick rejected Howard's effort, refusing to be drawn into sentimental bargaining.

'It's too easy to bring it all down to love,' he went on. 'Love has its duties and its responsibilities. Emotion isn't enough.'

It was late when they returned upstairs, unable to stop this skirmishing that wounded them both, knowing it was necessary.

There was no one else there. Only Harry, the barman, drying glasses behind the bar. They ordered a final brandy and silently he poured for them. Then they took them to the corner they had met in and sat down again.

'What am I doing here?' Howard asked. It was the question he had been wondering about all evening.

Nick had waited for it. And, just as he was about to tell him, his rigidity softened, and he suddenly felt sorry for Howard and for himself. Killing a friendship was not easy. It required an explanation. That was one of the reasons he had wanted to see Howard.

'We've been friends for a long time,' Nick started.

'Thirty years.'

'It requires a formal ending,' Nick said.

'Does it? Why does it have to end at all?' Howard said. 'We're still the same. Very much the same.'

'I don't feel the same.' Nick was sad. But nothing Howard could say would change his decision.

'No. It's true,' Howard agreed with him, 'you have changed a bit.' But he did not care. 'Does it really matter?' he asked.

'I don't trust you any more, Howard,' Nick said after a moment. He had wondered whether he should say it; but they had been friends and it needed to be said. 'I can't be friends with someone I don't trust,' he went on.

'Perhaps you are betrayed too easily,' he said.

There was a flash of anger from Nick's eyes.

'Perhaps,' he said. His voice was very controlled. 'Perhaps you betray people too easily.' If he could not be understood, then he would have no regrets.

'We might as well get this over with,' he added. Now he was being brisk and unemotional.

Howard said nothing. Nick's mood had changed. He was now going to say what he had wanted to say all evening.

'I want your resignation,' Nick said, very formally, 'from all the companies that Corpcom either owns or is a major holder of and of whose board you're a member.'

It was three months after Nick's victory. Roger was gone; he had sold out. Nick was now chairman of Corpcom.

Howard did not try to hide his consternation. He had never expected this. Earlier on this evening, Nick might have enjoyed it; now it brought him only distaste.

'Some revenge,' Howard said, and immediately he added, 'Of course. You'll have it tomorrow. What else do you have in store for me?'

He felt strangely liberated by this meeting now. It was all coming to a close. He felt relieved, as when a lover whom one does not know how to leave goes first. And Nick wanted to go and leave this bitterness behind.

Yet he could not resist showing Howard the quality of his

revenge. 'I'm not going to stay on with Corpcom,' he said. 'Now that Andrews has gone, I'm going to let Julian Campbell take over.'

'That's absurd.'

'I'm retiring from business,' Nick said.

Howard was amazed. 'This is theatrical,' he said.

'And that's my exit line,' Nick said. He was annoyed at Howard's remark.

'What are you going to do?' Howard asked.

'It doesn't matter,' Nick replied.

'What do you mean, "It doesn't matter"?' Howard said in disbelief.

'I don't care,' Nick went on. He drained his glass, stood up. 'I just don't want to do this any more.'

He looked down at Howard, whose face now expressed amusement – and growing understanding.

'Goodbye,' Nick said.

''Bye,' Howard said.

Nick turned and walked away.

'And good luck,' Howard called after him.

Nick was gone. It had all ended off the mark, somehow.

Howard watched him turn the corner and disappear. He shook his head. At last he had rediscovered the man he had always known and loved. It had been a noble gesture, but one filled with terrible pride.

FOR THE BEST IN PAPERBACKS, LOOK FOR THE 🐧

In every corner of the world, on every subject under the sun, Penguin represents quality and variety – the very best in publishing today.

For complete information about books available from Penguin – including Pelicans, Puffins, Peregrines and Penguin Classics – and how to order them, write to us at the appropriate address below. Please note that for copyright reasons the selection of books varies from country to country.

A CHOICE OF PENGUIN FICTION

Holy Mother   Gabrielle Donnelly

Every Friday night the Society of St Aquinas meets to discuss the Faith in the basement off London's sin-filled Soho Square. 'A raucously promising début . . . Full of intensity and high jinks, humour, warmth, crossness, crudity' – *Financial Times*

City of Spades   Colin MacInnes

'A splendid novel, sparklingly written, warm, wise and funny' – *Daily Mail*. *City of Spades*, *Absolute Beginners* and *Mr Love and Justice* make up Colin MacInnes's trilogy on London street life from the inside out.

Fiddle City   Dan Kavanagh

'Scary insider's data on the airport sub-world, customs knowhow and smugglers' more sickening dodges are marvellously aerated by bubbles of Mr Kavanagh's very dry, sly, wide-ranging and Eighties humour' – *Sunday Times*

The Rachel Papers   Martin Amis

A stylish, sexy and ribaldly funny novel by the author of *Money*. 'Remarkable' – *Listener*. 'Irreverent' – *Daily Telegraph* 'Very funny indeed' – *Spectator*

Scandal   A. N. Wilson

Sexual peccadilloes, treason and blackmail are all ingredients on the boil in A. N. Wilson's *cordon noir* comedy. 'Drily witty, deliciously nasty' – *Sunday Telegraph*

A Fatal Inversion   Barbara Vine

Ten years after the young people camped at Wyvis Hall, the bodies of a woman and child are found in the animal cemetery. Which woman? Whose child? 'Impossible to put down . . . she is a very remarkable writer' – Anita Brookner. 'I defy anyone to guess the conclusion, but looking back, the clues are seen to be there, unobtrusively but cunningly planted, so that it seems one should have known all along' – *Daily Telegraph*

A CHOICE OF PENGUIN FICTION

More Die of Heartbreak Saul Bellow

'What drives this book – and I mean *drives* – is the exultantly sour views of
modernity, sexuality, women, the local and international scene' – *The
New York Review of Books* 'Brilliant and funny . . . Bellow's ideas at their
most astute and trenchant' – *The New York Times*

Very Good, Jeeves! P. G. Wodehouse

When Bertie Wooster lands in the soup, only the 'infinite sagacity' of
Jeeves can pull him out. 'A riot . . . There are eleven tales in this volume
and each is the best' – *Observer*

The Good Apprentice Iris Murdoch

At Seegard there is something rich and strange, with the power to change
people's lives – for better or worse. 'Iris Murdoch is here very much at her
formidable, myth-making best; inventive, comic, moving' – Elaine Fein-
stein in *The Times* 'A heaving, sprawling, headlong spiritual thriller'
– *Observer*

Milk and Honey Elizabeth Jolley

'It is a novel about those who had to leave Europe and who never put down
roots in the earth of the new hemisphere into which they were blown . . . a
quirky, brilliantly written study on the amorality of ignoring reality' – *The
Times* 'A truly exotic mix, a little as though Edgar Allan Poe had been
transported to the outback and set to Straussian music' – *Guardian*

Charlotte's Row H. E. Bates

With its superbly realized industrial setting and cast of memorable characters, *Charlotte's Row* is one of H. E. Bates's best novels in which he reveals
his deep understanding of the ambitions and dreams of ordinary men and
women. 'He is the Renoir of the typewriter' – *Punch*

A CHOICE OF PENGUIN FICTION

Fireflies   Shiva Naipaul

The story of Trinidad's most venerated Hindu family, the Khojas, *Fireflies* is Shiva Naipaul's ferociously comic and profoundly sad first novel. 'A masterpiece . . . anyone who misses reading Shiva Naipaul's *Fireflies* will miss an entirely delightful experience' – Auberon Waugh in the *Spectator*

The News from Ireland   William Trevor

Twelve superb stories from William Trevor that exemplify his precision and subtlety. 'One may turn to him always for artistry, wisdom and wit' – *Sunday Telegraph*. 'Mr Trevor's imagination brings everything to life with a marvellous vividness and glow . . . voluptuously readable' – *Spectator*

Natives and Strangers   Louisa Dawkins

Only as she becomes a woman does Marietta, born in Songo, Tanganyika Territory, realize that she cannot change the whiteness of her skin. Just as marriage to the tormented Jonathan Sudbury cannot save her from loving Michael Kagia, the brilliant young African politician – and loving Michael cannot stop the tragedies of the future or correct the mistakes of the past.

Roger's Version   John Updike

'Updike at full power, a truly astonishing novel. It is a sort of modern fantasia on themes from Hawthorne's *Scarlet Letter*' – Frank Kermode in the *Guardian*. 'He is a writer of charm as well as one possessed of staggering gifts' – Anita Brookner in the *Spectator*. 'A complete original, and full of energy and optimism . . . a highly recommended read' – Lynton Lesserday in *Punch*

Maus   Art Spiegelman

'I can't find superlatives adequate to describe it. It's the best cartoon book I've ever read . . . Very direct, very powerful, very moving . . .' – Steve Bell. 'Anyone moved by *When the Wind Blows* . . . will appreciate Spiegelman's genius for dealing with a subject many would say cannot be dealt with at all' – *The Times*.